Iced Out

Lakewood Leopards #1
Jayme Hunt

Contents

To anyone who has ever seen someone knocked down, and
reached out a hand to lift them back up.
We need more of you in this world.
Never change.

Author's Note

This book contains offensive adult language, explicit sexual scenes, PTSD/flashbacks, discussions of grief and trauma, and graphic discussion of domestic violence (physical and mental, involving an ex-partner). If any of this content could be upsetting to you, please protect your wellbeing and do not continue.

Every second, three people in the U.S. become a victim of domestic violence. That means each year, more than 10 million Americans experience domestic abuse. If you or anyone you know is experiencing domestic violence, please know that help is available.

National Domestic Violence Hotline: Call 800-799-SAFE (7233) or text BEGIN to 88788

thehotline.org

Languages: English, Spanish and 200+ through interpretation service

Hours: 24/7

Team Roster

First Line:

Benjamin Estes (Benji) – #17 – center

Jordan Tremblay (Jordie) – #22 – right wing

Levi Anderson (Levi) – #84 – left wing

Grant Sanderson (Sando) – #29 – defenseman

Sam Highcloud (Highcloud) – #9 – defenseman

Second Line:

Daniel Nilsson (Nils) – #72 – center

JJ Clark (JJ) – #47 – right wing

Konner Moore (Kon-man) – #56 – left wing

Chris Goodman (Goody) – #33 – defenseman

Mason Berger (Bergsy) – #92 – defenseman

Third Line:

Ryan Larson (Rook) – #22 – center

Christian Larrivée (Frenchie) – #37 – right wing

Eli Forrester (Eli) – #64 – left wing

Lukas Laine (Lainey) – #18 – defenseman

Mike Sullivan (Sully) – #47 – defenseman

Goalies

Liam MacNeill (Mac) – #31

Sasha Novikov (Novi) – #6

PLAYLIST

Mind Games – Sickick

Where Did She Go – Saleka

How Do I Do This – Kelsea Ballerini

fuck, i'm lonely – Lauv, Anne-Marie

You Put a Spell on Me – Austin Giorgio

Figure You Out – VOILÀ

Easy to Love – Bryce Savage

THE DEATH OF PEACE OF MIND – Bad Omens

Little Girl Gone – CHINCHILLA

Call Out My Name – The Weeknd

Chapter 1

LISA

"This is your only chance. *Get out.*"

The last words my best friend said to me hammer home in time with my footfalls. I let out an exasperated huff and lower the speed on the treadmill until I'm walking. *In through the nose, out through the mouth.* I focus on breathing low and slow, recovering from the grueling pace I was pushing myself at. No matter how much I try to outrun this damn memory, it always keeps pace with me.

It's been weeks since she said those words. Weeks since I heeded them. I've put a thousand miles and several states between us, but the echo in my head is proof there are some things I just can't distance myself from.

I'd prefer to be running outside, where I'm able to distract myself with the world passing me by, but as it turns out, fall in Minnesota is volatile, swinging from sunny to frosty in a heartbeat. Today is even colder than usual, meaning I'm confined to the indoor gym in my apartment building. The second I step off the treadmill, the cool air envelops me like silk, chilling the sweat to my skin.

I shrug my hoodie back on and head up the elevator to my apartment, already daydreaming about the hot shower I'll take before my evening work shift. I have at least an hour before I need to leave, and all it will take is fifteen glorious minutes to warm back up, relax my sore muscles, and hopefully clear up my headspace, since my run clearly didn't cut it. Hell, I might even use a shower bomb.

The daydream is cut short, however, by the scent that hits me as soon as I push my door open. My eyes begin to water.

Shit – again. Literally.

"Winny," I groan, slumping against the door frame. "Really?"

The skittering of nails against hardwood in the other room tells me my dog heard the disapproval in my tone and is making a genuine attempt at escape. While my one-bedroom Minneapolis apartment is large, it isn't big enough for him to avoid my scolding...and it certainly isn't large enough to mask the scent of his third accident this week.

I tug my hoodie up over my nose as I locate the source of the offending odor, equipped with paper towels and floor cleaner. The clicking of nails comes closer, stopping a few feet away as my dog, Winston, pokes his head around the corner. I glance over to see his black ears tucked back, fawn-colored face furrowed in a genuine look of shame.

I snort and roll my eyes as I take in his apologetic expression, but I can't really blame him. Though I've had him for a few months now, he is a rescue, and he often experiences separation anxiety if I'm gone for more than an hour or two. Our recent move hasn't helped – something he's made abundantly clear with his shitscapades.

"You're okay, boy," I murmur, and hear the tentative thump of his tail against the wall in response. I stand to toss the soiled paper towels in a bag and wash my hands. When I reach for his leash, his tail thwaps come faster, threatening to put a hole in the drywall.

For what I spent on this apartment, I know I could have found a home with a yard for Winston instead of having to take him for quick walks every time he needed to relieve himself. But this apartment has fantastic amenities, grade A security, and honestly, the idea of maintaining an entire household by myself at twenty-four is too overwhelming.

Not to mention, the span of everything I own can – and did – fill two suitcases, so the idea of trying to fill multiple rooms is both unnecessary and depressing.

I sigh as I clip on Winny's leash. Only crazy people pack up and move to Minnesota, sight unseen, on the cusp of winter. Crazy people, and people who have to disappear.

Nope. Stop. Something in my chest twists painfully, and I squeeze my eyes shut for a moment as I will myself away from thoughts of my past. After a long minute, the feel of Winston brushing against my legs brings me back, reminding me he needs to go out, *now,* lest he give me a repeat of what I just cleaned up.

I hop in the elevator with him and press the button for the first lobby floor, watching as the numbers drop. After two, I close my eyes, steering my thoughts in a more positive direction.

I was able to find this great apartment, and not one, but two jobs that have flexible hours. I have Winston with me. I found a nearby boxing gym, and it's been surprisingly easy to build up my physical strength, especially since I've been so consistent. It's much harder to carve out my mental strength, though...especially when it feels like I'm starting from ground zero.

At the beep of the elevator, my eyes shoot open. I expect us to be on the bottom floor, but quickly see we've only traveled four floors down. I instinctively shift Winston to the corner of the elevator, tucking his small brown body behind my legs.

When I adopted him, I was hoping his company would ease my anxiety. Instead, he's a mixed-breed, 45-pound version of me, complete with his own brand of anxiety. We've conquered a lot together, from walking over strange surfaces to the fizz of a can being cracked open – something my sparkling water addiction greatly appreciates – but men are something he still fears deeply.

I can't say I feel any differently.

Unfortunately for both of us, they can't be avoided. Half the population and all that. I just *know* there will be one on the other side of the elevator door, and chances are high he will be wearing a hat, making Winny even more afraid.

Just my luck, when the door opens, there are *four* of them.

All in hats.

I feel Winston shrink further into the corner and reach a hand down to scratch behind his ears. Gratefully, none of them even seem to notice his small frame as they clamber in, too busy laughing with one another about something. All they do is glance at me with pleasant enough smiles.

My eyes travel over their sweatshirts, which all have matching logos. A snow leopard, from the looks of it, with a hockey stick in its teeth. The words "Lakewood Leopards" stretch across the top.

I blink, trying to place it. I haven't been here long enough to know the many cities that make up metropolitan Minneapolis, but I don't think Lakewood has a college. Besides, this apartment, with its fancy amenities and open floor plans, is not typically in a 'college student' price range. My college housing involved holes filled with toothpaste, peeling paint, and a fridge that never seemed to fully close.

They're all tall and fit, likely in their early to mid-twenties, like myself. One of the men – stocky, with thick, dark hair and an even thicker mustache – notes my gaze and grins. The movement lifts his mustache, and I can't help the way my own lip curls as I watch it move, like a hairy caterpillar.

"Oh, hey," he says, and I swear his voice sounds strained. Is he…trying to make it sound deeper?

My brow lifts, and my suspicions are confirmed as his friends snicker, shuffling and bumping into him. One murmurs, "Oh, hey," in a mocking tone, and Mustache Man punches him, dragging a wounded *"Ow!"* from his friend. The snickering intensifies.

I open my mouth to say something, but as my mind races, my throat closes, stopping any possible response.

Their jostling causes one of them – a fair-skinned blond man – to bump into me, and he mutters an apology. Sweat begins to prick my palms, but I still say nothing.

The tallest one in their group runs his hand over his face, clearly feeling secondhand embarrassment for his friends. He turns his head, and I brace for whatever comment is coming next. Probably a question as to why my mouth is open, but no words are coming out.

Instead, he glances down at Winston, who remains tucked on the other side of me.

"Cute dog," he says, his voice surprisingly soft.

There's a thumping against my leg. I look down to see Winston gazing up – not at me, but at the tall man. He's panting, but his ears are flopped forward, his tongue lolling happily.

I glance back at the man, my eyes going up his tall frame to land on his hat, resting on floppy, dark-brown hair. It's strange. He should be everything that sets Winny on edge, and yet, it's like he's already built some mysterious, silent bond with my dog.

I lock eyes with him. His are a deep, dark brown, and warmer than I expected. They crinkle at the edges with confusion, and I blink, realizing I'm still gaping at him.

My mouth snaps shut, but before I can say something like, "Thank you," or something more explanatory and reasonable, like *"Sorry, I'm just blown away, because he's never met a tall man in a hat he didn't want to run away from or bite in the nuts,"* the elevator beeps again, and the doors open on the ground floor.

The man smiles at us once more, though it looks a little uncertain this time. Before I can voice any of the thoughts flying through my head, he slips out of the elevator and disappears.

"Lisa? Lisa!" Fingers snap behind me.

I turn, blinking in surprise as I come face-to-face with a perky blonde – or, given her height, her even perkier chest.

"Didn't you hear me calling you?" My coworker, Julia, lets out an exasperated sigh.

We work together at a German sports bar, conveniently located only three blocks from my new apartment. The bar is incredibly cheesy – hell, it's literally named *Wunderbar* – but it has great beer, fun games, and since it closes at 11pm, it never gets too rowdy. I was lucky to jump on a bartender opening a few days after I moved in.

"Erm, sorry." I wipe my palms across my jeans and lean against the bar. "What's up?"

"The group over there just ordered some warm old fashioneds. Do you need some help with them, or are you good?" Julia motions at a group of four that just arrived.

I hear the concern in her voice and attempt not to roll my eyes. I bartended for a year in college when I first turned twenty-one, but despite being the one to hire me, that seems to slip Julia's mind every time someone orders something more complex than a Kölsch or a Pilsner. I'm still new-ish, so my guess is she'll hover until she finally decides I'm competent.

"An old fashioned topped with hot water? Solid choice in this weather." I pick up a towel and throw it over my shoulder, shooting Julia a smile. "Not a problem."

She grins at me. "Good deal. And, Lisa?"

"Yeah?"

"You look hot tonight. I hope you get a ton of tips."

I flush. "It's a Thursday night."

"Yeah, and? Plenty of people get drunk on a Thursday night." She flicks her apron string at me. "Like me, when I'm not working. You're always welcome to join."

I snort, but shoot her a smile. Getting close to people in this new life feels like opening a door to the past I haven't yet allowed myself to face. I worry they'll see those scars it left. But...I *do* want to make friends, so desperately it aches. I appreciate her nudging that door open when I'm too scared to do it myself.

I shift to lift four whiskey glasses from beneath the bar-top, lining them up for muddling and pouring. Despite Julia's conviction that Thursday night is prime drinking time, it's still early, so the bar is relatively slow. There are only a few people seated at the bar, while most opt for actual bench seating to eat dinner.

I locate the group Julia motioned toward, seated at a bench across the bar, and freeze as recognition floods me. It's the group from the elevator earlier.

As I wait for the water to heat up, I take a moment to really study them. They're still wearing their hoodies from earlier, and their hats, too – a mixture of the same leopard logo, and some hockey brand I'm only vaguely aware of. Mustache Man is gesturing wildly, which draws a whoop from the rest of the group.

The one who mocked him earlier – a shorter, red-haired guy with freckles splattered across his cheeks – punches his shoulder in response, and the two across the bench tilt their heads back to laugh. The booming sound of their laughter reaches me even over the noise of the TVs and other chatter from the bar.

When it dies down, Mustache Man and the red-haired guy lean their heads in, clearly deep in discussion. Across the table, the blond one turns to his side, saying something to the tall man Winston took a liking to. The man swivels to face his fair-haired friend as he replies, giving me a clear view of his face.

He tilts his head as he listens to whatever his friend has to say, his dark hair toppling over his forehead. His full lips twist into an amused smile, white teeth gleaming stark against the dark shadow of a beard beginning, as if he hasn't shaved for a few days. His intense, amused dark eyes gleam as he glances up, his gaze landing –

Directly on me.

Oh, crap.

For some bizarre reason, I'm tempted to duck behind the bar, as if I wouldn't have to resurface seconds later. I catch myself just in time and force a shaky smile before spinning around, eyes squeezed shut. It's been *years* since I've had a reaction like that to a man. Was I really just gawking at him, a complete stranger, like that? The thought leaves me unsettled.

Focus. In through the nose, out through the mouth.

I take a deep breath and move to get the hot water, forcibly turning my gaze so that the only person I stare at is Julia as I silently encourage her to come get the old fashioneds.

When she reaches me, she grins. "Aren't they cute? If I were single, I'd be all over that."

I follow her gaze to the bench where the four men are sitting, then look away quickly as I see the tall man still looking curiously at us. The air leaves my lungs under the weight of his gaze. First my bizarre behavior in the elevator, and now this? I can only imagine what he must think of me.

"What's that team on their hoodies?" I ask.

"Shit, girl. You really did just move here." Julia tsks. "That's the Lakewood Leopards. They're the local AHL team."

"AHL?"

"American Hockey League. Basically, the professional developmental league. A lot of these guys will end up playing in the show someday."

"The show?"

"The major leagues. As in, the NHL?" She blinks, clearly surprised by my lack of knowledge. I can't blame her; what I do know about Minnesota is that it's the State of Hockey. As a native Minnesotan, I'm sure hockey is in her blood. Hell, it's probably taught in the school curriculum. "The AHL is the step right under that."

I raise my brows. "Oh, wow. So they must be like... *really* good."

"Really good?" Julia laughs. "Try, some of the best there are." She shifts the old fashioneds so that she can carry all four in her grasp. "I don't know why they choose to come here; we usually just get grumpy old men. But they seem to like the food and the drinks, because they're here pretty regularly. I'm not mad about it – they tip well, and they're certainly not bad to look at."

She walks away with a wink, and I'm left with nothing in my hands and no one to talk to, opening my mind up to a flurry of thoughts.

I've seen them twice in one day, now. Does that mean all of them live in my apartment building? If they're in line to play in the NHL, does that mean they're important enough to be famous? My stomach plummets at the thought that they could bring media attention near me.

I moved here to escape notice. I want to become a nobody, not be surrounded by somebodies.

I don't care what Julia says about their tips and their looks. I just hope I'll never run into them again.

Chapter 2

BENJI

"You ready for this weekend, boys?" Coach Anders bellows, the slam of the heavy locker room door following his arrival. I push back my dripping hair and straighten as he continues, leaving my skates half-untied. "It's time to bring the game back home!"

"Hopefully not home to the sin bin," Levi says, shooting Grant a shit-eating grin. "We know our penalty box is always ready for Sando. It's been too long."

Grant simply grunts in response, rubbing sweat off his mustache. Coach ignores their exchange entirely, though he knows better than anyone that Sanderson leads the league in penalties, and tonight's game was no exception. Grant's a fucking nuisance sometimes, but when he's not in the box, he's an absolute unit on the ice, and that's what matters.

"First time back on home ice for the season. You all better show up with your game faces tomorrow night. Two hours before, as usual, and dressed like you mean business. Suits, ties, and *no hats.*" Coach pauses, giving us all a withering stare.

I know what's coming next, just as much as he knows it won't make a lick of difference to those who have heard and disregarded it for ages now.

"And behave tonight," he warns before stalking out of the locker room. A chorus of chuckles follows as the team continues tugging equipment off.

It's only nine in the morning, but a good ass-kicking on a freezing sheet of ice can wake anyone up, even if they aren't a morning person. I don't think I'm naturally a morning person, but years of routine changed that. I love getting a workout out of the way first thing in the morning, and hockey is the only thing that I'll wake up at the crack of dawn for.

Even though we don't have practice the morning of games – and therefore have tomorrow morning to sleep in – I tend to wake up and do a quick shakeout workout. We all have our pre-game rituals, and I like to stay consistent.

Jordie groans happily and snags a towel, heading to where steam is already spilling out from the locker room showers. "I'm so happy to have the night off."

I nod and follow him to the showers. Grant smacks my shoulder blade as I go.

Right over my brand new tattoo.

"Fuck, man! I know it's technically healed and all, but still." I rub it gently. "I don't want you ripping off parts of it."

He simply laughs. "Coffee after this? We need to get amped if we want to stay awake to celebrate tonight."

I grin. "Yes to the coffee, no to the night out."

"Seriously?" He groans. "Shit, man, I know you're trying to win the captain position back and all, but that doesn't mean you need to forget how to have fun. You've gotten boring, dude. It's painful to watch."

The jab at my goal for the season stings. I push it aside and attempt to get the fire off me. "You know what's painful? The way your sister threw herself all over me. I haven't had that kind of secondhand embarrassment since I turned down your ex."

Laughter echoes around the shower room, and Grant narrows his eyes. "Damn, dude, talk shit about my ex all you want, but leave my sister out of it."

I smirk. "No promises."

"We can leave your sister out of it, but we've gotta talk about your ex," Goody chimes in. "You always said her..." He pauses and gestures to his chest, both hands cupped. "Were unreal."

"Please," Levi scoffs, squirting a dollop of shampoo straight onto his red hair. "Everyone's seen photos. That was a free-for-all."

"There's a reason she's my ex," Grant says with a chuckle. "She showed those pics to *everyone.*"

I laugh along with everyone else, but keep a careful eye on Grant, unable to shake the role of captain that, as he mentioned, I had once before. It's all good fun now, but Grant *had* been cheated on, many times. Despite his violent tendencies on the ice, he has a soft heart, and it took him a while to get to the point where we can all joke about it.

It's something we all have to figure out about relationships, given what we do. It's far simpler to hook up, mostly outside of town, where we're less likely to be known. Women usually want to tag along for the fame, the clout, the bragging rights – and when they get what they want, they move on to something better. Sometimes, that includes other members of our team. Which can get...awkward.

It's simpler to take dating off the table entirely and just be clear up front that there are no expectations. That way, things don't get messy.

As ex-captain of the team, there are more eyes on me than on the others, especially after all the news articles from the past year. I've had to change how I get around town to avoid the kinds of people who sniff out news of me like hunting dogs. The heart of the city and the college area are the worst for it.

The silver lining is that now, I can basically become invisible in ten minutes. Ten minutes one way from our apartment? It's all the hustle and bustle. But ten minutes in the opposite direction? It's the older parts of the city, full of retirees who stay off of social media and follow the same routines that I've discovered: the same places, the same food, the same people. Low-stress, predictable environments where nobody new ever winds up. That's how I've operated for months.

And that's why her face stood so far apart yesterday.

Someone who interrupted the routine. Fair-skinned, light brown hair, long and pulled back into a ponytail. Big blue eyes, sharp and assessing as we all tumbled into the elevator the other day, with that cute dog velcroed to her side.

And again, later that night, when I noticed her eyeing me up from across the room at Wunderbar. She clearly knew who I was in a vague sense, but seemed to be trying to place me. Or maybe she was trying to find an in to talk to me without my friends around.

I'll admit, I was intrigued at first. Why wouldn't I be? She was fucking stunning. But the more I think about it, the more it rubs too closely at that old wound. She's more than likely a potential puck bunny, trying to make her way into my space. The space I've carefully crafted for myself and my teammates alone.

Those feelings kick around in my head as we walk to the coffee shop. There, they hit high speed as I see none other than the mystery girl herself, working behind the counter.

I skid to a stop, feeling Jordie bump into me from behind.

"Argh – what is it, dude?" he asks.

I swipe a hand over my face. "It's that *girl.*"

"What girl?"

"The girl with the dog," I say, motioning at the girl behind the counter. "She was in the elevator at our apartment, and then at the restaurant, and now here."

Grant lets out a low whistle. "Three run-ins in two days? That's...a lot of coincidences, man."

"Do you think she's...?" Levi ventures, letting the question trail off.

He doesn't need to finish it; I know exactly what he's asking. *Do you think she's like Sheila?*

"I don't know." I grit my teeth, scenes I'd tried to leave buried for months flashing through my mind before I can stop them. "But I'm about to find out."

I stalk up to the counter as she sorts through the cash from the last customer. When she looks up, I barely let the surprise register on her face before I practically shout at her. "Are you serious right now?"

The question I choose isn't eloquent, but it's effective. Even in my rage, I note that my tone *was* a bit harsher than intended, and I feel a pang of guilt as she visibly shrinks away from the question.

"W-what?" she stammers.

"You heard me. Are you kidding me? What are you doing here?"

"I... I work here. Today is my first day."

"Of course it is," I scoff. "Did you get this job because of me?"

"Excuse me?"

Irritation floods me as I'm forced to explain that I know exactly what's going on here. Does she think I'll be flattered? That I'll be impressed?

"It seems like quite the coincidence that we've had this many run-ins in the past day. In my experience, this has gone past chance and into something else. And I am *not* amused."

I watch as she sorts through this information, her cheeks coloring as she takes her time to answer. When she does, her posture is stiff, those wide blue eyes swimming with – what is it? I can't quite place the emotion.

"I don't know who you think you are, but I *work* here. And I work at Wunderbar. And in case you forgot, *you* climbed into *my* elevator ride, by chance." Her voice is soft but firm, trembling slightly with what I assume is embarrassment as she backtracks through our run-ins. "I'm not amused, either."

It's true. She doesn't look amused. She's leaning back as though the countertop is a person she can place between us, and her grip on the countertop has her knuckles growing white. Her eyes flash to her coworker, who is shooting her curious glances as he foams milk nearby.

"Today is my first day," she'd said.

I hesitate as I realize I may have gone a bit too far, storming in here and accusing her of stalking me. If she did just start, it's...entirely possible that this is a coincidence. One layered on top of several others, but a coincidence nonetheless.

I open my mouth to apologize, but then Grant claps a hand on my shoulder in solidarity, and I clamp it shut. Nope, there's no way this all happened by chance. Working at two places I frequent the most still means she likely got those jobs with an ulterior motive.

I can't afford *coincidences* anymore. Not after what my family has been through.

"You can't tell me you don't know me," I say, exasperated.

"I don't even know your name." Her eyes flick to Grant beside me. "All I know is that you're friends with young Tom Selleck here."

Grant clears his throat, but it's a strangled sound, as though he's covering a laugh.

"Funny," I continue, "but I'm still not convinced."

She sighs, gaze shifting to the line growing behind me. *"Please.* Order, or get out of the way."

I blink, taking in the obvious dismissal. Jordie leans in and whispers in my ear. "Dude, we can figure this out later. Just order."

I'm hit with a wave of embarrassment, thinking of the line I've held up behind me with my accusations. Not that I'll ever admit it was on me, though. It's on the cool-eyed barista behind the bar, the one who's currently fixing me with a steely look.

"I'll take a medium drip coffee," I mutter.

"Room for cream or sugar?" She oozes fake politeness.

I bite the inside of my lip. "No, thank you."

After I pay, I wait diligently at the other end of the bar to hear them call out our order, which she put under the name Tom, much to Grant's enjoyment.

Grant and Jordie keep looking between the girl and me, but I watch closely to make sure nobody spits in my drink for the shit I just pulled. I don't see anything, but I'm not entirely convinced. I might even deserve it.

Chapter 3

LISA

My heart rate doesn't slow for a solid thirty minutes after the men leave. I spend half of that time taking my break early, despite it being hours before noon. My fingers hurt from gripping the counter, looking for ways to get the tension out of my system. I'm just counting the minutes until I can leave so I can finally head to my new gym and gain back the control that completely fled me during that encounter.

What kind of douche canoe storms into someone's place of work and accuses *them* of stalking? When they're the one that walked into the place?

Benjamin *freaking* Estes, apparently.

I glanced at his credit card long enough to see his name when he paid. I *had* to know the identity of the person who clearly believed, with all his heart, that I already knew it. I have half a mind to print off images of his face to put on the punching bag at the gym.

Even though I've moved on to internal rage, my mouth is still dry from fear. I know, realistically, he barely raised his voice at me...but still. It took all of my willpower not to slip away at his initial tone, to force my flight instinct to fight instead.

I wonder when that knee-jerk reaction will go away. If ever.

I learned long ago that fear and anger are basically cousins. Fear can turn to anger, and vice versa. Both burn, though in different ways. Fear is like ice, shooting down your body like you're doused in it. Anger, on the other hand, burns white-hot, traveling through your veins like fire.

I thought for a long time that anger was the most effective tool – but fear? Fear is the best thing I've ever learned to master. Fear led me here, to safety, even if I've questioned that choice countless times. Including today.

"Lisa?"

The question jolts me out of my almost-spiral, and I turn to face my manager, Steve. The beginnings of a polite smile fade as I take in his nervous expression and the way he rings his hands together. He's young – younger than me – and it's clear he hasn't been in his position long. My eyes travel to my other coworker, who is conveniently immersed in some sort of latte art. Oh, god. I know what's about to happen.

"We can't have this kind of...*drama* in our workspace, Lisa." He pauses to fidget some more. "Given the fact that it was your first day, that doesn't bode well for what could happen in the future."

"I'm so sorry. I truly have no idea what that was about. I've never even *met* that man before." Not exactly true. We've now met three times, as Benjamin freaking Estes pointed out himself.

Steve hums but averts his eyes. "Look, I'm sorry, but I truly doubt that. We had several interested applicants who would jump at a second chance to work at this location, and with less...baggage."

I close my eyes at his use of the word *baggage.* I have it in spades, but not in any of the ways he can even begin to imagine.

"I'm afraid we're going to have to let you go," he finishes.

I open my eyes again, staring at him in disbelief. He's moved to cross his arms, his jaw set stubbornly. His mind is clearly made up, and even if it wasn't, I'm not about to argue with someone whose age still ends in a teen. I simply remove my apron.

"I understand," I say. "I wish you all the best. Thanks for the opportunity."

His relief at my lack of outburst is obvious. His arms drop to his sides, and he murmurs something about today's tips as I turn away, anger beginning to burn inside me. The anger isn't directed at teenage Steve, though.

It's reserved entirely for Benjamin freaking Estes.

"Get out of your head and into your body!" Paul calls out from the front of the room, and begins another series of movements: punching, driving, and twisting. The small class follows suit, and I exhale sharply with each punch, enjoying the feel of my muscles working to mirror the technique our instructor is demonstrating.

For at least sixty minutes almost every day for the past few weeks, Paul's advice has been exactly what I need. I came here for the self-defense classes, but stayed for the boxing. During these classes, all of my energy is focused on physical exertion, leaving my mind no room to wander. I'm too busy honing my form, stamina, and punching power.

I don't mind the small class sizes; in fact, I prefer them. I don't mind the fact that the gym, Punchline, is run down, with red and black paint peeling off the bricks and fraying rubber flooring. I don't even mind being screamed at by Paul, the lean, gruff owner, whose graying hair stands out in stark contrast to his tanned skin. For forty minutes, he grumps about our form as he leads shadowboxing, until finally, he unleashes us to the heavy bags.

"Come on, Andi! Twist that back leg, drive your hips up!" he hollers, staying true to his personality.

The short, curvy woman he called out groans audibly. "It doesn't feel natural," she complains.

His reply is immediate. "It's not going to feel natural. That's why you need to work at it until it's muscle memory."

Andi huffs, raising her fists once more, and I grin. She and I have become close over the past few classes. She's crass, blunt, and loud – all the things I wish I could be. I gravitated toward her instantly, and she accepted me with open arms.

For all the steps I've made to become more independent and strong, it still takes active work not to pull back inside myself every day. Most people would allow that to happen without question, but not Andi. She reaches in, yanks me back out of my shell, and somehow makes me cry laughing while she does it.

Once the class is over and we've sufficiently pummeled the heavy bags, Andi collapses against me, rubbing her arms.

"Remind me why we do this, Lisa?" She squirts a long stream of water into her mouth and then exhales dramatically.

"Because we want to be powerful, independent, and badass?"

She considers for a moment. "No, that's not it. I just want to see my abs again."

"Well, keep it up, and they'll be back in no time."

"Don't get me wrong, they're still there." She sits up and pokes at her stomach. "They're just hidden under a few...dozen drunken nights."

"Well, were the drunken nights at least worth it?" I ask, and grab the water bottle from her to take a long drink.

"Absolutely. But back then, my cardio just consisted of suffocating a man with my thighs."

I spit out the water, choking as I laugh. "Andi!"

"What?" she asks innocently. "I said it was worth it."

"Okay. Fair enough," I reason, shooting her a look of amazement. She's twenty-nine, and I hope that in my next five years, I can feel free and confident enough in myself to be like her. "So, tell me. What was your wildest hookup?"

"Ummm...a jester at a Renaissance Faire." She twirls a strand of blonde hair from her ponytail, clearly lost in the memory. Eventually, she breaks out into a grin. "He had all sorts of fun devices at his disposal."

I shake my head, smiling. "I take it back. I don't want to know more."

"What about you?" she asks, turning her bright, mischievous gaze on me. "Do you have any wild sexual adventures you want to share with the class?"

"Not really," I hedge. "My sex life has always been pretty mundane."

She watches me for a brief moment and then shrugs, grabbing the water bottle back from me. "Your loss! But you're young and hot; you'll find someone to give you all that freaky sex you deserve."

I chuckle, both from her comments and from relief. I love that she's so open with me but doesn't push for the same. She could easily bug and pry, but she seems to accept that there are things I keep close to my chest. Sometimes, I'd love nothing more than to confide in her. But I can't.

Instead, I decide to offer up another truth. "I got fired this morning."

"What?" She straightens. "What the hell did you do, girl?"

"That's just the thing. I didn't do anything! This guy in my apartment building and I had a couple of run-ins, which were *entirely on him,* I might add. When he came into the coffee shop, he blew up about it. Management decided I'm too much drama because of it, and let me go."

"Well, fuck. Do you want to go egg the place tonight? Or TP it?"

"What?" I laugh, incredulous. "Do people our age still do things like that?"

She shrugs. "If you decide it's necessary, I say yes. Just say the word and I'm there."

"Not necessary, but I appreciate the offer." I grin and check my watch. "All right. I've gotta go home and get ready for the job I have left."

"Go," she says, whipping my butt with a towel when I get up. "And be punctual, unless you want to get fired twice in one day!"

I stick my tongue out at her as I leave and she laughs, the sound providing a warmth I haven't felt in a long time. I can't remember the last friendship I had like this, where someone offered up all of themselves to it so entirely.

The warmth quickly descends into guilt as realization dawns on me, along with the words I couldn't shake yesterday – words from the last friendship I had.

This is your last chance. Get out.

Would Andi still be my friend if she discovered that nothing she knows about me is real?

Chapter 4

Benji

Unsurprisingly, my singular vote to change our bar scene was overruled. We ended up back at Wunderbar after our game, with more of the team in tow.

In a silent compromise, we're all sitting with our eyes fixated on the television. We're playing the Chicago Force tomorrow, but the real threat is the Washington Pirates, and they're currently playing, giving us the opportunity to scope them out before we face them. I sip my beer as comments fly around me.

"We'll have to keep an eye on that defenseman, Lee. He's an absolute beast."

"He's a fuckin' stud. He's definitely going to the show."

I smile to myself as I listen to the banter. Two years ago, when we lost several of our older bubble players to retirement and being called up to the major league, I assumed my first year as captain would simply be a season for rebuilding.

That hadn't been the case. The team bonded quickly, a talented combination of scrappy and motivated. On and off the ice, problems are resolved quickly and the team is tuned into one another's strengths and weaknesses.

In fact, I'm not even sure I'd still be on skates if it weren't for the amazing team I came back to. I wouldn't trade any of them for the world, especially Grant and Jordie.

They're both on the first line with me, and they were the sanity I needed the last few months. When we moved into our new apartment this summer, we got along just as well as hallmates as linemates. I'm the serious to Jordie's goofy, and Grant...well, Grant is as unhinged as they come. But we all fucking love it.

"What do you think of Roberts being the new Force captain, Benji?"

The question rips me from my thoughts. I blink and turn to see Highcloud eyeing me. "What?"

Sam Highcloud, Levi's roommate, motions at the TV on the side wall. I flick my eyes up in time to see a clip of a blond player, sporting blue and orange, making a beautiful goal against what looked to be the Avengers goalie. *Youngest player to captain the Pirates...* the anchor drones.

"Liam Roberts," he supplies. Jordie and Grant have gone quiet, but Highcloud is none the wiser as he continues on. "He's the new captain of the Pirates. You used to play with him, didn't you?"

"I did," I reply, clenching my jaw. Roberts is a pain in my ass, and we did our best to avoid interacting with one another any more than absolutely necessary while we played juniors together. But fuck if he isn't a good player. "I assume he'll come out with even more in the tank now that he has that letter on his sweater. We'll want to keep an eye on him for sure."

"If I remember right, he plays dirty," Grant says, cracking his knuckles. I catch the gleam in his eye and smirk. He's unofficially become known as our team's enforcer, a reputation he loves. Over the past year, other teams' members have learned – either slowly or very, very quickly – to keep away from him due to his fighting skills. If Roberts wants a fight, he'll get one with Grant.

"I don't know that he'll be dumb enough to pick that fight," I answer, swiping my beer back into my hand and draining it. "But by all means, if he tries anything with our players this season, get after him."

Enforcers are becoming less and less common in our sport, but I'm still of the mind that I'd rather have a single fight to settle things than face ongoing cheap shots all season. Those cause more injuries to players in the long run, and unfortunately, Liam Roberts is the type to deal those cheap shots out in spades.

Grant grins broadly. "Do we have to play the Force first?" He collapses dramatically against the back of his seat. "I think the Pirates are already due for another smackdown."

"All in due time." I sling an arm over both him and Jordie and smirk. "They'll get their reminder about who's on top soon enough."

"Hell yes," Jordie says, and Grant nods.

A chorus of belches and slams of glasses tells me we've all drained our beers or are close to empty. I rise from my seat, pointing to gauge who wants another, and turn back to the bar. My steps falter, however, as I see that the bartenders have switched over for a later shift.

The girl from the coffee shop is behind the bar now, talking with an older man seated across the bartop from her. Her eyes flick momentarily to me, as though sensing my approach from across the room. I swear they narrow slightly before she returns back to her conversation.

I settle myself on the opposite end of the bartop, listening half-heartedly to their conversion. Maybe I'll get a better idea of what kind of person she really is.

"So... are you from Tennessee?" the guy asks.

My god, so people actually use that line in real life? My throat closes, and my nose betrays me, an audible snort leaving my body before I can stop it. I spin on the barstool, leaning across the bartop so that my face is shielded from them. There is a lengthy pause before she responds, and I pray that it's not because they both heard me.

"I'm not, unfortunately. I'm from Wyoming. And even there, that line is surprisingly outdated." Another pause, and then she lets out a little laugh and adds, "But I have to commend the effort. Another beer, Joe?"

I frown, fighting the temptation to turn back around. Even to the man who has just used an abominable pickup line, she is being polite and warm – the opposite of her attitude with me this morning. What's her angle?

"Wyoming? I've been there! Whereabouts?" The man completely ignores the question clearly meant to move him along.

"Cody. Where have you been?" The question sounds light, but he notices the tightness in her tone. She's still being polite, but she wants the conversation to end.

"Cheyenne. I don't think that's close to Cody, though." The man sounds disappointed. "Have you been to Cheyenne?"

Damn. This conversation is becoming increasingly desperate, and my men are thirsty, though maybe not as thirsty as poor Joe here. When Levi shoots me a confused look, I decide it's time to interfere.

I stand and move toward the trainwreck down the bartop. The girl's gaze snaps to me as she notes my arrival, and I swear she deflates. My eyebrows raise, and I glance between her and the man at the bartop pointedly. Haven't I just given her an excellent out?

She averts her eyes and returns to her conversation. "Unfortunately not. Sorry, but can I get you another Dunkel? It looks like there's a line starting." She motions to me, and I return the gesture with a smirk.

Thirsty Joe visibly wilts, but nods. When she turns to pour him another beer, the man turns to frown at me, and I bristle. I've done nothing more than hurry up the service and save him from a failing conversation. I rest an arm on the bar and maintain eye contact, letting him know I'm thoroughly unimpressed.

Though I'm not wearing anything Leopards branded, I wonder if he knows who I am, because once he gives me a once-over, his frown turns to something like recognition. When the bartender slides him his beer, he grips the frothy mug tightly, mutters a soft thanks, and makes a quick exit.

Finally, the bartender turns to me. Instead of asking for my order, she places her hands on her hips. "Don't act like you're doing me any favors, after that stunt you pulled this morning."

None of the warmth she'd had with Joe, as fake and polite as it had been, remains in her tone. Though I know exactly what she's talking about, I'm caught off guard by her irritation. "I had my reasons," I reply. "This is...how many run-ins between us in the last three days? Four?"

"I can't help it if your habits bring you to the two exact places I work at. Maybe I should be the one accusing *you* of stalking *me* for everyone to hear." She gestures broadly to the full bar around us.

I can't believe this woman. Is that how it's going to be? "You plan on making a scene here, too? So you want attention from my whole team, then, not just me?"

Her mouth falls open for a moment, but she quickly snaps it shut, leaning over the bartop. I'm hit with a waft of a fresh, fruity scent, and despite myself, I inhale the scent deeply. It throws me off even more, and I blink as she gets closer to my face.

Her sharp blue eyes scan me, as if she's trying to answer some question, then narrow. "You got me fired, you know that? I was fired on my *very first day*. Do you know how embarrassing that is? The last thing I need is for you to ruin this for me, too. So." She leans back and rearranges her face into impeccable coldness. "What can I get you, sir?"

Despite the condescending tone, her use of the word *sir* only serves to rouse an unwanted reaction in my groin. I shift and clear my throat. "Three lagers, please."

She turns around, busying herself with lining glasses up. My mind turns over her words once, twice. Finally, I blurt out, "Did you really get fired over that?"

She pauses, analyzing me. I shift again under her scrutiny. There's something about it that feels deeper than a normal once-over, and it unnerves me.

"I'm sorry," I say. Even though I still feel justified over my reaction – and I still have many questions about this woman – I didn't know this would be the outcome. "They shouldn't have fired you over that. I can talk to them, if you'd like."

She shakes her head and turns to the tap wall behind her, grabbing one of the glasses. "I don't need your pity, and I don't want your support. I'll get by on my own."

I remain quiet as she fills the glasses. The tension thickens with each second of silence as I try to think of what to say, and how to make sense of the way her words and actions don't line up. Finally, she turns to set the first drink in front of me, and I clear my throat. "The rodeo capital."

She gives me a confused look. "Excuse me?"

"Cody. Wyoming," I explain. "It's the rodeo capital of the world."

She fills the second glass silently, and as she turns to set it in front of me, asks, "How did you know that?"

I shrug. "I had a few hockey tournaments there back in the day. All of our families

always wanted to visit the museums." I pause. "Did you rodeo?"

"Oh. No." She places the third glass next to the first two and busies herself with wiping up the leftover moisture. "I'm actually from Arizona. Sedona."

I let out a disbelieving huff, and the side of my lip quirks as I consider her answer. She doesn't raise her head, still focused on the bartop.

"So are you lying to him, or lying to me?"

She freezes at my question. Her eyes slowly rise to meet mine, and I'm startled by the sheer look of panic in her expression. I open my mouth, unsure what will come out, or if I'm even supposed to backtrack. I was teasing her, but clearly, I've said the wrong thing. I'm just not quite sure how.

Before I can say anything, she schools her face back into a neutral position and replies, her voice soft. "I guess you'll never know."

With that, she turns, her entire face brightening as she greets her next customer with the same fake politeness she gave Thirsty Joe, leaving me to collect the beers I've ordered.

I shake my head, replaying our conversation in my mind. I still have questions – more now than before, if that's even possible. But between her obvious anger at me and all that secrecy, I can't help thinking my reaction in the coffee shop might have been a huge mistake.

Entering the rink always has a calming effect on me, especially on our home ice. Within those four walls, I know exactly what to do. Even if the game goes poorly, I can pinpoint exactly what I will do differently moving forward. The end goal is simple: win.

The girl who has gotten inside my head? There's nothing simple about her. She cycles through my head on repeat as I go through the motions of our off-ice warm-ups, and then as I put my gear on. I can't help but wonder if I need to make a stop at the coffee shop after the game and clear her name – but then, I remember: I never even got her name. All I have is what she looks like and where she's from. And even that might not be the truth.

The more I think about it, the more her expressions when she crossed my path were nothing like Sheila's. Sheila had always been erratic, oscillating between awe and manic hostility. This girl, on the other hand, had been confused, reserved, irritated. Even when I made her mad, her anger had been a quiet, condescending sort. It was nothing like I've ever experienced, and I wasn't sure if I wanted to grovel or return the attitude in kind.

I'm still considering it as I toy with my helmet, waiting for Coach to come in for our pre-game talk. Conversation is whipping around the locker room, and I'm catching only snippets of it. Goody is on another rant about how he *almost* went pro in golf before he decided hockey was his true path. Nils is trying to convince Ryan, our newest player, that he should take in one of his many foster cats. Jordie shoves me, and when I glance up to meet his gaze, I read the question in his eyes.

Before I'm forced to explain, however, Coach Henderson strides into the room. He immediately points at Levi, who has his phone out. "Put that shit away. It's game time."

Levi flushes and silently obliges. Coach pulls a whiteboard marker out of his pocket, removing the cap with his teeth. He spits the cap at Levi and turns to face the white board, writing numbers as he calls out the names of the respective players.

I make a mental note of the lines, nodding along with his choices, unsurprised as he announces me playing center to Levi and Jordie. Levi is a newer addition to the team, young but talented, and we've had some seamless plays already. Jordie and I have been spending more time with him, anticipating his joining our line. I'm glad that Coach had seen the same. Unsurprisingly, Grant and Highcloud round out the first line as our defensive pair.

"Now." Coach turns, scanning the locker room. "This should be a relatively easy game for us all. The Force finished dead last at the end of last season, and they only have two new players. But that doesn't mean we need to go easy on them. If anything, this is our chance to really learn what we're all about. Jordie – got anything else to add?"

I don't miss the quick glance Jordie gives me, as if confirming it's okay for him to speak. The letter C stands out on the front of his jersey, signifying his Captain status this year. The ache in my own chest is located ironically close to where the C would have been on my own jersey.

Where it had been, just last year.

Jordie clears his throat and scans the room. "What Coach said. Let's really solidify these new lines, get some pretty goals, and bring back that W!"

Coach nods emphatically and slams his clipboard against the wall to punctuate the moment. "Let's fucking go, boys!"

His final words are met with a resounding chorus of whoops and bangs, and with that, we throw our helmets and gloves on, grabbing our sticks as we exit into the tunnel. The cheers meet our ears as we approach the ice, and I break out into a grin as I spot a small group of kids sporting tiny Leopards jerseys and bobbing on the balls of their feet. Their parents hang back in the shadows, sporting grins even larger than my own.

I lean over as we stride through the tunnel, giving each kid we've invited a high five. Their tiny fists ricochet off my glove, but bounce back eagerly to hit each player behind me. Their excitement warms me, replacing the ache in my chest.

I step out onto the rink, and every thought diminishes at the first hiss of my skates biting the ice. The roar of the crowd becomes a dull backdrop as I work my way through warmups, envisioning plays and enjoying the thrill building in my core at the anticipation of the first puck drop.

It doesn't disappoint.

I lose myself in the game, enjoying the way our line melds together. By the last few minutes of the game, we're up by four and Jordie, Levi and I are anticipating one another's plays at least two passes in advance. Even Grant manages to hold himself together – mostly. He did serve time at the start of the third period for starting a fight alongside two Force players, but Highcloud didn't seem to fault his defensive partner for it. Grant had been holding two of the players against the boards at once, laughing maniacally as they struggled to get at the puck between his skates until one of them lost their cool and took the first swing.

If you didn't know Grant, you'd assume it had all been an innocent play and he was the victim. But Goody – late to change out for Highcloud, but happy to get in on some of the action when the fight started – came back to the bench and proudly proclaimed the words exchanged between Grant and the Force players. Allegedly, he started with asking if the player's large A on his jersey was compensating for something in his breezers, and ended with telling him to check if his sack was still down there.

I swing over the boards and settle onto the bench, laughing breathlessly to myself as I remember Grant's broad grin as he saluted the players on his way out of the penalty box a few minutes ago. Jordie jumps over the boards to end his shift shortly after. He plops down on the bench next to me and reaches for his water bottle, pointing at the scoreboard as he squirts water on his face and into his mouth.

"Not a bad way to start the season," he says, and reaches over for another water bottle, unscrewing the cap just enough that it will fall off if tipped, but not enough to notice it at first glance.

I hum, eyeing the score. Five to one. "I think we could've gotten at least one more. We shouldn't let everyone off this easily."

Levi groans from my other side. "Does that mean we get angry Benji at tomorrow's praccy?"

"Depends," Jordie chimes in. "Will he be extra angry because of whatever was on his mind before the game?"

Grant, always the eavesdropper, leans past Highcloud to shoot me a quizzical look down the bench. "What happened before the game, bro?"

The buzzer goes off as they all turn to me, signaling the end of the game. Though we're all dripping sweat, an uncomfortable cold wave surges through me as I consider how to respond.

The rookie, Ryan, skates back to the bench, saving me the trouble of responding. We all watch out of the corners of our eyes as he goes for his water, tilting it back and squeezing. The cap pops off, exploding water down the front of his jersey.

"Awe, hell," he says, sputtering. "Who did that?"

Jordie slaps his back and tosses him a grin. "Just keeping you on your toes, rook."

We all chuckle, but it's clear that the conversation isn't over as Jordie turns back to me, brows raised. "Do you want to get a drink after this, buddy?" he asks, his brows raised. "Just us linies?"

I smile, grateful for his understanding, and rise to join the rest of the team as they empty out onto the ice to celebrate. "Actually," I reply, "how do you feel about a late night coffee?"

Chapter 5

LISA

My heavy breathing overpowers the sound of my footfalls as I slow the treadmill down, coming to a walking pace. I wipe the sweat from my brow and stare down at the number. Nine miles. The university's gym has all sorts of equipment, but the treadmill is my weapon of choice.

I grin triumphantly. "Patty, come check it out!"

My roommate, Patty, ambles over, still carrying her barbells. She gawks down at the treadmill screen. "Nice work. You'll be running a marathon in no time."

I groan and press stop, coming to a halt on the track. "I don't think I have the patience for that. I just want to keep up with Austin."

Patty's gaze slides past me and she smiles. "Speak of the devil."

Before I can glance behind me, I feel the strong, solid muscle of Austin's arm as it winds around me. He pinches my waist. "God damn! Look at how toned you're getting."

"Nine miles." I grin up at him and he gazes down at me, pride written across his face.

"Whew," he whistles. "My little workout machine. You're looking great."

"Gross," Patty gags. "Get a room, you two."

I smile and lean into Austin. "We already are, remember? I really can't wait to move in with you next year."

Patty swats at me playfully. "Hey!" she exclaims. "What about your amazing roommate? What were our first two years of college to you? Am I chopped liver?"

I roll my eyes at her and grin. "Oh, stop pretending I'm ditching you. We'll still be roommates next year, just not in the literal same room. Plus, you're the one who decided you wanted to move in with your hot, older boyfriend first."

"Well, I guess it was meant to be that your age-appropriate boyfriend is my boyfriend's brother." Patty grins. "The way I see it, since we'll still technically be roomies, we're all winning."

As I gaze back up at Austin, his face distorts. His smile turns into a sneer, and his eyes darken into something sinister. The hand on my waist tightens, and I squirm, but I can't escape the pain, which spreads up my entire side. A tingling sensation shoots through my veins and coats my mouth with a sour taste.

It feels like fear.

I shoot up, gasping for air. It takes me several long moments to register that I'm in bed, and I'm alone. No, scratch that – not alone. Winston is there, nudging at my arm with his cold, wet nose. I take several deep breaths and slide my hand over his head, scratching behind his ears. My hand is trembling, but he doesn't mind. He simply crawls forward, as close as he can get to me without physically crawling in my lap. He rests his head on my chest, and tears well in my eyes as I take in his soft, curious look.

After several long moments, I reach my other hand over to the nightstand and flip my phone over. 4:52. I sigh and close my eyes, but when my heart rate remains elevated, I decide that more sleep isn't in the cards for me again this morning.

I sit up in bed, then frown. Since I don't have a coffee shop gig to get ready for anymore, I've got several hours until I'm meeting Andi at the boxing gym. I wring my hands together, considering. I could run outside, but with the days getting shorter, it's pitch black outside, and I don't know the area well enough yet to navigate it in the dark. Not to mention, it's probably still a slipping hazard.

I can't sit here and read or watch television, either. My mind isn't strong enough not to wander into dangerous territory while my body is idle. I look back over at Winny and give him another scratch. "It's almost five, which means the gym will be open. I guess it's time to really check out those new amenities, huh? Maybe something other than the treadmill?"

I let Winny out, get dressed, and pack a swimsuit, ready for a quiet morning workout and follow-up swim. The second I enter the cycling studio, though, I come to a dead stop.

"You've got to be kidding me," I mutter under my breath and take a step back, but it's too late. The door opening has alerted the man in the studio of my arrival. His head shoots up, and my suspicions are confirmed: it's the Mustache Man, the friend I've seen with Benjamin Estes.

His expression shifts to one of recognition, but I really don't want to deal with another conversation, especially alone. I quickly turn on my heel and stride back out the door, heading for the pool instead. I change, keeping a careful eye on the locker room door on the off chance that I've been followed. When nothing happens, I relax slightly, and slip out the door into the pool area.

Laughter echoes off the water, filling my ears. It takes a minute for my eyes to adjust to the soft lighting – different from the bright, abrasive lighting in the locker room – and my gaze travels directly to the source of the laughter. The blond player is in the hot tub, arms draped over the side, talking to someone whose back is to me, towels stuffed under one arm.

A *tall* someone, broad-shouldered, with a large tattoo settled on one shoulder blade. I tilt my head, eyes tracing the lines of the bird in flight, spotted wings spread across his tanned skin. His swimming trunks cling to the tight curve of his ass, and my eyes drop to scan the outline despite myself. *Holy fuck...* I didn't realize a man's ass could be such an attractive feature until this very moment.

He turns, and when he tosses his dark, wavy hair out of his face, my heart sinks. Benjamin's expression twists from a broad, lopsided grin to one of disbelief. He faces me completely, and as he walks towards me, my gaze dips across his front of their own volition, scanning from his shoulders to his solid pecs, down his defined abs and to the waistband of his... *nope. Not going there.*

My eyes shoot back up to his, and as he gets closer, I can see the firm set of his mouth. A hard lump forms in my throat, and I clench my fists, feeling the prick of sweat in them. There's no one else around; no bartop or counter to separate me from him. My hand gravitates to my side, covering the phantom ache that twinges of its own volition.

I want to turn and sprint away, but that's not what I've spent the past several weeks training for. *In through the nose, out through the mouth.* I've worked to face my fears, and I remind myself that I'm safe here. I'm in my own apartment's indoor pool. I've faced far worse than this hockey boy. He just seems to have an irrational chip on his shoulder about how fate has been pushing us together. It's time to settle that.

I stand a bit straighter, watching carefully to see how close Benjamin gets. He stops before he reaches arm's length and glances down, as though he's also marking the distance. His gaze rakes over me and I cross my arms, hyper-aware that I'm in nothing more than a bikini. Finally, he surprises me by sighing.

"You can't be fucking serious." He runs a hand through his hair, sending droplets of water flying. "And to think I just talked with the manager at Rise & Grind to clear your name the other night."

"What?" I ask, my arms falling to my sides, caught off guard by this new information and his resigned tone. He went back to the coffee shop to speak to my manager. Did that mean I could get my job back? Does it mean he's gotten over whatever it was that had him so upset about me?

"What is it you want?" He tilts his head, studying me. "Is it a photo? A date?"

"I'm sorry, *what?*"

"What's your name?"

The question catches me off guard, and I have to bite back my knee-jerk answer for the first time in weeks. I swallow and reply, "Lisa."

"Lisa." He pauses, as if taking a moment to sort through a puzzle of his own. "Look, I'll give it to you, you almost had me convinced. But you can't blame this one on work. We're here before most of the building is even awake. It's always been quiet, until now. Tell me, who else gets up to swim at five in the morning? Especially when they don't have a coffee shop job to go to?"

Irritation bursts through my confusion and I scowl at him. "You don't own the early morning swim time. Don't you have your own gym at the ice rink, or something?"

He barks a laugh. "So you *do* know who I am!"

"I didn't, until you decided to yell at me over a cup of coffee." I cross my arms again and watch as his eyes travel down to my breasts. He takes another step forward and I stiffen, acutely aware of the fact that he's now within arm's reach. He leans in, close enough that he's nearly dripping on me, but doesn't make a move to reach out. I still lean back reflexively.

"Look, I'm down for some fun," he says, mouth turning upward in a dark and seductive smile. "I'll admit it. You look incredible. But then I need your word that you'll leave me alone."

My mouth falls open. Is this man seriously offering to fool around with me because he thinks I'm obsessed with him? Does he think I'm just trying to scratch an itch?

"So?" Benjamin pushes, raising a brow. "Do we have a deal, Lisa?"

I shake my head, incredulous. Is he really that big of a deal that he thinks I'm some sort of groupie? Clearly, he needs his ego brought down a peg or two.

"I *so* appreciate the offer, Benjamin," I begin, layering the sarcasm on as thickly as I can muster, "but I think the only fun you'll be having is with your own hand."

I step back, scanning the windows. There's the beginning of a soft glow outside, telling me sunrise is maybe thirty minutes away. I can change and take my morning run outside instead, and hopefully avoid running into more of these damn Leopards. They're like ticks at this point.

I turn back to face Benji and look past his puzzled expression, noticing his blond teammate. He's clearly pretending not to be invested in our conversation, and failing miserably. I nod to get his attention and call out, "I'm sure you can give him some solid pointers. He looks like he's in need of some guidance."

With that, I turn on my heel and stalk away.

"So, you just keep... running into him? Entirely by accident?" Andi asks. We're laying in a pool of our own sweat, our legs propped up against the wall under the guise of reducing swelling and promoting circulation. Bella, Paul's daughter, has joined us as well. She's currently in college, but her university is just a short drive into the city, so she still comes to classes here on the weekend. It's her chance to catch up with her dad, who I've come to know she's very close to, and she's been slowly folding into our little friendship circle as well. This post-stretch ritual doubles as our gossip time, since any other time we're breathing too heavily to hold productive conversation.

"Yes," I groan, wiping my arm across my forehead, which just ends up mixing my arm and head sweat together. "Apparently my coffee shop is the team's coffee shop, my bar is the team's bar, and my gym is the team's gym. I bet at least half of them live in my apartment."

"I have to admit, from his perspective, I can see why it would seem suspicious," Bella says, glancing my way. When I fix her with an openmouthed stare, she throws her hands up helplessly. "What? I'm sure he's had stalkers before. The best players on our team have them, for god's sake, and that's just college hockey. He's gotta protect himself from the more unhinged fans out there. Parasocial relationships these days and all that."

"And he was the captain," Andi puts in. "He's easily one of the best players. He's gotta be careful."

I clamp my mouth shut and consider her words. As much as I hate to admit it, she has a point. I'm no stranger to carefully crafting my surroundings to protect myself. From his perspective, I suddenly dropped in on all of his routines, someone he didn't know or trust. I could have been an undercover reporter, a superfan, or even a stalker.

But again, most *rational* beings would take a hot minute before reacting the way he did.

"Well, he didn't need to come out guns a-blazing," I mutter. "I mean, he got me fucking fired over it."

"True," Bella agrees. "But, he got you the job back. So, all's well that ends well?"

I hum, unwilling to go *that* far. But what Benji said was true – I stopped at Rise & Grind on my way to the gym, and they offered me the job back, apologizing profusely. If I didn't realize the celebrity status and power that Benjamin carried before, that told me what I needed to know.

That being said, it only makes me more nervous, knowing I somehow wandered so far into his circle. The last thing I want is to be associated with someone with such notoriety and influence.

"You said he *was* the captain," I begin, turning Andi's words over in my head. "Is he not anymore?"

"I don't think so," she replies and looks to Bella, our resident hockey expert.

She just shrugs. "Yeah, no. I think something happened at the end of last season, and they weren't sure if he'd be back. Don't quote me on that, though; I just remember reading something in passing."

I blink, absorbing her words. For all the anger I had when he got me fired, I hadn't actually bothered to do any real research that day. "Maybe I should really look him up."

"Do it. You know what they say about knowing your enemy."

Andi's timer goes off, and we roll our legs off the wall, reaching for our water bottles. "All right. I think it's time I visit your bar. I can be your wing woman or Benji's worst enemy," she says. "Or, you know, both. You just tell me what you need and I'm there for you, girl."

"Sure," I say, narrowing my eyes at her. "So you're not just going to get free drinks and stare at professional athletes?"

She grins conspiratorially and squirts water at me. "I said I'm there for you. I didn't say I'm not human."

Chapter 6

Benji

“T hank you, Jim,” I say, and hit end on the call. *What the fuck?*

“So?” Jordie plops down next to me and shovels popcorn into his mouth. “Anything?”

I shake my head, trying to sort the pieces together in my mind. Everything I've learned about Lisa in the past week has left me with more questions, and it's making me increasingly uneasy. But it also makes me more determined to uncover the truth.

The obvious answer would be to just drop the hunt and work to get her out of this building, but there's a piece of the puzzle missing, and I can't seem to let it go. Maybe it's because she's rejected me at every turn, going against all the obvious signs she would be stalking me. Or maybe it has to do with the way I can't get her piercing blue eyes or her stunning body out of my mind.

Or maybe it's because she's a goddamn mystery that just became a dead end.

“There's nothing,” I respond, scrubbing a hand over my face.

“Nothing?” Jordie echoes. *“At all?* That's impossible.”

"You're right. It's impossible." I stare at the slip of paper in my hand. Lisa Graham is written on it, alongside a phone number and an apartment number. The information cost me a hundred dollar bill and one of my most winning smiles, both given to the apartment receptionist. I have no doubt the information she gave me is accurate from Lisa's profile, but... "The phone number leads to a burner phone. The kind you buy minutes for."

"That's still a thing?" Grant asks, entering the room. He twists the lid off a beer and tosses it behind him as he saunters over to the couch. He plops down heavily, kicking his feet up onto the table in front of him, and takes a long drink. I narrow my eyes at him. We still have one more practice tonight, and if he shows up half-cocked, he'll end up sobering up halfway through practice. When that happens, his headaches become our headaches.

He sets the beer down on the side table and belches, keeping eye contact with me as he grins. I sigh and continue. "Yes, it's still a thing. Though I can't for the life of me understand why that's the kind of phone she would have. She lives on the top floor, so she's clearly not hurting for money, even though she's working shit-paying barista and bartender jobs. But," I lean in and both Jordie and Grant follow suit, raising their brows curiously. "Jim couldn't find *any* trace of online payments. So she's clearly paying in cash."

"What the fuck, dude!" Grant exclaims, slamming a palm down on the table.

"Right? I'm not sure how she's got things set up with her work, but he couldn't find a trace of those payments, either. And don't even get me started on her name."

"What do you mean?" Jordie asks.

"Jim couldn't find anyone by the name Lisa Graham that would be around her age in Cody or Sedona. Or here, outside of this apartment, for that matter." A nervousness bubbles up in me as I think through what our family's private investigator said. *"Keep an eye on this one. I don't know what her story is, but if she's got the same intentions as Sheila, she's going about it in a much cleverer way."*

"Look, I get the appeal. She's a fucking smoke show. But with all these loose ends, I don't think she's worth the trouble, brother," Jordie warns.

I simply blink at him, trying to sort out the weird mixture of apprehension and jealousy at his words. He saw her in that skimpy bikini, too, her body boasting all the same contradictions that the information about her did. She was slender and pale, but lined with hard muscle, giving possible truth to the fact that she did enjoy working out – possibly at odd hours, and probably too hard. Her light blue bikini top had barely hidden those perky breasts. Ones that I'd given thought to taking in my mouth when I threw out the idea of hooking up with her.

I'd thought about it a few times after, too, until I realized Lisa Graham was merely a ghost.

"I don't think Benji's trying to slam this one, Jordie," Grant puts in, and turns to face me. "I think he's just trying to figure out what her deal is. But, Benj... are you saying you don't even think it's her real name she's using?"

"I don't know," I say slowly, "but I plan to find out."

Gabbi: *Good luck today!!! Cheering you on from the couch. Love you*

I smile as I read the message, and type out a quick reply before Coach can come in and yell at me for having my phone out before the game.

Me: *Love you too, sis.*

Gabbi: *Kick Liam's ass for me.*

I smirk and put my phone away as Coach enters the room. He walks around, rubbing his chin and assessing us. He knows we're fired up; the Pirates are our biggest competition, and we've swapped more cheap shots with them than any other team. I can tell he's gauging whether or not to stoke the fire further or bring us down to ensure we're going to play with level heads.

"Listen," he begins. "This won't be as easy as last week's game. But we have three chances to beat these guys. One hundred and eighty minutes to fight against them, and sixty of those happen today. I know we're all eager, but don't come out too hard. We still have a whole season to get our legs under us. I want quick shifts. When we get tired, we get scrappy, and we take stupid penalties."

He pauses, eyes narrowing on Grant. Grant blinks back innocently.

"Keep your checking fair and play the puck, not just the body," he continues. "I don't want to see any of you taking a run into their numbers. Hurting them will only hurt us."

A murmur of assent goes up from the team and Coach nods, satisfied that he's made his point. "Now let's play some great fucking hockey!"

We cheer, leaving the locker room, but it becomes clear to me within minutes that our rough edges are still showing. Two periods of tense hockey have us down by one. The newer players, still riding the high that got them to the professional level, begin to try their hand at taking the puck all the way up the ice alone, forgetting to – or choosing not to – pass the puck. The game turns chippy as players begin hooking and tripping, attempting to cover ground with their sticks instead of moving their feet.

I can feel the Pirates gloating every time we face off, though I keep my eyes down. I like to think I've learned to remain calm on the ice, but an ill-timed chirp from the other team in moments like this, when we're down a goal, can still make me snap.

I throw my helmet down as we enter the locker room between the second and third period. I'm fine with losing if there are valid reasons, but this has been some shit hockey we've been playing, and I need to at least try to rectify it. The C that was on my jersey last year still meant something. Jordie locks eyes with me and nods, settling back into his cubby to let me speak. I shoot him a grateful look before I eye the rest of the players in the locker room.

"Listen," I begin, "I know this is going rough. But we can't keep playing selfish hockey. Games aren't just won north to

south, we need to be moving the puck east to west. Konner –
you've got JJ wide open on the other side of the ice every time
we break it out of our zone. Keep your head up and look for
him."

Konner and JJ exchange a look, and Konner bows his head
in acknowledgement. I continue. "Goody – keep battling for
control in the corners. Even if you're not the first to the puck,
that doesn't mean you won't win the fight for it. Don't just *give
up* on it."

Goody nods, and I turn to our last new addition, our goalie.
"Mac." Mac meets my gaze with a surprised expression. "Keep it
up. You're getting absolutely pummeled out there, and you've
let next to nothing in. It's on us to serve you this period."

He flushes at the praise, and I turn to the coaches, who
entered behind me while I was talking. "Anything to add?"

"Nope, that about covers it." Our goalie coach, Anders,
gives me a long, approving look, and turns to exit.

Coach Henderson nods in agreement, adding, "Let's take
this game back."

I settle in next to Jordie, who slaps my breezers with his
hand. "Good to have you back, captain," he murmurs. I toss
him a tight grin and duck my head, attempting to keep my
emotions in check. Jordie never wanted the leadership, but I
inadvertently handed it to him. It's on me to earn it back this
year, and we both know it. In the meantime, I couldn't ask for
a more supportive friend and teammate.

When the time comes to go back out on the ice, we toss our
helmets and gloves back on, silently focusing on what comes
next. As the last period commences, I'm relieved to see my ad-

vice has been taken seriously. As Konner and JJ tear down the ice as a unit, Konner looks up and passes the puck to JJ, making a beeline for the net. JJ skates to the side and then puts the brakes on, sending ice flying, and backhands the puck straight to where Konner is headed. Konner is there before any defensemen can reach him, and doesn't so much as catch the puck before redirecting it to the net.

It's wide open. The goalie didn't move in time to follow the play back in Konner's direction. The puck hits the back of the net with satisfying speed, popping right back out from the force, and the buzzer for the goal goes off. Our entire bench leaps to their feet, yelling and cheering.

"What a fucking beauty!"

"That's the way you do it!"

"Way to fucking take it, boys!"

I grin as they skate by, bumping gloves down the line of teammates. I can already see the trust settling in – they're discovering they can count on one another to be there, and from now on, they'll play as a team. No more selfish hockey. Coach Henderson slaps me on the shoulder, and when I turn to look at him, he bends over and murmurs, "That's why you're here, Benji. Keep it up, and you know what comes next."

I nod at him in thanks, but his implication tugs at knots inside me. *What comes next* is not just the C. It's getting called up to the NHL, and though I've been working all my life for that goal, it's become a complicated one over the past year. I distract myself by glancing at the scoreboard.

Tie game, with five minutes left. I surge forward as Konner comes back to the bench for a line change, ready to keep up the momentum – but during his shift, the tide has turned, and two Pirates players are now coming down the ice with only Highcloud to defend against them both. I tear after them.

Highcloud works to push the player with the puck to the corner and I go for the other player barreling to the net, noting belatedly that it's Liam. The player Highcloud is covering takes a shot on net, and Mac makes the save, dropping to the ice and covering the puck.

I begin to slow, but Liam doesn't. He continues full-speed toward the net, stopping hard and covering Mac's face in a spray of ice. Cries of outrage spring up from our bench as the players clock the insult. Rage burns its way up my throat. Before I can shove Liam to the side, he's at it again, slashing at Mac with his stick under the guise of going for the puck.

Abso-fucking-lutely not.

If there's one rule, it's that you do *not* fuck with the goalie.

Liam knows this, and he knows exactly what it means to do this to Mac in front of *me*. We lock eyes and he gives me that stupid fucking grin, one I've seen too many times over the years. My stick and gloves are on the ice in a flash, and I grab his jersey bare-fisted, tugging him into me. He shucks his gear off as well, but my fist connects with his face before he can so much as raise his hand.

Two, three hits in rapid succession, and I hear a sickening crack. Whether it's his nose or my knuckles, I don't know, and quite frankly I don't give a shit. Liam finally gets his first punch out, but it's laughably slow. I tilt my head to the side to avoid it, following through with my fourth punch. This time, his helmet goes flying, skittering across the ice. My eyes follow it for a moment, and I see other players are barreling towards us to join the fight. If the crowd is cheering or the refs are yelling, I'm not sure. All I hear is the blood pounding in my ears.

Liam fists my jersey in his hands, tugging me closer. "I'm surprised to see you're playing again, Estes," he sneers. Blood trickles from his nose, and I yank at his jersey, causing us to spin on the ice as we square up once more. "I thought after how last season ended, you'd be out for good. But here you are. How's it feel, getting demoted and *still* trying to take what was his?"

His eyes travel pointedly down to where the C used to be, and that's the final straw. I brace myself, twisting both hands in his jersey until I'm grabbing his shoulder pads, and I lift him straight off the ice, only to send him slamming into the ground. I'm on top of him before he can react, but I'm only able to get a few punches in before the refs are on me.

"All right, all right, break it up! Who wants to hurt their team more, huh?"

"He started shit out of nowhere." Liam spits, leaving red splatters on the ice where he lays.

Grant bursts through the two Pirates players he's got held up. He doesn't have a scratch on him, but I'm unsurprised to see the other players both sporting busted lips. "Oh, eat dog shit! You know better than to fuck with a tendy." He flicks something off his fist – someone's contact, maybe? – and fixes Liam with a glare. Liam at least has the sense to shrink back.

"Come on, Estes. Roberts. Let's go. Five for fighting." The ref looks resigned, as though he knows on some level that it's an unfair call. But it's the price to pay, and I did throw the first punch. I skate away with him, and the sounds of the crowd banging on the glass finally reach me as the rage dissipates into cold grief.

I barely register the goal the Pirates score in the last thirty seconds, officially clinching the win. Instead, Liam's words are on repeat in my head as I clench and unclench my fists.

How's it feel, getting demoted and still trying to take what was his?

Chapter 7

LISA

"*You really think I believe that bullshit?*"

Austin is towering over me, voice tight with barely contained rage. I instinctively shrink back, and he steps forward, filling the space I try to leave between us. He grabs the railing on the stairs, and his knuckles turn white in a matter of seconds.

"You think I don't see what's going on here?" Austin motions behind us. We're outside, but the thrum of the music is loud enough to hear through the closed doors. It's also loud enough that nobody inside can hear what's taking place out here.

"There's a reason I told you not to come to stupid shit like this. I saw you, all over the guys in there. You really can't keep away, can you?"

"I told you, Patty invited me." I hear the tremble in my voice, and though I know it will make me sound more guilty, I can't keep it from my tone. "She kept asking why I never come, so I figured one drink –"

"Enough!" He cuts me off with a roar. "Clearly you need to be reminded who you belong to, Alyssa."

He steps close enough for me to feel his hot breath on my face, and my heart sinks at his words. I risk a quick glance at his face and see all the rage he normally keeps so carefully contained in public. His restraint has officially snapped. "And how are you supposed to learn when you won't shut your goddamn mouth?"

The bitter taste of what I woke up from this morning hasn't gone away, even several hours later. I scrub furiously at a stain on the bartop and attempt to focus on Andi's words. If I can keep myself in the present, it won't be nearly as bad, and if anyone can help me with that, it's the animated blonde sitting on the barstool in front of me.

"I expected them to be…cheerier," Andi observes, taking a long sip of her radler. Most of the Leopards team is here, but they aren't nearly as rowdy as I'd expect a post-game hockey team to be. Instead, they're sitting around, drinking and murmuring amongst themselves. Some are playing pool, but most are on their phones, scrolling intently while spitting their dip every now and then into disposable cups. Gross *and* depressing.

"That might have something to do with it." I gesture to the screen, where a news cast is highlighting the score of the hockey game earlier today. The Pirates beat the Leopards, three to two. Andi glances up as the score switches to a snippet from the game, where #17 on the Leopards is squaring off with player #23 on the Pirates. They spin, and the name ESTES becomes clear as day on the back of the Leopards jersey.

"Holy shit," Andi breathes. "That's him, isn't it?"

I can only nod, watching as he lifts the Pirates player straight off his skates and slams him to the ground, going down on one knee himself to continue pummeling him. I wince and look away, scanning the sea of blue.

To my surprise, Benjamin Estes isn't watching the TV; he's watching me. I meet his gaze, and the intensity of it makes me pale. Unlike earlier this week, there is no soft contemplation. There's something dark there, as though the fight from the game earlier in the day only angered him further, rather than being an outlet. My stomach churns at the thought, and I look away.

"Excuse me. Do you mind changing the channel?"

I turn to see the teammate with the mustache at the bar, his face grim. "What?"

"Do you mind changing the channel?" he repeats. "It was a tough game. We'd rather not see the replays."

"Uh. Y-yeah."

He fixes me with a strange look, as though he has a question he wants to ask, but apparently thinks better of it. He shifts away, giving Andi a quick nod as he returns back to his teammates. I grab the remote and flip to a new channel, and Andi sidles back up to me on the other side of the bar, grinning.

"Oh my *god*. What I wouldn't give to take him for a ride," she says, giving a wistful, dramatic sigh.

I raise a brow at her. "Him? The one with the lip foliage?"

She nods. "Oh, I am an active member of the clit tickler fan club." I choke on a laugh, and she grins and taps the bartop. "Now get me another beer, so I can work up the courage to go ask him if I can suck his dick until I lose my voice. Respectfully, of course."

I snort and grab her empty glass. I'm ready to make a comment about what a vivid picture she paints, but the response dies in my throat when I see her frown, eyes flicking to someone out of my line of sight.

"If you phrase it like that, it doesn't matter how many beers you or Grant have. He'll say yes."

At this point, I'd recognize that voice anywhere, even with amusement in it I haven't heard before.

Andi flushes and stammers, uncharacteristically at a loss for words, and I take my time refilling her glass. I inhale deeply as I straighten the glass and fill it the remainder of the way up, mentally bracing myself. Finally, I pass the fresh beer to her and turn to face Benjamin.

He's leaning against the bar, a jacket over his Leopards sweater, and that trademark male baseball cap, turned backwards, because *of course* it is. He's got a half-smile fixed on his face, but it's more polite than genuine. That darkness I saw earlier is still a shadow behind his eyes, and it makes me tense.

"Can I get you anything?" I ask coolly. "Anything to drink, that is. Your last proposition didn't work that well."

He regards me for a long moment, then gives Andi a sidelong look. She meets it and then raises her brow at me in question. I give her a quick nod and pair it with a small smile. I'm okay – after all, what can he do here, other than yell again?

She shrugs and lifts her full glass in a salute. "I guess I'll go see if your theory about this Grant fellow is correct, then." She lifts herself off the barstool, but shoots me a pointed look before leaving. "I'll be right over here."

When she's out of earshot, Benjamin turns back to me. "Does she know?" he asks.

My stomach drops. He could mean several things, and none of them are good. I clutch the bartop and attempt to keep my voice level. "Know what?"

"That Lisa Graham isn't your real name."

What the fuck?

It's all I can take not to collapse behind the bar. My grip turns sweaty, there's a ringing that begins in my ears, and the edges of my vision go fuzzy. His eyes narrow as he takes in my response, and I know there's no talking my way out of it.

I had accounted for every piece of my past, ensuring there were no tie backs to my former life. I hadn't, however, counted on someone from my *future* digging as deep as Benjamin fucking Estes obviously had. Why the hell was he digging into me, anyway? Had our run-ins really upset him that much?

I lick my lips, willing moisture back into my mouth, now bone-dry. "How – how do you know?" I manage to ask.

"I have my ways." He leans over the bartop and lowers his voice. "Now, are you going to be honest with me, or do I need to scream your lies to the world?"

My heart begins pounding as I consider how to proceed. No – anything but a public announcement. It's as though he knows exactly what I didn't want to have happen. Maybe...*he* is the one planning these run-ins? The one stalking me?

Perhaps I have it all wrong, and he'd been hired to find me. Did hockey players have side gigs?

"I have money. I can pay you not to say anything," I plead.

He hesitates, and I jump on that. So, it *was* about the money then. Somebody hired him, and I can only think of one person who would want to. I lean in to meet him halfway across the bartop, and he tips his head in a way that tells me to continue.

"Seriously," I whisper urgently. "Whatever he's offering you, I can double it. Triple it. Just say the word. Just *please*, don't tell him I'm here."

His head jerks back. He opens his mouth, then closes it without a word. Is he…surprised that I'm willing to pay? That I can afford to? Well, joke's on them, then.

I scour his face for answers. Despite the fight that had happened earlier, he doesn't appear to have a single bruise, and he's cleaned up. I hate that I can smell a scent like leather and sandalwood coming off of him, because it smells amazing.

His hand twitches, reaching forward, and I pull back automatically. He pauses, then lifts the hand to rub his chin, almost looking…concerned? I blink rapidly, trying to make sense of his expression.

"Him? Who…who are you talking about?" He practically breathes the question, as though he's been punched in the gut. Suddenly, I feel the same.

Shit. Whatever just happened was a series of coincidences, leading to an admission that shouldn't have come out. If I wasn't screwed before, I certainly am now.

"Are you in trouble?" he asks, and oh, god. The look he's giving me – full lips pursed, those dark eyes wide and brimming with, yep, that's definitely concern now– tells me he's not going to drop this.

It was one thing when he was angry at me, wanting me to leave him alone. Now, I have a feeling I'll be the one convincing *him* to leave *me* alone. Maybe the dream I had this morning was a sign. No matter where I am, I haven't truly escaped anything.

I jolt away from the bartop as though it's started on fire. "I've gotta go."

I turn away and sidle to the corner of the bar where our coats hang, snagging mine. I'll have to find my manager, make some excuse about feeling sick, but it shouldn't be too difficult to fake. My hands feel clammy and I'm certain the blood hasn't yet returned to my face.

I glance back to see that Benjamin is standing straight up, watching me carefully. "Don't follow me," I say, my voice choppy, and slip away before he can respond.

Chapter 8

Benji

Of course I follow her.

Chapter 9

BENJI

The realization that I'd completely misjudged her – and the guilt that followed – hit me like a truck as we locked eyes across the bartop. I'd been so sure I'd pegged her correctly. The second I called her bluff on her name, she'd blanched, the paleness of her skin stark against her startled blue eyes.

The more I pushed, though, I realized her reaction wasn't like someone who had been busted at her own game. It was like someone who had been caught trying to flee. It startled and, quite honestly, scared me.

"Please, don't tell him I'm here," she'd said. Who is 'him'?

Is it possible that we're both running away from different pasts, and we just happened to run into one another?

Either way, I need some answers.

Thoughts swirl in my head as I follow after her, willing the crunch of snow under my footsteps to soften. She only makes it a block before she turns around a corner, tucking herself up against the building. I slow, and her panicked breathing reaches my ears before I see her. She has her arms wrapped around her middle, and hot breaths twist from her mouth into the cold air as she works to calm herself.

I halt, unsure how to approach now that she's come to a stop. A few steps closer, and I realize she's literally shaking, her eyes squeezed shut. *Fuck.* I did this to her, didn't I?

I've been such an asshole, pushing her, questioning her to the point that she feels like this. My skin feels itchy, the guilt manifesting itself to the point of making me feel physically uncomfortable.

I throw caution to the wind and take the final few steps, reaching out for her.

"Lisa, look –" I begin. Even though I know it's not her true name, it's the only one I've got, and all I want is to give her a scrap of comfort.

Instead of reaching her arm, I run face-first into a wall.

No, scratch that – not a wall. Her *fist.*

"Argh!" I yelp, stumbling back and clutching the side of my face. The hit was surprisingly solid, given her tiny frame. I can already feel the start of a bruise blossoming across my jaw. "What the *fuck* was that?"

"Oh my god, oh my god," she's muttering, sliding further down the wall. She covers herself with her arms, hiding her face, knees pulled up to her chest. "I'm sorry, I'm sorry, I'm sorry."

She keeps repeating those two words, even as they become muddled with her rapid breathing. Her whole body is moving, partly from the heaving breaths, and partly just from shaking.

I'm still standing here, unsure what to do next. Every fiber of my body is screaming to embrace her in an effort to comfort her, but a part of my brain – the one that's been hit awake, now – lights up with a warning sign to pause and think this through.

I flip back through our brief interactions in my mind, pieces I overlooked before sliding into place: her tense posture in the elevator, the fear and panic when I confronted her with a raised voice, the way she flinches away every time I shift toward her.

Something is very wrong. And though I didn't start it, I can see now that I haven't been helping. Instead of moving into her space again, I decide the safest option is to sit down across from her, crossing my legs and folding my hands in my lap. I don't speak, and I don't reach for her again. I simply wait.

It takes a minute, but her breathing becomes ragged as her words dissolve into choked sobs. Slowly, her trembling lessens, her sobs becoming small hiccups. That's when she turns her face enough to peek out at me from between her arms.

I give her a small smile. "Hey."

She simply eyes me, saying nothing. Fair enough – I deserve her apprehension.

I motion to my jaw. "That's a nice right hook you have there," I say. "I can't wait to explain this to the boys tomorrow."

She shrinks back against the wall. "I'm so sorry," she whispers, her voice hoarse.

"Nah. I had it coming." I flash her another small smile, hoping it conveys the *we're chill* message I want it to. "I shouldn't have blindsided you, especially in the state you were in."

She says nothing, and my mind races. I have so many questions, but clearly now is not the time to push it. Forcing these questions is what got us here in the first place.

Instead, I ask, "Can I get you anything? A water?" I hesitate. "A beer?"

She shakes her head and unfolds herself from the position she's been wrapped in. "I just need to go home," she mutters, and makes to stand, but stumbles back against the wall for a brief moment.

I'm up in a flash, ready to help her. She lifts a hand, stopping me with a quiet "please", and I purse my lips. She can have her space, but I'm not letting her walk home alone in the cold and the dark, especially not in this state.

"Can I at least walk you home?" I phrase the question as lightly as possible, but she still hesitates before nodding and pushing forward. I follow along silently, leaving just enough space between us that she has plenty of room, but not enough that I look like I'm doing anything creepy.

Her phone rings, and she digs in her coat pocket, fumbling for it. When she pulls it out, I see that it is in fact an old, clunky phone. Another piece of the mystery, confirmed. She flips the dinosaur phone open and answers.

"Hey, Andi," she says weakly, and pauses to listen. "No, I'm fine, I swear. I just started to feel sick, so I dipped out early."

Ah, so Andi is the friend from the bar. Clearly, she isn't aware of Lisa's situation and just now noticed our quick disappearance. I wonder if that meant her bold pickup line was successful with Grant. I make a mental note to bug him later to find out.

"No, no, stay," she's saying. "Have fun. I'll see you at Punchline tomorrow." She hangs up, and we're smothered in silence for several long moments. I shove my hands in my coat pockets as we walk and let the silence settle over us, listening to the crunch of our footsteps to preoccupy myself.

Finally, she speaks again. "Can I ask you something?"

I glance her way, feigning nonchalance. "Depends. Can I ask something in return?"

She bites her lip as she considers, and I can't help the way my eyes are drawn to the simple movement. "Fine," she agrees, and I take a hand from my pocket, motioning for her to start.

"How did you know Lisa Graham isn't my real name?" Her question is so soft I can barely hear it, as though saying it out loud will blow her cover once and for all.

"I have a private investigator that works for my family. It's his job to find things out when new people enter my life."

She frowns. "I didn't mean to enter your life."

"I know that, now. That's on me." I rub my neck, the shame coursing through me. "But when you're... well, me, you can't be too careful."

"What's it like?" she asks, and then flushes, as though realizing she's become too eager with her questions. "Sorry."

I bite back a smile. "Don't be. It's like...a big game of hide and seek." When she shoots me a confused look, I clarify. "Someone can be staring right at you, but not really see you."

"Sounds lonely," she murmurs, meeting my gaze. Her eyes are still puffy from crying, but they're wide and curious, the moonlight shining in them. There's an understanding there, one that makes me suddenly uncomfortable. I blink and look away.

"I guess. But I do have my team." I smile as I think about them, probably still licking their wounds at Wunderbar. Or, in Grant's case, having his wounds licked. We walk quietly for another minute, and then I motion behind us. "So. Does that happen often?"

Her lips press into a thin line, and for a moment, I think she's going to back out of our agreement, but then, she answers. "Every couple weeks. It used to happen more, though."

I raise my brows in surprise, both at her honestly and the frequency. "And...what's it like?" I echo her question from before.

She pulls her coat tighter around her as she thinks it over. "It's like leaning back too far in a chair. You know, the moment when it starts falling backwards? That feeling? But then that feeling just... keeps going."

I hum in response, taking in how truly shitty that sounds. I can only guess that it wasn't always like this for her. Someone did this to her, took that safe space inside of her and twisted it to the point that this is her new normal. I can guess, too, that it was the 'he' she was so worried about at the bar.

I'm burning with the need to know who she's so scared of, but I clench my jaw and swallow the question back down. I know I won't get that answer tonight, especially because she already avoided answering it earlier. Perhaps Jim can get the answer for me, and then I won't need to make her relive the trauma.

We come to a stop in front of our building and turn to face each other.

"Are you coming inside?" she asks.

I shake my head. "Nah. I'll probably head back to the bar. Join the boys for another round."

She looks relieved, and I try not to let that sting. She worries her lip back between her teeth and looks at the entrance of the apartment, then back at me. "If I ask why you were so concerned by the idea that I was stalking you, would you tell me the truth?"

My head jerks back in surprise. Damn, she's smart. She knows there's more to me digging into her than just covering the normal bases. "I'm...not ready to talk about that." I let out a long exhale, then add, "At least, not yet."

She nods, accepting the answer without question. I decide to push my luck, voicing my last question of the night. "If I ask for your real name, would you tell me the truth?"

She sighs, a frosty cloud billowing in the cold winter air. "Not yet."

The answer should be a blow, but it feels like a bridge. For the first time, she gives me a small, genuine smile. It's a sad smile, but it's a start.

Chapter 10

LISA

I t's freaking cold.

I knew moving to Minnesota would include seasons I wasn't prepared for, but I'd been pulled in by the allure of a white Christmas. Now, experiencing October weather – which includes the first snow of the season – I understand why hot dishes are so prevalent. Carbs and dairy swirled together in warm casserole pans? That's the light at the end of the long, bitterly cold tunnel they call winter.

I still will never understand how folks can stay so nice, though. The shorter days are already getting to me, and this weather certainly isn't helping.

I tug my coat in tighter around me and try not to slip on the slush surrounding the entrance to Punchline, vowing to get boots with more traction the next time I go to the store. If I ate shit right now, Andi would bribe Bella into the gym's video footage and hold it over my head forever.

The salt sprinkled on the path has reduced all of the previously pretty white snow to a disgusting brown sludge. I kick some out of the way with my high-tops and frown. It's so pretty when it's untouched, practically ethereal. But the second you mix it with something else, it's tarnished.

Huh. Just like me.

"Hey, wait up!"

I turn to see Andi jogging down the path towards me, hair flying from underneath her beanie. She pulls off the bundled look in the way only someone who was born here can, her clothing just worn in enough to look cozy as hell, but still cute as fuck. Half of my winter clothes still have tags on them, and even though I check the weather every day, I still don't know what temperature requires which item. The snow that's landing on top of my shoes is already melting into my socks, telling me I need to add *waterproof* to the requirements of my new snow boots.

Andi stops to join me at the top of the steps and grins. "I didn't know you were coming to help today."

"Help with what?" I ask, eyeing her curiously, and notice for the first time that she doesn't have her gym bag with her. "Wait, are you not practicing today?"

Her expression turns into a puzzled frown, and she opens the door. The second she does, the smell of fresh paint hits me. "None of us are," she answers. "Paul called to say that the painters he had scheduled for yesterday bailed. Apparently, they thought they were just supposed to deliver the paint, not...you know...paint." She shrugs. "He said he was spending the day doing the painting himself, and I said, fuck no, I'm coming to help."

"Oh. That's shitty of them. But great of you!"

"Did he not call you?"

"He might have," I hedge. "I'm not the best at answering phone calls."

Understatement of the year. I should probably save his number, because if I don't know the number, no force on earth can make me answer the phone. It's going *straight* to voicemail.

Andi simply laughs. "Well, look, I'm the only one on the hook for a few hours of labor. Paul hasn't seen you yet, so you can still escape."

"Oh, no, I don't mind." I move around Andi to open the door further. "I'm no artist, but I'm happy to help."

She eyes me dubiously. "Are you sure you don't have somewhere else you'd rather be?"

"Nope. No shift at the bar tonight." I smile, but it flickers a little. *And without staying busy, I'll go mad,* I want to say, but don't. "And Winny can last for a few more hours without me. He's gone a full week now without shitting on the floor."

"Really? Way to go, Winny! He's learning to be big brave."

Her genuine enthusiasm for my dog makes me laugh, and with that, we push our way out of the snow and into the gym.

"This looks wonderful, ladies," Paul says approvingly, gathering the drop cloth into his arms. "I can't tell you how much I appreciate this."

"Not a problem. I'm glad we were able to wrangle an extra helper. Now I still have time left in my day to do something fun," Andi says, and reaches out threateningly with the paint roller in her hand.

I jump back and laugh. "Seriously, I'm just happy to help. This place has been here for me since my first week here." I look around at the bright reds and blacks, alternating color across the brick walls. Though the faded look held its own kind of charm, the place now looks cheerful and proud, radiating an inviting energy. "And now it looks extra snazzy."

"Well, let's hope a fresh paint job and some social media posts do the trick. Business has been slow, and it'll keep slowing until the end of the year, at least. Don't tell Bella, but we're barely keeping our heads above water." Paul looks around, his face growing solemn. "I can't afford to do any more upgrades without more cash flow, but it's hard to get memberships without having something to offer that sets us apart. Everything's a streaming service now."

He rubs the back of his neck, frowning, and my heart sinks at his hopeless expression. He's clearly been working hard at making his dream come true, and sometimes, the shit reality is it comes down to dumb luck. You can grind your way forward for years, only to see someone else accidentally end up where you were aiming all along.

I thought I put in the work and landed a prize in my old life, but when I opened the treasure chest, it was completely empty. Now I'm figuring out how to fill that unexpected emptiness.

This gym really has become a safe place for me to begin filling that void, and I hate the idea that it might be taken from me, too. My fists curl tightly around my paint roller at the prospect, and I feel some of the paint drip across my fingers.

"Do you need money?" I ask. "I – I mean, my family – they love to make donations to small businesses like this."

Paul smiles sadly. "Well, thanks, kiddo. Money is always great, but the truth of it is, eventually it runs out. What we really need is awareness, and actual memberships. Without that lifetime value, we can't sustain this place long-term."

I chew on the inside of my lip, thinking of how I can slide him some money without raising questions. "What about some sort of event at Punchline? Like a fundraiser? That would garner awareness and cash flow."

When Paul nods in slow agreement, Andi gasps, causing both of us to blink in surprise. "Oh my god, Paul, we can totally do that for you! What about some sort of Halloween-themed event?"

Paul smirks, his eyes crinkling with amusement. "Like what? Get everyone here to eat candy and drink, and then get them hyped to join the gym?"

I glance over at Andi, who is now frowning at his words, second-guessing her scheme.

"It's not the worst idea," I put in. "Get them thinking about it now, and even if they don't sign up right away, it'll be on their minds when they're coming back from all the winter holidays ready to get fit. And the money you raise can tide you over to bridge that gap."

He tilts his head, considering. "You might be onto something there, ladies."

Andi and I exchange grins. I know she'll be talking my ear off about ideas for the next two weeks, and I don't mind it at all. For the first time in, well, I can't even remember how long, there's a pleasant flutter in my stomach. It's a warm tingle that starts at my core and works its way outward until it's brightening my cheeks. It's anticipation, purpose, *belonging*.

And my god, does it feel good.

The Minnesota cold during the day is its own beast, but the cold when it's dark out has an even worse bite. I had cut Winston's bedtime walk short to defrost my toes, seeing as my high-tops are still soggy from earlier. I'm already envisioning the perfect evening inside: a bath bomb in the steaming hot tub, a cup of tea, the electric fireplace on blast, a dive back into my book. As if hearing my thoughts, Winny starts tugging on his leash, eager to get to the elevator.

"Yes, yes." I laugh as I look down at him, picking up the pace through the lobby. "I know, you don't like the cold any more than I do."

"Funny that you live in Minnesota, in that case." The male voice comes from in front of me, and Winston gives an uncharacteristic wag of his tail. I grit my teeth as I look up, cursing the fact that the owner of the voice is the only male Winston's ever shown interest in.

Benjamin stands in front of the elevator, grinning at me. He's wearing a maroon beanie, a plain, charcoal gray sweater, and dark blue jeans. I note with surprise that it's the first time I've seen him without Leopards gear. Winston tugs on his leash to move forward and I let him, watching as Benjamin drops his gaze to the floor. He crouches down to get closer to Winston's level, and I frown.

"He doesn't really–"

My sentence is cut off as Winston's wiggles increase, and he shoves his body halfway into Benjamin's arms. Benjamin glides his hands over Winny's back and scratches as he reaches the base of his tail. Winston curves his body like a seal and pants happily, clearly overjoyed to be getting butt scritches.

"He doesn't really what?" Benjamin asks, but I just stare at him, openmouthed, and shake my head.

"...Nevermind." I watch as Benjamin moves back to scratch behind Winny's ears, accepting the kisses Winny assaults him with in stride. With a laugh, he finally straightens, and gives me an almost apologetic look.

"Sorry, I should have asked if I could pet him. I just miss my family's dogs, so I love when I can get some dog time."

"It's fine," I mutter, and sidle around him to press the elevator button.

"What's his name?"

"Winston." I pause, then add, "I call him Winny."

"Well, hi, Winny."

Winston wags his tail harder, and the bing sounds the arrival of the elevator. I meet Benjamin's eyes as the doors open, and he gestures to the elevator, stepping aside to let me go first.

After a pause, I enter, willing my chest to stop squeezing tighter at the prospect of being alone in a closed space with this man. My mind flicks back to the footage I saw of him during his game, literally lifting the other player in the air, just to slam him on the ice, and my throat threatens to close on my breaths.

Winny likes him, I remind myself. *And you already were alone with him once, and nothing bad happened. At least,* he *didn't do anything. You're the one who had a panic attack.*

I look down at Winston's relaxed face to calm myself. He gazes up at me, his warm brown eyes gleaming happily against the black fur that rims his eyes like eyeliner. My chest loosens. *Thanks, Winny.*

Benjamin clambers in and pushes 6, then glances at me with raised brows. Instead of telling him, I reach across him and press 8.

"Top floor," he notes, moving his gaze from the elevator buttons to me. "I'm in 604."

I don't respond, but he continues, ignoring the hint. "Care to explain how you can afford to live on the top floor off a barista and bartender salary?"

My jaw goes slack. "It's not polite to ask someone about their finances, you know."

"Some would argue it's not polite to punch people, either."

I blink in surprise at his retort. Another apology bubbles up, a reflex etched into my bones, too familiar to me now to be unlearned. When I meet his gaze, however, I see a twinkle of amusement. He's teasing me.

I bite back the apology and take a deep breath. "You said yourself you had it coming. But can we not do this?"

"Fair enough. I probably owe you one." He leans back against the wall of the elevator and opens his mouth again, unwilling to let us ride in silence. "Just so you know, your friend had a great night with Grant after we left. So you could say we made that happen."

"I heard." My gaze sidles to Benjamin, and I silently appreciate the distance he's put between us. It's just enough that I feel like I can breathe. "Did you know your friend is a snuggler?"

He chuckles. "I wish I could say I didn't, but unfortunately, yes. He's a known snuggler."

"Sounds like there's a story there." I can't help a faint smile. "Andi said she made him be the little spoon after a few minutes, because it was like being embraced by the sun."

"The male body," he agrees. "Generally known to be the same temperature as the sun."

A timely shiver climbs up my body, and I curl my arms into my jacket. "Running hot isn't the worst thing in this weather. I just want to get back upstairs to my bath and my book."

"A bath and a book, you say?" His brows rise. "Now that's an image that won't leave my head for quite some time."

I narrow my eyes at him. "Seriously? You accused me of stalking you not two weeks ago, and now here *you* are, fishing for information on me and envisioning me covered in bubbles."

"I didn't say there were bubbles involved." He beams at me, and despite myself, I flush. He's got a great smile, and he clearly knows it. "I seem to recall a conversation where you declined my initial offer and encouraged me to have fun with my own hand. Are you telling me I shouldn't do that now, either?"

My mouth drops open, and I toss my hair over my shoulder, turning away from him. "That's...neither here nor there. Just leave me out of it."

He's silent, and for a moment, I think I've finally gotten him to drop the conversation. When I glance at him again, though, his eyes are fixated on my neck, his expression dark. I back up a step.

"Did someone hurt you?" he asks, quietly.

I freeze, stunned silent.

He steps forward, and before I can react, his fingers are on my neck. I'm unable to move, my breath catching in my throat even as my heartbeat thrashes in my ears. I search his eyes for that rage, but find none of it – only a soft concern. His touch is featherlight, but I still refuse to breathe again until he's moved away from my neck.

When he does, realization floods through me. His fingers are covered in flakes of red and black, mixing together in what looks morbidly like darkened blood. His brow knits together as he inspects the dried concoction that somehow made its way onto my neck – probably from moving my hair out of the way when I had paint all over my fingers earlier.

"It's paint, you idiot," I snarl, and press my palms flat against his chest, shoving hard to get much-needed distance between us so I can clear my head. As I do, though, I can't help but notice how rock solid his chest is, and my traitorous emotions latch onto that line of thinking. I have the sudden urge to slide my hands under his sweater and feel my way over all those hard planes, letting the heat of his body warm my fingers.

I realize belatedly that I've kept my hands on him a bit too long and snatch them away, wrapping them back around myself protectively.

Instead of looking offended, he lets out a bark of laughter, startling me. "Well, I'm glad it's just paint. And at least when I touched you now you just shoved me, instead of punching me."

He leans in conspiratorially, and I lean back, but refuse to move my feet. "When will we move on to you begging for it?"

My god, this man is giving me whiplash. I shoot him my darkest possible glare. "Does begging for you to leave me alone count?"

"You're cute when you're irritated."

"Cute? I've heard it referred to as an attitude problem."

The elevator comes to a stop, and he smirks. "Maybe I like your attitude problem."

What a weird thing to say. Why do I kind of like that he likes it? But then I swallow, and remember his fingers at my throat.

"Benjamin."

He stops, holding a hand to the elevator door to keep it open as he faces me again. "Yes?"

"Don't ever touch my neck again."

He frowns in confusion. "Why?"

I simply purse my lips. Why can't he just agree to the simple demand, instead of asking invasive questions all the time? Instead, he shoots me an indecipherable look.

"Oh, sugar." He sighs and drops his hand away from the door. "What did you bury so deep you won't even let yourself uncover it?"

Chapter 11

LISA

"*I'm trying, baby. I'm trying to make this work for both of us.*"

I attempt to slide past Austin, but his body blocks me. He grabs my arm and forces me to spin, meeting his gaze. His eyes are bloodshot and watery, swimming with emotion and more than a little alcohol.

I immediately avert my gaze. Whatever he wants to find in my expression, I don't want him to. I just want this conversation over.

"I know. It's fine. I promise, it's fine."

"Well, of course it is, because you know I love you, baby girl. If you really believe everything I say to you when I'm angry, that's your problem. You really need to stop fixating on the negatives."

I don't answer. Instead, I drop to my knees and begin picking up shards of glass. The skunky smell of beer wafts up from the spilled drink, and I hiss as the sharp edge of the shattered glass pierces my hand. Blood wells from my finger, and I stare down at it in a daze. It doesn't hurt nearly as much as my heart.

It's been a few months since my mom passed, and though she and I rarely spoke, she was the only family I had to my name. I never knew my father, and I never had any siblings, so she filled a place in my heart that so many others took for granted. The only other person who worked their way that far into my heart was Austin, and it's times like these where I hate how much of my heart he has. If he ever leaves, I know there will be nothing left there. Just a black hole.

We're still in the same town as Patty and Austin's brother, Ethan, but I haven't spoken to either of them since they moved into their own place. Honestly, I don't mind that so much as of late, since I've been so busy wrapping up loose ends from my mother's passing. I gave up my bartending job months ago, but today was my first birthday without her, so all I'd wanted was a drink at the bar, drinking and disappearing into a crowd. Becoming one of the nameless. Someone who could pretend she was as carefree and happy as the rest of them.

I ball my hand into a fist, leaving the injured finger free. I watch as the blood wells and begins trickling down the side.

A towel appears in my peripheral, and I glance up to see Austin holding it out for me. He crouches down as I accept it, and runs his hands through his hair in exasperation.

"Why do you need anyone else in your life? Everyone at that bar was a fucking lowlife, anyways."

I choose not to respond. Trying to explain myself would only lead to more questions. Instead, I drape the towel over my hand and pick up more shards of glass. He continues, undeterred.

"I can't believe you did a shot with that random guy. He was so excited to talk to a pretty girl. It's just me you treat like shit, huh? Is that it?!"

He shoots up from his crouched position and begins pacing, my injury forgotten as his anger wells back up.

"Please don't yell," I whisper.

He whirls on me, his face contorted with rage. "I'm not yelling. Do you want to hear yelling?"

I instantly shake my head, and he scoffs. "Fuckin' unbelievable. You're always trying to make me look like the bad guy."

He stalks away, but before he exits the room, he slams his fist into the wall. Plaster goes flying with a resounding bang, and I duck my head, my heart racing. I don't look up, but I can feel his presence, still towering over me in the room. After a long moment, I hear his footsteps receding, along with his final, grumbled words.

"If you're not careful, you'll lose me. Then, you'll really have no one left."

I wake up gasping, sweat pooled in my collarbone. As usual, my senses haven't stayed with the dream. I can smell his scent, the sweat and beer and aftershave mixing in a pungent cocktail. His long, ashen hair, his dark eyes, the strain in his voice when he yells.

I go through the motions of the day in a haze, memories clinging to me like a shadow. I'm grateful that at least Benjamin has been leaving me alone. For the last few days, aside from polite smiles while taking his orders, he hasn't attempted another conversation. He's finally accepted that I'm not trying to get into his business, and in turn, it appears he's finally backed out of mine.

I glance over at him now where he sits with his teammates. They're all leaned over a table, brows furrowed. One of them – Grant – is gesturing wildly. Another slams his palm on the table in response to what he says.

"They look like they're having a pretty intense conversation," Andi comments, raising a brow at them.

I glance at her over the. "I bet it's something absolutely ridiculous, and they've just gotten themselves all heated over it."

"You're probably right. And speaking of heated," Andi begins, "has he been bothering you?"

I shake my head and grab a rag. "He's been surprisingly pleasant. I haven't had to see any more of him than necessary, which is ideal."

"Really?" She regards me carefully, then tosses her hair behind her shoulder. "You say he's been pleasant. And he certainly *looks* pleasant. Sooo...I'm counting two pros, no cons. Maybe you should ask him out?"

I give up on wiping down the bartop to flick the rag at her. "The pros don't cancel out the way he treated me when he thought I was stalking him. For all we know, he could have anger issues." I swallow down a lump, thinking of the fight I saw on the TV that night. "Plus, you know I'm not really in the dating scene."

"But why not?" she complains. "You're fucking hot."

"I'm twenty-four, not sixty," I remind her. "I've got plenty of time."

She groans. "That's the worst excuse I've ever heard. You're in the prime of your life. You deserve a whole team of hot hockey players knocking down your door." She glances over to see the group of the men headed toward the bar in their sea of Leopard blue, and tosses a wink over her shoulder. "Except Grant. He's mine."

I smirk. "I'm proud of you, babe. Get that dick."

"Look at you! I've been a bad influence…I love it." She pulls Grant to her side as the group arrives. He allows her to tug him to her without question, but turns to face me, an urgent look on his face.

"Lisa! Question for you. What kind of cheese is best on a burger?"

I blink, startled by the randomness of the question. "Umm. Colby jack?"

My answer, as soft and unsure as it is, sends the group into a spiral. There are yells of assent and disagreement, all of them loud. I lean back and lock eyes with Andi, and we swap knowing grins. This was definitely the *serious discussion* they'd been having, and the ridiculousness of it has just been brought to the bar, encouraged by my answer.

"It's obviously cheddar!"

"You'd seriously take cheddar when pepperjack is right there?"

"Fuckin' unbelievable."

"Jordie over here said Havarti. What kind of psychopath picks *Havarti?*"

"A Canadian psychopath, obviously. What do you expect from people who drink their milk from bags?"

I shake my head and lean into Andi. "And they say women are the emotional ones," I whisper. She chokes on her beer as she laughs.

"Hey," Grant interrupts and faces Andi. "Are you two coming to the game tomorrow?"

Andi taps her fingers on the bartop, considering. "Possibly. It's at six, right? We should be done boxing by then."

"Boxing?" Jordie asks, giving us a surprised look. "I didn't know I was in the presence of professional fighters here. Well, besides Grant."

"Lisa's got a pretty wicked right hook," Benjamin cuts in.

I meet his gaze, even as I feel Andi's questioning stare off to my side. My throat constricts as I remember the terror I felt at being grabbed that night, and what I did after.

Benjamin gazes right back at me, but I don't see any resentment or pity there. Instead, his lips curl into an amused smile, and I feel the pressure in my chest release slightly. Maybe the way he'd teased me in the elevator days ago was really how he feels, and there's no residual anger there. Perhaps he really believes he was in the wrong.

The memory of the way he sat across from me after I hit him pops into my head. He'd given me time and distance, and he was respectful and calm the whole way back to the apartment, too. He hadn't peppered me with questions like he had back at the bar.

Maybe he didn't have anger issues after all. Was the fighting something players could just leave on the ice?

"You can hit me any day," Grant says, and I snort. Well, maybe *some* players leave it on the ice. Grant clearly seems to like it rough, and his whole team knows it. But Andi is clearly into it, if the wicked grin she shoots him in response is any indication.

"Well, that certainly sounds like a treat," she says. "Maybe after you win tomorrow."

Gran's grin is borderline hungry. I chuckle, and Andi wiggles a suggestive eyebrow my way. "But what about poor Lisa? I can't leave my girl hanging. Anyone want to go on a double date with her?"

Damn it, Andi! My eyes widen in alarm, but it's not me who disagrees. It's Benjamin. "Something tells me Lisa's not in the dating scene right now."

I frown at him, unsure if I'm mad that he's speaking for me or that he's right. Andi narrows her eyes at him. "Be nice, Benji-boy, or I swear I'll fucking kick you."

Grant laughs, and Jordie clears his throat. "If you want to, Lisa, I'd love to take you out."

I freeze, staring at him for a moment, and then give a side-long glance over to Andi. She's nodding in encouragement as she leans into Grant, who simply looks amused by the whole ordeal. Then, for some reason, I look over at Benjamin.

He's regarding me with a cool curiosity, his lips pressed into a thin line. I think about how he spent so much time hung up on the idea of me following him around, and suddenly, the idea of me going on a date with one of his teammates instead sounds hilarious. Besides, Benjamin's offer had been a one night stand. At least Jordie has the decency to offer to take me out first.

I take a minute to really look at Jordie. He's tall and fit, with light blond hair that's carefully styled back, and kind blue eyes. He's always been the softest-spoken one of their group, always smiling. He seems...sweet.

I think back to Andi's words of encouragement. Maybe I *do* deserve this. Going on a date with a Canadian hockey boy. Is this a Minnesotan rite of passage?

"Well, even if we disagree on the best cheeseburger... that does sound like fun," I say.

Andi whoops, and Jordie offers me a broad grin, which I return hesitantly. Benjamin steps forward to order another round, his expression unreadable.

I begin pouring the beers, and Andi launches into plans for the following night, berating me for opinions until I laugh and tell her to just make a decision. And when I finally write down my phone number for Jordie, even I have to admit there is a flutter of excitement that starts deep in my stomach.

Chapter 12

BENJI

"Come on, Estes!" Coach Henderson roars from the bench, echoed by a handful of my teammates. I exhale forcefully, sending sweat droplets flying from my upper lip before they drip into my mouth, and skate to where the ref is lining us up.

"Vafan gör du?" Nilsson skates by, shooting me a disappointed look. I've played with him long enough to know most of his Swedish curses, and this one is nothing new: *"What the fuck, dude?"*

Nils has every right to be mad at me. He'd had full control of the puck, barreling down the boards, and I was the one who slipped up, darting into the offensive zone before him. The off-sides whistle drew us back out of their zone, restarting the play and losing Nils all of his momentum. Truly, it was a rookie mistake.

My head is not with it today and unfortunately, I know exactly why. Grant and Jordie spent twenty minutes before the game discussing their upcoming dates with Andi and Lisa, which of course dragged the rest of the locker room into it.

"What is this? Are you – are you texting her?" Goody had grabbed the phone out of Grant's hands, gaping in amazement down at it. "Who are you and what have you done with Sando?"

"Come on. There's something...I don't know. She's witty. Strong-willed. *Older,* man. She knows what she wants."

"Yeah, she wants that *dick!*" Berger crowed, shoving Grant from his other side. "For two whole minutes."

Grant picked up his skate, shaking it at Berger before tugging it on his foot. "I swear to god, I'll cut your dick off and feed it to Goody's dog."

"Hey! What did my dog ever do to you?"

"Give him a break," Highcloud cut in. "Haven't you ever met a girl and known your whole life is going to change?"

Goody snorted. "Yeah, every Friday night."

Jodie tossed a glove across the locker room at Grant. "Hey. What's the plan for tonight?"

Grant picked it up and tossed it back. "Pretty casual. Dinner at the All-Star, then off to the Barcade for some drinks and games."

When I heard that, the dark feeling clouding me eased slightly. A sports bar, an arcade – that's nothing serious. Just fun. I had to remind myself that she deserved some fun, even if I wouldn't be there to witness it.

As if he'd heard my thoughts, Jordie turned to me and patted my leg. "We'll probably end up back at the Wunderbar at some point, if you wanna meet us there for drinks."

"Yeah." I made an attempt to smile. Even if it was a pity offer, I'd probably take him up on it. "I'll think about it."

The ref blows the whistle, bringing me back to the present moment, and I square up. The puck drops and I win the face-off, tipping it back to Grant on defense. He lobs it over to Highcloud, who taps it up to Levi. Levi barrels into the O-zone, and I'm careful to enter after him.

We make a few valiant attempts to bury the puck in the net before someone on the other team eventually draws a penalty. I sigh and peel off for the bench, signaling to start with our second power play line. We're tied, but mentally, I'm not there, and I know it's affecting my game. I can admit to myself that I'm not the man for the job right now.

But as for who will be taking Lisa out tonight? I can't stop thinking about how strange it is, just how much I want to be that man.

Here I am, sitting like a fool, waiting for the conclusion of a date that I'm not a part of. For the hundredth time, I wonder why I'm so hung up on this girl. My apprehension turned into curiosity over the past two weeks, and now I'm forced to admit it's becoming a protectiveness that I have no right to.

Hell, I don't even know the girl's real name, and clearly, she won't give me the time of day to tell me. I shouldn't even want to get close to someone this embedded in my life. It can only become messy and complicated, two things I really don't need on my journey to the major league.

I've almost talked myself into returning back to the apartment when they stumble through the door, and I'm pulled back into my seat like it's magnetic and my ass is metal. My eyes are glued to Lisa as she enters. She's wearing black jeans and high tops – seriously, who wears high tops in the snow? – and a long-sleeved gray henley, topped with a khaki green jacket. Her silky, light brown hair is pulled back in a ponytail, and her makeup is minimal.

Despite her leisurely attire, it still looks stunning on her, as though she knows she can be comfortable and still knock men on their asses. Judging by Jordie's expression, it's working. He keeps sneaking glances at her, analyzing her expression, hunting for indications that she's having a good time with him. She's either oblivious or intentionally keeping her attention elsewhere, deep in a conversation with Andi.

Grant notices me and waves, jerking his head for me to join them. I grunt and peel myself from the barstool, contemplating the ridiculousness of me being here on my own, simply for the fact that I wanted to see Lisa after her date with Jordie. Pathetic.

I pull a chair up to their table and slide into it. Grant beams at me, and I make my best attempt at a smile.

"Hey, man! How's your night been?" he asks.

"Boring," I respond, willing my voice to be casual. I won't offer up any information on what I've been doing unless they ask. And even if they do, I won't admit that I was sitting here pining over a girl on a date with my best bud. "I bet you had more fun." It's the closest I'll let myself get to pleading for information.

Luckily, Andi is more than happy to provide it. "It was great! I didn't realize the All-Star had milkshakes, so Lisa and I split a strawberry one. It had literal pieces of strawberry in it. Ugh, I wanted to crawl inside it and live in it. One of the best I've ever had."

Lisa hums her agreement, and I glance over at Grant, catching him grinning as he gazes at Andi, watching her excited storytelling. Oh, wow, the man's in deep. I'm happy for him, though, especially after all he's been through.

"And then when we got to the Barcade, they had this punching bag machine," Andi continues, "and Lisa got the highest score by a *long shot.*"

Lisa and I lock eyes, and I flash her a teasing smile. She ducks her head, flushing, and I raise a brow. I find myself wondering if Jordie made her blush at all tonight. I'm basking in the sight of her rose-tinged cheeks, and I don't want to have to share.

God damn it. Am I really getting this jealous over a girl I barely know?

"I told her that if I had my boxing gloves, I could've at least given her a run for her money." Andi curls her fists in illustration, throwing a few air punches.

"I'd love to take up boxing on the side," Jordie muses. "Maybe I should get a pair."

"Funny, I was about to say the same thing about you," Grant puts in, smirking. Andi laughs, tossing her hair over her head and leaning into him. He wraps his arm around her possessively and tugs her closer. Oh yeah, the lucky bastard is getting laid tonight.

"And then the girls talked our ears off about their Halloween event," Jordie says, tossing Lisa an affectionate look before glancing back at me. "So I hope you don't have any plans the night before Halloween."

"Oh, yes! And we actually had something to ask you, Benji." Andi swivels in her chair to give Lisa a pointed look. Lisa ducks her head again, picking at her napkin.

"Something to ask me?" I urge, resting my chin on my hand. Lisa glances up at me, and I give her a sly grin, causing her to flush again. I kind of feel like a piece of shit for how much I love it. "Pray tell."

Lisa clears her throat. "Um, yeah, so...the gym kind of needs a popularity boost. And some people," she glares at Grant, who simply gives her a gleeful smile in return, "think that enlisting the most popular player on the Lakewood Leopards would be a good social media boost. Or whatever."

My grin widens. "Or whatever. So, you need my help?"

"No," Lisa grumbles, just as Andi exclaims, "Yes!"

I reach my hand out. Lisa blinks, and I waggle my fingers in emphasis. "Here. Give me your phone, and I'll put my number in. Give me a ring whenever you need me to sell my body for likes."

Andi snickers and Lisa rolls her eyes, but obliges. I create a contact and shoot a quick text to my own number – like hell I'll admit I already have her number through Jim – and return her phone. The conversation continues through the course of another round, and I watch the dynamic between Jordie and Lisa carefully.

He remains the unserious, fun Jordie I know. It's usually something I love about the guy, but at this moment, it makes him oblivious to the way Lisa tenses every time his body brushes against hers. It's subtle, but it's there in the way her brows pinch and her shoulders hunch, as though she can escape within herself.

For reasons I'm not ready to admit even to myself, my jaw clenches each time she flinches, my body vibrating with the need to pull her away and reassure her she's safe. As our beers near empty, Lisa taps her glass and straightens.

"I think I'm going to call it a night," she announces, and turns to Andi. "Are you gonna stay a while?"

Andi and Grant exchange a look, a wordless conversation passing between them, and Andi turns back to Lisa, nodding. "I think I'm gonna stay for another round. Will you be okay getting home?"

Jordie stands up instantly, offering Lisa his hand. "I'll take you home."

I clench my jaw, swallowing down the strange feeling rising in my throat. I remind myself that I should be happy she's being escorted home safely. I remind myself of that as I follow Grant to the bartop, sliding onto a stool next to him. I keep reminding myself of that as I order another beer. But even that can't keep me from keeping my eyes locked on them as they exit the bar, hovering outside for a moment as Jordie helps Lisa get her jacket back on.

Even after she's in her coat, Jordie is leaning over her, a slow smile across his face, making his intention crystal clear. I've never paid attention to another man's posture before outside of a game, but holy hell, I can see it now. While he's trying to make it come across as desirable, it's borderline threatening. The way she shrinks back from it ever so slightly speaks volumes. He leans in, and –

There's a clatter as my chair goes flying from behind me. I barely register the fact that I'm now standing as Grant clears his throat. "Dude?"

I glance his way only momentarily. He's gaping at me, his beer raised halfway to his mouth. My eyes shoot back to Jordie and Lisa outside, but she's turned her face, avoiding the impending kiss. Jordie pauses, and I exhale slowly. He's a great guy, I remind myself. One of the best. He won't push it.

As if reading my mind, he leans back, offering Lisa a smile and his hand. She takes it tentatively, and as they turn and walk away hand in hand, I slide back into my seat, the emotions roiling inside my settling slightly. Finally, I'm able to turn back to the bartop. I pick up my beer and sip slowly. I'm suddenly thankful Andi chose this moment to go to the restroom, but I can still feel Grant's stare burning into the side of my head.

But what am I supposed to say? That Jordie shouldn't be with her, because he doesn't know her like I do? The truth of the matter is, I still barely know her at all. So, I say nothing.

"I can tell you think about her a lot," Grant says eventually.

I run my hands through my hair and sigh, eyes still fixated on the spot where Jordie and Lisa walked away. "You have no idea, Grant," I rasp. "It's actually frustrating how much I think about her."

Chapter 13

LISA

"*Girl! This is amazing!*" *Patty gapes as she stares at the email I've printed out. "I don't know how you did it. I just don't understand how your brain works."*

I smile back at her, but it's half-hearted. "Yeah, well. A final project for a computer science degree, paired with losing a parent, can apparently make a pretty great app. I didn't want others to have to suffer their way through the aftermath the way I did."

"It's a great app with a great purpose. And one that people will pay a fuckton for, apparently." She pauses, giving me a once-over. "Are you sure you're not under too much stress, though? I say this with love, but... I've never seen you this thin. Even when you did your marathon two years ago."

Her concern is sweet, but she has no clue that it has nothing to do with the stress of the app and our upcoming graduation. I'm sure the change is jarring, considering she didn't see me the entire summer before our senior year. As for me, I've been staring at a ghost in the mirror for months. She has my hair, and she has my clothes, but she's starting to see the future. And while she's no longer excited for the way it's headed, she's even more terrified of the unknown. The one she dares to think of as an alternative to the now.

"Nope. I'm feeling better than ever." I try to smile again, fueling it with my happiness to be alone with her, if even for a moment. It feels like the good old days; the days before I started having to calculate every next step, measuring it against the potential rage I'd face when I was alone with Austin.

"Have you told Austin yet?" Patty asks, and the question sinks like a stone in the pit of my stomach.

"No, and I'd love to keep it between us." At her puzzled look, I add, "I want to make sure it's a done deal first. Surprise him."

I don't tell her that if it were up to him, I would have dropped out of college entirely. It was only the fear of student loans that amounted to an unfinished degree that convinced him it would be worthwhile for me to graduate. And, as it turned out, my senior project led to an offer on an app that could pay off my student loans ten times over. I haven't told him yet, because this feels like a new fork in the road of my future.

I'm still hoping to see a glimpse of the old Austin, the one I fell in love with. But if I can't, this may be my only chance at freedom.

The champagne fizzes in my mouth, cold and delightful, and I tip my head back to drain the flute. Andi came over to coordinate the logistics of the Halloween event at Punchline with donuts and mimosas in tow, and I was more than happy to accept both.

Andi commandeered the social media handles for Punchline from Paul. I listen as she gripes about how little he's posted and how hard it will be to garner up traction in the short time frame we've given ourselves. I fix us mimosas – mine, half champagne and half orange juice, Andi's, all champagne and a drop of orange juice – and lay out the donuts while she posts a teaser photo across multiple platforms. Finally, she sets her phone down and gives me a long, assessing look as she grabs the flute from my hand.

"What?" I ask.

"You need to record a hype video of Benjamin," she asserts, and takes a moment to chew on a donut. "We need his stamp of approval on the gym, and use his appearance at the party to entice others."

I groan and plop down on the couch next to her. "Yeah, I get it. I'll reach out to him."

She says nothing, just purses her lips. "What?" I ask again, weirdly nervous this time.

"How was your date last night?" The question is unexpected, a brusque pivot from our event discussions.

How was it? It was...pleasant. Jordie was kind, with a nice smile and all the right things to say. He'd been respectful but attentive, clearly interested but not pushy, something any girl would like. Every flaw in the night had been entirely due to me.

"It was good," I say. "I had a lot of fun."

"Because of my delightful presence, or because of a hand-some blond hockey player?"

I fiddle with the string of my hoodie and grin. "Can't it be both?"

"Of course it can. I would be offended if I hadn't been a part of it." She leans back and shoots me a conspiratorial look, one that tells me she's about to become the bane of my existence with her next comment. I brace myself. "I had to hear from you that you liked Jordie, though, because Benji went all lost puppy dog on you when you showed up at Wunderbar after the date.

He left not long after you and Jordie did. Grant wouldn't say much, other than that he was upset."

I digest the information slowly. "Benji?" I finally manage.

"Yes, Benji. As in, six foot three, dark and handsome, tattooed? A big, professional pain in your ass?"

"Okay, okay!" I throw my hands up, a laugh bubbling up in my throat. The image of him in his swimsuit, water running down those hard panes of muscle and gleaming against his tattoos pops into my head, and I attempt to shoo it away. "I just...always referred to him as Benjamin in my head."

"Well, Grant calls him Benji."

"Benji," I echo, swirling the nickname in my mouth. I hate how much it rolls off the tongue, how much it suits him. I hate how much I like it.

"Anyways. I just thought you should know," Andi continues, "in case that spark wasn't there with Jordie, and you might want to explore it with someone else. Someone you love to hate." She wiggles her eyebrows suggestively.

I take a long drink from my champagne flute, emptying it before I respond. "Nope," I murmur. "That spark is there with Jordie."

She squeals happily and refills our drinks. I take another sip, trying to ignore the fact that while my reply sounded genuine, it felt like a lie.

We move on to discuss the event further, and between rounds of mimosas, we argue over splitting the costs, the games and entertainment we'd put on during the event, and how to hype it up beforehand. Eventually, Andi concedes that I can foot the bill on catering, and I compromise that she and Paul will split the decor and drinks.

I'm not entirely sure what kind of income Andi has, but she didn't blink an eye at taking on a portion of the event budget. Luckily, she hasn't questioned my budget limits, either. Not like Benji had in the elevator, instantly clocking the discrepancy between my current jobs and my living situation. I know if I'd told him the truth – that I didn't even need to work, thanks to the app I sold over a year ago – he would have pried for more information on it. There are several news articles about it, tying back to my real name, and if he knew my real name...I don't want to think about what else he would find.

Eventually, the morning shifts to afternoon, and the champagne has been polished off. Andi orders a ride home and hugs me in front of the elevator.

"Don't forget." She boops my nose affectionately, in a way only she can pull off. I love her for it. "Shoot Benji a text."

I groan, but promise her I will, and decide to bite the bullet as soon as she leaves the apartment. It takes me a minute, but I find his name in my phone under "Winny's Handsomest Neighbor". I roll my eyes and quickly update his contact before shooting off a message.

Me: *Do you have time to record a hype video for the gym event?*

Cocky Shit: *Sure, I can make time for that.*

Me: *Great. Let me know if you need any sort of script. And just shoot it to Andi when it's ready.*

I pocket my phone and stare down at Winston. He's wiggling, and when we make eye contact, he skitters for the front door, glancing between me and his leash. I sigh and shrug on my coat. His wiggles gain momentum as he sees that he's going to get let outside, and I'm tugging on my right shoe when my phone vibrates.

"Hello?" I answer, bending over to slip on my left shoe and stumbling a bit. Damn, I probably should have had something more than a single donut to soak up the...three? four? mimosas. Slipping on the ice outside, half-drunk, would not be a great look for me. I can only pray Winny doesn't see anything he feels like chasing outside.

"Hey, sugar." The voice on the other line is deep and tinged with amusement, belonging to the only male I know who gets such joy from teasing me.

I bolt straight up. Winny's eyes go wide and he freezes, not sure what to expect, but anticipating something exciting. "Why are you calling me, Benji?"

"Benji? That's a first."

I can hear the smile in his voice, and fantasize for a moment about smacking it off his face. I shrug the phone against my ear with my shoulder and grab Winny's leash, bending down to snap it on his collar. He leaps up excitedly and bumps the phone from its perch on my shoulder. It goes clattering to the floor.

"Stop it, Winny," I hiss. "If you keep this up, I'm downgrading you to pee pads." He pants excitedly in response, and I scramble for the phone, raising it to my ear again. "Hey, sorry about that."

"Were you – were you just arguing with your dog?"

Fuck.

"What?"

Oh, shit – did I say that out loud? "Nothing. Nope. What do you want, Benji?"

"Benji again," he muses on the other end of the line. "I like that. I'm calling because we seem to have had a miscommunication about this video."

"Oh," I say, deflating a little. Though, why should I be surprised? Someone as high-profile as Benji wouldn't have the time of day to hype up a little mom and pop gym. It was a stupid idea to begin with. "No, I understand. You're a busy guy–"

"No, no. That's not it," he cuts me off with a laugh. "I'm not going to just record something and shoot it your way."

"Oh... kay?" It still sounds like he's backing out.

"If we're going to do it, we're going to do it right. Are you free to go to the gym right now? That way we have the right backdrop, and you can tell me all the right things to say?"

"That's... not a bad plan." I kind of hate that I didn't think of that first.

"Sometimes, I have good ideas." There it is again, the sound of his amused smile, shining through his words. "Are you free to head there now?"

I glance down at Winny, still dancing on the end of his leash. "Yeah, let me take Winny out quickly. And I need to grab something to eat."

"We can swing through somewhere on the way there," he offers.

I hesitate for a moment as I consider arguing, then sigh. "Fine. But you have to drive." I pause. "And I get to choose the place."

Twenty minutes later, we're on the way to Punchline, cheese-burgers and milkshakes in tow. The second we got into his car, Benji joked about his bad taste in music, and he didn't so much as bat an eye at my food request. Instead, he leaned into a ridiculous fast food order. He even looks as relaxed as he acts, wearing a black beanie, a blue Leopards shirt with a black puffy coat over the top, and gray sweatpants that he's tucked into boots.

I find myself sinking into his car's heated seats, lulled by his contagious mood and the smell of greasy fast food. "I didn't think you were allowed to have any of this," I say, shaking a fry at him.

He grins at me from around his straw, the other end attached to an excessively large strawberry-banana-chocolate milkshake. "It's all about balance. I can eat whatever I want, as long as I keep performing well. I'm an adult, after all." He wraps his lips around the straw and slurps from it, loudly, to underscore his point. It's supposed to be obnoxious, but I find my eyes drawn to his full mouth.

I bring my own milkshake to my mouth and glance away to reorganize my thoughts. Who knew a man sucking on a dairy beverage could be considered attractive? I didn't, until this very moment.

"Are you really an adult, though? I seem to remember a temper tantrum in the middle of a

coffee shop," I tease, and watch as he chokes on his next sip of milkshake before laughing.

He pulls up to a stoplight and eyes me for a long moment. "I like seeing this side of you."

I freeze. "Which side?"

"This... relaxed, joking side." He motions at me. "The side that calls me by my

nickname, offers up shitty jokes, and feels confident enough to kick her feet up on my dash. Even if they leave it covered in filth." He gives a pointed look at my shoes, which are covered in a slushy mixture of dirt and snow. I shoot him a guilty smile.

"Sorry," I say quickly, tucking my feet back down.

"No need to apologize," he replies, and I'm momentarily jarred by how easily the response slips past his lips. I'm not sure I've ever heard someone counter an apology by deeming it unnecessary. "I'm just concerned about the fact that you're still wearing high tops in the middle of winter."

I snort. "I'll use my next paycheck to buy some."

"Don't you have enough money for boots, Miss Penthouse?" He eyes me curiously, and I stiffen.

Instead of answering, I motion to a parking lot, then cross my arms tightly against myself. "You can park there."

Thankfully, he doesn't push the question. His eyes flick back to the road, and he twists the wheel silently, pulling into a parking spot. He puts the car in park before looking at me once more. "Ready?" he asks.

I smile and nod, leading him into the gym, but as I shrug open the door and motion him inside, a wave of self-consciousness suddenly hits me. Punchline is nothing like the gym at our luxury apartment building, and I'm certain it's a far cry from wherever he works out with his team off the ice. I'm glad for a moment that our timing has hit the late lunch hour, when Paul usually slips out to run errands and there are no classes in session. If Benji has something rude to say, at least I'll be the only one who has to hear it.

The gym is a large space, and it's got fresh paint, making it more vibrant, but the mats are still worn, some of the equipment is rusted, and half the punching bags have duct tape wound across them. Photos litter the space, taped simply against the wall, representing countless stories about Paul and Bella over the years, as well as some of the regular Punchline members. I watch carefully as Benji takes it in, walking along the wall, fingers brushing lightly against the photos.

He stops at one of the new ones, one I hadn't even seen yet. I step closer and peer over his shoulder. It's a photo of Andi and me, paint rollers in hand, heads thrown back as we laugh at something one of us must have said. I hadn't even realized Paul had taken the photo. Normally I'd be nervous about having my photo taken, but I'm surprised to find that this one doesn't bother me in the slightest.

Benji looks over at me, catching my soft smile. "This place means a lot to you, doesn't it?" he asks quietly.

I shrug, the wave of self-consciousness rushing back and causing me to flush slightly. "It's kind of my new home."

He considers me for a long moment, and my breath catches. Where the hell did that look come from? He was easier to manage when he was just being shallow and dickish, but this look, in this place...it's like he's stripping me bare, finding all of my most vulnerable pieces. I can't help but break eye contact first. "Well then, let's get recording."

As it turns out, because Benjamin freaking Estes has to be annoyingly perfect at, well, everything, he's a natural behind the camera. I'm trying to decide what sparkles more – his eyes or his smile – as he beams into the phone screen, walking around the gym before settling against a post of the boxing ring, providing an excellent backdrop.

"What better gift is there than the gift of a healthy start to the new year? So, if you're interested, join me on the thirtieth for a fun Halloween celebration and a chance to see if Punchline is the right fit for you." He grins for a long minute, oozing charisma and seduction, before straightening and clearing his throat. "So, do you think that was good?"

"Uh, yeah." I swallow, reminding myself that I don't have to revisit this footage, but then I frown. Andi will be editing and splicing it to post on social media, and then the whole world will be gushing at him. That feels even worse, somehow. My emotions are all mismatched, and I don't like it.

"Are you feeling all right?"

I glance up to see Benji standing in front of me, and school my expression into one of surprise. "Yeah," I reply quickly. "Why?"

"You seem a little distracted. It made me curious, how did your date go the other night?"

His words are careful, measured, nonchalant – but almost too much so, as if he'd been waiting all afternoon for a moment to ask this question. I remember Andi's words from earlier; that Benji went 'all lost puppy dog' when Jordie and I showed up.

Realization dawns on me: he's asking…because he's *jealous*. My lips curl up at the kernel of power I feel placed in my palm at this secret information.

"No, no, it was – it was good. Jordie's a wonderful guy."

Benji hums, toying with the line of boxing gloves. He tries one on before answering. "He is a great guy."

"Mhmmm." I watch him try another pair on, moving to a larger size. He straps a glove on experimentally and looks at me, his warm brown eyes narrowed and quizzical. I tense.

"I was just wondering, because I noticed you didn't let him kiss you." He lowers his gaze to grab the other glove and slip it on, as if he didn't just admit he had been watching us close enough to see my moment of weakness.

My mouth falls open. "Remind me, who accused whom of stalking?"

"I'm just saying." He shrugs, dismissing my question. "Must not have been that great of a date, if you wouldn't even let him give you a goodnight kiss."

"Who's to say I didn't let him kiss me after he walked me home?" I put my hands on my hips, feeling a spark of rebellion at the line of questioning. "Or more?"

I didn't, obviously. I had chickened out. It had nothing to do with Jordie, and everything to do with me. I thought I'd been ready to let someone close enough to allow that small piece of intimacy, but I'd been wrong. I wasn't ready to concede that much vulnerability to someone – even to someone as kind as Jordie clearly is.

I'm not ready to admit that to someone else, though. Especially not someone like Benji. And I have to admit, the way his eyes flash at the prospect of me making out with his teammate fans the embers of recklessness inside me, warming me to my toes. A prickle of jealousy, no matter how unwarranted, looks *good* on this man.

"If you did, he didn't say anything," Benji ventures, attempting to call my bluff.

But I won't concede. I'm in control, steering the conversation. "Maybe he's a gentleman, and doesn't kiss and tell." I bat my eyes at him innocently, and his own narrow in response.

"But you're not a lady, so I get the feeling you'd brag."

"Fine. Want me to brag?" I bite back a rebellious grin, enjoying where this game is headed. "I don't know why I questioned it, the first time he tried. He was *such* a good kisser. Just what I needed. He went in for that sweet goodbye. Soft lips, gentle touch, just enough tongue…" I fan myself in emphasis.

Benji chuckles and straightens, putting away the gloves and taking a few steps towards me. He moves slowly, his eyes glued on mine the entire time. My pulse instantly quickens, but I stand my ground, until he's standing over me, eyes scanning mine as if in question.

Finally, he lowers his head until his lips are practically pressed against my ear. I feel his warm breath fan against me when he speaks, and suppress a shiver, but don't give him the satisfaction of moving away. I know he's just taunting me.

"Sounds like a fun way to pass the time," he says, voice low. "If you're looking to fall asleep."

I blink. "What?"

"Come on. What you just described was a snooze fest, and I knew the second you said he went in for the kiss that it was a lie. You can't convince me that's what you did, let alone that it's what you needed."

I turn my head abruptly, brushing noses with him as I meet his gaze to glare at him. To my surprise, he's the one who pulls back slightly. "And what is it that I need?" I ask. "Enlighten me."

"You need someone that you don't have to question at all. You need someone you desire so much it pushes back on every fear you've ever had. You need to feel something, something far better than *good*. Something – or someone – that drives you crazy enough that *you* take full control. Take and take, until you're senseless with the pleasure of it all."

His eyes lower to my mouth as he speaks, and I realize with a start that my lips have parted as I listen to his words. I tear my eyes away from his own mouth and try to tamp down the ache that has settled low in my stomach, burning and reminding me that I can, in fact, still desire pleasure like that.

I want to run away from the feeling. It's too much.

Somehow, I manage a response. "Sounds like something I can handle all by myself, thanks." I smirk, but I'm not sure it's believable. "I told you to try it sometime. Seems like you still haven't learned."

"Oh, I've learned a lot, don't you worry about that. Seems like you're the one fixated on that image." He grins mischievously. "What is it you think I do? Call out your name as I pleasure myself?"

"Ugh!" I exclaim, even as I flush at his bold words. I shove him back, creating space between us, though I'm not sure if it's from disgust or to clear my own muddled head. "I should have hit you harder the first time."

Benji cocks a brow and gives me a slow smile. "Could you have?"

"Absolutely," I scoff.

He crosses his arms and regards me like the problem I am. Finally, he jerks his head at the boxing ring. "Prove it, little fighter."

Chapter 14

BENJI

There is so much more to this girl than I thought. Fuck, it terrifies me how intrigued I am. It's the reason I'm standing here, donned in boxing gloves and headgear, ready to get my ass handed to me. I can hear Coach Henderson screaming in my ear to stop being an idiot, but I'm not exactly known for my stellar choices. Why start now?

I had to call her bluff, knowing anything intimate would only have happened on her terms, and at her pace. The extra taunting had been a gamble, but it paid off. The fire in her eyes as she braids her hair and sizes me up is unlike anything I've seen before. I can see why she considers this place home. She's completely at ease here, not hunching down to make herself smaller or casting nervous glances around. She's showing me more of her confident, bold side, a side that I've only seen rare glimpses of here and there.

And if I'm being perfectly honest...the question about her date had been burning on the tip of my tongue since I woke up. I would have found any way to incorporate it into our conversation today. Jordie has been painfully silent about the date, and Grant has been watching me carefully since my admission about Lisa, as though any comment on the matter will set me off again.

I miscalculated when I taunted her, though. The thought of kissing her – and more – is burning me up inside, so I'm happy for the distraction of the ring. I'll follow her lead and see if I can pull any more of her real self out in the meantime. If I can leave with even one more truth, I'll be happy, and this seems like the place to get it.

She puts on some music and slips into the ring, motioning for me to follow. The music floods the ring and the strong, rhythmic beat echoes off the brick walls.

I raise a brow at her. "I didn't take you for a fan of rap," I comment, but she ignores me. Instead, she begins bouncing, her increasing energy palpable. Oh, yeah. She's in her zone now, and it's attractive as hell.

I duck into the ring, and she immediately approaches me. Whatever distance she'd been keeping before has completely cleared now that we're on her turf. The corner of my mouth curls up as she taps my hip, taking it upon herself to touch me.

"Take a step back with your dominant leg," she instructs, and raises a brow as I step back with my left, instead of the right hip she'd poked. "A southpaw, huh?"

I grin. "If you watched my games more closely, you would know that."

She simply rolls her eyes in response, and I find myself enjoying the casual dismissal. It's such a drastic change from the people who know all of my stats, keeping a closer eye on my future plans than even I do. It's my career, and where most of my best friends have come from, but it's not everything I am. It's refreshing to be with someone who can talk about other things – like coaching me in a new sport.

And on that front, she's an absolute drill sergeant.

"Raise your back toe and start bouncing," she barks, showing me as she twists her back foot and begins springing off it. Her braids fly in time with her bouncing, swinging across her shoulder blades. "Always keep your legs wide. You don't want them too close together, or you'll get off balance."

I snort, but comply, and she pulls up her fists, instructing me to keep them close to my chin. She then shows me how to step forward and backward, keeping my legs shoulder-width apart. When I make a mistake, she scolds me, I can't help the reply that slips out. "Always keep my legs spread. Got it, got it."

It catches her off guard, and a smile twitches at her lips for the briefest moment. I don't miss the flush that blooms across her cheeks, but then she shakes her head and continues.

"The jab – full extension, then retract it back close to your chin. This is important; it's how you know how far your opponent is from you. And now the cross. Shift your hips, twist and extend. Remember, your power comes from that dominant leg. Cross and rotate your fist – there you go!" Her praise is exuberant, and I'm struck by the warmth of it. Before I know it, I'm trying that much harder, working to get her approval once more.

She shows me the uppercut and the hook next, repeating, "Load – release." She glances at me. "Do you see that? My hips are driving up, and my feet are twisting."

'It's so technical," I comment.

She responds with a snort. "You're telling me hockey isn't? I'm sure there's a wrong way to skate, a wrong way to shoot, that loses power or momentum."

I mirror her movements for a few strikes, considering. "You're right. I suppose that's the case in every sport. You need the form down first, then you can build on the foundation."

She takes a swipe at me and grins as I step back and curse, realizing I've already lost the footwork. "Exactly. It needs to become muscle memory. Okay, now let's try it all together. Jab – back hook – front hook – back hook – jab – back upper – front upper."

I lose myself to the movements, trying to balance having the proper form with the way my eyes are devouring her in her element. She's small but toned, impressive muscle showing with each move, lightning quick. She's exuding confidence, and above all, *joy* as she works through the series of punches. Her cheeks are flushed again, now with the effort of coaching and going through the movements herself, but it almost seems like it energizes her more than slowing her down.

Her blue eyes shine as she steps closer into my space, and then she breaks out into a broad grin as I bounce back, keeping my fists tucked to my face. "There it is!" she exclaims proudly.

I want to claim it's the workout that has me breathless, but it's her grin that stuns me. It's broad, unburdened, genuine.

I'd come here every day and work out with her if it meant I could see that smile, especially when it's directed at me and something I've done to earn it.

Fuck.

The realization stuns me, and I drop my hands for a brief moment.

The whack against my left cheek is instant, loud and powerful against the synthetic leather of the headgear. I go stumbling to my right and trip over my own feet, landing with a thud on the ring floor.

I take a moment to gather my bearings, and from the other size of the ring, the muffled sound of a laugh reaches me. I shrug the headgear off before turning to narrow my eyes at Lisa. She takes a few steps forward and crouches down, unable to hide her grin as she assesses me. She's trying to contain her laughter now, but her body still shakes with the force of trying to fight it. As soon as we lock eyes, her composure shatters. She laughs openly, the sound growing louder until she lets out a ridiculous snort.

Her eyes widen as she realizes the sound she just made, and it sends me over the edge. I throw my head back as my own laugh bubbles up my chest. Our combined laughter ricochets off the walls of the gym, and I feel tears prick my eyes. I've just had my ass absolutely handed to me by a pint-sized fighter with big blue eyes and more secrets than I can even begin to unpack.

And it's fucking hilarious.

Finally, when my ribs begin to ache from the laughter, I take a deep breath and roll over, getting to my feet. I begin to strip the sparring equipment off, and my gaze travels back to her.

She's gone quiet, but while her gaze is still on me, her expression is distant. Again, I wonder what's going on behind those eyes – things she hasn't uttered aloud; memories she's bottled up into nightmares. Does she have *anyone* she shares her secrets with? I hate the thought of her being lonely.

"Well, you were right. You could punch me harder," I say, flashing her my most charming grin. The edge of her mouth ticks up, but it doesn't reach her eyes like it did mere minutes earlier. "I'm going to need to start calling you little fighter. And I think we might need to incorporate some of this into our dry land training. It's a better workout than half the stuff we do."

Again, that twitch at the corner of her mouth. "It would be fun to have a real opponent to spar with besides Andi. Though I think you'd still end up on the floor more often than not."

"Careful," I quip, "I might just like that." Then, before she can retreat further into herself, I jerk my head towards the front door. "Ready to head home?"

The ride home is fairly quiet, filled only by the soft stream of music. Lisa seems to be in her own thoughts, and I give her the space she needs to sort through whatever it is. Though she doesn't say as much, she seems grateful for it, content to tip her head back and rest her feet on the dash as she bobs along to my music. When we arrive home, I offer to take her all the way to her door, and she simply nods, giving me a small win that I wasn't expecting. As we go up the elevator, she lets out a sigh.

I slide my eyes over to her. "Everything okay?" I finally ask.

She tilts her head as she looks up at me. Finally, she shifts her feet and casts her gaze down. "I just can't figure you out."

I let out a soft chuckle. "Well, if that isn't the pot calling the kettle black."

"No. Seriously." The elevator halts and pings, the doors springing open. She exits, but turns back to face me, walking backwards down the hall. "You make all these... *comments,* and yet you don't make a single move to actually do anything."

"Comments?" I repeat, staring down at her curiously. Where is she going with this?

She comes to a stop, presumably at her door, and makes a helpless gesture. "You know. All these comments about...spreading legs, being on the floor, all that stuff. But even when you were suggesting we sleep together, you've never actually done anything about it."

My brows knit together. Is this what she was thinking about the whole drive home? "Like I said earlier, you seem like the type who needs to make the first move. And you've made it very clear in the past that if I wanted to do anything, that was strictly between me and my hand." I play it off with a small smile, though I can't help but add, "Do you *want* me to do something about it?"

She lowers her gaze to the floor and bites down on her bottom lip, worrying it between her teeth. *Christ.* My eyes narrow in on the movement, all the blood rushing to a singular point between my legs. Finally, she lifts her eyes to meet mine again. "I don't know. Maybe."

"Well." I step forward and put a hand on the door, watching her carefully. She doesn't step back or shrink down, but I catch the glance she gives my arm resting above her, eyes widening.

It's not quite the same reaction as she gave Jordie, but still...I purse my lips, considering. Finally, I add quietly, "I won't touch you unless you ask me to."

Her eyes dart back to mine, surprise etched in her every feature. Her lips part and her stare drops to my mouth, hovering there. She raises a hand to my face. It's cold and tentative, but the second she touches me, her lips come back together in a firm, decisive line, and she gives a slight nod.

I slowly move my arm from the door and place my palm over hers. Her eyes are back on mine, and I don't let go of her gaze as her other hand reaches for my shoulder. The touch is featherlight, as if she's just as surprised that she's doing it as I am, but then she steps into my space and I take the invitation, wrapping my other hand around her waist. I wait for her to jolt back or wince away, but she doesn't. The second my hand hits her waist, she bends into me, and my breath catches at the small but significant reaction.

I gently pull her closer so that we're flush against one another. Her hand drops from my cheek to my chest, leaving me to use my newly freed hand to brush the hair away from her face. It's just as soft as I imagined. I shift to graze my thumb across her cheek and watch as her eyes flutter. She tilts her head ever so slightly into my palm.

It feels like I've won a small, precious treasure, seeing how receptive she is to my touch. It makes me curious about running my hands everywhere else, to see how she'll move for me, but right now, I just want to kiss her. I want to feel how softly her mouth moves against mine and suck on the spot on her lip she bit just moments before. I want to breathe her name into her ear to praise her, like she praised me earlier.

It's then I realize one very important thing.

"I can't kiss you without knowing your real name," I murmur.

She goes rigid in my arms, and I realize we've come up to a hard line she's drawn in the sand between us. I scramble to stop her from shutting down completely, eager to bring back that warm, receptive side of her. I rub my thumb across her back and nuzzle my face against her ear, closing my eyes. "Tell me your name."

I'm borderline begging and if I'm being honest, I'm not above doing so.

We're still so intertwined that I hear the shaky breath she exhales and feel the soft shiver that follows. She pulls back, and just like that, the moment is shattered.

When our gazes collide again, her eyes are watery, shining against the light of the hallway. I open my mouth to question it, to take it all back, to ask what I can do to help – but before I can do any of that, she has her door open.

"I'm sorry," she whispers. The two words sound like a gavel pounding down, echoing with the finality of them. "I can't."

Just like that, she closes the door in my face. I can't help but feel like I've been closed off from so much more.

Chapter 15

LISA

"*A*re you sure?"

Ethan's eyes are wide, pleading. I know the silent question he's asking, but I also know it will only be worse if I answer it the way I want to. I can't even hint at what awaits me when I'm left alone with Austin. To admit that out loud would only make it so much worse. This is a damage control moment.

I school my expression into one of nonchalance, offering Ethan a soft, reassuring smile instead. "I'm fine. You can go home."

Still, Ethan doesn't move, his gaze sidling over to where Austin stands. Austin clears his throat. "You heard her, brother," he growls, crossing his arms. "You can go."

Ethan shakes his head but obliges, giving me a long look as he leaves to join his wife out in their car. It takes the door an eternity to close, as though it knows what will happen the second it's fully shut, too. My heart rate triples as I hear the final clink of the latch.

The sound of glass shattering makes me flinch, and I turn slowly, meeting Austin's glare, burning like two hot embers. "What the fuck was that, Lyssa?" he snarls. "You've got some nerve, inviting my family here for dinner and then talking like that!"

"We haven't seen them since their wedding, and Patty kept asking to come over. And all I said was that you were looking for a new job. You were the one talking about something in a new field, since this one isn't working out the way you'd hoped."

"You made me sound like a fucking failure, Lyss!" He stalks around the table towards me. I make the mistake of stepping back, keeping the table between us. The heated rage in his eyes is doused, instantly turning hard and ice cold. The shift is far worse.

"You've got that look on your face. What is it you want to say to me? Huh?" He stalks forward again, and this time I hold my ground, shaking my head.

"Nothing," I choke out. "I'm sorry. I'm sorry."

He's in my space now, his breath hot on my cheek. I turn my chin, eyes averted.

"Don't walk away from me," he says. "Even though I give you everything, it's always my fault, right? Am I not enough for you?"

"That's – that's not what I said."

He bristles, his nostrils flaring. "Are you calling me a liar?"

There's no reasoning my way out of this one. His mind is made up.

I open my mouth, unsure what I'll even say, but before I can get any words out, his hands close around my neck. I scramble against him, but my feet can't find purchase. He has me lifted off the ground, pressing me back against the wall by my throat. I scratch at his arms before clutching them, all my energy narrowing to the sole purpose of finding a way to pass breath. My vision blurs around the edges.

"You and your smart mouth," he hisses, dropping me. I collapse to my knees, gasping precious lungfuls of air. "You're lucky I love you. Stop provoking me, or nobody will."

I wake up choking, black dots swarming my vision as I regain my breathing. I'm not sure if it's the panic, but I swear everything was even more realistic than my last nightmare. I could feel every callous on his hands as they tightened around my throat, as though he reached through the dream to find me once more. I roll out of bed and check the mirror for marks, just in case, though I find none.

I brush my fingers against my throat, considering. This is exactly the reminder I needed. There are so many reasons I cannot allow myself to get close to someone again, this one chief among them. I wanted a physical escape, but Benji wanted more. And more is something I just can't give.

If I allow myself to get close to someone again, I will lose the freedom I fought tooth and nail for. I can't afford to give someone that kind of control over me again, body or mind.

I need something I can remove myself from, quickly and easily, and everything about Benji is messy.

We live in the same building, for starters. He towers an easy half foot over me, with at least another hundred pounds of sheer muscle to boot. And although all of his touches have been incredibly gentle, and he's given me permission to lead the way in that regard, that doesn't mean it won't change. Everyone has darkness inside them, it's just that some hide it better than others. I only need to look in the mirror for that painful reminder.

All of that aside, what's most terrifying is the way he genuinely *wants* to know the inner workings of my mind. He wants my name, my history, my deepest thoughts. He wants to pull them out of me, and if he ever did...there wouldn't be a snowball's chance in hell he'd stay, after knowing the whole story. Even if he didn't use it against me, it still wouldn't remove the fact that I'm damaged goods. I'm broken, shattered into sharp pieces that will cut anyone who tries to pick them up.

I begin getting ready for work and check my phone, rolling my eyes as I see the text from Andi.

Andi: *Girllll. Does the man never take a bad photo or video? I don't need to edit a thing. He's just too damn perfect.*

I roll my eyes and type out a response.

Me: *He's shit at boxing, if that helps. I sent him flying across the ring yesterday with one back hook.*

Andi: *Why tf would you do that? Poor guy probably gets hit enough at hockey!*

Andi: *His brains are probably half mush already. You just propelled them into full mush. Full mush, Lisa.*

Me: *See? He's not perfect. He's mush. Plus, I didn't give him anything he didn't ask for.*

Andi: *Ooooh... What else did he ask for?*

I pause, considering what to tell her. Benji wouldn't tell the others that he'd shut me down mid-kiss, would he? Especially not Jordie. The secret could safely stay between us and my doorway.

I continue getting dressed, ignoring my phone as it vibrates several more times. Finally, I grab Winny's leash and flip my phone open, reading the texts.

Andi: *Bitch. I know you read my text. What did you two do?!*

Andi: *I hope it was juicy.*

Andi: *I hope you washed your sheets afterwards.*

Andi: *Oh. Maybe you're still doing it...*

Andi: *USE PROTECTION!!!*

I snort and put my phone away, deciding to let her continue her spiral. I'm excited to see where it goes.

I open the door and Winny shoots out, pulling the leash taut in his excitement to get downstairs for his walk. I follow and stumble over something in the entryway, landing very ungracefully on the doormat.

I glance down and see a pair of black boots. The soles are thick and grippy, and they look brand new. There's a piece of paper sticking out of one of them. I snag it and read the handwritten note.

I saw the boxing shoes you put on yesterday and took a guess with the size here. Hope this helps keep you on your feet.

-Benji

"Are you freaking kidding me?" I mutter. I've never been good at receiving gifts; it always makes me uncomfortable. There are always strings attached. And this? From someone I've barely had a handful of conversations with? I grab the boot closest to me and scan the brand, cursing when I recognize it. These are top-tier boots, worth a few hundred dollars, at least.

I scramble back up and close my door, snagging both boots as I go. Instead of heading to the first floor, I hit Benji's floor, tapping my high-top-clad foot impatiently as I wait for the elevator to hit the sixth floor.

When it does, I storm out and pull Winny alongside me, who is clearly confused but happy to follow. I skid to a stop outside 604, banging on it for several long seconds. It's just after six in the morning, but considering I've caught him at the gym around now, I know he's an early riser. It can't be *that* much of an early wake-up call.

As I wait a beat, then bang again, I wonder briefly if he lives with his friends. A part of me will feel bad if Grant or Jordie answer – though the boots can just as easily be returned to either one of them.

But it's Benjamin freaking Estes himself who eventually opens the door, and it's clear I've woken him up. His hair stands on end and his eyes are foggy with sleep.

My mouth twists in a self-satisfied smirk until my eyes drop to his bare chest and boxers, which peek out from low-hanging sweats. Those bold tattoos swirl over his bare skin, and the v that teases out from his waistband, along with the dusting of dark hair leading below, is truly sinful.

"What time is it?" he asks, rubbing sleep from his eyes. "Is that Winny?"

Winny gives a happy wiggle at the sound of his name, and I force my eyes back up, reminding myself why I'm here. Just because he looks even better up close and personal doesn't mean I want everything else tied to his physical offers.

"Time for a gift return," I say. I move Winny's leash to the crook of my elbow and shove the boots into his arms, crossing my own once they're free of the offending gift.

He makes a grab for them before they can fall to the ground, blearily blinking down at them. His brow furrows. "This is because I bought you boots?"

"No," I reply. "It's because of *why* you bought me boots, and how much the boots *cost.*"

"Well, you said you couldn't afford them." He transfers the boots to one arm and rubs the back of his neck, clearly confused. "And not to sound like a douche, but I'm a professional athlete who lives alone. It's no NHL salary – yet – but most of my shit is sponsored. I can afford to give you a little something when you need it."

"I said I was waiting for my next paycheck, not that I couldn't afford it. And that's just it," I seethe, feeling my heart rate pick up. My hand trails to my throat, fingers brushing where the nightmare felt oh so real this morning. "I don't *need* anything from you. I can do this by myself. First it's just a 'little' gift, and then it's bigger gifts, and the invisible tally I don't know about will start. I'll start to feel safe, and I'll get complacent. Then, if I don't appreciate it enough, I'll hear about it. And you'll expect something in return – everything in return. I-I can't do that shit again."

Benji tilts his head. "Again?" His eyes are suddenly clear of all sleep, and they're focused on my hand. I realize it remains on my throat, and quickly lower it.

"Jesus –" I sputter. *Shit.* I was spiraling, and he's seeing everything. He's so attentive, and it's terrifying. I immediately go on the defensive. "Can you not turn everything into an interrogation?"

"Maybe if you stopped icing me out, I wouldn't have to keep asking questions."

I narrow my eyes at him. "I hate you."

"Okay." He shakes his head. "Except, I don't think you actually hate me. I think you just hate that you want me, and you don't know what to do about that."

"Excuse me?"

"Tell me I'm wrong." He shrugs and leans against the door-frame, boots still in hand, clearly willing to wait.

I open my mouth, then snap it closed as I look away. Benji clearly knows I want him – hell, I'd thrown myself at him last night, until he'd added conditions to it that were impossible to meet. I meet his gaze with an exasperated look of my own.

He smirks, dimples flashing at the way I'm meeting his challenge. "Go on," he urges. "Tell me I'm wrong."

"Fine," I spit back. "I want you, okay? But I want you with no strings attached. No boots, no names, no games. Is that something you can do?"

His expression grows serious, and a muscle in his jaw ticks as he contemplates my offer. Finally, he shakes his head. "Nope. You're too much, mystery girl. There needs to be some give and take here."

I huff. This man is impossible. "Fine. A truth for a truth?"

"So you'll give me your name?"

"Not that."

He lets out a humorless chuckle. "That's literally the bare minimum."

"Can we not just do, like, favorite colors? Favorite foods?" These are things we can bond over without investing too much. I search his face for agreement, but his expression is resigned and sad. It makes me feel like I've failed him, somehow, and I don't like it.

"You can trust me, you know," he says softly. "I just want to know the real name of the person I'm talking to."

I frown, confused. "It's still me, no matter what you call me."

"I could call you a lot of things, little fighter. They'd be mostly filthy. But I want one of them to be your real name."

I give a frustrated sigh. How could he say something sweet and turn me on at the same time? "Screw you."

He grins broadly. "That's my girl."

"Not what I meant. And I'm not your girl!" This conversation is clearly going nowhere. I straighten and wind Winny's leash around my hand, giving the boots in Benji's arms a final, pointed look. "I guess we have a stalemate, then."

With a final huff, I turn on my heel and pull on Winny. He seems reluctant to leave Benji, which only irritates me further.

"Come on, Winny," I say urgently. Finally, Winny lowers his head, trudging after me – but not without a dejected look back at Benji. Traitor. He's lucky he's so cute.

"Let me know if you change your mind, *Lisa,*" Benji calls after me, exaggerating the name in emphasis. "You know where to find me."

Chapter 16

Benji

I'm content. No, more than that – I'm happy. I'm fucking *ecstatic.*

At least, I keep telling myself that.

I tell myself that through every grinding practice over the next week, all the way through to Friday's game. We traveled down south to play the worst team in the league and fucking crushed them, so even though it was far from one of my best games, it wasn't like it took away the W.

That didn't matter to Coach Henderson, though. He came into the locker room after the game, yelling about how we should have had at least four more goals, and that he'd better see us show up for Sunday's game back in Minnesota or else we'd have a week of bag skates. The mood definitely went down after that, but not enough to stop a quiet celebration.

We're on the bus home, drinks being poured like we're headed to spring break in Cabo instead of the icy cold of a Minnesota winter. Everyone is already discussing hitting up a favorite local late-night bar, since we have all of Saturday to sleep off the hangover. Half the guys are texting their current girls to see who will show up and celebrate with them, Grant included. He's bribing her with the promise of vodka Red Bulls to keep everyone awake, and from the grin on his face, it's working. I wonder absently if that means Lisa will show up, then steer away from that line of thinking.

I haven't heard from Lisa, other than being on the receiving end of her professional attitude as she pours our morning coffees. Our only connection is through Grant and Andi, who have spent every minute together when he's home, despite their mutual claims that it's nothing serious.

Because Andi's always with Grant, I know exactly when I'll be needed at the gym for their Halloween fundraiser this week, what is on our *do* and *don't* do list, and what coordinating outfit I'm meant to wear with Grant. It came with the story of what had happened after Andi raided Grant's closet, which I wished I could scrub from my brain. Grant's a fucking freak, but good on him for finding someone to match his speed, I guess.

The only silver lining is that Lisa's distance has extended to Jordie as well, who hasn't heard from her since their date. He's happy as ever, currently making plans to use this weekend to move on, so the dismissal clearly hasn't affected him too much.

"Come on," he whines as he bribes Goody to give him some dip. "I can get you more tomorrow. I ran out, and you're being a wuss about going out tonight anyways."

"I told you," Goody says, rubbing his hand over his face. "I'll come for one beer. Two beers, max. I already agreed to go with my pops to pick up some lumber tomorrow morning. He needs help framing his basement."

"I can help," Nils cuts in, grinning. "I'm great with wood. Just ask your mom."

A chorus of hollers goes up, and Goody leans behind him to Nils's seat, smacking the back of his head. Then he settles back in and gestures to Ryan. "Hey, rook, give Jordie some of your dip."

Ryan sighs, but pulls a tin from his back pocket and tosses it to Jordie. Jordie catches it and salutes with the tin. "Thank you, good sir!"

I roll my eyes and sit back, but I'm only allowed a moment of peace before Grant pokes at me.

"What?" I groan, shifting to glare at him. He simply grins at me.

"Andi's coming out tonight. Want me to tell her to bring Lisa?"

I tug my cap down further on my head, covering my eyes. "I really don't care, Grant," I sigh.

"Hmmm. I'll take that as a yes."

I simply grunt in response, but my stomach is already churning with anticipation. *Fuck me.* This is gonna be a long night.

I take the shot handed to me without complaint, embracing the burn as I throw it back. I'm not usually a shot taker, but if it will take my mind off *that fucking top*, it'll be worth it.

Lisa's here with Andi, and she's come to kill. Kill me, specifically, if I had to guess.

She's all sleek lines and sinful looks, from her straightened hair and dark makeup down to her – yep, those are new boots, tucked into tight skinny jeans, which show off her muscular thighs and tight, round ass. They're even the same color and brand as the ones I bought her, which feels like a very intentional 'fuck you'. She doesn't usually wear much makeup when she works, so her blue eyes pop even more than normal. But... that *top*. It's some sort of bodysuit, pitch black with sheer sleeves, and a lacy front that teases over the swell of her breasts, dipping dangerously close to her navel. I want to drag my tongue down every curve.

But I can't. So I'll use my tongue to get wasted, instead.

"What's up, *Benji-boo?*" Jordie whispers in my ear.

It's a strange enough comment to make me finally rip my gaze from Lisa and eye him with alarm. "What?"

"Do you want one of these?" Jordie motions to his drink, which is some bright pink concoction. I spy chunks of fruit and – is that an *umbrella?* "The girls over there are buying rounds and convinced me to chug three of these. I'm sure they'd be happy to cover your drinks. And something else, too." He waggles his eyebrows suggestively.

"Ah." I blink. "So you're like this on purpose."

He nods and grins, opening his mouth to snag the straw again. He misses and tries again, this time sucking down half the sugary monstrosity that will surely give him a massive headache tomorrow morning. "Care to make poor decisions with me? Ha, get it – *pour* decisions?"

I can't help the snort that escapes me. "Nah. I'm good. But you're gonna have a great night, brother."

"Oh, I will," he replies, and sidles away with a wink.

I smirk and turn back around, skimming the crowd to find Lisa. I find Andi first, her blonde hair standing out brightly against a red crop top and a pair of black jeans. She's talking with Lisa, who has just appeared with two drinks for them. To my surprise, Grant is nowhere to be found, and there's a small group of men closing in on the two of them.

They surround the two women, one of them stepping forward to ask Andi something. I find myself standing a bit straighter, my gaze narrowing in on the interaction.

Andi tosses her hair and gives the man a quick half-smile, then turns to face Lisa, who pulls out her phone to show Andi something. The guys remain, clearly content to post up around them. It looks like one is still asking Andi questions, but she looks incredibly interested at whatever Lisa is showing her, oblivious to the guy next to her. I'm not sure if it's genuine, or a way to get the group of men to leave her alone. All I know is any guy half decent at picking up cues from women would know he'd been shut down, and move on to another group to try his luck.

Clearly, these guys don't fit the bill. The one who approached Andi taps her on the shoulder, and she glances back at him. He grabs her arm and *tugs,* and her polite smile dissolves, replaced with a frown and an angry shake of her head. Lisa steps closer to her, but another guy in the group intercepts Lisa, wrapping his arm around her waist.

She flinches, and before I know it I'm slamming my empty glass down on the nearby railing. I stalk forward, thinking of nothing other than getting this guy's greasy fucking hands off her. I'm not sure *what* I'm going to do when I get there, but before I can think of a plan, I see another figure steamrolling his way through the crowd.

It's Grant, and I follow where his eyes are trained: directly on a guy who is now soaking wet, drenched in Andi's drink. I have to give it to her – it was a direct hit, and Andi's drink was far from empty.

The guy looks livid, but it has nothing on the raging fire in Andi's expression. Her knuckles are white as they clench her empty glass. I'm not sure what he said to her, but it had to have been bad.

Not as bad as it gets, though, when Grant barrels into the guy whose grip is still laced around Andi's arm. Andi jumps back toward Lisa, now freed from the guy's grip.

I'm moving forward again, seconds away when the guy spins around and swings at Grant. Grant catches it and volleys a punch back, and with that, it's dissolved into a group brawl. *Fuck.*

My body reacts before my brain, catching a swing destined for Grant's face from the guy that touched Lisa. He turns to square up with me, and I ignore the feel of someone tugging on my jacket as I push forward, my fist connecting with his face in a satisfying crunch. I don't have time to celebrate it before someone clips the side of my face, and I spin to deflect the full blow.

From there, it's a flurry of swinging limbs and hollering. I'm dimly aware of the fact that Andi joins in, leaping on some guy's back and clawing to pull him away. The brawl only lasts a minute or two until someone else on the team – Levi, maybe?

– pulls me away. I pant as I shoo him off, glaring daggers at the soggy excuse for a man who started the whole ordeal.

"Out!" someone bellows. "All of you, out!"

We stumble outside, grumbling as we're ushered out before even shrugging our coats on. I wince against the flurries of snow that have started, even though the alcohol dulls the cold assault a bit.

There are muttered curses, and I turn at the sound of raised voices, ready in case we need to continue giving the lesson we started inside. To no surprise, it's Grant who's started it up again, but Highcloud tugs him away as he continues to spew insults at the man who grabbed Andi. Thankfully, the cold seems to have leveled that guy out, because he simply flicks Grant off and stalks away.

Grant and Highcloud stalk off in the opposite direction. Andi turns to follow them, then hesitates. Her gaze falls on me.

"Hey," she says, gesturing back to the bar. "Can you make sure Lisa is okay? I'm going to make sure Grant is all right. It looked like he was bleeding."

I nod, not bothering to tell her that Grant's blood leaves his body more often than not. She'll figure it out soon enough.

She shoots me a grateful smile and scurries off after Grant, disappearing into the dark and the snow. I take a moment to compose myself, and then stalk back to the bar.

I poke my head back inside, but after scanning the crowd for a brief moment, I see no trace of Lisa. Not wanting to get kicked out twice, I turn back outside and check around the corner of the building.

It takes a minute, but I find her tucked against the side of the bar. She has her coat on, but she's still shivering, eyes closed.

I pause, remembering the last time I approached her when she didn't want anyone near her. Finally, I decide to call out to her. "We've got to stop meeting like this."

She lets out a shaky exhale, and then peeks at me with one eye. She quickly snaps it shut again, and whispers, "You're bleeding."

I swipe a hand across my face and see that she's right. It must have happened from the hit I took on the side of my cheek. I swipe at my nose once more, and then sniffle. "Bloody nose. I'll live." I put my hands in my pockets and assess her. "Are *you* okay?"

I don't expect a response, so I'm startled when she answers me. Her voice is hoarse and quiet enough that I barely catch the words. "I don't do f-fighting."

I squint at her, unsure what she means by that. "But you...box?"

And you've got a mean right hook of your own. I want to add the comment to lift the mood, but I can see now's not the time.

She lets out a long exhale, and I watch it rise in the cold winter air. When she responds this time, her voice is steadier. "I box so I can feel strong and protect myself. Not to hurt others. There's a difference, Benji."

I remain quiet, try to put the pieces together in my mind.

Clearly, she's been hurt before. She doesn't like being touched. And she doesn't enjoy fighting. She doesn't trust anyone, not even with her name. Was it a stranger who hurt her, or someone close to her? Someone in her family, maybe? Is that why she is trying so hard to disappear into a life that isn't her own?

I take a cautious step forward. "Let me help. Let's order a ride and get you home."

She shakes her head, and when I extend my hand to her, she looks away, closing her eyes.

What is this girl running from? I hate to see her like this. I don't want her to be afraid anymore. I want her to know she's safe with me. "I won't let anyone hurt you," I promise.

Her eyes snap open, flicking from my face down at my hand. I leave the offer there, waiting patiently as the snow falls softly around us.

When she finally looks back up at me, her eyes are narrowed. "But *you* hurt people," she points out, and I can see the tears forming "You just did."

Ah. My hand drops. I open my mouth to say something more, then close it, because she's not wrong. She just witnessed it firsthand. And it's not just reserved for slimy dudes in dingy bars – it's something that happens frequently on the ice. All she has to do is search my name, and she'll probably find a compilation of my best hits, my best fights.

How do I let her know that there's a line I'd never cross when it comes to this? How do I win her trust, make her see this something I would never do to her?

I'm not sure there is a way.

"I protect my team, Lisa," I begin, struggling to find words that would make sense. "I protect my team, and I protect my – my team's girls." I fumble, barely avoiding the words *my girl*. She's made it clear that's something she'll never be.

"What did that guy say to Andi?" I continue. "That made her throw her drink at him?"

She quickly averts her gaze, but not before I see a dark expression cross her face. "Nothing worth repeating," she mutters.

I frown, but decide not to push it. "Maybe not worth repeating, but probably worth a cocktail to the face."

She gives a small smile, and it feels like a weight lifting off my chest. I offer my hand again and this time she takes it, stepping into my space. Her touch is barely there, and I try not to think of how big of a deal it must be for her. I've just used these hands to draw blood. She knows it, and I know it.

I pull her as gently as I can toward the sidewalk, ordering a ride on my phone as we walk. It's silent as we wait for our ride to arrive, but not uncomfortable. The snow is falling softly around us, lit up by the street lights. The night air is crisp, and the laughter and pulsing music emanating from the bar provides a soft background noise. It takes a few minutes before Lisa speaks again.

"It was a really expensive drink Andi threw." Her tone is wistful. "Such a waste."

I chuckle. "Something tells me Grant will reimburse her. Though he looks even worse than I do, if you can believe it."

"I can't," she says, looking my way and scanning me pointedly. I grin back, fully aware of the dried blood mixing with snowflakes falling on my face. It must be an interesting sight. "The guy Andi doused did throw the first punch. Though," she adds thoughtfully, "Grant was quick to punch back."

"He was," I agree. "And as his teammate, it was my duty to back him up."

She frowns. "Hockey players are weird."

I can't argue with that.

Chapter 17

LISA

It's the morning of our fundraiser for Punchline, and Andi has officially lost her mind. She's running around her condo, starting and stopping things halfway, muttering to herself as she goes. I try my best to follow after her and assist as much as possible, though her half-finished orders and multitasking make it difficult. At one point, she's so busy posting to social media that she runs into a chair in the kitchen. With a curse, she drops her phone and rubs her hip.

"All right, you've lost your phone privileges. Give me that." I duck down to retrieve her phone and read the post out loud. *"No tricks, just jabs. Halloween hits different at Punchline. Don't forget to join us in the ring for tonight's fundraiser event."* I look up and grin at her. "Good one, Andi. I can't wait to see what kind of engagement we get tonight."

"Thanks, babe!" She beams at me, even as she rubs her hip. "I always wonder why I wake up with random bruises. I guess I have the answer."

"Is that what those are from? I get them too, and I always thought I was just a wild sleeper."

"I was thinking tiny little leprechauns were kicking me in my sleep."

I laugh. "Angry fairies sound way more exciting than just having poor depth perception."

"Oh, well." Andi laughs and gives her hip one final rub. "I guess we can take the first load out to my car. Can you take that box?"

I eye the box dubiously. It's filled to the brim with beer and jars of pickles. "Not to question your shopping list, but...do we really need this many pickles?"

This, of all my questions this morning, causes her to skid to a dead-stop. "I don't think you truly understand the love between a midwesterner and their pickle beer."

I blink. "I suppose I don't."

"Seriously, girl, don't knock it till you've tried it." She adjusts an orange streamer in her box. "Back where I'm from in Wisconsin, that with some cheese curds is as close as you'll get to heaven."

A ding from her phone saves me from replying. I glance at it. "Grant wants to know if Nils can tag along tonight. He said his plans fell through."

Andi is already halfway out the door with her box of decorations. "Answer and tell him yes!" she calls back at me, reminding me of her passcode. "As long as Nils agrees to wear the same stuff as Grant and Benji."

I type out the response and scurry after her with the offending box of beer and pickles. "What *are* you making them wear?"

"Well, they need to bring their hockey sticks to play with any kiddos that show up. And they need to wear their Leopards logo, from head to toe. Their beanies, their jerseys, and gray sweatpants."

"Do they even have branded sweatpants?" I ask.

She shrugs. "Not sure. But I do know there's nothing that gets me going quite like a man in gray sweatpants."

I may question her taste in drinks, but she's got a point with that one.

Andi and I spend two hours before the event decorating, setting up games, putting out merchandise, organizing the raffles and ensuring the prizes are safely tucked away for their future winners. By the time the event is actually underway, my skeleton onesie is already damp with sweat, and I haven't even kicked off our impromptu boxing tournament.

People begin to file in, filling the space to near-capacity, and my nerves grow as my personal space shrinks. I wander my way over to the silent auction tables we've set up, scanning the items. Andi said we'd gotten some great donations, but hadn't specified what they were.

I spot a piece of artwork someone donated, a beautiful landscape photograph of a lake. The angle is positioned just so that a few rocks dot the bottom of the photo, with lush trees peeking in at the right corner. The sun is dipping under the horizon, winking narrow beams of light over the water as it goes down. The lake itself is glacially still, looking more like an expanse of glass than water. Even the bird floating in the middle of the lake is still, without so much as a ripple around it.

The moment captured feels serene, like I've been placed in someone's vulnerable memory. I'm immediately drawn to it. I put in the first bid, adding a cool hundred dollars to the minimum to ensure my win. I make a mental note to keep checking in as the night goes on. I secretly hope I get into a bidding war, so that Paul can't claim I'm just tossing money his way.

"Isn't this amazing?" Andi appears next to me, and when I glance over, she's nearly airborne with excitement. She's wearing a 70's workout costume, and her curls go flying as she bounces happily, restrained only by the neon blue sweatband drawn across her forehead. I just know her blue leotard and hot pink leggings will send Grant into a frenzy.

"Grant's going to lose his mind seeing you in this," I say. "I hope his sweatpants can contain all that excitement you're going to cause."

Andi flushes and gives a triumphant laugh. "Don't worry, we gave it a test run the other night. He'll behave today." She winks and gestures around her neck. "The sweatband may have ended up on him."

"Argh!" I hold my hands up. "Need-to-know basis, Andi. That was *not* a need-to-know."

She laughs harder, and dissolves into a shriek as the man in question appears behind her, swooping her into his arms. Their energy is contagious, and I grin as I take them in.

I glance over to see Nils and Benji have entered as well, standing back and smiling at the two lovebirds. I have to admit, Andi's rules for their wardrobe are doing wonders for these athletes. They look like the perfect combination of sporty-professional, the Leopards jerseys marking them as members of one of the most prestigious teams in the area. And those gray sweatpants? Damn, Andi made the right choice.

My eyes wander down Benji's body, my gaze freezing on his lower half. My thighs clench together as I allow my imagination to run wild, thoughts drifting to the little I haven't already seen of Benji's chiseled body.

As Andi drops back to her feet, my mind is jerked back to the present. *What are you doing?* I scold myself, my eyes darting back up to Benji's face. He's giving me a knowing grin, and heat floods my cheeks as I realize I've been caught ogling him at a public event.

"Come on, you guys," Andi says. "I want you to meet Paul!"

She drags Grant by the hand, and the others follow behind. I don't miss the wink Benji sends my way as he walks after the group. My cheeks are near-burning at this point.

News has clearly spread about the local celebrities. Most of the eyes follow them as they approach Paul and shake his hand. I sidle up to Bella, giving her a squeeze. She's wearing a Wonder Woman costume that's less revealing than most, but still gives her ample cleavage. The gold, red, and blue of the costume pop against the deep bronze of her skin, and her thick black curls fall elegantly down her shoulders. I give her a purposeful once-over and grin. "Damn, girl. You're about to break some hearts tonight."

"Pfft," she replies with a wave of her hand, but I don't miss the blush that tinges her cheeks. "I plan on going bar-hopping with my roommates later. I just figured I'd get as much use out of it as I can this weekend. Though," she adds, eyeing the hockey players, "I might stay a little longer tonight if they do."

"Well, it looks like they wouldn't mind if you do," Andi says, her eyes darting over to where Nils is standing with Paul and his other teammates. He keeps sneaking glances our way. "But I'll give you some advice my mom gave me when I moved here."

"What's that?"

"There are two things a woman should never chase. Whiskey and hockey players."

We both laugh, and Bella nods emphatically. "Says the one hooking up with one. But trust me, I learned that the hard way in high school. My poor dad had to deal with that. He looks pretty happy with these guys, though."

We all look at Paul and see that Bella's right. He's grinning broader than I've ever seen before, returning each handshake eagerly, cupping each hand offered with both of his. My heart squeezes at his grateful expression. People are raising their phones and snapping photos, and I hope it will lead to some awareness the gym so desperately needs. As for myself, I'm just grateful for my costume – complete with face paint – blurring me into obscurity.

The rest of the event goes beautifully. Andi and I are able to organize a mini boxing tournament for the children, split by age ranges, and I'm surprised by how much fun I have teaching them easy moves, then letting them loose on each other. It's the perfect blend of fun and competitive, and even those who 'lose' are rewarded with Halloween candy in the end.

I hand it over to Andi for a bit, and as she's leading a group through some simple motions, my eyes are drawn to the opposite corner of the gym, where the guys are leading their own activities. I wander closer, inspecting the game they have set up.

They're alternating as well: two of them are leading a mini game of hockey with the kids that aren't in the ring with us, and one is signing anything the adults shove their way. Andi – or Grant, I'm not entirely sure – has procured two small nets and a handful of tiny hockey sticks. The kids are running around, flailing the sticks in the air and at each other just as often as they're using them to whack at the rubber ball standing in as a hockey puck.

"Come on!" Grant is cheering his team of tiny weebles on, putting his own hockey stick in the fray every now and then in an entirely unproductive way. "We've got this!"

"Amazing!" Benji cheers as one of his kids sends the ball flying towards the net. Though, I'm pretty sure it's the wrong net.

There's a scramble as one of his kids works to fish it out of the net. One of Grant's kids swats at the ball, but gets her feet instead. The kid falls to the ground, and her face immediately crumples. I take a few steps forward, knowing what's about to happen.

The girl lets out a wail, and the game comes to a halt. A dad leaves the crowd, coming to get what I presume is his child as she begins crying, crocodile tears springing from her eyes and tumbling down her cheeks. Benji is at her side in an instant, crouching low to talk to her.

"Hey, hey," he murmurs. "What's your name?"

The girl's lip trembles, but she answers him. "Emma."

"Emma. That's a nice name." He smiles. "Can you tell me where it hurts, Emma?"

The girl sniffs, tears still streaming down her cheeks, and points at her leg. I shift to get a better look, my heart in my throat. If it's bad, not only is this poor girl going to be traumatized, but this event could be ruined, and by extension, Punchline could be done for. I exhale as I see a light pink mark on Emma's ankle. The poor girl might have a bruise, but thankfully, it doesn't look too bad.

"Ouch." Benji purses his lips. "We'll get some ice for that."

I see Paul nod and slip through the crowd, already on his way to get the ice. As he does, the girl's dad gathers her in his arms and lifts her from the ground. Benji rises alongside them and gives the girl a smile. "You know what we do when someone gets hurt on the ice?"

The girl shakes her head, and Benji continues. "Well, first, we make sure they're okay. And if they're okay, we bang our sticks on the ground to let them know how brave they are. Are you okay, Emma?"

Emma wipes at her tears, composing herself, and nods. Benji nods back, then turns to the rest of the kids and raises his stick. "She's okay! So, does everyone agree that Emma is brave?"

There's a chorus of agreement, and Benji bangs his stick on the ground, grinning proudly at Emma. Grant follows suit, banging enthusiastically, and soon everyone is slamming their sticks on the ground in a round of applause for Emma.

Paul returns with the ice, which the dad takes gratefully, and by the time the noise dies down, Emma looks back to normal, aside from the redness of her eyes. Benji grins and extends his fist, which she bumps excitedly.

There's murmuring throughout the crowd as everyone coos over the moment. "He's a wonderful person," someone says off to my side. "Such a shame, what happened last year."

Wait – what?

By the time I turn to ask the person to elaborate, the crowd is on the move again, shifting forward to get their chance to talk to the wonderful Benjamin Estes.

It takes another thirty minutes to shut down the remaining activities, then all that's left is the silent auction. People have five more minutes to get their bids in, and I'm sipping on my drink, keeping a close eye on the photograph of the lake, ready to swoop in if anyone adds a bid on top of my most recent one. Andi, Bella and I have formed a small group with the hockey players, who are getting a momentary reprieve from their autographing and polite chatter with the crowd.

"Tell me," I say. "Do you all understand the hype behind a pickle beer?"

"Me? Of course." Benji grins. "It's practically a midwestern mimosa. But if I had a choice, I'd put olives in my beer over pickles."

I gag. "What's wrong with beer the way it's meant to be?"

"I couldn't agree more, Lisa," Grant says. "But maybe that's just because we're from normal states. The cold isolation makes them weird here."

Benji and Andi swat his shoulders in tandem, and Bella laughs, though she's currently too shy to voice her opinion on the matter. I would guess as a native Minnesotan, she's probably on the pro-pickle-beer train.

Nils sips on his drink, contemplating. "Oh, that's nothing. In Sweden, we put raw eggs in our beer."

"Seriously?" Benji gapes at him, and he grins back.

"No. But I love how you will believe anything about Sweden."

Benji chuckles good-naturedly and rolls his eyes. I spot someone adding a bid to the photograph and excuse myself, slipping in to solidify my win. As I scan the other silent auction sheets, I'm happy to see that Paul will get a sizable chunk of change to sustain him through the end of the year. I can only hope the massive turnout today leads to more memberships as well.

When I return to the group, Andi is bouncing again, her curls still as voluminous as they were hours ago. I make a mental note to find out what hairspray she uses.

"Lisa! Lisa! Bella already shut me down, so *please* tell me you're not busy next weekend," she begs.

My gaze slides from her to Bella to the guys, trying to see what's brewing here. Their faces are the picture of innocence, giving nothing away. "I'm supposed to work at Wunderbar, but I could ask Julia for a shift change," I say slowly. "Why? What's up?"

"The guys just mentioned that their fall bye week lines up with the opening weekend at their favorite ski resort in Colorado." Andi claps. "It's next week. They're planning a trip there, and we're invited!"

My stomach bottoms out. Leaving, when I was just starting to feel comfortable here? Traveling out of the state? With a bunch of guys, most of whom I barely know? "Sounds expensive," I hedge.

"That's the best part." Andi looks like she's about to explode from excitement. "I guess their teammate's dad is a pilot. He's got his own plane, so a lot of them are going free of charge. Including us. Babes, we can't pass this up!"

Even though her excitement is contagious, I can't get the pit out of my gut. I try one last ditch excuse. "I can't ski, Andi."

"Ah, don't worry about that." Grant waves a hand. "You'll have a whole slew of people ready to teach you. And if you don't want to ski, the hot tub's always open. That's where a lot of the players' partners end up, anyways."

"And I'm sure Julia or Paul would be happy to watch Winny for you," Andi offers, her expression now pleading.

Shit. I get the feeling that if I don't go, she won't go. She needs a friend to be with, even if she wants to use part of this trip to further explore whatever she and Grant have going on. I realize with a start that I want to keep this friendship strong more than I want to avoid this trip. I haven't had a friendship like this ages, and I'll feel terrible if I deprive her of this trip. Plus, today with this group hasn't been awful. In fact, it's been kind of...fun.

I sigh. "Okay, okay. Yes! Count me in." Andi shrieks happily, and I hold a hand up. "But if you leave me on the mountain, I swear to god, I'll cut up all your best underwear."

She crosses her heart. "Ride or die, babes. I've got you."

A mic turns on, and we go quiet as Paul clears his throat and begins announcing the silent auction winners. Andi cheers as she wins a basket full of local wines, and Grant winks at her when he wins a similar basket with movie tickets and popcorn. A few more lackluster items go – an oil change, a fitness package to Punchline – and then my photo is up. I let out a small whoop as Paul calls my name, running up to claim my prize.

"You got it!" Bella cheers when I return. "Way to go!"

"I did indeed." I beam. "It's beautiful. I love it."

The boys exchange knowing looks, and I narrow my eyes. "What? What did you do?"

"It's not what we did," Grant says, smiling. "It's what you did. You bought Benji's donation."

My mouth falls open, and I turn to Benji. He smiles at me, but it's not as smug as I would've expected. Instead, he looks almost *shy.* "You donated this?"

He nods, and when he says nothing else, Grant shoves him good-naturedly. "Not only did he donate it, he took that photo."

I blink in surprise. "You *took* this?"

Again, he nods, but says nothing. Nils whistles. "Damn, dude. If the whole hockey thing doesn't work out, maybe you can be a photographer."

"No kidding," Andi puts in. "No wonder Lisa loves it. It's amazing."

I gaze down at the framed picture, refusing to meet the eyes of the photographer. I do love it. And I hate it, too.

I hate that I love everything I've learned today about the *wonderful* Benjamin Estes.

Chapter 18

Benji

We've stepped off the plane and into a winter wonderland. The ski-in ski-out townhomes we've rented every year for the last three years are mostly windows, offering a view of the endless, rolling mountains of snow, dotted with green. It's still light out, and it's a bluebird day, the bright blue of the sky contrasting with the expanse of white blanketing the mountains.

Within the rentals, everything is geared toward coziness. There are fluffy throws draped over every piece of furniture, and dark wood trim frames out a welcoming fireplace, ready to be turned on and enjoyed.

My gaze sweeps over the place, memories from previous years playing behind my eyes. Normally, coming to the mountains instantly transports me away from my regular worries and strains. This year, however, one lingers.

The last time I was here, I roomed with a couple of teammates that were getting called up to the show more often than not, including my brother. It was their last official rendezvous with the Leopards. That was just a few short weeks before...

"You have the list?" Jordie slaps my shoulder, pulling me away from a potential spiral. He and Levi are my roomies for this trip, with Grant, Nils, and Highcloud sharing the townhome next door, and Lisa and Andi on the other side. The rest of our team is scattered in other townhomes with their partners, or opted not to come. Though we're all a team, we do break off into different facets outside of the rink. It never bothered me as captain, personally. We all get along when the skates are put on, and there can be such a thing as too much team-building. If it's forced, people can grow resentful. So, I'm glad to see my team happily leading their own lives. Maybe I should have opted out of this weekend, too.

I try to shake that thought off and nod in response to Jordie's question. "Don't worry, bud, I'll see to it you're fed this weekend." I wave the slip of paper in my hand, lined with hyper-specific food requests.

"Wait, you're getting food for everyone?" Andi asks from the front of the townhome, her brow furrowing in confusion.

Highcloud gives her a one-shouldered shrug. "Well, we'll have our team-building dinner in town tonight, but otherwise, we have to follow our meal plans this weekend. If we don't eat what our nutritionist tells us to, we'll get in trouble when we get back."Lisa's mouth drops open. "You have a *nutritionist?*"

"We don't get these bodies by mistake," Grant croons, shooting Andi a wink. "The game is faster than ever. So we need to be better than ever. A good diet is the secret weapon."

"Not all of us can pull a Wayne Gretzky," Jordie puts in. At Andi's questioning look, he adds, "His pre-game ritual was to slam four hot dogs and a Diet Coke."

I snort, and Lisa gives me an imploring look. I know what she's thinking – why, then, did I house down a burger and milkshake with her, not long ago?

Something tells me I shouldn't admit that I would've done anything to put her at ease that day, including obliterating the meal plans our nutritionist had outlined for me, down to every macro.

Instead, I drawl, "Well, there's nothing wrong with a cheat day here and there."

"To each their own." Grant slings his bag back over his shoulder. "Should we go check out our separate digs, ladies?"

Andi nods and tugs on Lisa. "I can't wait!"

As they leave our townhome, Jordie turns to me, concern clear in his expression. When he speaks, his tone is low enough that only I can hear. "Are you doing all right? Seems like you're pretty in your head right now."

I hesitate for a moment, the lie of *I'm fine* jumping to the tip of my tongue. But it's just Jordie and me here. If anyone deserves the truth, it's him. He's been with me through it all.

I sigh and brace myself against the wall. "I don't know, man. There are so many memories here." I think it over for a minute, grief panging through me as I try to form words for what I'm feeling. "They're all such amazing memories, but I think that makes it harder. Knowing everything good that happened here won't happen again."

My voice cracks on the final words, and Jordie studies me silently for a long moment. Finally, he strides forward and tugs me roughly into an embrace. I'm caught off guard, but I tighten my arms around him, accepting the support he's offering.

He claps his hand across my back and whispers, "I get it, man. I miss him, too." When he pulls back, he gives me a grim smile. "But I think you're doing the right thing here. You're with us, ready to make some new memories. He'd want that, wouldn't he?"

"Yeah." I can barely form the words as emotion tightens my throat. "He would."

"So let's do it. Let's make sure you have an amazing time this weekend." Jordie's gaze lowers to the list in my hand, and he snatches it from me. "Starting with adding twice as much beer to this list. If we're going to make good memories, they're going to include some booze. Even if it's just us making sure Grant gets hammered enough to make a fool of himself in front of Andi."

My quick burst of laughter is choked, but this time from affection for my teammate. My best friend. "I think we can manage that."

When we arrive back from our full team dinner, we discover that our beer supply has already been tapped into by our two tag-alongs. That isn't nearly as surprising, however, as what they're doing while they drink.

They're watching *hockey.*

"Do my eyes deceive me, or is that a hockey game on your screen?" Grant plops down next to Andi on the couch, cracking a beer open and glancing between her and the screen. Sure enough, it's an NHL game, but to my knowledge, neither girl is a fan of either team playing.

"Well, see, we put it on because we wanted to understand the sport better," Andi explains, curling against Grant. He drapes an arm over her immediately, tucking her into him, and fuck if he doesn't look like the happiest guy in the world. I feel a pang of jealousy at the simple interaction. "But then we discovered something amazing."

"What's that?" Levi asks. He and Jordie grab a drink and plop down on the loveseat next to the sofa.

"That it can easily become a drinking game." Lisa giggles, and the sound is like music to my ears. I can't help but smile. The joy in her tone is absolutely infectious. There's an opening on the couch next to her, and I consider claiming it.

"A drinking game?" Grant asks.

"Yep," Andi says, popping the 'p' on the word. "The announcers are always saying something inappropriate. So we just drink every time there's an innuendo."

On cue, one announcer muses *"He goes down early,"* as the camera pans in on one team's goalie, replaying a save he made. The other announcer agrees. *"Yeah, he sure does."*

Andi hollers and lifts her drink, taking a dramatic swig. Lisa laughs again and snorts, reminding me of the last time she laughed with me, and that's it. I'm decided.

I swing by the counter to grab a beer, joining her on the couch. It shifts as I take a seat, pulling her in close enough that our thighs are nearly touching.

Lisa eyes my beer as I settle in beside her. I tense, waiting for her to ask me to move, but instead she asks, "If your diet is so strict, why are you allowed to drink?"

I take a long swig. "Because even though we're professional athletes, we're adults, and we can decide how we relieve our tension after a hard game. Even if it means a beer or two."

"Or five," Grant adds, "if it's a bye week."

"Do you not get in trouble for getting drunk?" Andi asks.

"The better you are, the more tolerant coaches are with the shit you do." Nils motions to the screen to highlight the best of the best, some of which are definitely known to overconsume off the ice. "As long as you stay out of trouble and get the job done, they generally turn a blind eye to any shenanigans."

"And morning skates keep *most* of us from wanting to be too hungover," Highcloud adds with a laugh.

The crowd suddenly roars at something on screen, and I glance up to see back-to-back hits taking place. "This is brutal," Lisa says, cringing as a massive hit makes the boards ripple, bowing in on the two players duking it out for the puck. "How do you deal with all that?"

"Lots of ice baths, ice bags, and acupuncture," Grant replies, cracking his neck in emphasis. "And it's worth every ache."

Lisa shakes her head with a soft laugh. "You all are a different breed."

We settle in to watch, taking turns answering the girls' questions about the game. I sip and observe Lisa, soaking in her curiosity. With all the questions, she seems to genuinely enjoy the game. Even as she cringes at some of the worst hits, she rarely turns her eyes from the screen.

As we sit and drink, our thighs gradually touch, and neither of us pull back from the contact. I'm tempted to test it, to push against her or place my hand on her thigh, but I don't risk it. Instead, I pretend I'm not focusing on the heat of her thigh against mine, channeling my interest into the game.

Lisa seems to be doing the same, whether on purpose like me or simply due to her newfound interest in the sport. She sucks in a breath at another hit, and I wonder absently if she would be concerned about me, if she were to watch another one of our games. I like the idea of her keeping an eye on me during the game, and offering to soothe my aches and pains afterwards. My mind ventures into dangerous territory, visualizing her hands on my body, and I have to shift slightly in my seat. I try to tune into the game they're playing, listening intently as the announcers dig themselves into an even larger hole.

"Their D is exceptional tonight; truly, outstanding work!"

The girls laugh again and this time, we're all joining in, raising our beers in unison. As the game goes on, it gets more ridiculous and harder to ignore how easily this game can become a dangerous – and hilarious – drinking game.

"It's really hard when they're coming at you from behind – "

The girls raise their drinks again, howling louder.

"There's a nice tight tunnel for them to get their sticks into – "

At this point, Andi is clutching her sides and Lisa is wiping tears from her eyes, each new breath triggering another bout of laughter. It's absolute chaos, but it's hysterical, and as I wheeze in an attempt to catch my own breath, my eyes meet Jordie's across the room. His eyes crinkle happily as he laughs along with us, and I know what we're both thinking.

It's only the first night, but already, these are the kind of memories we so desperately needed. This may turn out to be a wonderful weekend, after all.

"Do you think they even know who's winning?" Grant leans over to ask me with a chuckle.

Andi hiccups and raises her beer, clinking it against his. "We are, my friend. We are."

Chapter 19

Lisa

In the time it takes for me to wiggle into all of my ski gear and stagger out of the rental shop, nursing a hangover – thanks, altitude – I've decided I may, in fact, not be a mountain person. And by the time I hobble my way to the gondola line in the tight ski boots, juggling the heavy skis and poles in my arms, I've decided I am *most certainly* not meant for this sport.

I throw my skis on the snow with a groan. "People actually enjoy this?"

Andi laughs as she clicks into her skis, making the movement look enviously natural. "Enough to make it into several Olympic sports, at least."

"I'm already sweating," I complain.

She tosses me a sympathetic look. Before she can reply, the guys show up, carrying their skis and snowboards like they weigh no more than a tree twig. They look entirely at home in their snow gear, and – no surprise – they're all wearing some variation of a hockey jersey over their sweaters. None of them wear their Leopards jerseys, though, and a sense of relief washes over me. The last thing I want is for them to be a giant, light-blue beacon saying "Look over here!" while I'm busy looking like a baby deer trying to stand for the first time.

Even without any indication that they're professional athletes, their height and builds attract attention. I see a few gazes travel over from the lift line, scanning their fit bodies. More than one gaze snags on their backsides, and I can't blame them. These hockey players know how to fill out snowboard pants.

There's a lot of cheering and jostling, and somehow, we make our way through the gondola line. As we go up, shooters appear from various pockets, and the boys lunge forward to snag their favorites. When one is passed to me, I decline, instead rubbing my hands together nervously. "What if I run into a tree?" I ask. "Wait. Oh my god. What if I run into someone else?"

"Relax," Jordie says as he waves the shooter in front of Ryan, yanking it back before he can grab it. "There are barely any runs open this early in the season, so there aren't many people. A lot of them will be beginners, just like you."

I force a smile. I know he means well, but it doesn't make me feel any better. In my mind, I'm just visualizing a bunch of us running into each other and unable to control where we go.

Jordie finally tosses Ryan the shooter, and everyone else clinks them together before tossing them back. There's a moment of silence, and then the coughs start, interspersed with more whooping.

Andi crinkles her nose and passes the empty shooter back to Grant, who pockets it. "Just take it slow, and you'll be okay," she assures me. "We'll be sure to wait for you. You're in good company."

At that, my smile is genuine. "You're right. Just take it slow. Okay."

As it turns out, *slow* is an understatement. I barely get going down the slope before I whip myself to the side, slamming on the brakes. I'm sure I look a bit like a caterpillar, inching its way down the snowy mountainside.

By the time I make it down the first run, my back aches from hunching over, and I'm grateful for the rest going back up the lift will allow, even if it's only for five minutes. The second run goes about as well as the first, and I apologize each time I catch up to the group, all huddled against the side of the run, waiting patiently and staring at my solo journey down.

By our third run, I am thoroughly embarrassed and more than a little frustrated. I attempt to focus on the path I'm carving in the snow – nope, nope, *too fast* – when a kid who can't be more than six flies past me on his skis, his dinosaur helmet covered with red spikes standing out against the snow.

I'm so startled by his appearance that I try whipping to my side to stop. Instead, I go flailing forward, ending up face-first in the snow. My legs bend at an awkward angle, the strange, massive contraptions attached to them making it impossible to get back in a normal position.

"Are you kidding me?" I groan. I attempt to flip over three times before I'm successful. Then, panting, I just lay there, summoning the courage to attempt *actually* standing up. It's entirely too much work.

I gaze up at the evergreens above me, contemplating if I can just stay here for the remainder of the day. It's actually pretty peaceful.

There's a whoosh as snow goes skidding next to me. "Need some help up?"

I shift as much as I can and crane my neck to look up at Benji, towering over me on his snowboard. A helmet and goggles cover most of his face, but all it seems to do is accentuate his full lips and shapely jawline. He clearly hasn't shaved in a day or two, and the five o'clock shadow almost hides his dimples as he smirks down at me. *Almost.*

That smirk fuels my frustration, and I attempt to get up on my own, but it just makes me start to ski down the mountain while still on my ass. In a panic, I flail myself to the side, tumbling to a stop.

My eyes find Benji once more, who has patiently scooted down the mountain to where I just crash landed again. He bends over and extends a gloved hand to me. I eye it cautiously. "Won't I just drag you down here with me?"

He huffs out a laugh. "Try me."

I do, and he pulls me back to my feet with surprising ease, not letting go until he's certain I've readjusted my poles and have my skis firmly under me. His grip is powerful, but gentle. I'm startled to find that it doesn't scare me. Instead, I feel protected, supported.

He lets go as soon as I'm steady, standing back to give me space, but close enough to catch me in case I fall back into the snowy abyss. "Ready?" he asks.

"I'm not sure." I bite my lip. "Every time I start to speed up, I get scared and jerk to a stop. I'm scared I'm going to hit someone, or fall hard."

He's quiet for a moment, then asks, "Do you want advice?"

He's asking *permission* to give me advice? Who is this guy?

"Please," I say, and he gives me a smile.

"Your turns are really jerky right now, which makes sense, since you're nervous." His understanding words soften the critique. "If you make bigger, sweeping turns, it'll help you control your speed without stopping. It'll also be easier on your legs. Picture making a giant C in the snow."

"And if I get going too fast?" I ask.

"Then stop. Going fast comes with time. But if you want to go faster, just keep your eyes further ahead of where you want to go. That will help."

"And if I fall?"

He smiles again. "Then I'll be there to pick you up."

The nerves eating away at me disappear at the thought of someone going down the slope with me, rather than leaving me behind. I glance down the mountain, to the small dots that make up the rest of the group, waiting at the lift line. They seem to be chucking snowballs at one another. "Are you sure you don't want to go join them? You don't have to wait for me."

"You're worth the wait."

I pause at his comment, delivered with a note of seriousness, but he doesn't allow me any kind of response. Instead, he scoots backward down the hill, still facing me expectantly. He motions with his gloved hands for me to follow.

I take a deep breath, repeat his advice in my head, and take off. It's slow-going, and I'm still shaky, but the change is instant. Benji shouts out sporadic praises, inspiring me to keep working at it. By the time we reach the group at the bottom, I've fallen twice more, but I feel slightly more confident, and Andi is cheering for me.

"That looked so good, girl!" she exclaims. "You'll be a pro by the end of the day!"

I smile, but grimace at the thought of several more hours of this. "I don't know that I have a full day left in me. Maybe a few more runs, but that's it."

She nods in understanding. "And I hate to say it, but you'll probably be sore tomorrow."

"You'll have muscles complaining that you didn't even know you had," Highcloud says, picking up a pine cone and chucking it at Grant.

Grant yelps. "Can you fuck off with the tree poop?" He fakes chucking the pine cone back at Highcloud, but fires it off at Ryan instead, who ducks it at the last second. "But yeah, she's right. The hot tub will be your best friend today."

I'm tempted to call it quits right then and there at the prospect of a hot tub, ready and waiting for me at the base of the mountain. But then I think of Benji's encouragement on the last run, and the urge to continue improving outweighs the comfort. "Well then, let's make these last runs the best ones."

I'm back in my apartment, showered, stomach full of a delicious dinner – who knew hockey players could cook? – and facing down what to do for the remainder of the night. Though Andi slept in our townhome the first night, she and Grant had been all over each other after dinner, and I don't expect her to be back tonight. Which leaves me with a giant ski lodge to myself and limited options for what to do.

I alternate between the idea of staying inside by the fire and removing my cozy pajamas to brave the hot tub on the patio. I think back to the others' warnings about how sore I'll be and decide on the latter. I'm already starting to feel my muscles tighten.

I only brought one simple red two-piece swimsuit with me, and I eye the falling snow outside as I consider what it will feel like getting out of the hot tub afterward. They don't expect people to just wander in the snow in their bathing suits, do they? Do I have to wear my ski jacket out there?

Luckily, a quick sweep of the townhome uncovers some thick, fluffy robes, and I bundle up to open the hot tub and start it up. I wait until the last minute to fling my robe aside and dive into the hot tub, bracing against the cold mountain air. It takes a second, but then I sigh and sink deeper into the water, letting the heat and the jets work on loosening my muscles.

A few minutes go by, and my mind begins to wander, giving me warning signs that it's moving to dangerous places. I brought books I could read, and I could put on a podcast, or music, but none of those sound appealing right now.

Then, it hits me: I'm lonely. I want someone to be with.

And I think...I think I want that person to be Benjamin Estes.

I grab my phone and smile when I see his name in my phone, deciding to change it. He's successfully fought off his Cocky Shit moniker. My fingers hover over the keyboard as I consider what to type next, or if it's even something I should do. After a minute, I sigh and hit send. No going back now.

Me: What're you guys up to?

Benji: Just hanging w/Jordie and Highcloud. Grant's off duty and on booty next door.

Me: I know. Had to go out to the hot tub to escape any potential thumping against the wall.

Benji: A little hot tub sesh, you say?

I pause, summoning the courage for what I want to ask. I know I'm comfortable with him, but am I ready for where this might head?

I think back to our almost-kiss, and my toes curl. Yep...I'm definitely ready for that. The question is just if he will be ready, or if he's still planning to keep his word on his ultimatum. We'll see about that.

Me: Interested in taking a dip?

Benji: I thought you'd never ask. Be there in 2.

I stumble out of the hot tub to dry off, then slide into my robe. By the time I open the door, Benji is already there. He's in a matching robe, and he smiles down at me, holding up peppermint schnapps and marshmallows. "Hot chocolate?"

Before I can answer, he breezes into the room, and I stare at the large, dark man towering in my kitchen, set on making cocoa. It's a jarring image, but he doesn't seem deterred at all. Instead, he turns and leans over the kitchen counter with a questioning look. "Big or small mug?"

"Big mug, for sure."

I watch him plop marshmallows into the two mugs, and he motions to the patio. I follow him outside and he halts, both mugs in hand, waiting for me to get into the hot tub first. I hesitate for a moment, but it's too cold to delay the inevitable for long. I throw the robe off and step into the hot tub, keeping Benji in my line of sight.

His gaze grows molten, shamelessly devouring me in my swimsuit, but he stays where he is. I sink into the water, grateful. Somehow in the many small moments where we've interacted, he's met my moods where they're at – quiet when I'm overwhelmed, teasing when I was able, ready to help me let off steam when needed. When I'm fully situated, he comes up next to me, handing me both mugs.

"Thanks." I take the hot chocolate from him, and he shrugs his robe off. I've seen him shirtless twice now, but the sight again, at such close proximity, makes my fingers itch with the urge to run them over his broad shoulders and across the planes of his abs. He's absolutely magnificent. Instead, I curl my fingers tighter around the mugs.

"Penny for your thoughts?" Benji asks, settling into the hot tub on the opposite side. He leans forward, motioning for his hot chocolate. I hand him his mug and sip my own, the minty schnapps adding a boost to the beverage.

Am I bold enough to share my thoughts out loud?

Not yet, I decide. "I'm thinking about Winny," I say instead. "I hope he's doing all right."

Benji nods thoughtfully, taking a large gulp from his own drink. "I miss my parents' dog," he says absently. "I used to get home to visit so often, but it's been months now. I barely even talk to them, let alone visit."

I take in this information and sink lower into the hot tub. Benjamin strikes me as someone who has his whole life put together, which includes the perfect family. Someone who goes home for every holiday and calls his family weekly, if not daily. I imagine everyone in his life being supportive and loving. What caused him to pull back?

"I'm sorry," I finally say, curiosity getting the best of me. "Do you mind if I ask why?"

"Ah." Benji pauses, his mug stalled on its way to his mouth. Finally, he raises it fully, takes another long sip. When he continues speaking, he's focused on the soft snow falling around us, rather than meeting my gaze. His voice is soft, strained. "My brother passed away. Ten months ago. It's been tough on my family."

"Oh." I say the word on an exhale, assessing him. The grief is so plain to see in his expression now, as if every line of it has built up over the last ten months. How did I not see it before?

He kept it so well hidden beneath his smirks and well-placed quips. Though, now that I think about it, we spent most of our time circling around the topic of my background. I never pushed him to talk about his. He's choosing to share it with me now, and I only had to ask once. "I'm so sorry, Benji."

He gives me an off-kilter smile, one that I realize is practiced for moments like these. "It's not your fault. Though," he adds thoughtfully, "it was part of the reason I was so mad at you when we first met."

I must look as startled as I feel, because he continues haltingly. "Jake was amazing at hockey. He was two years older than me, but we both played hockey together for a bit in high school, and then even at the same university. I knew I was following in his footsteps, just trying to keep up, but how could I not? He was a once in a lifetime talent." Benji shakes his head affectionately. I take a long drink from my own mug, waiting for him to continue.

"It was amazing, getting to play my favorite sport with my favorite person. And he was really making a name for himself. I ended up as captain of the Leopards, but he easily would have been, it's just, he was already getting called up to play in the show more often than not. Hell, his first season with the Minnesota Chill, he was making headlines for his great plays every game. But with that attention came the fans."

At this, his smile fades, his expression growing dark. "He ended up with a stalker. It started off almost...funny? But over time, she grew more and more intense. The day he...he died, she was following him in an ice storm. He couldn't brake at a red light because he was going too fast, trying to outrun her, and someone T-boned him."

"Oh my god," I murmur, and scoot closer, reaching for his hand. He puts his mug down and takes it, turning it over thoughtfully. I replay his words in my head, stunned. I can't imagine what it must feel like to have a sibling you not only love but share a career with, play on the same team with. And to lose that person, in such a gruesome way? All I can think to do is squeeze his hand, hoping to convey a bit of comfort.

"I wasn't able to finish last season, after that." He takes a deep breath. "I wasn't even sure I would play again this year, but my team was there to pick me up, and make sure I didn't sink too far into the grief. They convinced me that my brother would've wanted me to get back out there. And it made me realize...grief isn't meant to be carried alone."

I hum my agreement, his words hitting uncomfortably close to home. For so many years, I'd been alone without even realizing it. It's only now that the loneliness is starting to fade.

"And then you showed up. And I was worried the same thing would happen to me, or one of my teammates, when we kept running into each other." He shoots me a guilty look. "I know now how crazy that sounds."

I shake my head. "No. It makes a lot of sense, actually." I pause, gazing down at our intertwined hands. "My mom died in a car accident, too."

His head jerks up. "What? When?"

"Almost four years ago. But it still...it still hurts, sometimes." I answer honestly, and I'm surprised by how *good* it feels to share it with someone else, someone I know will be gentle with it.

"I'm sorry," he replies quietly. "Were you close with her?"

I take a moment, then nod. "She was everything good I had."

He doesn't push, but suddenly, the silence feels overwhelming. I pull my hand from his and grab our mugs. "This feels like a good time to refill these. You want some more?"

He takes them from me. "I'll handle it."

I watch him as he re-enters the kitchen, still only wearing his swimming trunks, and consider what he told me. The comments the people at the gym made suddenly make so much more sense – and so does his initial reaction to me. In a way, it seems, we were both sizing each other up, just waiting for the other shoe to drop. Little did we know what the other was going through...and, at least on my part, I didn't even bother to ask. The thought makes me frown.

Benji gives the living room a scan before he returns outside, and when he does, he eyes me conspiratorially. "Looks like the place has no card games or anything."

"Yeah, I don't think so. Why?"

"Well. Now I don't know how we're going to play any drinking games with our exciting cocktails." He lifts the mugs and grins before settling back in the hot tub and passing me mine.

"Well, we can always play our game," I say, my heart rate spiking even as I utter it out loud. When he tilts his head at me, I add, "Truth for a truth. If we don't want to answer, we drink."

He purses his lips in consideration, and I hold my breath as I wait. Finally, he shrugs and extends his mug. "I'm in. Cheers."

We move quickly through the easy questions, like our favorite colors and animals, all the way into shows and music. He asks if he can list several favorite movies instead of just one, and drinks when I say no, but I have to do the same when I can't decide on just one favorite book.

We've reached the end of our third spiked cocoa when we run out of simple favorites, and we've drawn closer to one another with each question. Our thighs are touching, invisible under the steam and bubbles, and I've begun dragging my foot along his leg. One of his hands has drifted under the water, fingertips grazing every now and then across my bare skin. Each point of contact sends delicious shock waves to my core.

"First kiss?" I ask, and he makes a face.

"Geneva Samson. Second grade. We literally knocked teeth, and I lost one of those teeth the next day. Clearly, we had no idea what kissing actually was." He smirks, and I smile in response as I watch his dimples flash. "Last ex?" he asks.

I draw in a sharp breath and duck my head to my mug, polishing off the last drops. I put the mug down pointedly, and he gives me an apologetic look. His hand travels to my cheek, turning my head back to him with barely a touch. "Sorry. Touchy subject?"

"Uh." I wave dismissively and avert my eyes, even as the room is starting to spin. "It's fine." I scramble for another question, but at this point, I only have one left that's been bouncing around in my head for the past five minutes. I blurt it out. "So. Are you going to kiss me?"

His hand slips away from my cheek as quickly as he put it there, his expression shuttering. "No."

My heart dives from my throat to the pit of my stomach. "Why not?"

"You know why. Besides, little fighter," he says, "I want you to make that decision for yourself. I'm not going to force anything on you. Every step is going to be dictated by you." He leans back until no part of us is touching anymore. "So until you take that leap of faith, I'll be here, waiting."

I bit my lip, considering him. I want to crawl onto him, try to see if I can kiss him without having to open the door to my past, but I can't handle another rejection. So I remain frozen, unable to close the gap he created between us.

Emptiness, I realize, can take up so much physical space. The mere inches between us are filled with it – empty promises, empty wishes and empty dreams. Empty hearts.

Finally, he gives me a sad smile. "I hope someday, you'll choose not to ice me out. I hope you'll choose me."

He puts his mug down, his intention clear. Our drinks are empty, the game is over, and he's planning to leave. Through my haze of uncertainty, the realization slams into me: I don't want him to leave. The disappointment of him leaving after everything suddenly overwhelms every anxiety I have about my secrets.

"Well," he says, shifting, and I place a hand on his chest to stop him. He pauses and I open my mouth, but the words catch in my throat. After a long moment, he removes my hand and rises from the hot tub. I rise with him.

"Alyssa," I blurt.

Benji turns back around, staring down at me. We both exhale, the heaviness of the moment mingling in the cold winter air.

I repeat the words I thought would never pass my lips again. "My real name is Alyssa."

Chapter 20

Lyssa

For a moment, time freezes. Benji looks at me like he's turning an idea over in his head, trying to decide what to do with it. I tense, my breath catching in my throat. I'm about to step away from something like terror, humiliation, or a mixture of the two – how bad is the process of starting somewhere new again, really? – but then he's in my space.

He towers over me, and his hands are on me, but his touch is soft and gentle. One wraps around my waist, the other winding in my hair, and he pauses for a moment, those dark eyes soft as he peers down at me. The tip of his nose brushes against mine, his mouth a mere hair's breadth from mine. Almost a kiss, but more of a question. And then I remember what he said: *Every step is going to be dictated by you.*

I take a beat to think. I haven't done this in ages. I can't remember the last time it was completely on my own terms. Am I ready for this?

It feels like stepping off a ledge, not quite sure what is on the other side. My heart pounds in my chest, the panic from my past threatening to surge forth.

But when my gaze rises from his lips to his eyes, I see the warmth in them as he waits, patient as ever. In that look, I find all that I need to know. I shove my worries down and answer his question by closing the remaining distance to his mouth.

The second our lips touch, every anxious voice in my mind goes silent. It's like I'm taking a long overdue breath, filling myself with fresh air, and I give myself over to the kiss entirely.

It's like Benji can feel what's going on inside me. He mirrors my energy, letting the moment pull him in. His hand tightens on my waist, tugging me against his body. I shudder at the contact of our bare skin against each other, warm against the cold winter air. His other hand drops from my hair to my jaw, tilting my chin up to ask for more from the kiss.

It starts soft as we explore each other's lips, but quickly dissolves to something raw and urgent. He kisses me like he's branding me with his mouth, and I answer in turn, stretching up on my tiptoes as I throw my arms around his neck, pulling him down to me just to feel the heat of his mouth on mine. *More, more.*

I don't even realize how hard I'm tugging on him until I slip, and we both go careening back into the hot tub. He twists so that he lands first, but we're both hit with hot splashes of water.

There's a moment of breathless laughter, and then he locks eyes with me once more. His hungry look has me biting my lip, and he winds his arm around me readily, hauling me on top of his lap. I settle across him and lean back in, running my hands through his luscious, dark hair as I kiss him again. The fact that there's barely any fabric between us is erotic as hell, and I can feel just how much he enjoys having me on his lap.

I sigh at the strong, hard feel of every inch of him beneath me, and he takes it as an invitation, parting my lips with his tongue. I open for him willingly, relishing in the expert sweep of his tongue against mine.

His fingers dig in at my waist and his thumb grazes lightly over bare hip bone, turning my core molten with desire. I grind against his lap in response, working to release some of the frustration between my legs, and he tightens his hold, moaning softly against my mouth. He nips at my bottom lip, tugging lightly with his teeth, then lets go and runs his tongue over the soft hurt.

My head falls back, and he takes the opportunity, skipping my throat to move his mouth down to my shoulder and collarbone, soft lips and warm tongue grazing my skin as he kisses his way across them. He nuzzles the strap of my swimsuit with his nose, nearly pushing it aside. I arch my back, pressing my chest closer to him in invitation. I'm drunk on the feeling he's giving me.

He murmurs against my skin, his voice dropping to a low, husky tone that instantly becomes the most erotic thing I've ever heard. "I haven't been able to get you out of my head." Another pass of his lips over my bare skin, skimming over the strap of my swimsuit. He grabs it with his teeth and tugs, sending it snapping softly back against my skin. "Every night, I imagine the things I can do to make you moan. To make you cry out for me."

I sigh again, and he continues. "I imagine what it's like to taste these perfect lips." He moves back up to my mouth, tipping my head back for a long, passionate kiss. It's deep and devouring, leaving me breathless when his mouth leaves mine to pass back over my shoulder. He trails his fingers down my top, skimming the bottom and grabbing hold before pausing for a reaction.

I simply raise my arms over my head, encouraging him to continue. A soft sound of approval rumbles deep in his throat, and his hands work swiftly to pull the top over my head as he continues his narration. "I imagine what it's like to run my hands over your perfect body."

When it's off, he leans back for a moment, drinking me in. Then he does exactly as he said, palming my breasts in his large hands before sweeping his thumbs across each nipple. I sigh and melt further into him, and he moves his hands to my back, pulling me in close. He lowers his head, hot breath fanning its way down and over my bare chest.

"To replace my hand with the warm, tight feel of you."

Good god, the *mouth* on him. I never knew words could be so damn sexy. I squeeze my eyes shut and try to control my breathing as desire pools low in my belly. The sensations rippling through me are nearly unbearable – the heat of the water, the crisp, cold air, and his hot breath on my bare skin.

When he adds his warm, wet tongue, dragging over an already sensitive nipple, I can't help but cry out. I rock my hips against him, harder this time, and hear him curse under his breath. I can't help it, though. My every nerve is going haywire at the light touches he's delivering with his mouth and his fingers. I want it. I want *him*.

"Please," I whimper.

He raises his head and meets my gaze, running a thumb over my bottom lip. "Please what, Alyssa?" he murmurs.

The name is like cold ice water. I rear back, my every muscle stiffening.

Alyssa. The name, no matter how softly it's said, sends memories streaming through my consciousness. I squeeze my eyes shut against them, but it only brings them to the front of my closed lids.

Benji picks up on it instantly, halting his movements, but it doesn't matter. He's no longer the one I'm with. The strong hands holding me are suddenly seconds away from locking me in an iron grip meant to bruise and break. I need them off of me, and I need to be able to *breathe*. As long as I'm trapped here, it feels like a vise has clamped over my lungs.

My previous name never brought about anything good. It was only ever twisted, wielded like a weapon, reminding me of everything I've done to deserve the pain.

Alyssa doesn't exist anymore, *can't* exist anymore.

He doesn't realize he's trying to resurrect a ghost.

"I need to – to get away," I rasp, scrabbling for purchase on the slick side of the hot tub. I meet his gaze briefly as I navigate around him, and I wonder what he sees there. I'm sure I look like a caged animal, attempting to flee.

His eyes are wide, and he scans my face, trying to figure out the answer to whatever question I'm giving him. Another emotion takes root and blossoms in the pit of my stomach: shame. I blink, feeling hot tears well in my eyes. Even when I think I'm thousands of miles away from my past, it's still right here, with me.

"I..." His jaw stiffens, and he glances away, shifting to allow the distance between us to grow. "I'm sorry. I didn't think."

I hear his words distantly, but they're layered under the roaring in my ears. I rise from the hot tub and reach for the robe, refusing to meet his gaze. Suddenly, everything that had my body alive with electricity feels painfully exposed, from the goosebumps trailing my arms to the heat pooling between my legs. I get out and quickly cover myself, stalking inside, but the memories follow me in.

"Enough, Alyssa!"

I can practically hear Austin's roar following me as I pace through the kitchen, and I flinch at the memory of dishes flying, shattering into a thousand pieces on the tile. I switch tactics and dart into my room to change into my pajamas, needing to replace the feel of the wet swimsuit with something thick and protective. It's useless against the way I'm beginning to tremble, though.

When I return to the living room, I hear the patio door slide open and close again, and know Benji has joined me inside. I wait for him to say something, but after a moment passes, it's clear he's waiting for me to be the first to speak.

"Don't call me that," I warn him without turning around. "Please." I hate the way my voice wavers. "I could handle Lyss, or even Lyssa, but...if I never have to hear someone call me by that full name again, it will be too soon."

I brace myself, waiting for him to explode, to storm out, or to do anything that would make sense. I just cut off the sex tap so abruptly, and I'm sure he's upset.

Instead, he remains quiet. I turn to find him gazing at me with that soft, assessing expression of his. I shiver again, and of course, he notices immediately. He moves across the room to turn on the fireplace without a word. After a moment, I settle in front of the fireplace with a blanket, picking at the tassels nervously.

Benji moves to the couch, purposefully giving me distance. When he speaks again, his voice is quiet. "I want to take this slow, for you," he rasps. "I swear, I do. But you are driving me out of my mind."

I brace myself again and turn to face him, eyes wide. What does he mean by that? There are far too many men in the world who have never properly learned to deal with their emotions, especially the ones that follow rejection. A man claiming he's out of his mind can use that to excuse a lot of things.

But Benji simply places his elbows on his knees as he leans forward. "I don't mean this," he continues, gesturing between us. "Not physically. Say the word, and we'll stop right here, right now. But...I can't keep playing these mind games without knowing what I'm getting into. It's confusing me, and it's hurting you." He levels me with a pointed, borderline desperate stare. "The truth, little fighter. I need it now, or nothing at all."

Chapter 21

Benji

My body feels like it's been set aflame and promptly doused. I'm not sure what to do with this girl that's sitting in front of me except force her hand. Because fuck, I want everything she has to offer, but it's clear we're not going to truly get anywhere until this bridge is crossed. And I *can't* go any further until she's shared her truth with me. I don't want to accidentally do anything else that harms her.

I'm questioning my logic as she sits in front of me now, though. Her bottom lip trembles as she wrings her blanket in her hands, clenching and unclenching her fists. I move off the couch to join her on the floor in front of the fireplace, being sure to move slowly. There's still distance between us, but as I reach around her to grab another blanket, I can see the way she stiffens, and hear the way the breath catches in her throat.

"Which do you want?" I ask softly. "Do you want me to leave?"

She shakes her head and then tilts it up, clearly trying to force her emotions back down. Despite her attempt, the tears I saw in her eyes earlier spill over, leaving a trail across her cheeks. My fingers twitch, aching to wipe her tears away, but I busy my hands with my blanket instead, waiting for her answer. I need her to tell me where this will go.

Her mouth opens and closes as she fights for words that won't come out and in a way, I can relate. The words that spilled past my lips earlier, about my brother, were ones that I didn't think I would say out loud again. Telling my team had been an experience I never wanted to relive. Aside from my sister, Jordie is the only one I talk to these days about Jake, and those days are few and far between.

But something told me I needed to be the first to open up to Lisa – *Alyssa,* though I know now it was a mistake to call her that – and show her she could trust me. The deepest scars aren't the ones you can see. So it stands to reason that one of the hardest things a person can do is willingly share those wounds with someone else.

But with her, sharing my past wasn't quite as difficult as I thought it would be. She clearly understands hurt, and she knows how to handle what I shared with her. I study her now, wondering if she will understand that and allow the same of me.

She meets my gaze, looks away, and sniffs. Finally, she lets out a shaky exhale. "Everyone always said that they never had to worry about me being abused, because I was so strong. They couldn't have been more wrong. Just because I was strong with most things didn't mean I saw that value in myself."

A cold wave hits me as I realize she's choosing to give me the truth. *Abused.* The word tells me what's coming, something I already suspected, but that I had somehow convinced myself couldn't be the reality. I remain stock-still, barely daring to breathe as she continues.

"I kept telling myself that I could change enough, be enough to make him stop. I thought that I kept deserving it with something I did, that I had to stop doing the things that triggered him, but...it didn't make it hurt any less. All those years, I cared more about making him happy than my own happiness. Especially once I lost my mom, and I had no one left to turn to. I told myself I'd figure out how to be okay, as long as it was making him happy."

The truth might be worse than never knowing at all, but now that it's started, I'm desperate for answers. "Who was he to you?" I manage.

She picks at her blanket, feigning intense interest in the fabric. Then she swallows. "Austin." The word is barely more than a breath. It leaves her lips hoarsely, like a warning. "My ex."

I inhale deeply, then ask the question I'm dreading the most. "And what did he do to you?"

Finally, she lifts her eyes to mine, and instead of tears, what I see there is much worse. It's cold, distant, emotionless. "I think you already know."

I grind my teeth so hard I can hear the sound, a muscle popping in my jaw from the force of it. But I say nothing, allowing her the space to tell me more if she wants to. It seems like the right thing to do.

After a brief moment of silence, she continues. Her voice remains quiet and detached, but it's as though the gates have opened. Her words come quicker as she recounts her memories, her fingers moving over her body while she speaks.

"It started with him hitting walls. Smashing bottles. I stopped going out, stopped talking to people, just to keep him from getting angry. But it only progressed from there." She runs her fingers over her arms, almost absently. "Anything could set him off. He would grab and shake me. And then he slapped me. When he started choking me, though... that's when I really got scared."

Her fingers drift over her neck, and bile coats my throat, burning just as hot as the anger that courses through my veins. I swallow it down forcefully and watch as she buries her hands in her blanket for a long moment, as though she's gathering the courage for what's next. But what could possibly be next?

"But it wasn't until he b-broke my rib that I realized how much danger I was in." She trips over the words and twists her arms around her middle, as though she can wrap herself in bubble wrap. I want nothing more than to do the same. "I realized I might end up alone, but at least I would be alive. And if something was going to kill me, I want to fight for it to be something in my control. I mean... I know that's not guaranteed, but I'd rather be doing something that matters. Be living a life that matters. Have it be something that at least makes me feel alive."

Hearing her talk about life and death in such a matter-of-fact, detached way, is astounding. How could someone beat her down to such a point? Who could possibly lay hands on her in such a way in the first place? My muscles are shaking from the force of being tensed for so long.

"And he's still around?" I ask, my voice hushed and vibrating with anger. "Where is he?"

"I'm not sure," she whispers. "Probably still at the home we lived in."

"He didn't go to jail?" I growl. How could this fucker get away with breaking someone's *bones* and not get jail time?

She shakes her head and stares furiously into the fireplace. "I never asked them to arrest him, so they didn't. I just got a civil order of protection."

I'm silent for a long moment, digesting the information. As though she can sense the questions burning off of me, she adds softly, "My lawyer told me going for jail time with assault charges in criminal court just tends to make them more violent."

Them. Abusers. People who choose to beat their partners into submission, rather than foster an equal partnership. People who would rather enjoy the shadow of a person than everything that makes them whole, unique, and perfect. She tosses the word out like they're a general population, rather than the stain on earth that they are. And her defeated, accepting tone splits my chest in two.

I clench my fists and mutter, "How long does your civil order last?"

"Six months."

I curse. "And that's why you left. Because changing your name and starting over was more protection than the court could give you."

She winces. "Yeah. And that's why I...don't like having my throat touched," she says, "or fighting."

I nod slowly as the pieces finally click into place. She's gazing at me, clutching the blanket against her like a barrier, as though the information is a live grenade that she's just thrown down in front of me.

And well, fuck, it kind of is, but not in the way she's thinking. I scooch closer to her, closing the gap that she's slowly been creating between us, and reach my hand out. My fingertips brush against her arm, and she squeezes her eyes shut, but I can't tell if it's from relief or apprehension.

"How many months?" I ask.

"What do you mean?"

"How many months has it been since the order was put in place?"

She hesitates. "It's been four months. A little more. I didn't get everything in place to move until about halfway through the order."

I release a slow breath, considering. "And you think he'll come looking for you when the order is lifted?"

She glances back at me, and then quickly back at the fireplace. She shifts the blanket around herself to tuck her knees up into her chest, folding herself into them before she responds.

"I'm sure he will. He thinks of me as his property. This is just a minor setback for him. It probably made him so much angrier that I disappeared." Her bottom lip starts trembling again, her composure shattering in front of my eyes. "At the end of the day, I'm still his."

Like hell she is. I clear my throat at her words, wanting to argue.

She draws in a sharp, ragged breath and looks back up at me, her eyes swimming with tears once more. "I am so, *so* sorry for dragging you into this. You deserve so much more than this. Than me. Please. You need to leave before things get any messier."

Screw that. I'm not leaving her. Even before hearing all of this, my draw to her was inevitable. I'm definitely not abandoning her now, knowing how hurt she's been, and the possible danger she's still in.

I reach for her, gently drawing her into me. She folds into me, and I'm flooded with relief at how easily she molds against my body. The blanket is draped over her, leaving only her fuzzy pink socks poking out and fuck me, I'm a goner. There's nothing I won't do to protect this girl.

"I'm not leaving you. You hear me?" I murmur into her hair. "And don't think for one second you deserve what he let you believe. You are not what he told you you are. You are so, so much more."

"I don't know if I'm strong enough, Benji." She twists to stare up at me, those bright blue eyes wide as saucers. "I'm working every day at it, but I... I still don't know if I'm strong enough to leave my past behind."

"Sometimes the strongest people are the ones who just make it through the next day." I smile down at her. "I call you my little fighter for more than one reason, you know."

She lets out another shaky exhale. "I'm so scared."

"Don't be. Please? Not anymore. I'm not going to let him hurt you anymore." I kiss the top of her head and run my hands down her arms. If wishes could turn back time, she'd never have known an unpleasant touch. "As long as you're here with me, everything will be okay. You'll be okay."

Chapter 22

Lyssa

"Well, isn't this cozy?"

I wake to the sound of Andi's voice, but I'm so disoriented that it takes me several long seconds to get a sense of my surroundings. I blink groggily, wondering why I'm on the couch instead of my bed, and why I'm twisted around a space heater.

Not a space heater – a hockey player. A very large, very warm, very cozy hockey player. One of his arms is tucked under my head, wrist dangling off the side of the couch, and the other is draped over my chest. One of his legs has mine pinned in place, though I'm surprised to find it isn't unpleasant. Still, when I meet Andi's shit-eating grin, I begin to squirm, anxious to remove myself from this compromising position.

"Hrrrrmph?" Benji groans, shifting. I allow myself a minute to move with him, basking in how good it feels, how we fit together just right. He must feel the same, because his arm slides from where it's draped over me to grab my hip, squeezing.

I close my eyes, indulging in the moment for another second before I ask, "What time is it?"

"Two in the morning," Andi replies. "I would say sorry for being out so long, but it seems you were preoccupied." She waggles her eyebrows at me.

I shake my head. "We were just sleeping."

And we were. After I'd confessed what transpired with Austin, we'd simply remained curled up by the fireplace, and I'd been so exhausted from admitting my story to him that I just listened to him tell me stories softly in my ear until I fell asleep. I know now that he played the trombone as a kid, and that his childhood dream, if hockey hadn't worked out, had been to own an alpaca farm.

What I also know now is that I'm falling for him, and it absolutely terrifies me.

This realization has me shifting as he wakes up, removing myself from his arms and quickly slipping from the couch. Benji lifts himself onto his elbows, blinking blearily up at us.

"Did you say two in the morning?" he asks, and the gravelly husk in his tone does something to me. I want to bottle the sound and play it on repeat.

"I did," Andi replies with a laugh, but something about it sounds off. I frown at her, but she's looking at Benji, not me.

"Jesus Christ," he mutters, ambling to his feet. "Didn't know Grant had that kind of stamina."

"I'd have questions if you did," Andi retorts. "But don't worry, if you two want the bedroom, I can take the couch."

"No!" I reply, so quickly and loudly that they both look at me. I see confusion and a touch of hurt cross Benji's face, and the wave of guilt is immediate. I clear my throat. "I'm sorry. I mean, we all have an early flight tomorrow. We should get some sleep in our own beds and be up early to pack."

"That's a good point," Andi puts in. I can't tell if she is actually following my logic or just making sure I'm comfortable. "Sorry, Benji. It's girls-only in here for the rest of the night." She smiles but fixes him with a look that leaves no room for argument, and the love I have for her triples instantly.

Benji rubs the back of his neck, his gaze flicking from her to me. "Ah, yeah, sure. Makes sense."

As he gathers his things, Andi tosses me a curious look, but I simply shake my head. *Tomorrow,* I mouth, and she nods. Not only does that give me time to think up what I'll tell her, but I can sort out my own thoughts on this whole ordeal. I also want to question her on why *she* didn't spend the night with Grant.

I open the door for Benji and offer him a shy smile as he approaches. He stops, eyeing me carefully. "See you tomorrow?" he asks.

"Of course."

He moves forward – to do what, I'm not sure – and I step back, averting my eyes. I'm confused, and my heart feels raw and vulnerable from everything I've admitted to him. I'm not sure I have the space to invite any more emotions into this tonight.

Instead of voicing all of this, I simply whisper, "Sorry."

He tilts his head, considering me. "You sure do say that a lot, don't you?"

"I guess so," I reply with a shrug. *Because I feel it, all the time.* "But I mean it."

"I wish you wouldn't."

I meet his gaze and give him a half-hearted smile. "Good night, Benji."

This plane ride is fucking awkward.

Benji keeps looking at me as if he wants to ask me something, but thinks better of it. The attention makes me alternate between wanting to crawl into a hole and crawl into his lap. I don't know what to make of how conflicted I am, so I do my best to ignore it, instead sidling up to Andi. The more space I give him, the easier it is to think clearly.

I'll give it to the boys, though: they know how to pass the time and keep things amusing. They're playing an aggressive game of spoons, and each time they dive for one, I'm surprised the pilot – one of their dads, though I'm not sure whose – doesn't yell at them for causing unnecessary turbulence. It's not a tiny plane, but it's not necessarily a jumbo jet, either. Levi's girlfriend was given control of the music, and Andi and I holler with approval every time a song we know and love comes on. The woman – Jessica, I think? – shoots us a grin every time it happens.

"We're earning our way into their good graces," Andi says, giving me a sideways nudge and waggling her eyebrows at me suggestively.

I laugh. "As if that's hard for you to do."

"True." She considers this. "I'm like a virus. Easy to catch and hard to get rid of."

I spit out my drink, spraying part of Ryan's shoulder. I go to apologize to him, only to be met with cries of disapproval. "Andi, don't let her apologize to the rook!" Grant shouts.

I cover my face, which is quickly growing warm, and whisper the words to Ryan regardless. He simply laughs, shrugging, and turns back to their game. My eyes flit over the group, catching on Benji's face.

I'm unsurprised to see he's already looking at me, a thousand questions behind that intense gaze. Like I've done several times on this ride home already, I shift my eyes away, then back again, unsure if I can face what I see in his expression. Unsure if I want him to read what's in mine.

We're interrupted by the pilot calling back and telling us to prepare for landing, causing the players to groan and shuffle to their feet. Grateful for the break in eye contact, I sigh and face Andi, taking another long sip of my water and reminding myself where we left our conversation off. "If you're a virus, you're the only one I'd enjoy having."

Andi beams and puts her hand to her heart. "Lisa, that may be the best compliment I've ever received."

Grant whirls around in his seat, stopped only by the buckle he's just attached around his lap. "What's this I'm hearing about Andi and viruses?"

"Hate to break it to you, but your lover has VD," I deadpan.

Andi groans, but Grant simply takes it in stride. "Ah, hell, I knew she was too excited when I didn't want to wrap it anymore."

"Grant!" she shrieks, lunging to smack at his shoulder. He darts forward to avoid it, his booming laughter carrying over the seats, and I take small satisfaction in shaming her for a change.

Their bickering keeps me happily distracted through our descent, and when we land, I text Julia that she can drop Winston off at my apartment. The ride home is filled with Andi's happy recollections from the weekend, and I sit on the edge of my seat, anxious to get back to the furry face that has always been the best at helping me cling to my sanity.

When we arrive back at the building, I expect Andi to break off and leave with Grant, but she wordlessly follows me up to my apartment. I'm grateful for her presence, especially when I see the way Benji takes note and leaves alongside his friends while she stays in the elevator with me.

I'm grateful, that is, up until the moment we get to my apartment and she closes the door softly behind us. I hear Winston's feet skittering across the floors, racing to greet us, but I can't look away from Andi's expression. It's more serious than I've ever seen her: a mixture of stern and concerned, devoid of any sarcastic, bubbly humor I'm so used to seeing from her. We stay that way for a long moment, saying nothing, simply looking at each other.

"Do you want to talk about it?" she finally asks, and her voice is so quiet that I finally tip over the edge. I sink down to grab Winston and burst into tears.

Chapter 23

BENJI

"He really got his stick in the way of that one."

A collective cheer goes up around the living room as we all raise our glasses, taking large gulps. We're watching our professional team, the Minnesota Chill, as they play against the Colorado Summits, critiquing the plays and chirping nonsense at the TV as we nurse our last beers before a long five days on the road. We like to keep tabs on where we see our futures heading. Most of us already have a two-way contract with the Minnesota Chill, since the Leopards are the AHL team they're tied to, but some of us have a one-way contract, and there's always a chance to get traded. So while we keep a closer eye on the Chill, there's always a chance players from the other teams may soon become our linemates.

Normally, that's where our focus is when we watch these games, but all it took was a few short days for Lyssa and her friend to make their impact. Now we can't unhear the double entendres in everything the announcers say.

I smirk into my glass, then frown. What had been shaping up to be an amazing weekend had turned sour overnight, and I'm not sure what I did wrong. Clearly, saying her name had been a misstep – but it led to the answers I've been desperate to have for weeks. I slowed things down, gave her reassurances. I promised she'd be okay with me. Had sleeping next to her scared her off? Was this strange distance the price of her honesty, or mine?

I wanted to talk to her and understand where her head was at, but she hadn't given me the chance. And now... now, we're about to be shoved on a bus and carted off for the next several days. I run a hand over my face, groaning inwardly. This girl is a flight risk, and the last thing I want is to put this distance between us, when what we have is so fragile and new. Well, *whatever* this thing is...just another bullet point to add on our ever-growing list of things to discuss.

Jordie, ever observant, notices my silent suffering. "Anything you wanna talk about, buddy?"

The room goes quiet as the others eye me up, and I shift uncomfortably. These guys can't be bothered to shut up and listen when the rideshare outside the bar is leaving in two minutes, but sure, the second Jordie murmurs something interesting that involves my sex life, they're all ears? Fucking figures.

"Is it Lisa?" Highcloud asks, and I bite the inside of my cheek at the use of her fake name. She clearly chose a pseudonym that would be as close to her old nickname as she could find. *Lyssa.*

"Yeah, she kind of ignored you that whole flight home." Grant eyes me up. "Didn't you spend the night with her?"

If the guys weren't fully invested already, they are now. Nils even reaches for the remote, turning the volume down on the TV. Well, so much for our drinking game.

Even so, I stand up and fetch another beer, tugging at my chain as I go. I take my time rummaging in the fridge, considering what to say. I make my way back to the living room, but opt to stand, shifting on my feet. Finally, I clear my throat. "Yeah, we fell asleep together, but we didn't *sleep* together."

"So you two didn't do...anything?" Grant raises a brow at me.

"I mean, we started to." I take a sip of my beer, turning the words over in my head again before I voice them. "But we stopped. She's been through some shit in the past."

Sympathetic murmurs ripple across the room. "Bad ex?" Nils asks.

"The worst," I reply, flexing my jaw.

"I'm sorry, dude," Jordie says. "She told you about it?"

I nod, and a flicker of surprise ripples across Jordie's face. He knows how hard it's been for me to get information on Lyssa, so he knows how huge this is for me. How long I've been vying for these details to make it make sense; make *her* make sense. Then, I see the moment it registers, and guilt floods his expression. I can tell he's putting two and two together – the fact she put so much distance between them when they hung out, the way she reacted to the fight in the bar. I give him a tight smile, hoping he understands it's behind us.

Levi's brow furrows in confusion. "So...that's it? It's done?"

"I don't know." I huff. "That's what I'm trying to figure out. We talked, and I thought we were cool. But then she kicked me out of bed and hasn't spoken to me since."

The guys exchange weighted looks, and I hate the silent message it conveys. I can practically hear them screaming that it's a lost cause. I set my beer down and begin to pace.

"Well, it's official," Grant announces, watching me. I pause, blinking at him, and he clarifies, "You must just suck in bed."

Highcloud punches him. "That's a shit joke, even for you."

It does what I suspect he wanted it to, though, and the guys begin shifting and talking again.

"Maybe she's just scared," Jordie offers, as Nils puts in, "She probably just needs some time to think."

Yeah, that's what I'm hoping for. I'm glad to hear it's where their minds went, too. "But if that's the case, how much time do I give her?" I ask, then hesitate, feeling pathetic as I add, "Do I text her, or let her come to me?"

Everyone exchanges another long look. Jordie shrugs, and Highcloud runs his hand through his hair. Grant excuses himself to get another beer and Levi coughs, I suspect just to break the silence.

I swear to god. This group can learn a new power play after one walkthrough on the white board – with near-indecipherable marker lines, I might add; Coach isn't known for his stellar handwriting – but the second a girl's involved, we're all fucking useless.

Finally, Jordie sighs. "Fuck, man," he says. "I know you like her and all, but this season is huge for you. And you going after this girl is huge, too. I mean, we've all noticed that you haven't really been hooking up."

Everyone nods in agreement, and even though nobody looks judgemental, the faces of sympathy are almost worse. I feel my cheeks begin to burn as Levi asks, "Are you sure you don't want to get back in the saddle with something more, I dunno, simple?"

My head is shaking before I've even answered the question aloud. "Nah, man," I say. "It might not be simple, but it feels...right."

The team might be useless, but I know one person who can give me the female perspective I desperately need.

I dial my sister's number, praying I can catch her at an off time. I have about forty minutes to pack and be on the bus, and I want this conversation to happen away from the team, seeing how dismal our last attempt at discussing it went.

I don't want simple. I want *her*. I just don't know how to make it a reality.

"Yeeah-loh? What's wrong?" My sister's voice comes through the speaker, and I grin as I shove sweatpants into my duffel.

"What, I can't just call my sister out of the blue to check in?"

There's the sound of a bag crinkling, and then crunching. "No," Gabi replies, her voice muffled as she speaks around a mouthful of what I presume are chips. "If it's not a text, I have to assume something terrible has happened. That's the only reason people call each other these days."

I frown. "That makes no sense."

"*You* make no sense." Her reply is quick and snappy, but I can tell she's smiling as she speaks again. "Seriously, though, is something up?"

I clear my throat, bracing myself for the conversation. "Yeah." I exhale deeply. "There's this girl, and I need your advice."

The crunching stops, and her voice comes closer, as though she's tugged the phone against her ear now. "What happened? Are you okay? Is it like–"

"No." I cut her off, feeling a pang of regret course through me from causing her alarm. "No, no, this is...this is a good one, Gabs.""Oh," she says, then: *"Oh.* Benji, are you in love? What did you do?"

I laugh and shake my head at her immediate accusation. She's not wrong, though – she's seen me through all of my dating years, and I haven't always been a class act. I certainly pissed a few women off as I was growing up, fueled by a cockiness at my abilities and my good looks. By the time I got to this level of professional hockey, the women understood – more or less – that I didn't want anything serious. I didn't know where I'd end up, and I wasn't ready to settle down.

And then...everything with our brother happened.

And then, *she* happened.

My mind fixates on the other part of her question. *Are you in love?* Well, fuck, I can't even think about that. First I have to get this impossible, complex, beautiful girl to even go out with me. "I don't know what I did, Gabs," I say.

She must hear the desperation in my tone, because her own switches from accusatory to soft. "Oh, Benj. Tell me what happened."

And so I do. I tell her how I fucked up at the beginning – earning a stern *hmmm* in the process of my explanation – and how, while I was busy figuring out who she really is, I found myself falling for the pieces of her that I could grasp onto, every side of herself that she's slowly revealed to me. The side that held firm on telling me off and met me with ferocious punches in the ring. The side that wanted to save her local gym, laughed so hard she cried while watching hockey with Andi, that sweet-talks her dog like a human.

"Hold on, she's got a dog?" Gabi asks. "I already approve."

I smile as I tell her about Winston, and think back to Lyssa's face on the plane when she realized she'd have Winston waiting for her when she got home. I've never owned pets, and neither does most of our team. It's not that we don't love them, but we just don't have the time to look after them. A few have cats, but my sister has one, and I've seen the way it looks at me. I don't need to willingly adopt something that's plotting my death while I sleep.

I even tell my sister about the side of Lyssa that comes from her dark past, that has her flinching away from raised voices and abrupt touches. I don't tell Gabi every single detail I was given, but just enough that she understands why Lyssa has been pulling away from me, and why I need to tread carefully.

I throw my toothbrush and toothpaste into my duffel and zip it with a sigh. "And now...I don't know where we stand. She barely acknowledged me on the flight home, and she hasn't messaged me since."

There's a pause on the other end of the line, and I hear a door slam in the background. Gabi's voice fades as she turns to greet her wife, then comes back clearly. "All right, Benj. Were you calling for my advice, or just to have someone to talk to?"

This is what I love about my sister. Somewhere along the line, she got fed up with the passive-aggressive, midwestern niceties. Maybe it's because she's the middle child and got sick of being the go-between for my brother and me growing up. She's not afraid to ask point-blank what it is that people want from her, and set boundaries if it doesn't line up with what she's willing to give. You know exactly where you stand with her, and while that can be terrifying to some, it makes her the easiest person in the world to talk to, at least for me. I don't know why I didn't call her sooner.

"I really could use your advice," I say.

"Okay. Well. First off, I think you were a dumbass for how you treated her at first, but you already know you fucked up. But as for how you reacted after she told you the truth...I think you did everything right. I'm proud of you, little brother." My heart warms at her praise, and then I immediately roll my eyes as she adds, "I taught you well."

"Yeah, yeah, you're the best, I know," I shoot back.

"And you'll do well to remember it." The crunching sound is back, and I wait as she chews, likely pondering her next words. "And she didn't *say* she doesn't want to see you anymore, or not to message you? She didn't look angry?"

I think back to the plane ride, and how she avoided even looking at me. "No, she didn't say anything like that, and no, just...maybe embarrassed? Definitely not angry. I know her angry face."

There's a smile in Gabi's voice as she answers. "Then my guess is she's just processing. This has to be a lot for her to reconcile with. You're her first step back into the real world after what sounds like a horrible relationship." She pauses, then lowers her voice. "And if I'm not mistaken, this is your first relationship since everything that happened with Jake, isn't it?"

I swallow around the hard lump in my throat. "Yeah."

Gabi makes a noncommittal noise. "I think you both want the same thing, you're just going to need to be gentle with each other. Until you or her call it quits, to me, it sounds like the door is still open."

"So...what should I do?" I ask, feeling my heart lift.

Gabi laughs. "Text her, you idiot! I mean," she amends, "Don't like, bombard her with texts. Don't be that guy. Just shoot her one to know the door is still open on your end, when she's ready."

"Okay." I nod. "Thanks, Gabs."

"Anytime," she replies. "Oh, and Benj?"

"Yeah?"

"*Text* her. Don't call her. Nobody calls anymore."

I chuckle, and we say our goodbyes. I sling my duffel over my shoulder and head for the bus, my fingers typing and deleting a text to Lyssa as I go. Finally, as we board the bus, I decide to stop overthinking it and shoot off the single sentence, praying it's enough to show her that I'm ready if she is.

Me: *Can I take you on a date when I get back?*

Chapter 24

Lyssa

I tell Andi everything.

Everything, that is, that I told Benji. Some secrets are still too dark to voice, even to myself. But at this moment, what I share can at least help her understand what I'm feeling and why I'm currently using Winny as a tissue. For his part, Winston remains still, only turning every now and then to climb further into my lap or to lick at my cheeks. We really don't deserve dogs.

As soon as I began crying, Andi collapsed on the floor next to me, giving my shoulder a gentle rub and murmuing a soft, "It's okay, it's okay." When I began explaining myself, she leaned back, allowing me to cling onto Winston. Despite all the exuberance and intensity I know her for, she remains surprisingly quiet now. She simply listens as I recount my past with Austin, my hidden identity, and the reason I keep everyone at arm's length. When I tell her about my injuries, she ducks her head, but I still see the discreet movement of her wiping a tear away.

"I'm so sorry I didn't know," she says quietly. "I wish I had noticed. I wish I could have done something."

"It's not always something you can see." I give her a wobbly smile. "Even when he hurt me, he made sure it wasn't visible."

She blows a heavy breath out from between her lips. "You're so fucking strong. I'm so proud of you for getting away."

My gaze trails to the window, where I see other skyscrapers in the distance. Strong isn't the word I'd use for what I did.

How often have I heard girls just like Andi say that they wouldn't allow such things to happen? Women with fiery tempers and very active gym memberships, adamant that they would kick their man's ass if he so much as touched them.

Even when I'd been at my strongest physically, I didn't give a second thought to other ways I could be taken advantage of. I'd allowed him to infiltrate my mind, make me feel small. I'd shaped myself around him and allowed him to convince me to wilt. By the time he started being more than emotionally abusive, I'd lost enough weight that he could lift me with one hand. My desire for him to find me beautiful walked me right into his powerful, violent hands.

How often had I chastised myself for allowing it to get to that? I'd been a successful athlete when I started college. If I'd fought back with the strength and size I'd had when we first started dating, could I have won? Or would he have found another way to hurt me, aside from his words and his fists?

I'll never know, now. Instead I ran, praying I could leave it all behind. And here I am now, still allowing the past to find me and haunt me.

"I wasn't strong," I whisper. "I was cowardly."

"No." Andi's tone is sharp, and the seriousness of it makes me jerk my head up in surprise. "Don't you dare say that. You were able to see your worth, how much better you can be away from him, and that you didn't deserve what he did to you. You did that all by yourself. You left on your first try, and you didn't look back."

False. I'd actually tried leaving twice, but she didn't know that. She never would.

"And I can't believe you did that all on your own. Girl, you are so fucking strong." The sheen in her eyes makes my chest twinge painfully, and I glance away. I don't deserve her praise. "If you don't mind me asking, what name do you want me to use?" she asks.

I blink in surprise. Of all the things, I wasn't expecting her to ask that. I assumed she would just want to use my real name, and I wasn't sure yet how it would make me feel. But...part of me *does* want to be called by my real name. "You can call me Lyssa. Or Lyss." I swallow. "But please, never Alyssa."

She gives a sage nod. "Even around others?"

"No, I–I'm not sure I'm ready to tell anyone else this story." I shake my head. "The only other person I've told is Benji."

"How about this? Can I just call you L? That could mean anything, and encompasses all of you. Then and now." She gestures in a circle and beams at me, and I feel my hesitant smile grow. The way her enthusiasm manages to pull me up from the darkness is something to be admired. It's infectious in the best way.

"Yes." I huff out a soft laugh. "That sounds perfect."

Her grin grows triumphant. She scoots closer and gives Winny a scratch, considering me for a long moment. "Do you wanna talk about Benji?"

For some reason, the simple question has tears springing to my eyes again. I sigh and blink them away. "I don't know, Andi."

"You don't know if you want to talk about it, or you don't know what's happening with him?"

I shrug. "Both?"

She gives a sad, soft laugh. "Oh, L." The nickname rolls easily off her tongue, and warmth blooms inside me. She slides an arm across my shoulders, and Winny moves across my lap so that he has some body part touching both of us, the greedy little lover he is. "What happened?"

I mull over the past weeks, starting with Benji discovering my hidden identity. How he refused to take things any further until he knew my real name. What happened last night, with me giving in and sharing my name. How he used it as we made out, stopping me short.

As I recount our night in Colordado, I skirt over Benji's story about his brother. Andi could probably easily look it up, but it's his story to share. I hold it close, knowing he showed the same vulnerability that he asked of me.

I also skim over the more graphic details of our moment in the hot tub, even though my cheeks flame, and she gives me a knowing smirk that says she absolutely knows what happened. Even now, I can feel his large, calloused hands skimming over me, and the soft warmth of his lips against my skin. It's a heady feeling. Desire and fear are sitting on two ends of the same scale, nearly equal in how much they're overwhelming me.

I didn't think anything could match the unease always curled in my gut, ready to pounce. But when his hands and lips were on me, those feelings became quiet. Not gone – never gone. Just...quiet. And, I realize now with a jolt: I didn't have a nightmare that night on the couch. I slept soundly with him next to me.

"He sounds...incredibly sweet," Andi says. "I'm telling you as someone who is always looking for the worst in men. But, really, it sounds like he's taking it all in stride, and he wants you. The question is, do you want him?"

"I don't know. I mean, I did last night. I do, still. But that's just physical desire. Then he went and said my name, and when I told him the truth, and it didn't scare him away, it made me feel like things were heading somewhere...deeper. But I don't think I'm ready for all of that." I gesture broadly. "Look at where that ended up last time."

This is the centering conversation I needed. The reminder to get out before this beautiful thing twists into something dark and painful. Every happy memory I should've had with Austin is stained by the fear and violence that grew over the years, overshadowing anything else. At least with Benji now, I can hold the memory of that moment in the hot tub and the time after, curled together on the couch, suspended in time, forever unblemished.

Andi's look is full of concern. "I hate that he did this to you."

"Did what?" I gnaw at my lip, hating her expression.

"That he made you think that any relationship you have from here on out will end with you needing to run away. I mean, what if you end up losing someone you could really care for?"

"The hardest part isn't losing someone you care for," I say. "It's realizing they weren't who you thought they were in the first place."

Austin had been good once; amazing, even. To this day, I wrack my brain, wondering if there was something from the very beginning that could have warned me. If I had been able to see past his generosity, his charm, and his humor, would I have found a piece of that darkness underneath his handsome exterior?

The more terrifying reality is that he kept it carefully hidden until he knew he had me in his grasp. It was like another person had emerged, far too late for me to get away unscathed.

"I know how that feels," Andi says, her voice quiet. My eyes widen and shoot to hers, but she shakes her head. "Not what you went through. But how it feels when someone you love isn't who you thought they were." She pauses. "I was engaged once."

"You were?" I can't help my shocked tone.

She nods. "I was young, and naive. We were high school sweethearts. But the week before we were supposed to be married, I found out he was cheating. And to think," she lets out a rueful laugh, "we were talking about having kids."

I need a moment to digest the information. I can't imagine who could have this bubbly, charming, beautiful woman next to me as their partner and actively choose to hurt her, over and over again. "Where is he now?"

"I don't know." She shrugs. "Buried under a gaggle of women? Choking on a ball gag? Oh, hopefully dying a slow death from one of his numerous STDs. A girl can dream."

I snort, but grab one of her hands and squeeze it. So, Andi doesn't just make jokes to make others feel better – she does it when she's hurting, too. I remind myself to pay closer attention. "Do you want to talk about it?"

"Not now." She shakes her head and gives me a sad smile. "But maybe someday."

"Whenever you're ready, I'm here," I say. "But you're doing okay, now?" When she nods, I add, "What am I saying? You're banging a professional hockey player 24/7. I'd say you came out on top."

"That's true. I come on top a lot." She pauses as I laugh again. "But see? The point is, not every man is going to be like the one that ruined our pasts. Grant and I have a wonderful, consensual, no-strings-attached relationship. Nobody's getting hurt, but everyone's getting laid. It's fucking great."

I consider this and frown. "Something tells me Benji's not as into the idea of friends with benefits as Grant. Strangely, he seems like the relationship type."

And I'm not sure I can give that to him.

"Well...you're not looking to date anyone else, are you?"

"I mean, no?"

"Then I bet you can both agree to not see other people while you see where this is going. Just take it slow. You both have your own apartments, jobs, lives. Hell, his job keeps him away half the time as it is. If you decide it's not for you, all you have to do is say so." As if she can see the panic rising in me, she bumps my shoulder. "And the best part? You'll have me here to back you up. Just say the word, and I'll come get you, day or night."

"Okay. Take it slow. Yeah. I think I can do that." I inhale slowly through my nose, willing my heart rate to stop spiking.

Andi grins at me. "Baby steps, L."

Again, the nickname sends warmth tingling through me. I let the breath out on a deep exhale and take out my phone. As

Andi watches, I pull up my conversation with Benji, where I left his question on read, and type out one word.

Me: *Yes.*

I hit send. "Baby steps."

Chapter 25

BENJI

"You're not going to try to take me cross country skiing, are you?" Lyssa asks as she climbs into my truck, shooting me a distrustful look.

I choke out a disbelieving laugh. "Not thirty seconds in, and you're already questioning our date?"

"Well, all I'm saying is, even with gravity on my side, I sucked at skiing," she grumbles. "I can't imagine doing it on a parallel surface would improve things."

"No skiing," I promise. "Though, my sister was on the cross country ski team in high school. If you ever want to learn."

"Really? That's a thing here?"

"Of course!" Her eyes widen at my response, and I smile, wondering what kinds of things she did in high school. There's so much to learn about her, and I'm genuinely excited to start. Her feet slide up the dash immediately as we pull out of the apartment garage, and my smiles widens, remembering the last time we drove together.

I pass her my phone to turn on some music. "1788."

She looks at me, confused, and I motion at the phone. "That's my passcode. Feel free to turn on some music. Whatever you're into. Even if it's what we listened to in the gym."

I expect her to laugh, or say something snarky in response, but she remains quiet. When I steal a glance at her, she's scrolling through my music app, but her brow is furrowed.

"Can't find what you're looking for?" I ask.

"It's not that." She shakes her head. "I just...it caught me off guard. You letting me use your phone so freely."

I frown. "Why wouldn't I? There's nothing on there to hide."

The long beat it takes her to respond is filled with everything she doesn't say, and I can't help but tighten my hands on the steering wheel. I can only imagine what her dynamic with phones was like with her ex, but I don't know if I'm ready to hear that answer.

"So, there aren't any nudes on here or anything?" Her joke is weak, but clearly an attempt to deflect, and I try to take it in stride.

"I mean, you might see Grant's pale little asscheeks if you go digging, but that's about it."

She chuckles, the sound genuine, and I relax slightly. "I'll leave those to Andi," she says, putting on some music. We drive along for a few minutes in companiable silence, but then I feel her gaze on me, assessing.

The side of my mouth quirks up. "What?"

"I just realized, you're not using a map." It's a statement, not a question.

"I'm not."

"Did you grow up here?" she asks.

"Nah, but northwest of here. Near Pelican Rapids."

"Is it even colder up there than it is here?"

"Most winters, yeah." I glance at her, and she blinks back at me, eyes wide. "Great for the ice, though. My dad would flood our backyard and build it up so that we had our own personal rink."

"So that's how you and your brother got so good at hockey," she says, then grimaces. "I'm sorry. I didn't mean to bring him up."

"No, it's...it's good." I think back to those winters, smiling to myself. The ice was choppy and at times soft, but it was ours. We spent weekends out there with our teammates, and evenings, working on tricks until our wrists ached and our mom was yelling to get inside before we got sick. "We were on skates before we could walk. Sometimes my mom had to bribe us with cookies just to get us back inside."

"Chocolate chip?"

I nod, and she sighs. "A classic. Top tier. I was worried you were going to say oatmeal raisin."

"Hey, don't knock oatmeal raisin. Those have their place."

"Oh no. Are you a closet oatmeal raisin sympathizer?" She clutches her chest in mock horror, and I chuckle.

"I could be. So keep that in mind before you throw out such reckless opinions."

I drive for another minute in silence, and then she says, "Bristol."

"What?" I glance at her.

"Bristol, Tennessee. That's where I grew up."

I know this moment is significant – she's giving me another piece of herself that she's held back from everyone else. I feel special for it, but I also can't help the laugh that works its way up my throat. Before I know it, I'm bent over the steering wheel, wiping a tear from my eye.

"What's so funny?"

"You're telling me, when that guy used the terrible pickup line on you at the bar –" I choke on another laugh. "– he was *right?*"

"I..." she trails off, and then giggles as realization dawns. "Yeah, I guess he was." She joins me, laughing in earnest now, and I'll be damned if it isn't music to my ears.

We pull into the parking garage, and she leans over in her seat to peer out the window, frowning as she reads the sign we pass. "The Mall of America?"

I hum in response, rotating the steering wheel as I back into a spot.

"Are you taking me on a shopping date?"

I grin, throwing the car into park and turning the ignition off. "That depends. Do you want to go shopping?"

Her nose crinkles. "I'm not big on shopping."

"I know." I laugh. "I remember the boot debacle. Vividly."

She huffs and unbuckles her seatbelt. "So what are we doing at a mall?"

"This isn't just any mall. This is the *Mall of America*. You can do far more than shopping here. Hell, people even get married here." At her look of alarm, I laugh again. "Easy, little fighter. We're not doing that, either."

We exit the car and I guide her into the mall, enjoying her genuine look of amazement as we weave through the crowd. Even though it's a weekday, it's still busy, and we find ourselves turning, twisting our shoulders and pivoting around groups of people. She doesn't seem to mind, though. In fact, she seems to enjoy it, taking in the various groups that pass us by, smiling to herself as snippets of conversation float past our ears. Between the chatter, the colorful storefronts, and the sweet and savory smells wafting from restaurants, some might consider it sensory overload, but it all reminds me of my childhood.

Whenever my parents agreed to a splurge growing up – whether it be hunting for Halloween costumes, looking for my sister's perfect prom dress, a birthday celebration, or even a wedding for a cousin here and there – this became a full day trip for our family.

It certainly isn't the same place it was ten or twenty years ago, but as I take in the families here now, I know they're here for the same type of experience. Our family could spend hours shopping on one floor alone, and there are multiple – not to mention the ever-changing theme park. When Lisa spots that particular jewel, she steps forward as if to explore it further, then stops and turns to me, eyes wide. "Holy shit," she breathes. "You weren't kidding."

The corners of my mouth twitch in amusement. "I *never* kid about a Minnesota staple."

"Are we going in there?" she asks, stepping a few feet closer. Her eyes track an orange roller coaster as it flips upside down on a bright blue track. Excitement is written all across her face, and my stomach plummets. Shit. Did I choose the wrong date activity? Should I try to pivot?

"I didn't know if you were into those kinds of rides," I admit, feeling defeated. When she turns to me, though, she doesn't look disappointed.

"That's fair. I don't see why you would." She pauses and relief sweeps over me as I realize she's not upset. She eyes me, and I wonder if she's thinking the same as me; how little we really know about one another. "I love roller coasters. Big drops, twists, loops, all of them. I guess you could call me an adrenaline junkie," she adds with a smile.

I grin back. "I should've guessed. But in that case, I know a place with way better roller coasters to take you when it's warmer out."

Her brows raise. "Oh, really?"

"Mmm. Just be prepared to scream."

"I have no doubt you can find a way to make me scream," she teases, and there I find myself, blushing like a teenager in the middle of a mall filled with people. At her laugh, I know she's noticed.

"Come on," I say, offering my hand. When she takes it, a different warmth fills me. Damn this woman. She's my own personal roller coaster.

I guide her through the chaos to our actual date location: the mall's aquarium. When she sees the signs, she twists to face me, leaving her hand in mine. "There's an aquarium in here, too?" she exclaims. "What doesn't this place have?"

"I truly don't know," I reply with a laugh. "Maybe... archery dodgeball?"

She squints up at me, attempting to gauge my seriousness. "Is that a thing?"

"It is. Can't say I've seen it here, yet, though."

"Give it time. I'm sure it'll be the next pop-up."

We descend the escalator, and her eyes shine as she takes in the initial ponds, alive with the movement of dozens of fish. A weight lifts off my shoulders at the sight. If she's already excited by this, she'll love the rest of the experience.

"If they did do a pop-up, is it something you'd want to do?" I ask.

She pulls her gaze away from the ponds. "Archery dodge-ball?"

"Yeah."

"Oh, absolutely." The grin that spreads over her face is mischievous. "But be prepared to lose."

I feign a look of betrayal. "You wouldn't want to be on my team?"

"Absolutely not!" We pause to scan our tickets, and she adds, "Well, I guess it depends. I want to be on whatever team Grant isn't on. I feel like he needs a good ass-kicking."

"Oh, he would definitely be on the other team. I need to kick his ass every now and then, too. Just to keep him in line. Well, as in line as Grant can ever be."

She giggles, and I want to bottle the sound. "In that case, I guess I'll be on your team. If I'm allowed."

I give her hand a squeeze. "Always."

We make our way through the first portion of the aquarium, and while I love watching sea life as much as anyone, my attention keeps slipping from the colorful fish to Lisa's expressions. Her blue eyes are wide and excited, darting every which way to take in the creatures. Every now and then, she drops my hand to explore something, but to my immense delight, she keeps returning to slide her hand into mine, intertwining her fingers with mine.

She even pauses at each sign, absorbing the information, her lips moving as she reads. Her excitement is palpable and contagious. As we make our way to the tunnel, I can't help but ask, "Have you been to an aquarium before?"

She studies me for a moment and, seeing no judgement in my question, shakes her head. "Never been to the coast, either. Maybe as a baby," she amends. "But nothing I can remember. My mom did her best, but she was a single mom without much extra income. There wasn't much left over for vacations."

I turn my head away to hide a frown, feigning extra interest in a passing fish as we enter the tunnel. The thought of her being robbed of a childhood experience like this, paired with what I know of her recent experiences, unsettles me. I don't like the thought of her being unhappy at any point in her life.

But the second she grabs my arm, inhaling sharply and whispering "Oh my *god,*" all I can feel is selfish gratitude. She tracks a shark as it swims overhead, lips slightly parted in awe. I simply watch her until we're parted by a kid bursting through the tunnel to get to what's on the other side. I'm just stupidly happy to be giving her this new adventure.

There's a pond in the next room, and kids and adults alike surround the edge, dipping their fingers into the water as small stingrays glide around. We're ushered to a station where we're instructed to wash our hands and given guidance on how to gently touch the rays.

"And it isn't stressful for them? They don't mind it?" Lyssa asks the employee, her brows furrowed in concern.

"They're swapped so that they don't spend too much time in the tank, and they have enough space in there and places to hide. That way, if they don't like it, they can avoid being touched," he assures her. When she still doesn't look convinced, he adds, "There's research to suggest they actually enjoy the stimulation and being petted. See for yourself – go put your hand in the water and don't seek them out; just wait for one to rise up to meet it."

We both follow his instructions, placing our pointer and middle fingers in the water and waiting. Sure enough, one of the next rays swims up our edge of the pond and surges up to the surface, its back grazing against our palms. Lyssa stiffens in surprise next to me.

"It's like a cat!" she shrieks. "But it feels...I don't even know!"

I grin. "Weird, huh?"

"It's like...slick sandpaper." Her voice is filled with wonder.

"Be careful you don't touch them where they're sensitive," she cautions as another passes by, and I chuckle but oblige. It's endearing how she cares for these creatures, but not surprising, given how she is with Winny. We stay like that for a few minutes, waiting for a couple more rays to glide by.

I thought it would be the highlight of the trip. What Lyssa ends up loving the most, however, is the seahorse exhibit. She traces her fingertips along the glass as she moves along, marveling at all the different colors and species of seahorses.

"I had no idea they were so tiny!" she whisper-shouts, peering at the small creatures. "Look at them, curling their tails around the seagrass."

"It looks like that's how they sleep," I reply, peering at a sign on the wall stating fun facts about seahorses. Lyssa sidles up next to me, her lips moving with the words again as she scans the sign.

"They're one of few fish species that mate for life," she reads out loud, and smiles. "Look – they do little courtship dances with their tails! That's too freaking adorable."

We continue through the tanks of seahorses, Lyssa excitedly calling out every fact she finds interesting. Apparently, seahorses are awful swimmers, but they're fantastic at eating, even though they lack teeth. Once we've seen every inch of the exhibit, I know more about sea life than ever before, but more importantly, I've witnessed another new side of Lyssa, one that I desperately want to see more of.

As we come to the end of the aquarium – which, naturally, dumped us into a gift shop packed with stuffed sea creatures, t-shirts, and keychains – I can't help the question that's burning at the tip of my tongue. "So, was this an acceptable date?"

She pauses her perusal of the shelf laden with seahorses and gives me a genuine smile, one so bright and wide my heart swells with victory. "It was," she replies, and picks up a tiny orange seahorse plushie, stroking it absentmindedly. She begins to walk around the rest of the store, still holding it.

I watch her for a moment, then follow. When she's done a full lap around the gift store, still holding the seahorse, I hold out my hand, and ask, "Does this mean we'll have a second date?"

When she looks at me, I gesture to the stuffed animal. After a moment, she tentatively places it in my hand. I carefully bring it up to the cash register, keeping an eye on her. When she doesn't argue, I relax, pulling out cash to pay for it. She watches, not stopping me, but not replying to my question, either.

When I finally place the seahorse back in her hands, she does something that knocks me completely off kilter.

She reaches up, winds her free hand around my neck, and kisses me.

The feel of her soft lips pressing against mine is enough to knock the air from my lungs. It's all I can do to reciprocate and wrap my head around the moment as we explore each other's mouths. On the outside, it's chaste – we are in a kid-friendly aquarium, after all – but it's also slow, sensual, and intimate. By the time I regain enough air to want more, she's pulling away, but the look in her eyes tells me she's restraining herself, too. As we create distance, we both seem to recall where we are.

I clear my throat, attempting to break the heated moment for both our sakes. Because fuck, I've had a taste. Twice, now.

I want to devour the dish and lick the spoon.

"So... is that a yes?"

Her laugh is soft, breathy, telling me she's just as affected by our kiss as I am. "Yes."

We head up the escalator to the exit, and she fiddles with the orange plushie as we ascend. After a minute, she glances up at me, a question in her eyes. When I tilt my head in encouragement, she blurts out, "Why this? Why did you take me here?"

I lift my eyes to the levels above us, filled with families making memories, and smile warmly. "I wanted to take you somewhere different, but still show you something that's a piece of Minnesota. A piece of my upbringing." At her raised brows, I continue. "This is where a lot of our fun family outings happened. Shopping for important moments, shoving our faces with cinnamon rolls, whipping around on rides until the cinnamon rolls nearly came back up."

"That sounds...nauseating, but also wonderful." She smiles, but it wavers after a moment. I can't help but wonder if she's thinking of her childhood, of her own parents.

I bump her lightly, hoping to shake any unpleasant memory away. "Plus, I know you're not quite used to a northern winter yet. Didn't want to freeze you out before I got to show you all this place has to offer."

"I don't know," she muses, leaning against me. "With you here to keep me warm, it doesn't feel all that bad."

Chapter 26

LYSSA

"Do you want cash back?"

The cashier at the grocery store looks at me expectantly, and I swallow, quickly selecting the option for $50. I will the older lady to move faster as she opens the register, passing me two twenties and a ten. I slip them deftly into my front pocket, eyes on the entrance to the store. Austin will have pulled around by now, but if I take too long, it's not out of the question for him to come back inside, arms crossed and a frown painted on his face. I gather the bags and turn my plan over in my head again.

I've collected cash back for a couple of months now. Austin doesn't pay close attention to the grocery bill, and costs have been rising, so he hasn't questioned the fact that our weekly runs have increased in price. It's also one of the few places he lets me out of his sight, either opting not to go with or simply dropping me off to run the errand. It's a funny feeling, the fact that I breathe easiest when I'm weaving in and out of aisles of chips and cereals. There's a dangerous whisper of freedom to it, and when I watch the others in the store, I sometimes imagine I'm them. On the phone with a friend, confirming ingredients for a party. Leaning into a loved one, planning a romantic night in. Holding hands with a small child, rolling my eyes at their endless attempts at sneaking junk food into the cart.

Most days, I block out the whispers. But today, I let them grow and blossom into what could almost be called hope. Because today, I have a plan.

When we get home, I unpack the groceries and run upstairs to change for the night. It's Patty's graduation party – and technically, mine, though I don't expect any acknowledgment there. Ethan bugged Austin to the point that he gave in, agreeing to bring me with to celebrate, too. The fact that they want to include me in the celebration, even with the distance that has grown between us, both warms and pains me.

"Let's go, Alyssa!" Austin bellows from the front door, and I hesitate for only a second before grabbing the money I've saved up – carefully folded into an unused sock at the bottom of my drawer – and tuck it into my bra. Tonight is the night we graduate from one life, and I can only pray the one I graduate to next looks wildly different.

As we leave, the road swirls and blurs, time skipping forward until I find myself on a deck.

It's dark out, and Austin is clutching a handful of bills in his hand. Shadows move in the background, milling about, but I don't take my eyes off the predator in front of me.

"What the fuck is this?" It comes out as a whisper, low and soft. To anyone else, he simply sounds surprised, but I know better. I know the violence that tone promises.

Why did I listen to the whispers that told me I could get away and find freedom? His words are the only ones that matter. The ones that remind me where I really am, where I will always be.

I may have graduated, but I'll never escape this.

A knock at the door pulls me out of my thoughts. I shake my head and gather my things, knowing exactly who will be on the other side of that door, because it's ten minutes before our scheduled date time. For the past two weeks, that knock has sent my pulse skittering and launched butterflies in my stomach. For the first week, the nightmares let up, as if the excitement from being with Benji simply took up all my headspace.

This past week, however, they've come back with full force. I'm not sure if it's because things are getting more serious, or if I'm just getting too deep into my feelings. I *know* it's not because of anything physical.

Things have remained frustratingly stagnant on that front. Two weeks ago, we had dinner outside during a snowfall. The dining space was enclosed and heated, but it was transparent, so it felt like we were eating in a snowglobe. It was romantic as all hell, but at the end of it, when he dropped me off at home, we shared a long kiss. Afterwards, he simply placed a brief kiss on my forehead and said goodnight.

I almost wondered if he'd given up on me, but then he texted for another date, and we ended up walking through a botanical gardens light display. The lights were set up like flowers in bloom, and lit the snow around us in a beautiful display of colors. We ended up kissing on a bridge, listening to the water rush beneath our feet, but it went no further. When we came back to the apartment, he did the same thing as before: a kiss to the forehead and a goodnight.

Maybe my dreams are warning me that it's too good to be true?

I bite my lip and open the door, trying to drive away that negative train of thought. Just because he's backtracked on the physical aspect doesn't mean he's regretting his choices. He's here, isn't he? And all of our dates have been fantastic. I've never experienced anything like this before.

I can't tell if he's trying to sell me on his home state, or on himself. Either way, I'm steadily growing fonder of both. Just because he's been a little hot and cold on the physical front doesn't mean the dates weren't still wonderful.

"Hey," Benji says, leaning against my door frame.

I give him a once-over, soaking him in. He's got on a beanie, smothering his wavy, soft locks, and a dark Leopards sweatshirt. Pair that with his boots and his gray sweatpants – *fuck,* those really do wonders – he's the perfect combination of sexy and cozy that has me wanting to crawl into those clothes with him.

I wet my lips and drag my eyes back to his, which are crinkling in the corner from amusement. "Everything okay?" he asks.

"More than," I reply. "But I don't think I got the casual dress memo. What are we doing tonight?"

He shakes his head. "Nope. That's a surprise. But you have time to change, if you want to."

I give him another once over and nod, inviting him in.

"You really don't own much, do you?" he calls after me. I glance back to see him looking around, assessing my space.

I know what he sees. No photos on the walls, no invitations on the fridge, not even any mail left on the counters. A television, but no DVDs or video games stacked in the corner.

A bookshelf that I've slowly been stocking, but it still only contains a handful of novels.

"Yeah, well. Minimalism is a side-effect of reinventing yourself." I call through the half-closed door to my bedroom as I shuffle through my drawers, selecting my own sweater and a pair of leggings. The pants go first so I can tug the leggings on, and then I throw my nicer shirt in the corner of the room. I grab the sweater from the bed and turn back to the living room.

As I'm tugging it over my bra, I catch sight of Benji through the crack in my bedroom door. He's facing me, but his gaze is lowered, tracing the curve of my breasts. There's a heated look in his eyes, and his entire body has gone taut. When he realizes I've caught him looking, he glances away, rubbing a hand over his face. As he does, a muscle in his jaw flexes, and he clears his throat. "Sorry about that."

I flush, but not from embarrassment. It feels like a victory, knowing I do still have an effect on him. It feels like a question has been answered, and it makes me want to stride out of the room, strip back down, and wrap myself around him, see if he would replace his eyes with his hands, or even his mouth. And god...I know the things his mouth can do.

Given his reaction to being caught, though, something is still holding him back. I'm determined to find out what it is and change that.

"Are we going to a baseball game?" I ask, frowning at the stadium we pull up to. Could this place even be open in the dead of winter?

Benji shakes his head with a smile. "No. We're going roller skating. They open this place up for runners and skating during the winter." He pauses. "Does that sound okay?"

I've noticed he does this a lot. Though I've assured him I like the surprise of a date, he's always checking in on what makes me comfortable, just like his gentle touches. It's like he's creating a mental blueprint of what makes me feel safe, and pushing me to set up boundaries if I need them. It's strange, feeling so cared for. The butterflies he's been giving me for the past two weeks pick up pace at the thought, but it also makes my heart race anxiously.

I swallow. "That sounds amazing."

Ten minutes later, we're strapped into our roller skates and being told which direction to skate in by a teenage boy with a clipboard and a tone that says he takes his job *very* seriously. We both chuckle as he walks away to give instructions to someone else, and Benji stands, motioning for me to do the same and follow him.

Normally, I like to think I'm an athletic person. I've been working day and night to regain the strength and stamina I lost in those years with Austin. But the second I stand on these roller skates, I realize I'm about to be the laughing stock of the arena. I wobble like a deer on ice, sending my hands flailing out to grab onto something before my face makes friends with the floor. Just before I topple over, my hands meet Benji's large, warm ones. His grip is rock-solid, and I'm able to regain balance.

"Easy, little fighter," he says with a laugh. "Have you never done this before?"

"No," I admit, cheeks flushing, and brace for judgement. The more I'm out in the real world, past Austin's clutches, the more I realize there are so many things that I never experienced. I'm so behind on what a lot of people would consider common adventures. Skiing was one thing, but this feels like a simple and obvious failure.

His eyes simply twinkle with amusement, no trace of criticism to be found. "Well, I'm happy to give you another first, then."

He guides my movements with soft directions and gentle corrections, the absolute picture of patience. It's similar to our ski weekend, but unlike then, I catch on fairly quickly. When I can finally hold my own and notice something other than my own clumsy feet, I sneak a peek at him.

It's one thing to see Benji skating from a distance, whether in person or on the screen. I haven't missed a game since our first date at the aquarium, and I can admire his fierceness, his athleticism, and the way he finds his teammates on the ice. But when everyone on the ice is at roughly the same skill level, it's hard to notice just how much *more* talent he has than the average person.

Skating next to him now, I can see all the strength he possesses. Even hidden under sweats, moving slowly to keep pace with me, his graceful movements are obvious. His toned legs stride out flawlessly, and I have no doubt he could pick me up and make endless laps around the people skating alongside us. And when he skates ahead of me, and his strides cause his sweats to frame his ass? Well, that's just fucking distracting.

"You're so natural," I manage, trying my best not to ogle his perfect ass too much in public. There are children here, after all. "I think you're even more comfortable on skates than your own feet."

He crosses over to face me, skating backwards – *show-off* – and grins. "I might have been skating before I walked. I'm not even sure."

"Is that normal for a Minnesota boy?" I tease, attempting to catch up to him. I trip as I pick up speed, and he catches my hand again. In one swift movement, he's pivoted to my side, skating forward once more, but he doesn't let go of my hand.

"Pretty common, I'd say," he says. "Just thinking about the amount of friends that would join us in our backyard when my dad flooded the rink. We could all skate pretty young."

His brother. I gaze up at him, wondering if I should ask more about him or not. Instead, I play it safe and ask, "What about your sister?"

"Oh, she can skate, too. She just never wanted to make a career out of it." He pauses. "Not that there were that many opportunities back then, anyways. When she was fifteen, she basically had to decide if she wanted to try to work up to the Olympics or play it safe."

"That early?" I ask, and he nods.

"That's about when your life changes as an athlete. At least in hockey, anyways. That's when you're getting picked up for Juniors."

"So that's what you did?" I imagine him as a little fifteen-year-old, all gangly, with floppy hair and braces, trying his best to make the best team.

"Nah. My brother and I didn't have to. The high school hockey scene for guys in Minnesota is already super competitive. Throw in summer camps, and you're on the right track." He stops and smiles to himself, but it's a bit sad. "Then we made it work so that we ended up on the same college team."

"That's right," I murmur. "You mentioned you played in college together."

He turns that sad smile on me. "Yep. Couldn't keep the two of us separated for too long. That's when local news caught wind of us, and we kind of became a package deal. 'The golden brothers from Minnesota.' The headlines wrote themselves."

He's somehow slowed to my exact speed, our hands still intertwined and moving at the same pace. I'm amazed at his openness. Whereas I keep everything close to my chest, he offers this up to me as if it's normal to share such vulnerabilities.

"It's incredible you could play on the same teams for so long."

"Yeah," he says, but there's a new tightness to his voice, and I tell he's getting emotional.

I squeeze his hand. "What did you go to college for?"

The corner of his mouth twitches. "Business management."

"No way." I choke on a laugh. "You're such a cliché. The athlete who goes to college for his sport and skates by with a business degree on the side. Pun intended."

He laughs in earnest now, the sound deep and rich. "I'll have you know I was an aggressively average student. B's all the way."

"Hmmm. I suppose that's impressive, given how much time you probably spent flirting with women," I tease.

He shoots me an amused look. "Little fighter, is that jealousy I see?"

"Just trying to figure out how much of the college athlete cliché you fit."

"A lot of it," he admits, and the candidness of his answer briefly stuns me. "But the excitement wore off quickly. I spent most of my last two years in the gym, just trying to get drafted like my brother...and then everything happened with him."

I squeeze his hand tighter. "For what it's worth, I can see where your business major would come in handy," I say. "If you ever consider selling your photography."

Benji seems to genuinely consider this. "I never thought about it that way."

"You should. Your work is beautiful."

"Well, that's a compliment I never saw coming." He shoots me a warm look, then asks, "What did you major in?"

"Computer science."

He raises a brow. "Let me guess. Honors student?"

"Maybe," I hedge, a flush creeping over my cheeks. "Mostly out of necessity. I needed to keep my scholarships."

"And do you ever think about doing something in that field anymore?"

"Not really." My answer comes so quickly, I don't even consider hiding the truth. "I made an app and sold it off. Because of that, I'm well enough off that I don't really need to work. I just work to stay busy."

His brow rises even higher, but the question he asks next startles me. "Why the service industries? I can't imagine you get treated that well."

"Some people suck," I admit. "But it also allows me to meet so many wonderful new people, and hear so many stories. For every terrible customer, there are three more that restore my faith in humanity."

His expression turns unreadable. Before I can question it, though, a group of kids zoom by, darting around us, whooping and hollering.

"Shit!" I stumble into Benji as I attempt to avoid a collision with the pint-sized terrors. His arms immediately wrap around me from behind, warm and toned. He pulls me in close, his grip just tight enough to keep me in place, but not uncomfortable. I wobble on my skates, attempting to regain my bearings.

For a brief moment, my ass lines up with his hips, and I slow, enjoying the feel of how our bodies meld together. I can't help but push back into him, and I hear his sharp inhale next to my ear. His body tenses and his arms tighten further around me, almost imperceptibly, but it's the hard length I feel against me that tells me it's had the effect I want.

I push my luck and grind back into him, harder, just enough that he knows it's intentional. He grunts and pulls himself back away from me, forcing distance between us. My heart plummets in my chest, but when I turn to face him, I can see the strained look on his face as he shakes his head at me. There's desire there, mixed with amusement. In one stride, he's right up at my side once more, and when he leans in to murmur in my ear, one hand slides down, giving my ass a soft squeeze. "You're going to get me in trouble, aren't you?" he murmurs.

Desire pools in my stomach at his touch, and I meet his mischievous gaze with one of my own. "A girl can hope."

He pulls back with a chuckle, and we continue our skate around the arena for several more laps, making idle chatter. But the heat his one touch stoked in my core never quite goes away, and I decide that hoping isn't enough. I'm going to have to take matters into my own hands.

When we get back to the apartment, I press the button for his floor first. He shoots me a confused look, but doesn't question it, and when the elevator doors open, I take his hand, pulling him to his apartment. He follows willingly and opens the door, inviting me in.

The second the door closes, I press myself flush against him, pushing him to the wall. Though he could easily stand his ground, he allows me to guide him there, hitting the wall with a thud. I pull his face down to mine and meet his lips, kissing him with enough urgency to let him know I don't want this to end with a forehead kiss.

It takes him a moment to respond, just long enough for panic to build in my mind that I've missed the mark, that I've misinterpreted the signals. But in the next second, he's groaning into my mouth, winding his arms around my waist. My heart leaps at the small victory, and I dare to push it further. My tongue darts out, skimming across his lips. To my relief, he lets me in instantly, tugging me closer and responding with a sweep of his own tongue.

I kiss him back like a woman starved, my hands running over his jaw and winding into his hair, pushing his beanie off. One of his hands dips down, his thumb dragging across the waistband of my leggings. More. I need *more.* I arch into him, lifting a leg to wind around him.

He moans, and in a flash, I'm lifted in the air. My legs wrap fully around him on instinct, my hips lined up at the perfect angle to feel him, harder now than he was earlier. I sling my arms over his shoulder and give his silky hair a tug.

He pulls back to rest his forehead against mine. "Jesus," he mutters. "I need you to tell me – what do you want from me?"

The air is thick with tension and desire, and I'm determined to cut through it. I don't want to lose my nerve now.

"I want you to sleep with me."

Chapter 27

Lyssa

Benji lowers me to the ground. We stare at each other, like two competitors sizing each other up. I tip my chin up, holding firm, but Benji is the first one to speak.

"Are you sure?" he asks. "We don't have to – I mean, I'm trying to take it slow with you, for you–"

"Stop. Please," I say, cutting off wherever he's headed, not only for him but for myself. I'm grateful to finally understand he's been holding back purely for my sake. Even now as he strokes his thumb across my palm, I can see plainly that he has no reservations, only curiosity and desire.

But a part of me worries that I'll take the out he's given me. When he only kissed me on our previous dates, my emotions ranged from guilt to relief to frustration. Perhaps I really *wasn't* ready.

The barrier I had up in the hot tub is gone. I'm no longer hiding behind another identity, pretending to be confident, carefree Lisa, fueled by liquor and lust. We aren't just going to part ways after this, with him being none the wiser about my past. This is real, and vulnerable, and *terrifying*.

"I want to," I say, and watch as Benji blinks. "I want to do this with you. But I need..." I trail off and swallow.

"What do you need, little fighter?" Benji winds his fingers into mine, holding me steady. "Tell me, and I'll give it to you."

As I stare at this beautiful, patient man before me, I'm surprised to feel anger bubbling up. How *dare* Austin take this from me for so long? I can't stand how much space he's taken up in my mind, especially when I have something so potentially wonderful in front of me.

I want to change it. I want to think of nothing but the pleasure I can chase with Benji. And that starts, completely, today.

"Make me forget," I whisper. "Make me forget everything but you."

He squeezes his eyes shut and remains silent, letting the words linger for a long moment. Just as I'm about to question him, he mutters a soft curse and leans forward, his lips crashing into mine.

He devours me like if he didn't, it might be our last kiss. He backs us into his bedroom, his lips barely leaving mine as we go. Every stroke of his tongue is a reclaiming, and his fingers skim over my body like he's inspecting a piece of art, tracing each dip and curve. In a few soft touches, my sweatshirt has been lifted over my head, and he's shed his as well.

We find our way onto the bed, and I skim my hands over his warm, muscular shoulders, shuddering as he runs a finger under one strap of my bra. "What do you like?" he murmurs against my mouth. "Tell me how to make you feel good."

"I...I don't know," I stammer. My mind tumbles down the dark path of my memories, searching for an answer that isn't there. I can't even get back to the early days with Austin, trying to remember if the sex was good or if I just didn't know better. Had I ever really examined what felt good for me, or had I always let it be about *him?*

I squeeze my eyes shut, unsure how to voice this as an answer.

There's a soft brush of fingertips against my hair, pushing it behind my ear. I open my eyes to see Benji's warm, brown gaze. "Don't ice me out," he says. "Don't do that to me. Not now."

"I..." My voice is little more than a whisper. "I don't know what to tell you. I've never...thought about it that way. Thought about it as something for me."

His lips purse in the barest sign of disapproval, and when he glances away, I notice his jaw tick. "I'm sorry," I whisper. *Shit.* A swell of emotion threatens to consume me. I can't believe I've disappointed him already.

"What? No." He shakes his head. "Don't apologize. Please. I'm just upset nobody has ever asked you that question. You should know exactly what you want, and you should be able to ask for it." His expression is heated as he fixes his gaze back on me. "And when you ask for it, I want to be able to give it to you. However you want, whenever you want."

My breath catches at his words, and I lick my lips. He tracks the movement and shakes his head again, running a hand over his face. "I guess we'll just have to learn as we go." He shifts on the bed to position himself between my legs, his hands hovering at the waistband of my leggings. His eyes flick to mine, looking for silent permission, and I nod.

He tugs them down, running his hands over my bare skin as he goes. I shiver at the touch, but he's careful to leave my panties on. I can tell restraint is warring in him as he eyes the blue lace, dragging his eyes over the two pieces of fabric keeping me from being entirely exposed to him. After a moment, he shifts forward to kiss me again. As he deepens the kiss, he runs a hand over the fabric of my bra, then down to my panties, his hand dipping between my legs.

"Fuck," he groans, breaking our kiss and ducking his head. I feel his hot breath fanning against my ear. "You're already wet. Is this all for me?"

I arch against him as he drags his thumb over my clit, rubbing in a firm circle over the fabric. "All for you," I gasp.

"Jesus," he hisses out through clenched teeth, his hands trailing to my back, reaching the clasp of my bra. He pauses, the question back in his eyes. My breath is coming in short pants now, and it's all I can do to nod. The second I do, the pressure of the band releases, and my bra drops to the ground, leaving my chest exposed to him. He gazes hungrily at me, a reverence to his look that has me flushing hot before he even puts his hands on me.

In the next second he does, though, taking my breasts in his hands and palming them. When he brushes his thumbs over the peaks of my nipples, I moan softly. "There we go," he murmurs, his eyes shuttering with desire. "Found something. Let's keep going, then."

He replaces one hand with his mouth, and I press into the feel of his warm lips against my breast, gasping when he circles his tongue over my nipple. *More,* I think, lifting my hips to chase the surge of feeling he's giving me. *I need more.*

As if I said the thought out loud, he gives one last flick of his tongue and moves to settle lower, trailing kisses across my skin as he goes. I eye him with a combination of desire and apprehension.

"Tell me if you want me to stop," he says, slowly curling his fingers around the sides of my panties. When I simply squirm, he grins and tugs them down my legs, putting them in the pocket of his sweatpants. *Unfair,* I think, *that he still has those on.*

Before I can voice this, though, he's moving up the bed and shifting my legs, situating himself between them, my heels resting on his shoulders. He gives me a wicked smirk as I realize his intentions. "You don't have to –"

I'm cut off as the warm pad of his tongue is pressed to my core. He trails his way up at a leisurely pace, the pressure deliriously perfect. My protest twists into a moan, and his hum of approval vibrates against me, adding a spark to the pleasure already coursing through me. His tongue swirls around my clit, and then he *sucks,* causing me to arch and reach for him, desperate to cling on.

I find his soft locks of hair and run my fingers through them, gripping tightly as he combines his sucking kisses with firm passes of his tongue. He wraps his large hands around my thighs, gentle but firm enough to hold me in place as I grind against him.

"Benji, I..." I trail off into a garbled sigh as the pressure builds. I squeeze my legs against him tighter, rolling my hips into him, and he responds by sucking harder, followed by insistent strokes of his tongue. I chase the pleasure, crying out as I rushing toward the edge. He moans into me at the noise, a deep, throaty sound against my core that causes me to topple right over that edge.

But still, Benji doesn't relent, carrying me through the orgasm with warm, firm lashes of his tongue that drag the pleasure out longer than I thought possible. When I finally come back down to earth, he's resting his face against the inside of my thigh, dark eyes watching me expectantly.

"Holy shit," is all I can manage.

Benji grins and rubs his face against my thigh, the scruff from the shadow of a beard he carries tickling my leg. "So we've found another thing you like," he says, a low note of triumph in his voice.

I'm tempted to kick him for the cocky tone, but my legs are closer to Jell-O than bone at the moment, so all I can do is roll my eyes and smile. He works his way out from between my legs and stands. I eye the evidence of his own desire, straining to free itself from his sweatpants. I reach for him, but he catches my hands before I can reach his waistband. He shakes his head. "We don't have to," he says.

Not this again.

"But..." I trail off, insecurity rearing its ugly head. "Do you not want to?"

"Fuck, babe, of course I want to." He runs a hand through his hair, and my eyes can't seem to decide where they want to land. The stretch of his ab muscles, the flex of his arm as it drops from his hair, the divots that dance over his hips and into his sweatpants. "The sound of you saying my name while I ate your delicious pussy...fuck, of course I want to know what it would be like to have you doing that while I'm inside of you."

This man and his words. My legs clench, already in anticipation of more. "Then why not?"

He settles onto the bed next to me and fixes me with an intense look. "Because I'm not sure I can control myself. It's been a long time for me, too, and you're..." His gaze drops to my body, completely bare to him, and he trails a finger from my shoulder down between my breasts, then over my hip. I shiver, and his gaze darkens. "Well, you're you. God, just look at you. You're fucking stunning."

His words make my heart swell, and I pull him into me, kissing him with a fervor I hope explains how much I want him, tasting what he's already done to me. He groans, and his hands wrap around me, pulling me into his chest so that I'm straddling him.

I grind into him, and his grip tightens for a moment before he releases me. He settles back into the pillows, eyeing me as I stay seated above him, and murmurs, "There's a condom in the nightstand."

I immediately lean over to locate it. His gaze follows me the whole time, and when I go to remove his pants, my hands shaking slightly, he shifts me off of him, taking the condom from my hands as he does. I can't help but stare at his cock as he removes the rest of his clothes. It's beautiful but intimidating, the cumulation of all that corded muscle above. He rolls the condom on with ease and leans back, head resting on the pillow as he slides his arms underneath.

I simply stare at him. What now?

As if he can read my mind, he swallows. "I told you...I can't be the one in control here. You have to be. This all happens at your pace."

"Okay."

I can do this...right? This is what I wanted. And I see what he's doing here. He doesn't want to get too caught up and do something that's too much for me. But that doesn't stop me from wanting this. Wanting him.

I swing my leg over him, straddling him once more, and sigh as my clit touches the hard length of him. His cock twitches in response, and he hisses through his teeth, but doesn't move a muscle. Instead, I'm left to rock against his erection at my pace. I grind up and down on him, getting a feel for just how much will be inside of me. Free to do what I want, I trail my fingers up and down his bare skin as I go, tracing his impressive expanse of muscles, the beautiful detailing in his tattoos, the trail of curled hair leading down to where my own desire is pooling.

The anticipation is making me halfway delirious, but there's an insidious part of me that's still afraid to let go, to potentially have everything change. There's power in sex, especially with emotions attached, and what if I give up too much of mine in this? There's no going back once it's done. My hands go still on his chest and my movements slow.

"Little fighter. Look at me."

I do, taking in his warm, sincere expression as he continues. "If you want me to talk you through this, I can do that. You're with me. It's you and me. Is this still what you want?"

He shifts his hips, rolling me over him once more, and desire sparks anew, turning my core liquid. "Yes," I say around a moan. "Hell yes."

"Then have me," he says, his voice husky. "Use me. Take the pleasure you need. It's all yours."

His encouragement spurs me on, and I skim a hand over his broad, firm chest, lifting my hips and positioning him with my other hand. He inhales at my touch, then exhales sharply as his cock brushes against my entrance. When I sink down onto him, we groan in unison.

It takes a precious minute to get all the way seated as I adjust to him stretching me. Once I am, I'm so absorbed in the feeling of his size inside me that I almost don't register the way his body trembles beneath me. "Benji?"

"I'm fine," he says, but his voice is noticeably strained. "God, just look at you. You take me so fucking well."

Confidence blooms in me at his words. I smile and, slowly, begin moving. The pleasure is immediate, unfurling inside me with each rock of my hips, and I experiment with different ways to roll and move. And fuck, the control is intoxicating. The way my movements cause Benji to curse or groan softly, the heated lust sparkling in his gaze as he stares up at me, encouraging me to take more. I sink down on top of him, moving faster, chasing the pleasure burning and building inside me for the second time.

"Jesus Christ," he rasps, his arms twitching as he fights the urge to remove them from behind his head. "Such a good girl. Use me to make yourself come."

His words, paired with the fullness inside me and the brushing of my clit against him as I rock forward once more sends me straight off the deep end. I arch my back and cry out, tightening around him. His throat works and he squeezes his eyes shut, his hips lifting to meet me as I come all over him. It's euphoric, and it's all I can do to hang on, my hands and thighs gripping him beneath me.

"Can I touch you?" he asks after a long moment. It sounds like his throat has been coated in sandpaper. My chest rises and falls as I nod, attempting to catch my breath. With a throaty growl, Benji pushes up and pulls me flush against him, sliding a wet kiss across my mouth before transferring his hands to my hips, lifting me off him just slightly. It's then that I realize he is still rock hard.

"Wait – you didn't –?" I ask, but my question transforms into a cry as he thrusts up into me. "Oh, *god!*"

"I didn't, because I wanted one more from you," he murmurs, slamming his cock back up into me. "And I told you, I wanted to hear you scream my name."

Another thrust, and pleasure shoots through my body, rendering me limp, but it doesn't matter, because he's holding me up, driving himself upward and into me, over and over again.

I collapse forward, bracing myself on his chest, and when the new angle he's hitting makes my nerves go from sizzling to full-on ablaze, I cry out the only words I have left. "Oh – god – please – *Benji!*"

I squeeze around him and this time he explodes with me, his breathing choppy in my ear as he holds me tightly. We ride it out together, nearly frozen in the moment, before collapsing next to each other.

We're both too hot to remain fully joined, but we're still touching with a hand here, a foot there. I focus on catching my breath, enjoying the aftershock of pleasure still coursing through me. When the ecstasy subsides, I roll to my side, taking stock of how Benji is faring.

He mirrors my movement, shifting so that we're facing each other. His eyes are gleaming with a sated expression and another, deeply affectionate one that I don't try to analyze, because it's a dangerous thing to put to much too thought into. As we gaze at one another, his expression becomes tender, and he moves to cover me with the blanket. His hand hovers at the top of the blanket and, seeing his indecision, I grab his hand first.

I fiddle with his fingers, taking note of how large and calloused his hands are. I've watched him use them for sport and for violence. Yet tonight, he waited until I felt completely in control and came not once, but twice, before using them to chase his own pleasure.

When I raise my gaze from his hands back to his face, I find an adorable shyness there. "Was that...was that okay?" he asks.

I huff a soft laugh, too exhausted to do much more. "It was more than okay, Benji. It was amazing. It was..."

It was perfect.

Shit.

Chapter 28

Benji

"So, I have an idea." Grant plops down next to me, shoveling tater tots into his mouth. We're in Nevada for the weekend to play against the Cavaliers, but it feels strange. Jordie's been called up for a few games with the Minnesota Chill, so we're watching his NHL game from the couch, cheering him on while we chow down on some wings. It's what we all dream of, so even though I don't love the way it feels being here without him, I'm stoked for the guy. It just sucks to be without him *and* without Lyssa.

I know it's not realistic to expect her to want to hop on the road with me after a handful of dates, but after this week, I'm having a hard time keeping away from her, even for the game I love. I'm states away, but she's still in my head and under my skin. I'm finding myself constantly replaying the view from between her legs, how responsive she was to my mouth, her hands gripping my hair. The way she looked, rocking on top of me, her mouth parted on a sigh as the pleasure overtook her. The way she squeezed my cock, causing me to nearly black out from the feeling as she screamed my name.

It's never been like that for me. On one hand, it's fucking terrifying. On the other...I'm just counting the hours until I get to do it again.

"Yo," Grant says, snapping his fingers in front of my face.

"Sorry, man." I cough, returning my focus to him. "Idea?"

"So, I think we should pull one more prank on the rook. He's been racking up the goals, getting all full of himself. How's this sound: We swap numbers in his phone before our next night out, and switch his sweetie with Coach's number. Then we play some truth or dare type game, and tell him to text his girl "I can't wait to see you in bed later tonight" or something like that. He'll think, huh, this isn't so bad, but he won't realize he's actually texting Coach." Grant beams. "Can you imagine the look on Coach's face during practice the next morning?"

I grab a wing and frown at him. "You came up with this whole idea while taking a shit?"

"It's when I do my best thinking."

My phone lights up, and I see "L" pop up on the screen.

Lyssa told me how Andi calls her that to avoid confusion, and I immediately jumped on it. Not only is it easier, but I'm also happy to know I'm also not the only person she's confided in. "Look, as long as you keep it safe and fun," I say to Grant. "We're better than that old school shit. Don't take it too far."

Grant salutes me, and I swipe across on my phone, smiling as Lisa's face pops up. She's on her couch, and I can see the tip of Winston's tail in the corner of the screen. "Well, hey, stranger," she says.

"Well, hey yourself," I respond. Winston's tail starts thumping at the sound of my voice, and I feel the couch shift as Grant leans over.

"Hey, Lisa!" he shouts, waving a wing at her from over my shoulder.

"So this is your natural state," she says with a grin. "Sitting on a couch, wings in hand."

"You got me," he replies around a mouthful of chicken, and returns his attention to the TV.

I lean back with a smile. "Are you watching the game, too?"

She nods, her eyes drifting over the phone, I assume to her own TV. "I am. I've only seen Jordie once or twice, though." She pauses, then says, "I have been hearing the name Polk a lot, though. If only I had you here to drink with."

"Oh, don't you worry." I shift to pick up my beer and waggle it in front of my phone. "We can play a long distance drinking game."

She grins and as if on cue, the announcer yells, *"Oh, god, what a great opportunity between the legs there!"*

At this, we all laugh and cheer, and Lyssa gets up to walk to her fridge, putting her phone down to search for a drink. The way her phone sits, propped up on her counter, gives me the perfect view of her tiny lounge shorts, which pull tight over her ass as she bends over to locate a beer. My mind drifts to the thought of bending her over in that position the next time we're together, and I'm forced to adjust myself in my pants.

"So, remind me again. Jordie's being called up for just a few games with the Chill to start?" she asks, fully vertical again and cracking her beer. I'm grateful for the change in subject, even if the sound of her speaking my language makes something flutter in my stomach.

"Yep. He's really holding his own, though. If he keeps crushing it, he'll be in the league full time sooner rather than later."

"Good for him," she muses. "But that's a bummer for you if you lose him."

"No bummer." Okay, *small* bummer, but I'm beyond proud of him. "That's the end goal for all of us."

"You're such a good friend." She smiles at me, and I swear, I damn near flush at the praise. I'm used to getting compliments on my game, but the way she talks about me as a person makes me happy on a deeper level.

We sit there for a little while, simply drinking and cheering every time Jordie takes the ice or something sexual is said. It feels like it could be a new normal for me, and it does funny things to my chest.

So, that's why when I ask what her plans are for Thanksgiving this coming week, and she doesn't have any, I find myself saying, "Come to mine. Everyone would love you."

She's silent for so long, I wonder if the connection has been lost. Finally, she shifts on the screen, and I realize she simply hasn't said anything, which makes it so, *so* much worse. "Benji...I don't think that's such a good idea."

My heart sinks, even as my head realizes it's a perfectly logical response. "Yeah, no, sorry," I reply, clearing my throat. "I just don't want you to be alone on a holiday."

She shoots me a tentative smile. "I won't be. I'll probably end up going with Andi, or maybe Paul and his family. Don't worry about me; I'll find something to do." She pauses, then says, "I should probably go clean up around here. I'll see you when you get back, though, yeah?"

"Yeah." I swallow. "I'll see you when I get back."

Grant stares at me as I hang up the phone.

"Did you just invite a girl that you've been on three dates with – that took ages to convince to go out with you – to come to your family Thanksgiving?"

I know he's right, but the embarrassment of the situation makes me go on the defensive. "Oh, yeah? At least I'm shooting my shot with my girl. When are you going to admit your feelings to the girl you've been sleeping with for months?"

"Oh, get fucked."

I scrub a hand over my face. "I did. That's how I got here."

It's been a long few days, and today is looking like it'll be another one. Ever since I offered for Lyssa to come to my family's place for Thanksgiving, she's pulled back, claiming she's been too busy to see me, even after we got back from Nevada. We still talk every day, sure, but I can tell she's put more distance between us.

I've been working hard to keep my mind focused on our last few games, and at least that's been paying off. This is the last game before Thanksgiving, but of course, it's against the Pirates. I work my way through our warm-ups, trying to keep my mind off the fact that Roberts is back on my ice and that Lyssa is in the crowd.

I avoid glancing to the other side of the ice, but my eyes can't help but travel up to find Lyssa in the crowd. She's sitting with Andi, wearing a black Leopards sweater.

Wait. Is that my sweater? I think back to the last time we were together, and wonder if she snagged my sweater on the way out. The thought makes me grin. The fact she's claiming me as hers in this small way has my body wanting to respond in kind. The only thing hotter would be to see her up there in my jersey. Fuck...now there's an idea.

I shake off the thought and work to keep my head in the moment as we transition into the game.

If anything, having her in the stands makes me work harder. We set up beautiful plays, moving the puck like a dream, and it's a tie game at the end of the first. When we enter the second period, it's clear that there's a shift in the energy. We're dominating, spending most of the period in the Pirates' zone, leaving our end of the ice looking pristine. It's almost laughable, and I can tell Roberts is flustered, which makes it all the better.

In the middle of the chaos, there's a sudden break in the traffic, and I see a straight line to Levi in front of the net. I send the puck sailing his way, and watch out of the corner of my eye as the goalie follows the pass, squaring up to Levi to make the save. Levi sees it too and fakes a shot, only to send the puck back my way instead.

I catch his pass and shoot in the same breath, sending the puck spiraling into the net. It clinks decisively against one bar before pinging off the other, finally settling into the back of the net. God, that is one of my favorite sounds in the world.

My linemates barrel into me to celebrate, but as we break apart and skate to center ice to line back up, I can't help but look for Lyssa in the crowd. She's leaning forward, a proud smile painted on her face as she gazes at me. When the announcer roars, "Gooooallll, number seventeen, Benjamin Esteeessss!" she gives me a subtle thumbs up, and I can't help but point at her and return the thumbs up.

Her responding blush is a favorite view of mine.

"That your new sweetie, Estes?" Roberts skates up behind me, taking his time lining back up.

I don't respond, so he continues. "I wouldn't mind taking a run at her. She's a sniper."

I clench my jaw and take a beat to respond. When I do, I work to keep my tone level. "Yeah, it must suck that you can't get your dick wet. They usually take one look at that ugly mug and run the other way."

He sputters angrily, but the ref blows the whistle, and his attention is forced to the puck drop. I keep a careful distance from him the rest of the period, knowing it's only a matter of time before he blows up.

Grant is easy to rile up, but quick to calm down, and you always see him coming. He has his limits and he fights fair. Roberts, on the other hand, is sneaky and cheap. And man, that fucker can hold a grudge.

I start relaxing halfway through the third, and that's where my mistake is made. Grant makes a beautiful pass up the ice to me, and it's just me, the Pirates goalie, and one Pirates player –

Roberts. I turn on the gas, barreling up the ice to put distance between me and Roberts, but even as I approach the goalie, I can hear him working to catch up to me. The crowd's roaring grows, and I adjust the puck on my stick, gearing up to shoot.

A gloved hand whips out, grabbing at my jersey.

I lose my balance, just enough that the puck fires off my stick as nothing more than a wobble. The Pirates goalie saves it easily, and I turn my momentum away from the net to the corner. I'm able to slow myself, and note the ref's hand, raised high in the air. *Penalty.*

"Penalty shot!" The crowd screams, and I grin.

Just as I fully put on the brakes, ready to head back up to center ice, I'm shoved firmly in the back – two hands, one stick – and the boards rush up to greet my face with a sickening crack. There's angry shouting in the crowd, but all I can hear is Roberts as he leans over me, saying, "I'll get my dick wet when I fuck your girl. Just imagine those pretty lips wrapped around my –"

There's an oomph and the shuddering of boards as he's – presumably – slammed into them. I scramble to my feet with a groan, but I'm pushed back against the boards as both teams join the fray. I note the warmth trickling down to my upper lip and blink to clear my vision. Grant has Roberts by the jersey, and he's working to free his other arm, which is being held back by other players. "Finish that sentence," he snarls at Roberts. "Finish it, and see how many teeth you'll have left."

I'm tempted to join in, but my gaze slides involuntarily into the crowd, where I find Lyssa's face. Her eyes are wide and worried, and all I can think of is finding her the night of the bar fight, working to recollect herself. I don't want to give her another reason to shut down on me.

By the time I turn back, the refs are already breaking up the fight, making the decision for me. Roberts is led to the penalty box and I'm led back to the bench, where I'm handed a wet washcloth. I pat my face as they decide what to do with all of us, and peer down at the bright crimson that immediately takes over the fabric. I groan inwardly. I'm not ready to deal with another broken nose.

The decision comes back – five minute major for Roberts, penalty shot for me – and I toss the cloth back on the bench, sliding my gloves back on. The puck is placed in center ice, and it's just me and the Pirates goalie. I size him up, ignoring the warmth already trickling slowly back down my nose. It's easy to tune everything else out when there's just one obstacle to focus on ahead of me. I've practiced this so many times I could do it in my sleep.

I start by swinging wide across the ice, picking up the puck as I go, fast at first and then slowing down as I approach the goalie, dribbling the puck carefully. At the last minute, I fake a shot, kicking my leg out. When the goalie bites, I swoop to the side, sinking the puck in the back of the net.

I can hear the roar of the crowd, and I smile to myself. I'll be proud of that one later, but right now, I just need to make sure I don't bleed on the fucking ice.

When I settle back on the bench, Highcloud sidles up to me and hands me a fresh washcloth. "Up by two, three minutes left. And you put Roberts out for the game." He gives me a congratulatory nudge, and I nod in thanks.

"You know he did that because you're pissing him off, right?" Coach says as he comes up behind me. I nod, checking the washcloth. It's still pink, but at least it isn't taking over the fabric like it was before. He continues. "You're beating his game on every level tonight, and it was the only thing he could think of doing to keep up."

"He wants to get in my head," I mutter, and toss the cloth to the side. My nose is still throbbing, but at least the worst of the bleeding has stopped. I'll be able to finish the game.

"And you didn't let him. Keep up the good work, kid." He claps me on the shoulder. "Things are looking good for Jordie. We might be needing you to finish out the season as our captain. Get eyes back on you as the next Leopards call-up." I turn to look up at him, and the pride in his eyes is clear as he adds, "You've earned it."

Chapter 29

Benji

The knock comes *far* too fast for the game we're playing.

I groan, shooting a glare down the table at my sister. She tosses a sickly sweet smile back at me, ignoring the complaints that come from all the others around the table. She's just announced that we all get one more chance to swap our cards before we have to show them, and her knock means she's convinced she's got the best hand.

We're playing our family's version of Golf, a card game that involves memory, luck, and – most importantly – money. It's the perfect sedentary game for a post-Thanksgiving meal, which is why it's been our tradition for as long as I can remember. Anyone who gets invited has two rules: They need to bring cash to play Golf, and they need to pretend they don't see our great-grandma Catherine cheating at it. Every year, she gets a bit more obvious as she peeks at her cards and slides one or two up her sleeves, but at ninety-four, it's an unspoken rule that she can do whatever the hell she wants. I think she knows it, which is why she doesn't bother to be sneaky anymore.

"God, really, Gabi?" Her friend Mia groans as she flips her cards over. They're all high numbers, and they don't match, so she's easily got a score in the twenties or more. "You wrecked me."

Gabi smirks, and I can't help but wonder if we have the same shit-eating grin. We have the same dark hair and eyes, and I've been known to make a similar face when I think I have a round of Golf in the bag. "Can't help it, I was dealt a good hand. You know the rules."

And she does. Mia has been coming to our Thanksgiving for the past three years. Her family life is rough, and we have a firm open-door policy for anyone: friends, family, and acquaintances alike. The food is always overflowing, and our parents are warm and welcoming. There's a reason us kids keep coming back to the area, even when life takes us to another state for a while. It's rare to look at your family and realize they've done it right, but we're blessed enough to have that. Even when a piece of that family is now missing.

My eyes skim over the seat where my brother always used to sit, and I draw in a ragged breath. Fucking hell. Grief tends to hit hardest when you think you're doing *so* well, painting the happiest moments over in shades of grey. I flip my cards over and count, forcing my thoughts back to the present. "Eleven," I announce.

Everyone takes their turn announcing their scores, with the winner being my great-grandma Catherine. The rest of us fold down a corner of our bills, accepting the loss, and say nothing about the ace that drops out of her cardigan as she collects the money that's had all four corners fully folded.

"How's your nose?" Alice, Gabi's wife, asks as the cards are shuffled and redealt. She's leaning over Gabi, her blonde bob shifting as she tilts her head to examine my nose. She tucks stray pieces of hair behind her ear again and frowns at whatever she sees on my face.

I shrug, brushing off her scrutiny. She's a nurse, and she's always worrying over my inuries. "The medical team checked it out after the game. It's sore, but it's not broken."

"I can't believe that Roberts is still such an asshole," Gabi scoffs. "You'd think he'd grow out of that."

"Yeah, well, I think when you're that kind of asshole, you stay that kind of asshole for life. It's a permanent condition."

"It's a shame he's actually good," Alice puts in. "If you're gonna be a dick, you shouldn't be allowed to have talent, too."

I laugh at that, and Gabi tosses me a card, giving me a long look before moving to toss more cards down the table.

"What's that look for?"

"I don't know," she says. "Is there something else you want to tell us about the other night?"

"What do you mean?"

"Oooh, right," Alice gasps, her face brightening. "Did you point at someone in the crowd after your first goal? We saw it on TV."

Shit. I feel my cheeks burn. "I think you're both seeing things."

"Yeah, no." Gabi hums, exchanging a knowing look with Alice. One of them interrogating me is hard to navigate, and they become supercharged when they're together. It's impressive, but scary. "I don't think so. I think it has to do with that girl you were hung up on a few weeks ago."

"There's nothing to tell," I argue, even though I know it's already useless.

"Sure. Agree to disagree."

"That's just because you like to disagree with me, don't you?"

Gabi pins me with that classic smirk. "No."

I sigh and organize my cards, peeking at the bottom two – only once, as allowed – though I promptly forget what they are as my mind wanders to Lyssa. We talked briefly the other day, so I know she'll be celebrating Thanksgiving at Andi's place. I hope she has a good time there, but I still can't help but wish she were here at my side. My mom would have fawned over her, and my dad would've given his curt nod of approval. She would have held her own with Alice and Gabi, made friends with Mia, and we could have all laughed at how obvious great-grandma Catherine is with her cards.

I know it was too soon to invite her into this world, but I also know this world is ready for her when she is.

"I invited her here," I mutter.

"What?" Gabi barks out a laugh. "Oh, Benj. Way to scare her off."

"Why would that scare her off?" Mia shoots us a quizzical look. "The Estes Thanksgiving is awesome!"

"Well, *she* doesn't know that," Gabi replies. "All she knows is Benji just invited her to meet our entire family. As awesome as we are, that's a big step."

"Who wants pie?" my mom calls, as if to underscore the point. "We've got apple and pumpkin, with ice cream or whipped cream."

We all raise our hands obediently, and she takes our orders, heading back to the kitchen. Mia and Alice go to help, and while we wait for dessert, I type out a message to Lyssa.

Me: What's your Thanksgiving dessert of choice? Apple or pumpkin pie?

L: Hmmm. Depends. Is the apple pie warmed up?

Me: Let's say yes.

L: Do I get ice cream with it?

Me: Obviously.

L: Then how could I say no to that?

Me: But pumpkin's the classic!

L: NOTHING is more classic than good old apple pie, a la mode

Me: Pumpkin hater.

L:

I grin down at my phone, and Gabi pokes my shoulder. "It's good to see you like this."

"Careful, now," I say. "Don't want to jinx anything."

"Ah, how can she resist? You just have to turn up that Estes charm."

"She's right," Alice says, sliding two plates piled high with pie in our direction. She leans down and gives Gabi a kiss. "We can't resist that Estes charm."

My phone buzzes, and I look down to see another text from Lyssa.

L: Want to hang out tomorrow?

"See?" Gabi exclaims, shamelessly leaning over to read my texts. "Can't resist. Oh, and she's right," she adds, shoveling a piece of pie onto her spoon. "Apple all the way."

Chapter 30

BENJI

The moment Lyssa's door swings open, there's fire in her gaze, and I'm momentarily stunned by the deep blue of her eyes.

My first thought is *fuck, she's beautiful.* Even in leggings and a t-shirt, this woman is breathtaking.

My second thought as the fire in her eyes registers is *fuck, I'm in trouble.*

"I can't believe you," she says.

I'm thrown off by how she can put so much intensity into her tone without so much as raising her voice. "What?"

I truly don't understand where this is going. Is she mad that I couldn't come over until late? It's a little after nine, but we had a team meeting to discuss Jordie's transition and a celebratory send-off. I'd told her as much, but perhaps she's sick of my unpredictable schedule. My chest constricts at the thought that this might be her deal-breaker.

"You just expected me to stand by and watch while you get tossed into the boards like a sack of potatoes?"

I wince. Not gonna lie, that visual is a hit to the ego.

She continues. "And you gushed blood all over, probably broke your nose, then just – nothing? You say nothing about it, just move right on the next day to talk about *pie?*"

Ah, shit. Yeah, that probably wasn't the best move.

I rub the back of my neck. "It ended up being just fine. Nothing was actually broken."

"Nothing was actually broken?" She stares at me like I've sprouted an additional head. "Did you say something to set him off?"

What the hell?

I cross my arms, more than a little offended at the insinuation. "Why would you say that?"

"I don't know, why else would he do something like that unprovoked?"

"He *was* provoked," I scoff. "I was scoring, riding high, and he didn't want to see me back at the top of my game."

Her brow furrows, as though this concept is entirely new to her. I sigh.

"Listen. I've played with Roberts before. We have a history, and it's not a great one. We were always competing for the same slots, and pressure like that...it makes some into diamonds, and it cracks others. We both made it pro in the end, but let's just say, it left some cracks in Roberts."

I gesture into her apartment in a silent question, and after a second, she moves aside, letting me in.

"Do you want some water?" she asks, her tone softer now. I nod, taking the peace offering.

While she wanders to the kitchen, I go to her couch and Winston hops up beside me. My hand automatically goes to scratch behind his ears. He wiggles closer, tongue lolling happily out, fanning me with his disgusting breath. I grin at him and do my best not to inhale.

"So, he's just jealous," Lyssa says, giving me the glass of water and taking a seat next to me.

I shrug and stare into the water glass. "Maybe? He's made it very clear he doesn't think I deserve everything my brother had."

And sometimes, I don't, either. I don't voice this portion out loud.

"Jealousy, in my experience, boils down to fear. He's just afraid he's not as good as you." Lyssa takes a thoughtful sip of her own water. "And he's using everything he can to tear you down. Including being a piece of shit about your brother. That's the lowest of the low."

I hum. She's right – I don't know many guys in the league that would stoop that low. In fact, talking shit about my brother is something nobody else has ever done. My own team is reluctant to mention him to me, even if it's something positive. It's just not done.

"True. Even though Grant's a menace out there, he's not going to take it off the ice. He'll give a guy ten stitches on the ice during a fight, and then they'll be grabbing beers together later that night."

She shoots me a disbelieving look, and I toss back a half-smile. "We're just wired that way, I guess. We know when it's gone too far, and even when we're riled up, we can leave it all on the ice. But some guys...they're just rats, through and through. It's cutthroat out there in the AHL, and they don't have any lines they won't cross."

She bites her lip. "So you really didn't say anything? Did Grant, when he got there?"

"No," I shake my head. "Grant was just protecting me. Actually –" I give a soft laugh. "–he was protecting *you.*"

"What?" Lyssa straightens, the water in her glass sloshing.

"Roberts was trying to start shit by talking about you."

"Oh. Wow."

"Yeah."

She glances down at her glass, then peers back up at me through her lashes. "And you're really okay, then?"

"I am." My lips twitch in amusement. "Sweetheart, were you worried for me?"

"Of course I was!" She sets her glass down to glare at me, but this time, her expression is no fire and all wide-eyed concern. "I watched you turn an entire washcloth red with your blood! They put it on the big screen!"

"Ah." I wave a hand dismissively. "I'm sure you've caused a few bloody noses while boxing."

"I haven't, actually," she huffs. "Though I'm considering it now, just to knock the stupidity out of you."

I fake a dramatic gasp. "You'd *give me* a bloody nose, just to teach me a lesson about *getting* a bloody nose?"

She gives a nod so serious I can't help but grin.

"Such beautiful ways you show me you care." I put a hand over my heart, and her expression turns mischievous.

"You want me to show you just how much I care?"

It's my turn to give a solemn nod.

She takes the glass from my hand and puts it on the table, moving to straddle me as soon as her hands are free.

When she slides against me, I let out a soft groan and wind my hands around her waist. *Fuck,* she's perfect, warm and round as she settles into my lap. Her hands skate up my chest, where I'm sure she can feel my heart pounding against my chest. I can already hear it, picking up pace, sending blood rushing to my head and far lower places.

"The whole time I was watching you out there, I was just thinking of how much I wanted these talented hands on me again," she murmurs, gazing down at me through her eyelashes.

I squeeze my hands against her waist, and she responds by rolling her hips against me. I'm wearing sweats, and the barrier is somehow not enough and also way too fucking much.

"Anything else?" I ask, gravel in my voice.

"I wanted your lips on me," she breathes, her eyes going to my mouth. "Though when you got hurt, I wasn't sure if you'd be able to anymore."

A raw sound escapes me. "I can show you just how well they still work."

A smile brightens her face, and she leans forward to kiss me. I sink into it, allowing her to feel just how much I want her with each sweep of my tongue.

I'm dying to peel her clothes off and sink my cock into her soft wet heat again, but I'm determined to savor this. It's a beautiful form of torture, watching this new confident, sexy side of her emerge. Knowing *I've* had a part in making her feel safe enough to show it to me.

I slide my hands across her skin, careful to keep the touch gentle and away from any area that could replace her pleasure with pain. "What else do you want?" I ask when we both lean back, panting slightly.

She gives a thoughtful hum, and then closes her hand over one of mine. I let her bring it up from her side, watching, mesmerized. She closes her lips over two of my fingers, and a hiss escapes through my clenched teeth, the sight of her mouth on me immediately sending fantasies racing through my mind.

Her lips curl into a wicked grin, as if she can read my thoughts, and her tongue flicks over my fingers. My cock, already aching painfully in my sweats, jerks at the movement. It takes everything in me not to grab her and carry her to her bed.

I will give her anything she wants, and more.

With one final sweep of her tongue, she removes her mouth from my fingers and backs off of my lap. Without removing her eyes from mine, she shimmies out of her leggings and panties, and reaches her hands under her shirt. I hear the snap of a clasp, and her bra drops to the ground. All that's left on her is a soft, loose T-shirt.

"Fucking hell," I mutter, drinking her in. Her nipples are hard under that shirt, telling me her teasing has just as much of an effect on her as it does on me.

She saunters back to me, bare from the waist down. I bite down a groan as she settles back onto my lap, but her next words are my undoing.

"I want you to touch me."

"I thought you'd never ask," I rasp, running the fingers she's moistened down to her core. I slide them across her entrance and curse. *"Fuck,* baby, you're already so wet for me."

She lets out a desperate whimper, a noise that's been burned into my memory since our first time. It's an addictive sound. I slide one finger into her, pull out, and plunge two in. I'm immediately lost in the feel of her soft, warm pussy. My gaze slides to hers, and I watch her eyelids flutter, her lips parting as I move inside her. The sight of her losing control over my motions is intoxicating. I increase my tempo, curling the tips of my fingers to bring her to the edge.

She responds instantly, rolling her hips against my hand, and I feel her walls begin to clench around my fingers. "Yes, baby," I whisper hoarsely, adding the pressure of my thumb against her clit. "Come for me. Let go."

Another thrust, another curl, and she shatters around me with a cry. I carry her through it, savoring the flush that enters her face, the beautiful shape her mouth makes, the way her chest heaves from her pants.

When she's come back down, I slide my glistening fingers out of her and bring them to my mouth. She stares as I suck them clean, still catching her breath.

"See?" I murmur. "My mouth works just fine."

She leans into me, giving a breathless chuckle. As she does, she brushes against my hard cock, and I can hear her breath catch. She fists my shirt.

"Bedroom, Benji." It's an order, and one I'm happy to oblige. *"Now."*

"Demanding, are we?" I ask through a laugh. There's a moment of terror that flicks across her face, and I immediately regret my words. "Don't worry," I reassure her. "I fucking love it."

She relaxes and I pull her against me, lifting her to carry her into the bedroom. She curls her legs around me and squeals when I hop, jostling her against my hips.

I deposit her on the bed and step back, running a hand over my face as I admire her: the way her hair spills over the bedsheets, the flush still streaked across her face from her first orgasm. Goddamn, the sight of her is too much. Lyssa is quiet for a moment, embracing my examination, but when she squirms, I give her a smirk, attempting to smother the desire I can feel turning into something more. "Impatient?" I ask.

Her answering frown is fucking adorable. "You have entirely too many clothes on."

With a laugh, I grab the back of my shirt and tug it over my shoulders. My sweats and briefs follow suit, and I fist my cock as I step toward her on the bed.

Her hands find my bare chest, and she drags her fingers down them, eyes wide. "You're unbelievable," she says. "I could just...lick you."

A startled laugh escapes me, and I lean over her on the side of the bed. "So do it," I challenge.

Those big blue eyes narrow, then turn mischievous. The next thing I know, she's dragging the pad of her tongue along my abs, and my blood turns to fire.

"Jesus," I moan, my hands finding her hips. I curl my fingers and barely have the presence of mind to ask, "Condom?"

She pauses for a moment to glance up at me, her expression shuttered. "I'm on the pill," she says, haltingly. "And I'm clean. I just got tested – well, I felt like I had to, when –" her voice breaks, but she doesn't need to finish her sentence.

I remove my hands from her hips, but only so that I can clench them into fists. I'm sure her bastard ex had been with other women, and that's why she felt the need to be tested. He had no idea that the prize was right in front of him. And she's willing to share it all with *me.*

"I get routine testing," I say carefully. "And it's been a long time since I've been with someone else. But–" I hesitate. I don't want her to do this just because she thinks she has to. "Are you sure you want this?"

She gives me a determined nod and reaches for the hem of her shirt, pulling it off and leaving her completely naked in front of me on the bed.

"Fucking hell." The breath shudders out of me and I find her hips again, pulling her to the edge of the bed. I run my hands up her bare legs. "You're really going to test my stamina tonight, aren't you?"

Her laugh reaches my ears, but dies off as I part her legs, position myself at her entrance, and wait. One more desperate noise from her, and I'm plunging into her heat. We groan simultaneously, and the sensation is *euphoric.*

We're both still for a moment, and then she runs her hands up my arms, tracing my muscles with her fingertips. I push in deeper, pressing myself flush against her body.

"God, Benji," she whispers, throwing her head back. "I feel –"

"I know, baby," I murmur. "I know."

I don't remember anyone feeling as good as she feels. And every time I'm with her, I just feel more. The emotions I smothered a mere minute ago threaten to consume me – and this time, I don't give a fuck. I'm burning with them.

I pull back and thrust in again to the sound of her gasp. I run a hand over her side, coming up to cup her breast, taking slow strokes inside her as I go. I flick my thumb over her nipple and relish the way her back arches into my touch.

With a grin, I lean forward, sucking her peaked nipple into my mouth. The sound of her soft curse urges me on, and I slide back into her, harder this time.

"Yes," she chants.

I shift back to observe her, arms bracketed on either side of her naked body.

"Yes, what?" I ask, though I already know the answer. I slide nearly all the way out of her, then flick my eyes down to where we're joined, savoring the sight. "This?" I slam back in to the hilt, and good god, the way she clenches around me has pleasure shooting down my spine.

"Yes, that," she says, though the words are choked out on a sigh. "More of *that.*"

Every stroke follows her commands for *harder, deeper, faster*, and I know I'll never get enough of her. Her body responds and she rocks back into me, her legs trembling against my hips.

My palm runs down her stomach to where we're joined, and my thumb finds her clit. I circle there, and her response is instant, squeezing me to the point I'm nearly seeing stars. Through the haze of desire, I have a thought, one I should have had at the very beginning. I lean forward.

"Where do you want me to come?" I murmur, pausing the circling of my thumb.

She whimpers, dissatisfied, and I grin, giving her one more sweep. "Where do you want me to come, baby?" I ask again.

"In me," she moans. "Come in me."

"Fuuuuck." Her words are like gasoline poured on a fire. I lean back and work her faster, pumping deeper, claiming her with each thrust. My thumb circles her clit in practiced strokes, and she grips me, digging her fingernails into my arms as she unravels around me.

She starts to bite her lip again, but then she's tightening around me more than ever before, and her mouth opens as she cries out. It's a chorus of "Oh, god" and "Holy shit," and, my favorite, *"Benji".* The second the last one passes her lips, I erupt with a groan of my own, spilling into her.

She comes in tandem with me, and our erratic breaths mingle as we both slowly descend back to reality. I take my time withdrawing, and the moment I do, I miss the warmth of her. My heart is pounding in my ears, but somehow, my mind is quieter than ever, filled with nothing but pleasure and relief. We stay like that for a long moment, our gazes locked on each other. I wonder if she's feeling even a small part of what I'm feeling, but I don't dare voice that question. I'm not sure I want the answer.

"Do you want me to get you a washcloth?" I finally ask, straightening.

Lyssa sits up with me and shakes her head. "No...I'm just going to shower, I think."

I nod and watch as she stands, crossing the room. I'm prepared to just sit and wait, to give her privacy, so I'm startled when her head pops around the bathroom door. The sound of the shower hisses behind her.

"Are you coming?"

I blink, then grin. "Absolutely."

The shower is large, but we're still forced to stand nearly toe-to-toe, and I have a hard time looking away from the way the water glides over her soft skin, following her curves. She laughs at the way I hunch over to grab her body wash, then squeals when I drip it down her chest. When she returns the favor, she takes her time tracing the muscles of my chest, nearly making me carry her back out to her bed for a repeat performance.

As we're drying off, though, I sense her mood change. She fiddles with the corner of her robe, her face downcast. With her hair hanging in damp strings around her face, she looks so damn vulnerable.

I draw a deep breath, my sternum suddenly aching. "Is something wrong, little fighter?" I ask, tugging on my sweats.

She's silent for a beat. Then her eyes rise up to meet mine, and she whispers, "Will you stay the night?"

Of all the things I imagined she would ask, this one catches me off guard. "Do you want me to?"

She nods, and relief courses through me. I beam at her. "I thought you'd never ask."

Lyssa takes her time getting ready for bed, and I steal some toothpaste and an extra charger, making myself at home. By the time she lets Winston in the room, I've already made us a small pillow fort on the bed and turned on her TV. Winston gives us both a serious side eye, as if he knows exactly what we've been up to.

"Come on, dude," I tell him. "Can you blame me?"

Apparently he doesn't, because a second later, he hops up onto the bed and curls into a tight ball at our feet. Lyssa gives him a fond smile as she climbs into bed next to me. I offer my arm to her, and after a second of hesitation, she slides her way into the nook of my shoulder.

I bury my nose into her hair, inhaling the scent of her shampoo, and she snuggles deeper. My heart lurches.

I take the chance while I'm riding the high, and ask, "Does this mean we're exclusive?"

A small laugh comes from my armpit. "Were we not before?"

"Well, I was." I grin into her hair. "I was just waiting for you to choose me."

She's silent, but I can feel her smile against my arm, and I bask in the win.

We watch TV for a little while, until the sound of Winston's snores and Lyssa's weight against me tell me they're both asleep. I slide my arm out from under her as carefully as I can, hissing as the blood flow returns to it. *Worth it.*

I'm setting my alarm just as the texts come in.

Coach: Be at the rink 10 minutes early tomorrow. I've got a new sweater with your name on it.

Coach: Oh...it may have a C on it, too.

I put my phone down and turn back to face Lyssa, face nearly splitting in two from my grin. Life doesn't get much better than this.

Chapter 31

Lyssa

"I can't believe this is our standing date now." Andi plops down in the seat next to me, shuffling her concession stand goodies around. "Free seats, junk food, and watching our guys kick some ass."

"We're certainly living the life," I agree, and pop an M&M in my mouth, even as my stomach does a funny little flip at the thought of *my guy* being out on the ice. He's still just warming up, but even from here, I can see the confidence in him as he skates around, flashing the fancy new C on his jersey. The sight sends a warm flush of pride through me, and I trace the C on my own new jersey, the one I splurged on. I know he would've gotten me one himself, but I wanted to surprise him with it today.

I know how hard he's worked for this, winning, losing, and then winning the honor back. I also know he's earned it. The way he cares for his team – and the way they listen to him in turn – makes the distinction natural. Overdue. He's already had the C for two weeks, but it's their first home game where he's wearing it, and I know that makes it extra special for him. I only hope this will add to it.

"Though...*our guys?*" I waggle my eyebrows at her. "Is there something more you need to tell me about you and Grant?"

Andi scoffs. "You know what I mean." She waves a dismissive hand, but she looks uncharacteristically flustered. "Mine to use, selfishly, when I'm feeling horny. It's a mutually beneficial agreement. Low stakes."

"Uh huh. And...are you using anybody else, or is this an exclusive low stakes agreement?"

"Well, you don't see me wearing his jersey, unlike some people. God, this is gonna be the best surprise for Benji," Andi says, gesturing to me. "I feel like a teenage boy. I just can't stop staring at your chest!"

I giggle, then blush as Benji catches sight of us in the stands. He slows to a stop, eyes laser-focused on me. I hold his gaze, and time feels frozen for several long heartbeats. Me wearing this feels like a big step, and with the way he looks up at me from the ice, I think he knows it. He owns the name, the number, and the letter C, and now I own the jersey. I'm wearing him tonight, declaring that we're officially together. Not just with words exchanged in the night, but publicly.

I blow him a kiss, which he catches unabashedly. The warmth spreads further in my core. He stares for another moment longer, until the spell is broken by a teammate slapping his shoulder, causing him to shake his head and skate away.

"It sounds like Jordie's doing great in the big leagues," Andi says as the warmup winds down and the starting lineup is introduced.

"Yeah," I agree, my eyes glued to the ice. "He's had some goals already. Sounds like he's set to spend the rest of the season there." I'm happy for him, but even happier for what it means for Benji in this moment.

"And back on home ice wearing the captain's mark, Beeenn-jamin Estesss!" the announcer roars, and there's murmuring in the crowd. People are definitely starting to take notice, and it makes me both proud and anxious. I hear snippets of conversation between plays, most revolving around him.

"So good to see him really coming back to himself –"

"Remember what happened with his brother, it's just the saddest thing –"

"Did you see his goal last week against Vegas? Insane –"

"Seen a couple articles about him –"

I try to ignore the commentary and follow the game. The Leopards have learned to shape their game around the loss of Jordie, and the crowd would never know he was an integral part of the lineup just a few weeks ago. They're passing beautifully, setting the momentum for the beginning of the game in their favor.

Eight minutes go by with nobody scoring, then there's a rush down the ice with Benji at the lead. He barrels into the offensive zone, deftly moves the puck out of another player's reach, and circles behind the net, never losing speed. Somewhere in the chaos, he finds Grant, scooting closer to the net, undetected by the other team's defense. Benji flips the puck to him, and Grant doesn't even bother with the time it takes to catch it. He fires a one-timer, redirecting Benji's pass toward the net.

The puck flies past the goalie, the ref blows the whistle and gestures to the net, and there's a flurry of motion in the crowd as toys go sailing toward the ice. They come in every color, every size, and range from mundane stuffed animals to hilarious plushies shaped like beer bottles.

Andi and I grin at each other, then lift the toys from our laps and chuck them over the ice to join the growing pile. Today's game is to raise awareness for local animal shelters, so everyone is encouraged to bring a toy. Once the first goal is scored, we're supposed to toss the toys to the ice, and volunteers will collect them after the chaos ends. I chose a multicolored fuzzball, and Andi chose a plush toy that looks like a hot dog.

"I hope they give my toy to a wiener dog," Andi says, settling back into her seat and shoving a handful of popcorn into her mouth. "Damn, I love hockey."

I watch as Benji and Grant pile into the pit of toys, which is growing larger by the second. Levi tackles them both, causing most of the toys underneath them to squeak, and they flail like they're drowning.

I join Andi in our seats and laugh. "I couldn't agree more."

Ryan's voice cracks on a note and I wince. He's on stage doing karaoke while the rest of the team gets drinks, and though any Queen song is catchy, he's certainly not doing it any favors tonight. He doesn't seem to mind, though – the Leopards won five to two, and he was able to get his first hat trick. Given that the team doesn't play again until after Christmas, I'm sure he, along with everyone else on the team, will be doing their best to get hammered tonight and cleared up in time to see their families a week from now.

Andi and Bella slide into the booth alongside me, and I feel something slip into my hands. I grip it on instinct and look down to see a flask.

"Whose is this?" I ask.

"Certainly not mine," Andi replies automatically, and I snort.

"Drink up!" Bella says.

I eye her, but oblige. "Who are you to peer pressure me? What are you, eighteen?"

She rolls her eyes and snags the flask from me, giving a cautious look around before she takes a swig. The guys come back toward us as a unit. Their large group draws looks, mostly from the other women in the bar. They're in their element, though, celebrating the win together as a team.

I sit back and chat with Andi and Bella, listening as the karaoke rounds run to their end and change to dance music. My head grows fuzzy as I alternate between the bar cocktails and not-Andi's-flask.

Finally, Benji sidles my way, leaning over the table booth. His eyes flicker from the strobing lights. "Dance?" he asks, reaching for me.

I glance at the girls for confirmation, and when they nod encouragingly, I slip out of the booth to join Benji. His hand in mine is warm and immediately intoxicating – far more than the alcohol. He guides me toward the stage, where everyone is dancing, some singing along with what the DJ has put on. The crowd closes in, and when I'm shoved from one side, I begin to stiffen.

Benji pulls his hand from mine, putting both on my waist instead. His lips come to the shell of my ear. "We'll stay back here," he murmurs. "Is that okay?"

I nod, comforted by the distance from the crowd; close enough to be a part of the music and dancing, but far enough away that we're not constantly bumping into people.

His hands tug my waist closer to him, and I'm momentarily stunned by how well we fit together. The music thrums, and I swear it's matching my heartbeat, pumping the alcohol and lust through my veins. The lights flash, and I squeeze my eyes shut, swaying to the rhythm of the beat with Benji following suit, moving in sync behind me. His hands shift on my waist, moving under the hem of the jersey, and a thumb dips into my waistband. My breath stutters at the simple movement, and I swear he notices, because I hear him chuckle at my ear, sending my hair fluttering.

"You look so fucking good in my jersey," he whispers, running his thumb along the waist of my jeans, dipping low enough to trace the lace of my panties. "I bet you'd taste even better right now."

I whimper and force myself to turn around in his arms, trying to clear my thoughts. "What are you doing?" I want the words to sound forceful, but desire has my voice unsteady and hoarse. I'm completely off-kilter, and he grins as he sees it.

"Just having a little fun with my girl," he says, and then his face transforms into the picture of innocence. "But I can behave if you need me to."

I nod, attempting seriousness, even as I'm left reeling from the way he said *my girl* so matter-of-factly. "We're in public. And I'd hate to traumatize your rookie. He's having such a great night."

We both look over to where Ryan is on the dance floor. He's got at least three women surrounding him, all moving in a way that suggests they wouldn't mind being his dance partner for the rest of the night. He looks ecstatic, if somewhat oblivious, and it's clear from the way he's moving that if he doesn't stop drinking, he'll be spending the night in the bathroom rather than the bedroom.

Benji clucks his tongue sympathetically. "Poor guy is going to *wish* he remembered tonight."

I let out a loud snort that dissolves into laughter, my own inebriation making me giddy at the thought of Ryan's drunkenness. Benji tugs me a little closer, grinning down at me. His smile is so genuine, so tender, and all I can think about is how much I want to kiss his gorgeous face.

So I do.

The way Benji responds, sinking just as deeply into it as I do, feels like a personal victory. *Mine,* my body screams. I'm wearing his jersey, I'm kissing his beautiful lips, and I don't want it to end. I love this. I love...

"What was that for?" he asks when we both come up for air.

*I love...*the words feel loose on my tongue, driven forward by alcohol and emotion. Benji'i face looks light, expectant

It would be so easy to say. And to mean it.

But so, so hard to take back.

I'm saved from having to answer as Andi bounds up, Grant and Bella in tow. "Hey, you two lovebirds!" she coos, then looks at Benji. "No drink in your hand? You must not be taking this pre-Christmas celebration seriously enough." She cuts a glance at Grant. "You should get your captain a drink."

Grant smirks. "Want anything?" he asks Bella.

She shakes her head, looking pointedly at Ryan. "There are about two drinks closing the gap between my drunk and his, and I don't want to be there."

Grant laughs and looks at me in question. When I shake my head too, he salutes and slides off toward the bar.

"So what's your plan for Christmas, Benji?" Andi asks.

He shifts so that we're both facing her and Bella, and slings a casual arm over my shoulder. I surprise myself when I lean into it, and Andi beams at the sight.

"Just my normal Christmas with family," he replies. "You?"

She shrugs. "Same. Bella?"

"My dad and I have some fun traditions," Bella says with a smile. "I'm also just enjoying the break from school, so I'll be sleeping in."

Andi groans. "Christ, I always forget you're practically an infant."

"Shut up!" Bella shoves her good-naturedly. "What about you, Lisa?"

I'm momentarily caught off-guard. "Um, I don't have any plans."

They gaze at me – Bella in surprise, Andi in sympathy – and I feel my face flush. Is this what every holiday is going to be like?

Andi opens her mouth, presumably to invite me to her place, when Benji cuts in.

"I'd love it if you'd come to my Christmas."

I step away and blink up at him, searching for any signs of pity or regret. But his face is entirely earnest; hopeful, even. "You would?"

He nods. "I know it's only been a couple weeks, and Thanksgiving was a bit much, but so much has changed, and –" he clears his throat, shifting on his feet. "I just...if you want to, I'd love it. If you came with me."

I open and close my mouth, unsure what to say.

I want to be excited by the offer, and he's right. Since Thanksgiving, we've begun an actual relationship. The last few weeks together have been phenomenal. But the second I think about what could be a fun time with Benji, another family comes to mind – one that I had lost myself in, claiming as my own. What had been a replacement for all I'd lost became something I lost all over again. Because of *him*, because of *me*, the illusion shattered the day I left.

Home. I want one here, and this feels like another step to making it one. But is it really home if the second you settle down, all you feel are the walls closing in?

I'm suddenly aware that Andi and Bella are witnessing this, and I haven't answered him. I go for the safest option in the moment. "Yeah, I'll think about it."

Benji smiles, but it's a smile tinged with sadness. I want to pull him away, maybe try to explain myself, but Grant comes barreling back at that exact moment, no drinks in hand.

"Dude," he pants. "Ryan is spewing and we need someone to help get him home."

Bella rolls her eyes and whispers a quiet *called it*. Andi smothers a laugh behind her hand. Benji groans. "Why can't you handle it?" he asks.

"You know me! If you puke –" he gags and clasps a hand over his mouth for a moment before continuing. "– I'll puke."

"Fucking unreal," Benji mutters with a shake of his head. Then, he looks from me to the girls. "You all good to make it home together?"

"Yeah," I say, the conversation having sobered me up significantly. I'm ready to get home and curl up with Winny. "I'm probably gonna head back now."

Andi and Bella voice their agreement, and as we all shuffle to the door to wait for the rideshare, Andi nudges me. "You okay?"

I nod. "It's just…Christmas is a big step, is all. I'm not sure about it yet."

Bella leans against the wall and studies us, like we're a question she hasn't quite figured out the answer to yet. "Benji seems like a great guy. What's the holdup?"

"Baggage, kiddo," Andi says. "Sometimes you can meet a great guy, but it's after quite a few shitty ones."

Bella frowns. "I hope I never have to deal with a shitty guy. First bad thing he does, I'd kick his ass to the curb."

Andi tenses and glances at me, waiting for the blow to hit. And yes, it does hit a sore spot – I can't count how many times have I heard someone say in passing, *I could never let a man treat me that way* – but it's Bella, and I know she means well.

So I just say, "There are a lot of ways to end up in a shitty situation without even realizing it until you're in too deep. And not everyone can kick ass the way you do, Bella."

She flushes and ducks her head. "Sorry, that was probably a stupid thing to say," she mumbles. "I've just had too much to drink." I gather her into a hug. The last thing I want is to make her feel bad for her questions. She's young, and I really do hope she'd never have to deal with any of the things Andi and I have been through.

"Sometimes, you fall in love with a man and build a life as equals, and that's fucking amazing. Other times, you lose yourself in a man." I pause and sigh. "And some men...well, some, you're lucky if you simply survive them."

Chapter 32

I know I could call Andi to talk this out with her. She would come over in an instant, wine in hand, and encourage me to say yes to Benji and everything it entails. It would dissolve into a night of binge-watching some show or another, ultimately giving in to our cravings and ordering our favorite desserts from the local restaurants.

In theory, it sounds delightful, and I might need it later this week. But tonight, it would only make me wake up in the middle of the night with a sugar headache to accompany my already racing thoughts. What I need is to sweat this out, and push myself to the point that my body is too tired to allow my mind to take over.

Because if I allow my mind to take over, I'll spiral over the fact that saying yes to Benji means choosing not only him, but his family. To take another step toward melding myself into his life, losing the carefully built control and freedom I've recently gained. To make the choice to cross the distance I've purposefully put in our relationship to keep me safe. To keep us *both* safe.

If we go further, that means more, and more leads to a key point of my worst years. And even those years started with something I thought was wonderful. I can't trust what I'm feeling right now.

So here I am, pummeling a punching bag, ignoring the way my arms, back and core all complain at me in unison. I have the gym to myself, so I'm free to get lost in the effort. My phone was burning a hole in my pocket, so it's laying in a locker nearby, my playlist synched up to the Bluetooth. The music thrums in time with my heartbeat.

A shadow moves in the corner of the gym, and I whirl, gloves up, only to relax when I realize who it is.

Paul leans against the brick wall, keys in hand, his face expectant. After a long moment, I realize he doesn't just plan to leave me to exercise. I make my way over to my phone, removing my gloves along the way. I wipe a sweaty palm across my leggings and pause my music, wincing as the time on my screen registers. The gym closed nine minutes ago.

I turn to face him. "Shit, Paul, I'm sorry. I lost track of time."

"No worries. You've really improved your technique." He crosses his arms, nodding at the punching bag. "So. Are you training to become the next Sylvester Stallone, or are you looking to get something off your chest?"

I smile, but don't reply. Instead, I set to work cleaning up the space.

"Don't think I haven't noticed what you're doing, kiddo."

His words pull me up short, and I can't help the panic in my expression when I face him. He's moved to help me clean up, and his face is inscrutable as he continues.

"All sorts of people come through this gym, and you don't get to my age without a good understanding of them: what motivates them, and how I can help them. Some, they just want to get in shape. Some are looking to cross-train, work some new muscles, learn a new sport. Those are always fun people to work with, and they want to be here, sure, but they're not the most important people I meet."

He motions for me to sit on the side of the ring, and I oblige.

"People like you are the most important. People who *need* to be here. People who need to feel safe, strong and capable." He studies me. It's hard to hold his gaze, but even harder to look away. "Am I right so far?"

I swallow and nod, unable to form words.

He nods in return, though something in his expression softens. It's a strange look on someone who usually swings between stern intensity and fierce motivation during his classes. "I'm so sorry that I haven't been able to help the way I thought I could."

"What do you mean?" I blink rapidly, unable to process where this conversation is going.

"I figured, when you came through these doors for the first time, you needed a way to feel safe again. It's not my place to ask why – " he holds his hands up in a patient gesture "–but I always hoped this could be a place where young women could feel safe and learn how to defend themselves. I mean, that's what I want for Bella, and I always feel better knowing she can hold her own. I thought this was helping you work through whatever you needed to. But tonight..." he trails off for a moment. "This reminds me of the way you attacked your first few lessons. With better posture, of course."

I wipe the sweat off my brow and let out a choked laugh, torn between amusement and affection. I had no idea just how much he's been looking out for me all this time. "It's not that," I manage. "Back then, I was running from something."

He nods patiently, and I'm grateful he doesn't dig for specifics. "And now?"

And now? I turn his question over in my head, looking for the right words. "Now, I'm trying to decide whether I need to run again. Or if I'm staying put."

Paul hums thoughtfully, his gaze far away. "Does this have to do with a certain hockey player that bent over backwards to help you with our fundraiser?"

"What?" My stomach flips. "He was helping *you!*"

"That poor boy didn't know the name of my gym until he showed up to promote it," Paul chides. "Everything he did for me, he did because you asked him to." His eyes slide to mine. "Don't get me wrong. I'm beyond grateful for everything you did. But if you had asked him to promote a porta-potty, he would have."

I groan, because he's *right,* and that causes a new wave of terror to crash over me. I bury my face in my hands. "You're not helping."

He frowns, and I can see him trying to work out my words in a way that makes sense. "If you don't want to be with him…"

"No," I blurt out. "I do."

He pauses, his pale blue eyes searching mine. "And he's good to you?"

My heart lurches. They're such simple words – such an obvious question – and yet, in this moment, they mean more to me than Paul will ever know.

"Yes," I whisper, then add in a voice so soft it's barely audible, "for now."

I see the realization dawn over him in flickers of surprise, then anger, then sadness. He runs a hand through his graying hair and sighs. "You know, there are a lot of people in this world that will try their best to bury you. Whether it's because they want to keep you, take from you, or just beat you down. And I can't claim to know everything, but this is a truth I know, deep in my bones. Deeper than my early arthritis." He smiles, the wrinkles on his face crinkling in a calming, familiar way. "The best way to get back at those kinds of people is to simply live your life, and live it damn well."

"But what if –" I start, but he cuts me off with a wave of his hand.

"The only *if* you should be asking yourself is if it's worth giving up over whatever's got you in such a fit tonight. Because if there's one thing I know about you, it's that you're not a quitter." He says it so matter-of-factly, as if this should be obvious. "Whatever had you running in the first place, you knew you'd find a better life getting away from it. You fought for that." He gestures around. "You fought for this. For happiness. A life full of people who treat you the way you deserve to be treated. And you even giving Mr. Estes the time of day means you're still fighting for that."

"Benji," I correct him with a soft smile. "He'd hate to hear you call him Mr. Estes."

"See?" Paul tilts his head te. "Clearly, you care for him."

"I do," I reply. "But...caring for him means opening myself up for all the hurt that might come next."

"Yes. Caring means you give someone the opportunity to break you. And trust me, there are so many ways it can break you." He pauses, and I remember what Bella told me; how her own mother had passed when she was young. I wonder if he's thinking of her. Before I can ask, he continues. "Besides, from what I tell, whatever you ran from didn't break you, even then."

But it did, a voice in my mind says. As if he can read my thoughts, Paul shakes his head. "No, you're not broken. Maybe a little battered and bruised, but you've never let that stop you. In the ring or out."

I attempt to roll my eyes at him, but I'm forced to blink and look away instead as the tears well up. "I think you're giving me entirely too much credit, Paul."

He bumps my shoulder with his and places my gloves in my lap. "Nah. Like I said. Giving up before you even try is still quitting. And I would never let a quitter in my gym."

I slide through the doors of the Wunderbar, scanning the crowd for the familiar, broad figures of the Leopards. It's easy to pick them out in their normal booth, hats on, jostling each other while they play some sort of card game. My gaze rakes over the bodies, and I frown when I don't see Benji among them.

"Hey, stranger."

I jump at the voice next to my ear and spin. Benji gives me an apologetic look, raising his phone in his hand before pocketing it.

"I was on a call and saw you walk in." His face is flushed, and I wonder if he took the call out in the cold. "What's up?"

I smile, but it falters as the nerves sweep in. Walking in here, I'd been so sure of this next step, but staring at him now, that step feels like a leap again. I try to remind myself of Paul's words and how confident I'd felt leaving the gym.

His gaze rakes over my face, and he frowns. "What's wrong?"

"Nothing." I shake my head and swallow. "I–I actually just wanted to let you know I made up my mind. About Christmas."

He cocks his head, and I continue, the words rushing out before I lose my nerve. "I'd love to join your Christmas. If you'll still have me."

His expression is unreadable for a long moment, and the breath catches in my throat. Oh, god. Did he change his mind? I never even considered that option in all my hypothetical scenarios, but it's just as bad as some of them.

But then, he *laughs.* "If I'll still have you?" He shakes his head, still chuckling. "Of course I want you there. I wouldn't have asked if I wasn't completely sure."

"And your family?" I ask, though the relief of his reaction already has a weight lifting off my chest. "They're okay with it, too?"

"Of course they are. Gabi will be beyond thrilled." Benji lifts up his cap and runs a hand through his hair, beaming. "And here I was, thinking I'd already gotten the best news I could today."

"What do you mean?" I blink, confused.

"I got the call," he says, eyes gleaming. "One of the Minnesota Chill players is out with a concussion. At least a month, maybe two."

I frown. "I don't understand. How is that a good thing?"

"It's not, I mean, not for him. Well, in a way it's good because they're taking the recovery seriously, which the league only started to recently –"

He pauses, inhaling to reorient himself, and I can't help but smile at the contagious energy of his babbling. He's acting like Winston when he's excited for a walk, but forced to sit still so I can leash him up. I can almost picture Benji tippy-tapping his feet like Winston, and my grin widens. I bite the inside of my cheek to keep from giggling.

"It means they need another player for the next few weeks," he continues, "and they called *me.*" He picks me up and swings me around, and I start laughing outright, my heart near bursting with happiness for him, because now I know what he's going to say before he even says it.

"I'm going to the show!"

Chapter 33

BENJI

"Are you sure I shouldn't get anything else?" Lyssa asks.

"No, this is more than enough," I assure her for the third time, attempting to hide my amused grin. If I didn't know better, I would assume that Lyssa had grown up in Minnesota. It seems like the entire state's love language is gift giving, and the table in front of us is overflowing with them. She's selected a thank-you gift for my family hosting her, as well as individual gifts for my sister, mom, dad, and great-grandma, and a tin of cookies she baked the night before. Now, she shoves all the goodies carefully into a bag, double-checking that the bows remain intact.

"You know, when I asked you to join us for Christmas, I thought we would just head over for a few hours of fun," I say. "I wasn't expecting...well, *this.*"

She ignores me completely, spinning in a circle as she assesses everything. Her hair is curled, and I can tell she took extra care with her makeup – something Gabi would be proud I noticed, since as she likes to point out, I'm usually terrible with those things. She's wearing a knitted evergreen sweater and jeans, something she decided on after I insisted my family is casual. The sight of it made me go back to my apartment and change out of my standard Grinch t-shirt into a nice cream long-sleeve and green flannel, just so she didn't feel overdressed.

"We match," she says absently, tugging on my shirt, and I pull her to me and kiss the top of her head. Fuck, she even smells like Christmas, some delicious scent of sugar cookies.

"We do," I agree. "They're going to think we're sickeningly adorable."

We put our shoes on, and out of the corner of my eye. I notice her fingers shaking slightly as she laces up her boots. When she straightens, I pull her to me again.

"Hey," I say, rubbing her arms. "Deep breaths." She nods, closing her eyes for a moment. While she follows my advice, I take the moment to study her. I can tell it's a big step for her, and I want to ask how I can help make it better, but I don't think she would have the answer for me, either. I can only hope the warm embrace of my family will give her what she needs. We've experienced our share of losses, too, but we've healed around the cracks, becoming closer than before, and I know Lyssa will be welcomed in with open arms.

She opens her eyes, and I'm relieved to see a steadiness in her blue gaze. She nods at me, and I return it with a smile. I grab the overflowing bag of goodies and motion for her to head out the door ahead of me, giving Winston a scratch as we go.

"There's only one rule in the Estes household," I say as I shut the door behind me.

She looks back at me, alarmed. "What's that?"

"You have to let Grandma cheat at cards."

"I told you, it wasn't me who took your Pokémon game!" I scrub a hand down my face. We're a few drinks deep, and the reminiscing has gone as far back as elementary school, where things quickly turned combative.

"Then who did?" Gabi taps her fingers on her wine glass, quirking a brow at me.

Lyssa and Alice are both holding glasses of wine as well, their eyes darting between the two of us. Alice looks entirely unsurprised, having witnessed several holidays with us, but Lyssa's expression is attentive and, to my relief, amused. While my sister and I tend to default to bickering, it's how we show our affection for each other. I wouldn't have it any other way.

"I don't know, who was your little friend who followed you around everywhere until you came out?" I wave my hand. "Lucas something-or-other?"

Gabi scoffs. "You think he stole my game out of spite?"

"Yes." This time Alice and I answer in unison, and I shoot her a grateful look for the backup.

Gabi shakes her head. "I don't think so. You were even more obsessed with those games than I was. And you were mad that I got the new game for Christmas that year."

"There's a reason they're still making new games. They're timeless. But," I add pointedly, "he was more obsessed with you than I ever was with those games."

"I don't think so."

"You just want to argue with me here, don't you?" I ask, exasperated.

She grins. "Maybe."

Alice and Lyssa laugh, and then my mom pops her head in from around the corner. "It's time to play ball!"

She taps her knuckles on the wall and disappears. Gabi and I scramble up, and Alice giggles as my sister grabs her hand, shoving past me in her rush to get to the living room.

Lyssa sidles up to me, her brow adorably wrinkled in confusion. "Does your family play basketball too?"

"No." I chuckle. "This is a game left over from our younger years. We didn't...well, every spare dollar went to making sure my siblings and I could chase our dreams. So, our Christmases didn't always look as flashy as my friends'."

Lyssa bites her lip and nods. "I get it. All the other kids at school got such amazing presents from Santa. I used to wonder what I did to make Santa upset."

My heart twists painfully, but in a weird way, it feels good to talk about this. It's something we both can relate to, despite all the other completely different journeys that led us to where we are now.

"I understood why my parents prioritized certain things when I got older, but when I was young, it wasn't like I could unwrap all the training camps and select team fees." I pick at a piece of the label on my beer that's peeling off. "My biggest gifts were always hand-me-down equipment from my brother, but even those were usually a size or two too big. I had to wear two sets of socks, and even then, I got some gnarly blisters."

"What?" She gapes at me. "What did you do about the blisters?"

I shrug. "Super glue works wonders."

She opens her mouth, ready to argue or ask questions, but Gabi pops back around the corner. "Head's up!"

A giant white ball comes hurtling my way, and I barely get my free hand around it in time to catch the awkward object.

"God, this gets bigger every year," I complain, shifting it in my arm. "I kind of miss when it was just lollipops and stickers."

"Pffft. If that were true, you wouldn't have dropped off five of your own gifts and a metric fuck ton of shrink wrap."

Lisa shoots me a curious look, and I feel my face growing warm. "We had a bunch of swag dropped off at the rink, and they were just going to throw out the shrink wrap. I didn't want to be wasteful."

"My eco-friendly brother-in-law," Alice coos. "I appreciate it."

"All right, kiddos, let's play!" My mom ushers my dad into the room and gathers us all around, holding oven mitts and a cup filled with two dice. Great-grandma, having had her three glasses of wine and sufficiently cheated her way through cards, is still on the chair nearest the TV. Judging by the soft snores I hear, she's not going to join us anytime soon.

"So...how do we play this?" Lyssa's voice is soft and timid, but my mom doesn't miss a beat.

"Oh, it's super silly. Give it a few rounds, and you'll have the hang of it." She beams at Lyssa, who flushes, giving her a shy smile in return. "Benji here will start with the oven mitts. Gabi will start with the dice. Benji has to wear the oven mitts and try to pull apart as much of the shrink wrap as he can before Gabi rolls doubles. Once she does, she gets the mitts and the ball, and then you get the dice. And so on."

"Don't worry about Benji snagging any of the good gifts from the ball." Gabi nudges Lyssa with her shoulder. "For someone who wears gloves professionally, he can't unwrap that thing to save his life. One year when he was little, he barely got through two layers the whole night."

Alice leans in and whispers to Lyssa, "I hope he's better with his bare hands than those oven mitts. That's *super* embarrassing for a professional athlete."

I choke, whipping my head toward Gabi as she bursts out laughing at her wife's comment. Lyssa's face has turned a shade of crimson, and I pray she's not ready to bolt.

"Okay, children!" My mom claps. "Let's get started!"

Gabi grabs the cup and I grab the oven mitts, determined to shake my bad reputation – on my first holiday bringing a significant other home, no less. I grit my teeth and get to work, but it only takes three rolls for Gabi to get doubles. She rips the mitts off of me, cackling.

Around we go, little goodies being peeled off in rapid succession. Candy, gift cards, face masks, and jewelry come flying out, as well as little pieces of paper that say things like *STEAL* or *REVERSE.*

Eventually, a mini wrapped ball pops out of the larger one, and it gets sent around the circle counter-clockwise with its own pair of dice.

"This is so intricate!" Lyssa huffs, fiddling intently with the wrapping of the mini ball. She sucks her lower lip into her mouth in concentration, and it's so adorable I have to remind myself not to tug her into my lap. She's competitive enough that I think she would hate me for it.

"We've had quite some time to perfect the game," my dad says with a chuckle. "Every few years we think of something new to add to it."

A game card pops out of the larger ball, and Gabi lets out a victorious shriek. "Ohmygod, Benji, did you do this?"

"I knew that damn game would come up again this year. And even though it *wasn't me,*" I pause for emphasis, "I figured this might put an end to you blaming me for it."

She throws her arms around me, laughing. "This is the best gift. Thank you!"

"You're welcome." I squeeze her back.

When I turn around, I find Lyssa grinning at me.

"So that's one of the five gifts you dropped off," she notes. "What other goodies are hiding in here?"

"I guess you'll just have to dig in and see, L."

"Well, as luck would have it, I seem to be far better with these mitts than you are." Lyssa digs into the shrink wrap with gusto, then yelps when a bracelet comes flying out, skittering across the floor from the force of her ripping the ball apart. She scrambles across the floor on her hands and knees, still wearing the oven mitts, to chase the item down.

The entire scene sends a chuckle busting out of me, and Lyssa shoots me a sheepish glance that only makes it worse. I laugh harder. She flushes, but then lets out a giggle of her own, followed by one of her little snorts. Within seconds, we're both laughing uncontrollably.

By the time we catch our breath moments later, Lyssa's lost her round with the mitts. Alice tugs them off her hands, grinning as she does. My gaze bounces off Alice and around the circle, surprised to find everyone giving us warm, knowing smiles.

It's not the kind of smile where I'm in the dark about an inside joke, though. I know exactly what they're thinking, and I feel the same.

This feels like something I would happily experience, every year.

When we say our goodbyes later that night, they come with all the classics I've come to learn from my family. Everyone thanks Lyssa for their gifts, and she thanks them in return for hosting her. My mother gives her a recipe on a notecard that they discussed earlier in the night. My dad and I make plans to play some indoor golf, and Gabi asks if I'm still free to cat-sit in two weeks. We hug everyone goodbye at least three times, because another conversation started from the living room to the front door, and from the front door to the porch. Even Grandma wakes up long enough for the parting hugs.

I worry it was all too much for Lyssa, but the flushed smile on her face looks truly genuine. When we slide into my car, I blast the heat, giving it a minute to warm up.

"Did you...have fun?" I ask, and I'm surprised by important her answer is to me.

"I really, really did." She smiles to herself, taking off her hat and mittens. "I can see how much your family loves you."

"Well, most of them. Gabi is fifty-fifty."

Lyssa chuckles. I carefully pull out of the driveway, turning the evening over in my mind. "And now, they love you."

When I'm met with silence, I glance over at Lyssa.

Her smile has faltered, and she's fiddling with her hat in her lap, gaze turned downward. Shit, was that too much?

"They don't know me," she says softly.

"What do you mean?" Does this mean she'd rather they know her real name? Her backstory? I can't tell if it's because she's withholding information from them, or from me. For some reason, I feel like it's both.

She shakes her head and turns on the radio, answering with a soft, "Nevermind."

I want to press her on the matter, but she's already long gone, her thoughts carrying her somewhere I can't reach.

Chapter 34

Lyssa

*T*he lights are swirling, flashes of red and blue taking turns passing over my vision. I stopped registering them ages ago, thanks to the mysterious cocktail of medication administered by the paramedics who arrived first on the scene. We're waiting for the police, and everyone is mulling around, assessing the scene and working to keep bystanders back. Everyone except me. I couldn't walk around, even if I wanted to.

Someone breaks through the crowd, rushing towards me, and when I glance up, it's Patty's face that appears over me. "Alyssa..."

She glances around, taking in the scene, and freezes as she notices the broken stair railing. The gap is large enough for two people, and the weather has turned dark and nasty, sending the splintered edges waving in the wind. Slowly, she turns back to face me. "What happened?"

After years of her being the closest thing I had to a sibling, I thought I knew all of my best friend's expressions. I'd seen her joy, anger, stress, and disappointment. But this is a new one.

The expression I see on her face now is sheer terror.

I simply close my eyes.

Awareness comes to me slowly. I take a minute to gather my senses while my eyes remain closed. The distant sound of sirens is gone, replaced by the soft ticking of an overhead fan. The sticky summer air has been replaced by the crisp, winter air, threatening to cut through my apartment's heat. There's a band of warmth encircling me, and in my disoriented state, it takes me a moment to place it.

"Lyssa?"

Benji's voice snaps everything into focus.

That's right – he's here. I remember now that he spent the night. His arm is wrapped around me, just like it was when we originally fell asleep.

I crack my eyes open, tilting my head to meet him. It's still dark out, but in the moonlight, I can see that his face is drawn tight in concern.

"What's wrong?" I shift off of his arm, blinking rapidly to clear the sleep away. Is his arm asleep? Does he need to move it?

"You were crying."

"Crying?"

Benji gives a slow nod, studying me closely. "Were you asleep?"

"I...yeah."

"Was it a nightmare?"

I bite my lip, and he takes this as his answer. "Do you have those a lot?" he asks.

I pause, then figure there's no way to sugarcoat it. I've woken up to a wet pillowcase enough to know this isn't the first time this has happened. Sleep is the one place I can't truly hide from my feelings. "Yeah. Probably once a week or so."

He goes silent at that. I can't make out much of his face, but I'm sure he's putting the pieces together in his mind. My pulse begins to race alongside my mind as I consider what he could be thinking about. Did I say something in my sleep?

I turn over the glimpses of the nightmare in my head, panic constricting my throat. I wait for him to say something.

"Do you...want to talk about it?" he ventures.

I almost laugh at the question, even as my answer comes instantly. "No, I *really* don't."

"Okay." There's a pause. "But...maybe you should, with someone, eventually. If you're comfortable with it, of course," he adds hurriedly.

I sigh, trying to brush away the defensiveness that jumps up on instinct. I know he's right, and he and Andi have both skirted around the subject of therapy with me before. Andi went to therapy following her breakup, and Benji has mentioned his whole family going to someone after his brother's passing.

So far, I've taken it upon myself to do my own research. I've gotten deep into podcasts and ventured into forums. It's helped to an extent – mostly with knowing that I'm not alone – but I know that someday I'll need more tools to get me back on my feet. These nightmares are just another clear sign that my brain is still processing everything.

"I will," I promise. "I just wanted to feel more...established first, I suppose. I need the newness of this life to settle a bit more before I try getting vulnerable with someone I don't know."

Benji brushes the hair back from my face. "If you need some space..."

"No," I cut in, realizing how my words sounded.

"No?"

"I need the opposite of that," I say, snuggling closer to him. He wastes no time winding his arms back around me, and I bury my head in his chest, breathing in the fresh, crisp smell of soap on his skin.

"In that case, do you want me to get Winny off the ground to join the slumber party, or...?"

I give his shoulder a light smack and feel the vibration in his chest as he chuckles in response.

After the first night Benji slept over, he bought a high-end dog bed for Winston, complete with its own blankets for him. Winston spent ten minutes nosing the blankets into the perfect position, circled exactly five times, and then passed out in doggie bliss. I can't blame him. I mean, the material inside his bed is definitely more expensive than what my own bed is made of. But I still bring him up on the bed on the nights when Benji isn't here.

One of Benji's hands rests against my head, and his thumb strokes slowly against my temple. My eyelids are already growing heavy again, and I feel drunk on the feeling of him surrounding me. My own personal safety net. Part of me registers how fascinating it is, to feel so safe with another person that I want nothing more than to fall asleep in his arms. I nuzzle closer and press a soft kiss to the nape of his neck.

"Thank you," I whisper.

He shifts and hums, dropping a kiss against the top of my head. "Any time, little fighter."

I spend a few minutes enjoying the rise and fall of his chest and the way it feels against my own body. My own breathing slows in tandem with his, and I close my eyes, ready to give in to the weightless sensation of sleep.

Just before I drift off, I think he murmurs something against my hair, but I've floated too far from awareness to decipher it, instead enjoying the simple bliss of being with him.

It's only been two days since Christmas, but Benji's new schedule has been even crazier than his old one with the Leopards. Instead of the break he thought he'd get with his old team, he's been practicing with the Chill every day since he received the call, Christmas aside. Even today, he's already been busy with a morning skate and pre-game meeting with the team. His first game with the Chill is tonight – a home game against Calgary – but I haven't had much of a chance to ask him about it.

I slide my gaze over to him as he drives, taking in his handsome suit and combed-over hair. Even though he needs to be at the rink three hours early, I wanted to come with and see him off; to wish him good luck. Andi, Grant and I all have tickets to the game, and they're planning to meet me for a pre-game meal and drinks at the restaurant attached to the rink. I don't want to risk missing even a minute of his first game here, and I think they feel the same.

What I see on Benji's face makes me frown. I expected him to be amped up, talking excitedly about tonight like he had when he first got the call. Instead of someone buzzing in their seat, I'm met with someone who looks borderline...sullen. His mouth is drawn into a thin line, his brows pinched, and he grips the steering wheel tightly. He hasn't said much, but I figured he was focusing on the drive. Maybe there's something more going on here.

"You get to play with Jordie again tonight." I attempt to start a conversation, eyeing him carefully.

He nods. "I do."

The words are light, but I detect a note of strain underneath them. I can sense that he's in his head, so I remain quiet for the next few minutes as we make our way to the rink, simply choosing some music to break up the silence. At a stoplight, his hand comes down off the wheel, and I take the opportunity to grab it and squeeze it, trying to convey my support for him. He flashes me a grateful smile, but I can see the flicker of nerves and something else underneath.

When we pull up to the rink, I'm surprised to see a small crowd outside. Benji curses under his breath and turns to me. "I think those are reporters. God, they're probably here for me." He eyes them, and then me, rubbing the back of his neck. "They haven't noticed us yet. You can take my car and leave."

I take in his expression and shake my head. "No. I'm not leaving." I can tell he's nervous, and I don't want his send-off to be his girlfriend ditching him. The idea of attention makes me anxious, but it pales in comparison to him and what he needs right now. Especially with reporters, who are basically a paid version of stalkers.

The thought clicks everything into place, and I eye him. He turns off the ignition, but I stop him with a hand on his leg. He pauses, tilting his head at me.

"How are you doing today?" I ask quietly. "I bet this is...kind of a mixed bag of emotions for you."

Benji glances down, fiddling with his keys in his lap. I wait patiently. He's given me the space to talk with him, countless times. I want to be able to return the favor.

"Yeah, it is," he says quietly. "When this day came, I thought...I thought I'd be playing with him."

His Adam's apple works in his throat as he swallows, glancing out the window. There's some chatter, people shifting and taking interest, but at this moment, I couldn't care less.

I thought I'd be playing with him. He doesn't mean Jordie. He means his brother.

My chest aches as I notice the sheen to his eyes. The pain he's been in today is suddenly so clear, and I hate that I didn't notice it sooner.

"You *are,* though," I whisper. "Any time you play, you're playing with him. You're playing the game the two of you grew up learning together. You're playing the game that made you both so unbelievably happy." I put my hand on his cheek and gently pull his face in line with mine. "You'll be playing with him, and just as importantly, you'll be playing *for* him. Because this is exactly what he wanted for you."

Benji squeezes his eyes shut at my words, and a single tear escapes, trailing down his chin. I brush it away and pull him as close as I can across the car, kissing the path it took.

Benji's breath comes out as a shaky gasp, bordering on a sob, and then his lips are on mine, desperately seeking a comfort I'm more than happy to give. By the time we pull apart, we're both breathless.

We gaze at each other, and then he glances back out the window. The group has grown curious, venturing closer. Benji sighs and shoots me another look. "Thank you." His words are low but sincere, and I give him a small, reassuring smile.

As we get out and walk toward the rink, the small crowd grows excited. It's clear now that they are, in fact, here to report on Benji's first game tonight. They begin shouting out questions, camera lenses fluttering.

"Benjamin Estes! Back up to captain of the Leopards, and now making your debut with the Chill. You're certainly making a name for yourself."

"How does it feel, being the Golden Boy again?"

"Minnesota missed you, Benji! Glad to see you're coming back!"

"Benji! Benjamin Estes, who's this young lady on your arm?" Someone calls, and through the chaos, this makes the breath catch in my throat. Even though I know he wouldn't breathe my real name aloud, not even to his closest teammates, I feel as though I've been caught. I shrink into his side, trying to stay out of sight of the small but tenacious group of reporters.

Benji doesn't answer any of them. Instead, he pulls me protectively against him as he makes his way inside.

The door closes on them decisively, and the silence that follows is jarring. I choose the first random thing that flits through my head to break it. "Does this mean I can get a new jersey with your name on it?"

He scoffs and shakes his head. "That's a bit presumptuous. I'm basically being leased on a game-by-game basis. It's not like I belong here."

"They certainly seem to think so. And so do I. Benji." I frown and pause, forcing him to look at me. I give him a final, firm kiss and make sure he knows I mean it when I say the next words. "You absolutely belong out there."

Chapter 35

LYSSA

G rant and Andi are talking about something, but I only have eyes for #17 down below, watching the blue-green and grey of his jersey flashing across the ice.

My breath catches as one of the Chill defensemen lobs a puck in the air. Benji turns on the gas, determined to be the first one there when it lands in the center of the ice. His effort pays off and he flies into the offensive zone, a player on the other team hot on his heels.

Then he turns so fast that ice sprays, knee-high, and sends the puck sailing back to the middle lane of the ice, where another team member intercepts it. His teammate fakes one way and then buries the puck behind the goalie in the opposite direction, so fast I can barely comprehend what just happened.

Holy shit, this team is *good*. And Benji is matching their talent in stride.

The red light goes off, a horn blares, and the roar of the crowd borders on deafening. My phone vibrates in my pocket, and I know it's from Bella. She and Paul are watching the game at home, and she's been texting me every time Benji is out on the ice, telling me they're cheering him on. They must have just seen his fantastic assist. I know Andi and Grant did. She's screaming, he is hollering, and the energy all around us is so contagious I feel drunk on it.

I twist in my seat to meet Andi's gaze, and from her grin I can tell she feels the same. Yeah, we could get used to this whole professional hockey thing.

I'm still riding the high later that night when Benji arrives back home. Minnesota took home the win, and he had not one, but *two* assists. I could tell by the end of the game that he'd settled into his rhythm, celebrating with his new line – which, to my delight and Grant's, included Jordie. I'm sure he received all sorts of celebratory words from the team after they left the ice.

I'm excited to celebrate with him now, too.

"Come in!" I call out, rushing to my bedroom. I leave the door open a crack and dart over to the bed, situating myself on it. I attempt to strike a seductive pose, but quickly pivot as I begin sliding off the pillow. The door to my apartment closes, and I hear Benji's footsteps as he enters, then pauses. Winny's skittering footsteps tell me he was excited to be the first one to greet Benji.

"I'm in here!" I shout, opting to simply tuck myself under the covers.

The door to my bedroom opens, and Benji pops in, his hair still damp from his shower. He has his suit back on, and he looks puzzled. "Were you sleeping?"

"Not exactly," I say. I try to make it sound sultry, but it comes out phlegmy. Good god, I really am *not* good at this. I clear my throat. "I was waiting. To celebrate your win."

He smiles down at me, the innocent lump in bed. "I can't believe we won tonight."

His tone is laced with triumph, and I feel a secondhand pride swell up in me on his behalf. He worked so hard for this, and it makes me beyond happy to see him reaping the fruits of his labor.

"You were a big part of that, Benji." I shift the blanket down a notch, showing a glimpse of one breast, covered in pink lace. Benji's eyes snap to the movement, and he stills.

"I just hope it doesn't mean you're too tired to celebrate…in other ways." The blanket pools at my waist, exposing both of my lace-clad breasts to him. It's just see-through enough that I know he can see my nipples, and from the way he licks his lips, I know he likes what he sees.

"Oh, I'm never too tired for that kind of celebration." He prowls forward, shrugging his suit jacket off in one deft motion. He's already got his shirt untucked from his pants in the two strides it takes him to get to the side of my bed. In response, I remove the blanket entirely, flashing my matching lace underwear directly in his line of sight.

"*This* is the only thing that could possibly make this night more perfect," he says, his voice husky. His eyes rake over me, and I flush at the admiration and hunger in his gaze. He makes me feel so wanted, so treasured. I don't know if I'll ever get enough of him. The thought both scares and thrills me.

All thoughts leave my head, however, as he wraps his hands around my thighs and tugs me to the edge of the bed. "You stay right here while I catch up," he growls, unbuttoning his shirt. "Don't move a muscle."

There's a feral gleam in his eyes as he undresses, and it sends a molten heat searing down to my core. I love how he changes ever so slightly during sex; his words becoming more crass, his movements choppy and intense. Never enough to feel unsafe, but just enough to feel the carnal desire he doesn't bother to hide.

When he's down to his briefs, he kneels at the side of the bed, coaxing my legs open. He drags a finger across my panties, down over my core, and I shiver at the touch. He drags his finger back up and hooks both pointer fingers over the sides of my panties, dragging them down in one swift movement. Then he pauses, gazing at me.

"No, no, this won't do." He shakes his head and rises. I rise with him, feeling panic shoot through my veins.

"What? What is it?"

He gets on the bed and reaches for me, tugging me to him until I'm straddling him. "I need you to sit on my face."

I stare at him. "Sit on your face?"

He nods, his gaze heated. "Get over here and sit on me, baby. I want you to come in my mouth."

My heart thrums at his words and I scan the space between us, thinking. Finally, I grab the headboard with both hands and situate myself over him, listening as he murmurs encouraging words, his hands running over my bare legs as I move.

His nose brushes the inside of my thigh, and I shudder, my knees going weak at the touch. I pause, hovering over him. "Should I stop here?"

An impatient sound rumbles in his throat, and his hands grip my waist, pulling me down further against his face. "I swear to god, L. Don't. You. Dare. Stop."

After just a moment's hesitation, I settle down onto his face, leaning into his warm lips. The second he starts moving his mouth against me, I don't even bother stifling the whimper that escapes me.

I can tell from the way his hands tighten on me that he heard the noise, and before I can ask if I'm suffocating him, his tongue lashes against me. Any thought I had leaves my brain as my eyes roll back, the pleasure overtaking everything else.

I grind against him, encouraged by the hard strokes of his tongue, chasing the mounting feeling soaring inside me. Benji hums deeply in approval, and the vibration sends me even higher.

"I'm gonna–" My voice cuts off on a gasp as Benji sucks my clit into his mouth. "Fuck, Benji, I'm going to –"

Before I can finish my sentence, I explode, the burning pleasure shooting through my body and pulsing down my spine. I collapse shamelessly against Benji, but he doesn't seem at all bothered by it. Instead, when I slip off to his side, still catching my breath, he grins wolfishly at me, wiping his glistening face. Somehow, it's the hottest thing I've ever seen.

"God, I love the way you scream my name." He kicks off his underwear, his cock springing loose, hard and ready. I eye him greedily, even though I'm still winded from seconds before. He shifts over me, his eyes burning as he takes me in.

"I love the way your mouth works," I whisper, stupidly, but he gives an unsteady laugh against my skin as he kisses his way down my body, lining himself up with my entrance.

"Do you love how this works?" he asks, hooking one of my legs around his waist.

I nod emphatically, and he grins, but the second he pushes inside me, the grin dissolves and he groans. *"Shit.* I'll never get enough of you."

I can't manage a response, so I simply squeeze around him in answer, pulling another curse from him.

He withdraws, almost to the tip, and then thrusts back in, so hard that I don't think either of us breathe for a moment. Then he picks up the pace, angling me so that he goes deeper, answering my whispered pleas for *harder* and *faster* until I'm not even sure I'm saying words, just garbled cries of pleasure.

When I come for a second time, he follows me over that edge, and between his ragged breaths I hear my name pass his lips in a low murmur.

I think I love the way he says my name, too.

Chapter 36

LYSSA

I wake up to the soft vibration of my phone going off. My phone is normally set to sleep, but I must have completely overslept that mode. I know I can blame it on the dark-haired space heater in bed with me, since he got back late from his game, and I kept him up even later. Even the memory of what happened last night has me growing warm, and I glance over to where he's still sleeping peacefully. His expression is soft with sleep, his mouth slightly parted. His hair, which was still wet from his shower last night, has dried into unruly curls. I resist the urge to reach over and stroke it away from his forehead, not wanting to wake him.

Another buzz from my phone snatches my attention away from him. I stretch across the bed to snag it from my nightstand, scrolling through the notifications. They're all from Andi – unsurprising, since she tends to text sporadic thoughts in quick succession, rather than one long text. My heart begins to pound as I read through them.

Andi: GIRL

Andi: Check this out!!! <u>Article: Golden Boy Back in Action</u>

Andi: Ur boi is first page news!!!

Andi: And from the looks of it, so are you

Andi: Is this a good thing or a bad thing?? Lmk

Andi: I'm here for you if you wanna talk

I click into the article. It leads with two images: one of Benji in his Chill jersey, presumably taken last night during the game. He's mid-turn, ice spraying everywhere in the perfect action shot. The other is a photo of *us,* walking hand in hand, and I can tell it was taken right as we walked into the rink the other night. My heart goes from pounding to full-on galloping as I realize that my face is on full display, paired with a headline that has me feeling faint.

Rising hockey superstar makes debut in professional and romantic life!

Benjamin Estes, who has long been known as one of the Minnesota "Golden Boys" alongside his late brother, Jacob Estes, made his debut with the Minnesota Chill last night. It brought a moment of nostalgia for many hockey fans, who remember his brother, Jake, and his climb to the same team, before his untimely death almost a year ago.

It was speculated that Benjamin may not continue his hockey career, but it appears he is back and better than ever – complete with a new romantic partner! He was spotted entering the rink for his first NHL game with a mystery woman on his arm. Cameras caught the pair sharing a kiss, sparking speculation about the young hockey star's love life. He then went on to get two assists in his debut game, indicating early promise as a permanent member of the team.

We haven't been able to reach him for comment, but fans are buzzing about his future with the Minnesota Chill and, just as importantly, who the mystery woman on his arm might be.

My mouth feels dry, and I lower my phone, unable to read any further. Somehow, I didn't put the pieces together last night, when the crowd had gathered, eager for Benji's commentary. I thought they may try to quote him in some article, and he hadn't even said anything, but to plaster *photos* across the internet...

God, how far could these reach? A reverse image search is easy. These could get back to *him*. And who knows what else these reporters could dig up. They're clearly thirsty for any information they can uncover. What if they dig deep enough to find –

"What time is it?"

Benji's voice breaks through the blood pounding in my ears. I jolt and glance over at him. He's blinking, clearly still half-asleep, but whatever he sees in my face has him wide awake in seconds.

"What's wrong?"

I hand him my phone wordlessly, and he takes it, glancing down at the screen. His brow furrows as he reads the article, and by the time he's finished, he's sitting upright in bed, the blankets pooling around his waist.

"I can't believe..." he trails off, turning his gaze on me. "Are you okay?"

I shake my head, the panic bubbling up to a breaking point. "What if they find out, Benji?" My voice cracks on the question. Winston raises his head off his bed, sensing the fear in my tone. "What if they find out who I really am?"

"They won't. I won't breathe a word."

"But there are still ways, Benji. It's what they do for a living." My palms are sweating, and I clutch at the blanket, using it like a thin layer of protection. Winny has padded over to the side of the bed now, his chin resting on the mattress, ears back and eyes wide as he observes me. "It's only a matter of time."

"Then we deal with it. Whatever happens, I'm here for you." Benji drops the phone and reaches for me. "You're my girlfriend, and this changes nothing."

"It changes everything! What if – what if *he* –" My voice cracks, and I'm unable to finish the sentence.

I can see the moment realization dawns on him, rearranging his expression. "If he finds you, I'll be here." He says the words slowly, his voice thick and low. "I won't let him hurt you. I promise."

"It's not just that. It's…"

"What is it, L?" His gaze is bright and intense, begging in a way his words can't reach. "What…what aren't you telling me?"

I shake my head, and Winston jumps on the bed, shoving his nose underneath my hand. Tears well up in my eyes at the small support, the probing question, and the memory that's been haunting me for weeks, repeating itself in the back of my mind even now.

I inhale sharply. "I can't."

"Please." A quiet plea. "Whatever you're facing, you don't have to face it alone. Please tell me."

I know I have to. I didn't want to; I never wanted to have to share this memory, the darkest part of me, but…I know deep down that it's going to come out eventually. Benji is asking now, and I have to answer him. I can't ice him out of this piece of my past forever.

A vice clamps around my throat, and it takes several moments to free the words. "He got hurt. Because of me."

I can't look at Benji, but I can feel the weight of his gaze as he looks at me. "Austin?"

"No." I exhale a shuddering breath, barely able to say his name. "His brother. Ethan."

It's silent, and when I'm finally able to venture a glance over at Benji, I can see the confusion written all over his face. He's waiting for me to continue, but he has questions. I wrap the blanket in my hands, bracing to choke the words out.

"He...he saw what Austin was doing. He was trying to help me get away. Austin and I were arguing, and he tried to split it up. He pulled me off the balcony, back inside, and confronted Austin. The balcony broke, and..." I blink rapidly, and the tears fall freely, racing down my cheeks. "He and Austin both fell. Austin broke an arm, but Ethan hit his head. H – he was in a coma for a week."

I brush the tears away, though they're quickly replaced by fresh ones. Winston nuzzles at me, but I ignore him this time. "It was all over the news. He pressed charges against Austin, and that's when I got my restraining order. His wife, Patty, told me to get out. That it would be my only chance." I sniffle. "I knew I had to listen, after what Ethan did to help me."

I don't voice the part that still guts me the most to this day. The way Patty looked at me after realizing what had happened. The way she said to *get out*. I'm still not sure if it was from a place of pity or anger, and to be honest, I'm not sure which is worse: the idea of her being scared for me, or hating me for what I allowed Austin to do.

I look at Benji, but he's almost completely blurred by the tears swarming my vision. "He was Austin's own brother, and still, he came to help me. And look what Austin did to him! I can't bear anything happening to you."

I'm met with silence. I've grown so used to Benji's quiet side – his patience while he waits for me to open up, his long pauses while he absorbs information – and it's been one of the things that makes me so comfortable with him.

This silence, though? It physically hurts.

I can't imagine what he thinks of me right now. I was so weak back then. I had been cowardly and unable to leave on my own. It took someone going to a hospital and policemen asking questions right to my face to get me to leave. If I had just been able to leave the first time I tried; if I had been smarter, or stronger, none of that would have happened. Nobody else would have been hurt.

I can't let that happen a second time.

Finally, Benji speaks. "None of that is your fault, little fighter." Before I can interject, he continues. "Blame Austin; hell, blame the shitty balcony. But whatever you do, you can't blame yourself."

"Yes, I can!" I shout, balling my hands into fists.

"Would you blame Jake for his stalker?" Benji asks.

I blink, confused by the turn in conversation. "What? No –"

"He had as much control over his stalker as you had over Austin." Benji interrupts me, his tone firm. "They are both terrible people who did terrible things, in the name of what they saw in their heads as a fucked-up version of love. But you and I know that's not love. Their version of it is what gets people hurt...or worse."

"But then, don't you see?" My voice is nothing more than a whisper. "I can't let you be dragged into this, any more than you already have been."

Benji's lips curl up into a sad smile. "That ship has sailed. I'm in it for the long haul."

I look at him, alarmed. Doesn't he understand what I *just* said? I'm giving him an out here, and if he was smart, he would take it and run. I don't want him to feel like he's stuck in this situation with me.

I whip the covers off and get out of bed, needing to move and quell the uneasy energy building in me. As I tug on a pair of pants, he moves off the bed to mirror me.

"I'm serious, little fighter. We'll deal with this together. I won't let him hurt you, L."

"It's not just that I'm worried about!" I say, exasperated, even as my heart tugs at his protective words. I pull on a shirt and gesture between us. "Why don't you understand? I don't want him to hurt you, either. This is my problem to solve, and mine alone."

Benji frowns. "He can't hurt me. And I won't let him hurt you. What about that can't *you* understand? You don't have to deal with this alone. I'm here for you. *I love you.*"

Those three words are a bomb dropped between us.

My mouth falls open. I feel knocked sideways with surprise, and then a rush of joy floods through me. That sideways feeling turns into one of me falling forward, into him. Don't I feel the same?

I jerk myself back to reality.

Those three words have never been anything but a weapon. He said it himself; people twist those feelings to meet their own selfish needs, and hurt people in the process. The fact that he's using them in the middle of an argument says it all, and that realization makes my chest squeeze painfully. "You can't say that. You don't mean it. You barely know me!"

"But I do know you." He prowls closer. "I know you bite your lip when you're stressed. I know you snort when you laugh. I know you have to read every fact on a sign. I know you love Winston more than anything, and I'm happy to take second place to him."

"Stop," I plead, but he keeps going.

"And I know how I feel. Before you, I was in a dark place. Meeting you..." He blows out a breath. "When you came into my life, I don't know. It was like the lights came on."

I felt the same way.

It's what I want to say, but I'm frozen. This conversation is entirely too much right now, and I'm torn between believing all the beautiful things he's saying to me, and the fear that it's just a way to keep me from running. Maybe I'm even afraid that the things he's saying to me are the truth.

"What do you want me to say right now?" I plead.

"I'm not asking you to say it back right now. All I ask is that if you're going to give your heart to someone again, you pick me. Choose me."

"I – can't do that." I hate the way my voice trembles, and I lower it to a whisper. "I can't have you hurt, too."

Benji levels me with a somber stare. "You're hurting me right now."

It's on the tip of my tongue to apologize, but I can't. I'm not. I know this is for the best.

For a long moment, we gaze at each other, neither of us saying a word. It's clear we aren't going to change each other's minds, but the final fallout hasn't occurred yet.

Finally, Winston whines, and the moment is shattered. Benji shakes his head and, with one more long look at me, leaves the apartment. He doesn't say another word.

Chapter 37

Benji

"Only eight minutes left!" The captain of the Chill, Matias Halko, bellows down the bench. His Finnish accent is heavy with excitement. "Let's hold this lead! We can do anything for eight minutes!"

My new linemate, Nate, bumps me. "Well, not *anything*. Some things, he can only do for one."

Jordie chuckles, and I offer Nate a brief smile, though my heart isn't in it. I've been going through the motions during this game, and it shows. My performance isn't as dazzling as the last game, but I'm just happy I'm still holding my own. Having Jordie here provides the element of familiarity I need. It's pulled me out of my head just enough to play a decent game.

I haven't heard from Lyssa in a day and a half. I've picked up my phone to message her at least a dozen times, but each time I end up putting it away. She hasn't made any attempt to reach out to me, and her parting words are still ringing in my head.

She didn't choose me. I tried my best to let her know that I chose her, that I would be there for her, and she couldn't do the same. I'm trying to understand that her background has more pain in it than I knew before, but I'm also frustrated that she wouldn't let me help her. There's nothing I can do about it if she wants to handle it alone.

"Four miles left!" Matias bellows as the clock hits the four minute mark, and I do my best to funnel all my focus into the end of the game. We're able to squeak out the win, and my chest decompresses somewhat as we head into the locker room.

"Only one more game of the year," Jordie says as he peels off his jersey and tosses it into the laundry bin. He runs a hand through his hair and then squirts water into his mouth. "Isn't that wild?"

I nod, muttering, "And what a year it's been."

Jordie studies me, like he can't tell if the comment is a good or a bad thing, and I'm not sure, either. On one hand, my career dreams came true. I'm playing for the team I always dreamed of playing for, something most who work their whole lives for will never be able to say. I met a great girl who turned my world upside down.

But on the other hand... I may have lost the girl, and my brother isn't here for any of it. Not to cheer me on, not to skate with, not to talk about the girl with. Jake's gone, and grief burns through me like alcohol on a fresh wound. That's the part of losing someone that nobody ever tells you about; the way that a single memory or a single moment can bring the pain rushing back like it was yesterday, no matter how much time has passed.

I throw my helmet to the ground, too confused to voice it all, but too tired to get up and try to walk it off in the moment.

Jordie's eyes go from the helmet to me, his lips pursing. "Beers with the boys tonight?"

"Fuck yes," I groan. "You have no idea how badly I need that."

The mood at the bar is sour across the board. The Leopards had another game against the Pirates today, and they lost to them, 4 to 1. It was a solid ass-kicking, according to our old linemates.

"It's cruel to make us play so often against them," Highcloud mutters. "Why do they have to be in our division?"

"Because life's a bitch, that's why." Grant takes a long pull from his beer, and Jordie and I exchange a glance.

"Who pissed in your cereal, Sando?" Jordie asks slowly. Grant is the perpetual optimist of the group. He's always ready with a joke to lighten the mood. When he's in a mood, we know it's something serious.

Grant blows out a long breath through pursed lips, staring hard into his glass. "I don't know, man. I'm just trying to figure out what's going on with Andi. I feel like we're not on the same page."

My laugh is short and hard. "Welcome to the club, bro."

"It's a terrible club, Benji. I want out."

"Wait. Didn't you say she was engaged before?" Highcloud asks, and Grant nods.

"Yeah. That's why we kept it so casual. But, I don't know. Lately it feels like something more. I just don't know how to bring it up to her. We agreed on one thing, and I think she wants to keep it that way."

"But you don't?" I ask.

"No, man. I want more." The look on his face is so sincere and new. God damn. We're both just fools in love. My heart goes out to him, and I pray it's not one-sided.

"Then you've gotta tell her how you feel," Jordie says.

"I know, I know. I will. But we've both been so busy, we've barely been able to see each other, and when we do, it's just for quick hook-ups. You're not making things any easier, by the way." He levels me with a glare, but it doesn't have any heat behind it. Even so, I cringe. We're at Wunderbar, but I only agreed to come here once Grant confirmed with Andi that Lyssa would not be working tonight.

Grant gives me a long look. "Just ask about her, dude. You know you want to."

"Fine." I sigh. "Have you heard anything?"

He shrugs, pushing his empty glass to the corner of the table. "I don't know, man. I can tell you she's still upset. Andi says Lisa's trying not to bother her with her problems, but she can tell Lisa's all bent out of shape." He pauses. "I still don't quite get it, though. You just told her you loved her, and she flipped out on you?"

I make a noncommittal noise, taking another sip. I know Andi probably knows the truth by now, but clearly she's still keeping Lyssa's secrets. I hate not being able to tell my friends everything, but...I shift in my seat, resigned. It's not my place to say more.

"Well, for what it's worth, Andi is positive Lisa loves you, too. She's probably just dealing with some shit in her head."

My eyes meet his over my glass, and he gives me a half-smile. "I mean, come on. It makes sense. Who wouldn't love you, bro?"

The others make obnoxious cooing noises, shoving me, and it's enough to force a laugh out of me. For the first time in almost forty-eight hours, I feel light again. This is exactly what I needed.

"What kind of weird bromance am I witnessing here?" A voice says, and we all glance over from our table to see Liam there, flanked by two other Pirates players.

Well, if this isn't a fucking bucket of cold water on what was about to be a good evening.

"What are you doing here, Roberts?" Grant asks, his tone laced with ice.

Liam looks around, feigning surprise. "It's a free country, isn't it? And what a happy coincidence we ran into you all."

"Well, you saw us." Jordie waves him away. "Now you can go do your thing, and we'll do ours."

"Too good for us now, Tremblay?" Liam asks, dropping his fake politeness. "You make it to the show, and suddenly you can't be seen talking to us little people?" Jordie frowns, but before he can answer, Liam continues, zeroing in on me. "Now, you I can understand, but Estes here has to know better. He was just a pity call-up, to give the newspapers something to talk about."

The words are like lightning to my veins, and I feel my palms begin to prickle with sweat. Fucking hell. How does this guy always know how to hit where it'll hurt the most?

"That's it." Grant stands from the table, sending his chair skittering out behind him. He squares up with Liam, and the rest of us are quick to follow suit, rising out of our seats to flank him in silent support. "Get the fuck out of our faces, Roberts."

Liam simply smirks. "Looking for another ass kicking? I would've thought you had enough today."

"You're such a piece of shit, you know that?" I grind out.

Liam simply shrugs. "Hey man, at least I don't have a girl-friend running around on me."

I freeze. "What do you mean?"

He waves his hand. "There was some guy in here earlier, showing the manager a photo of you and your girl, asking where he could find her. Said she was *his* girlfriend."

My breath catches. It feels like I've been dunked in an ice bath. *His girlfriend...*

Liam says something and laughs, but I can't reply. The pho-tographs – the article – her ex must have put two and two together. Maybe it was shit luck. Or maybe he'd been searching for this kind of slip-up ever since she left.

I look down, stunned to see that my hands are trembling as the surge of adrenaline hits. I barely even notice as Grant and Jordie turn, closing in on either side of me. Liam slips away, shaking his head.

"What did that fucking loser mean?" Grant asks, but I don't answer. I'm busy pulling my cell phone out, fumbling as I find

Lyssa's contact. I press call and bring the phone to my ear, praying for her to pick up.

"The number you have dialed has not set up their voice mailbox..."

I curse and hang up, searching for Andi's number. When she doesn't answer either, I pivot to Grant. He takes in my expression, alarmed.

"Do you know where Andi is right now?" I demand.

He shrugs. "She was at the gym with Bella and Lisa, but she should be home by now. Why?"

Jordie grabs my shoulder, eyeing me carefully when I meet his gaze. "Hey, what's wrong?"

"It's Lyssa." I swallow, too frantic to realize my slip up. "Her ex is here. And he's..." I trail off, unable to form the words as fear floods my veins.

Jordie's hand drops from my shoulder in surprise, but then he gives me a firm nod of understanding. "Let's go find her before he does."

Chapter 38

Lyssa

"Great session today, everyone," Paul says, tossing a towel over his shoulder. "We'll pick this back up on Tuesday."

The entire class lets out a collective sigh, happy to be released from the intense workout. Andi and I glance at each other, still working to catch our breath. "Is it just me, or is he getting stronger as he gets older?" she asks.

I squirt a steady stream of water into my mouth and nod. "At this rate, he's going to do a marathon for his birthday this year."

"And then for his sixtieth, he'll be ultra-marathoning."

"He'll be asking us to join him for an Iron Man at his retirement party."

We laugh and continue firing off scenarios as we cool down. It feels good to discuss something so simple. Andi came over yesterday as soon as I called, and she hasn't left my side since. Though it's been nice to have company, of course she wanted to know what happened, and so I had to tell her. Admitting the worst parts of my past, twice over, left me mentally drained.

I think she knows it, because she didn't push about the argument with Benji that followed. She simply listened, then hugged me and offered up a movie marathon. I'd gratefully accepted, but my mind kept racing, even after the movies finished and we went to bed.

I know Andi has been trying her best to keep me preoccupied – she stuck with me through brunch this afternoon, and now the gym this evening – but I think we both know I really just need to have another conversation with Benji. Everything about yesterday caught me off guard, and I know I wasn't thinking rationally when I pretty much kicked him out of my apartment. It was just too much, too fast, and I told Andi that.

"Trust me, girl," she'd said, a knowing frown on her face. "I get not being on the same page with your partner. You've just got to figure out where your head's at first, then take it from there."

If only that was the easy part.

I sigh as I turn over the conversation in my head for the hundredth time, Andi seemingly lost in thought next to me as well. We're just about done stretching when Paul ambles over to us.

"Hey, I've got a dinner with Bella to get to. Does one of you mind locking up on your way out?"

Andi shakes her head. "Sorry, but I've got to run to the pharmacy before it closes."

"No worries," I say. "I can lock up."

"Thanks, kiddo." Pauls shoots me a grateful smile. Andi looks at me guiltily, clearly not wanting to leave me in my current state. I give her a reassuring nod, and after a moment's hesitation, she packs up to leave.

I take my time closing up, giving my boxing gloves a deep clean and leaving them to air dry. The extra love the gym has received in the past few weeks makes it even more peaceful now, and I relish the alone time in one of my favorite places.

The second I step outside and lock up the back exit, however, the mood changes. The quiet feels pressurized, like a balloon about to pop, and the hair on the back of my neck stands on end.

Am I being watched?

I freeze, immediately on high alert. There's nobody around – at least, not that I can see. It's past sunset, but the street is well-lit, and there are no figures on the sidewalk. Still, I decide to wait a little while longer in the gym, hoping the ominous feeling will go away.

I unlock the back door to the gym and slip back inside. Not thirty seconds later, I hear the crunch of footsteps on snow pass by the door. My breath catches, and I hold it, listening as the steps subside.

Even though I've lost the sound of the footfalls, I can still feel the weight of someone's presence.

I wait five minutes, then peer out the window of the gym. Everything is silent. I will myself to relax.

For so long, I've been jumpy, anticipating the worst. It was probably just someone passing by at an inappropriate time. I'll be back on the main road in a block, and from there it's a quick walk home. I gather my keys and phone and take a deep breath, opening the door again.

I don't make it more than two steps outside before a crushing weight slams into me from the side. My phone clatters to the ground, and I claw against the arm that wraps around my waist, though it's like trying to move iron. A startled cry slips past my lips, but it's cut short with a palm that slaps over my mouth.

All I can do is kick out helplessly as I'm dragged back into the gym. The voice that reaches my ears is the one that's haunted my nightmares for months, and my life for years before that.

"Did you really think I wouldn't find you?"

Austin stands between me and the gym exit. His eyes are wild, reddened as if he hasn't slept well, has been drinking, or both.

I'm frozen, taking in the scene in front of me with a detached sense of reality.

He paces like a caged animal, even though I'm the one who's trapped. "Do you think this is some kind of game, Alyssa?"

He pulls my name out in three long syllables, in that familiar way he always did when he was about to strike. I shake my head, my pulse hammering in overdrive as my mind races.

The front of the gym is behind me, but it's already locked, and in the time it would take me to unlock it and run out, he'd be on me. A fresh wave of terror dawns on me as I realize I don't even know if he's got a weapon on him. I'm beginning to feel dizzy from the rush of panic.

Through the flood of sensations, a rational thought flits by, and I grab onto it. *You're panicking. But you knew this could happen. You prepared for this. What will you do now?*

I grasp that question and try to breathe, forcing back the hyperventilation. Austin has stopped pacing, his eyes fixated on me as he runs his hands through his hair.

I clench my own hands into fists, the tingling, balmy sensation of fear having traveled all the way through my fingertips. *Focus. What's the next step?*

"Whatever this is—" he gestures wildly around him. "—it's over. It's time to come home."

A sour taste coats my mouth. He won't simply let me go, but even if I escape him, won't he just keep coming back?

"This is my home now," I answer carefully. I take a few steps, positioning myself just far enough away that he can't grab for me, but I can reach him with a well-placed kick. He shifts with me, his face contorting in confused rage.

"This place?" He laughs without humor. "This freezing shithole?"

"Yes," I reply quietly. "This is my home. I'm staying here. We're done, Austin."

"No."

His voice raises only slightly, but my gut reaction is immediate, telling me I need to be more alert. I step back once more, trying to gain more distance between us.

The difference between Austin and Benji is so clear now, I'm amazed I didn't see it before. No matter how loud Benji and his teammates get, it never has the dark undercurrent of violence that Austin's tone has. His entire demeanor is a stark contrast to everyone in my life now, the sense of wrongness in him so apparent after letting my instincts guide me freely for the past few months, rather than tamping them down to safely accommodate him.

"Is this because of him?" he spits out.

Benji. He knows about Benji. Of course he does; he had to have seen the article of us together. The one that mentioned us kissing.

I blink.My mouth opens to answer, but nothing comes out. Do I say yes? Will knowing there's another man in my life hold more weight than me denying him for myself? Or will it only add another victim to his list?

It doesn't end up mattering. I've taken too long to respond. He's back to pacing, but this time it's toward me. "No," he mutters. "You belong to me, and we're going home, now."

I stumble back, but he swallows up the ground between us. He lunges for my wrists and on instinct, I whip them up, bracketing my face as I would in any boxing class. Something inside me clicks, and my focus narrows, muscle memory barreling forward and banishing my fear to the back recesses of my mind.

As his palms curl around my wrists, I plant my feet firmly and tug one hand to lay flat across my chest. His hand comes with, still on my wrist, but I twist my elbow over his hand and bring it down, breaking his hold.

Without missing a beat, I ram my freed hand into the arm that's still gripping my opposite wrist, and add an elbow to his chest. He stumbles back a step, his hold broken, but it's not *enough*, not enough distance, and not enough to fill the growing rage and terror roiling in me. I ground my feet and lash out with a firm side kick to his solar plexus. He doubles over, gagging.

Go, go! Again, that rational voice commands from the back of my mind, and I take a precious second to compare my options. Do I try to go around him, to the back exit, or go unlock the front door?

Front door, I decide, and spin around, making a dash for it. I hear a wheeze behind me, and then footsteps following, gaining traction. My heart leaps into my throat as I skid to a stop in front of the door, turning the latch over.

I'm twisting the handle just as arms reach around me, solid as steel, wrapping me so tightly I can feel my bones grind together. I'm lifted off the ground, and my kicks land helplessly as I squirm in his arms.

"You're going to pay for that," he snarls. "When we get back–"

"*No!*" I gasp, lashing harder. Finally, a kick against his loin lands. His grip loosens, and I use that to escape out of his grasp.

I scramble to my feet, gaze locked on the front door, but as I take the first steps, I'm wrenched back from my ponytail. I cry out from the pain, tears springing to my eyes.

I reach back to loosen his grasp, but it's already gone. I'm being spun around, my back slamming into the wall. His hands reach for my neck, and I duck my chin down, attempting to stave off what I know is coming. Even before he wraps his fingers around me, I feel my throat constricting, the impending pain imprinted on my brain like a cruel tattoo.

I wrap my hands around his wrists, but my grip doesn't even reach all the way around. His arms and hands are too large, too impenetrable.

I should have known; should have known that even with months of training, I would be no match for him at his worst. I send out a silent apology to all those who tried to help me become stronger these past few months. Andi. Bella. Paul. Benji. They wouldn't want to see me like this.

No, I realize. They wouldn't. They would want me to be a fighter.

Fight.

With one final gasp, I grit my teeth and twist, raising my arm and slamming my elbow down on his grip. As it loosens enough for me to tilt toward the ground, I lash out, punching him square in the groin. Again, he grunts and bends over in pain.

But I don't stop there. I send a knee to his chest, followed by a kick. Then I use my fists. I go for him out of a combination of fear and rage, knowing that if I leave him with enough energy to follow me this time, I might not escape. I have to do whatever it takes to get free of him, here and now.

When he's finally the one backing away from me, I take a few tentative steps back, my chest heaving and eyes glued to him. He doesn't meet my gaze, and I can feel the power shift in this moment. He wasn't expecting me to put up a fight like this.

"I'll say this for the last time, Austin," I choke out. "Leave me alone. Forever."

With that, I turn and sprint out of the gym. Pain is blossoming across my body, both from where I've been grabbed and where I've dealt blows, but I barely acknowledge it. All I care about is getting to a public space where I know I'll be safe.

I see three figures moving toward the gym, and head their way at a clip faster than a normal walk, but not fast enough to alarm them.

When I see who the figure in front is, however, I break out in a dead run, at the same time he does.

Benji.

I skid to a stop in front of him, emotion rendering me incapable of speech. Benji's gaze sweeps over me hurriedly. He doesn't say a word, but as he takes in my face and my neck, his eyes grow noticeably darker.

He begins to twist away, already focusing on the gym behind me, but I grab his jacket like it's a lifeline. "Please."

It's a single word, but he hears everything behind it. He stops to face me once more, and a choked sob slips past my lips when he reaches a hand up to my face. His rigid expression softens, and he gathers me into his chest, the movement so tender that the mental wall I threw up in the gym shatters completely.

I begin to cry in earnest. Great, heaving sobs rip from my throat as I allow myself to be swallowed up in Benji's embrace. I barely hear the approaching footsteps, the sound of Benji's muffled voice as he says gruffly, "I've got her. He's in the gym."

Two voices respond – Grant, maybe Jordie? – and then it's just Benji and me again. He's a solid, immovable force, holding up against the waves of my emotions. The only movement is the palm of his hand, rubbing softly against my back. My sobs subside into hiccups, and then disappear altogether. Still, he doesn't move, waiting for me to pull back.

I do eventually, but not all the way. It feels like gravity is resting its center between the two of us, and if I pull away too quickly, the security I feel being in his arms will disappear. Instead, I lean back to see his face, still clutching his jacket in my grip.

"You came," I say, wincing at the rawness of my voice.

Benji moves one arm away, but only to cradle my cheek in his palm. "Of course I came." He exhales shakily. "I'm only sorry I couldn't be here sooner to keep you safe."

"I am safe," I whisper. "Now."

His eyes skim over my face once more, but this time, his gaze is all tender affection. He's reassured himself that I'm here, and I'm okay.

I'm here.

I'm safe.

I survived.

A few final tears well in my eyes at the thought, and I sniff, trying to chase them away.

"I've got you, little fighter." Benji swipes a tear away with the pad of his thumb. "I'm here for you. Always."

Chapter 39

Lyssa

"I can't believe you've never been up here," Benji says, passing me a flute of sparkling wine.

"Ah, yes. Because naturally, the first thing I want to do when it's thirty degrees out is come hang out on the rooftop."

I gesture around, and Andi slings an arm over me, rubbing my shoulder in a mock attempt to warm me up. "Actually, I think it's closer to twenty degrees. But I do agree with Benji. This rooftop is *sick.*"

I have to admit, she's right. There are lights strung out across the space, lighting the way like little stars. The walls are a mixture of wood paneling and fake vines on all sides except one, which offers an unobstructed view of the city skyline in the distance. A giant round fireplace is roaring at the center of the space, the flames licking up toward the sky doing their best to fight off the frigid temp, alongside a half dozen patio heaters. The floor is cleared, but there are still some snow piles tucked in the corners where the heat can't quite hit them.

Between that and the body heat of our group, it's bearable, but I can't imagine we'll stay up here much longer than the ten minutes we have until midnight rolls around. It's New Year's Eve, and Benji wanted us to celebrate the ball drop from the rooftop of our apartment. So we followed, throwing thick winter coats, hats, and gloves over our shiny outfits, and following him back here.

Grant groans. "It's cool and all, but seriously. I can't believe you dragged us away from the bar to do the countdown up here."

"Yeah, dude, we're missing the bobber drop!" Levi chimes in.

I stare at him. "A bobber drop? Like, with fishing?"

He nods excitedly, and all I can do is snort. Clearly, there's still some things I have to learn about Minnesota. But I do kind of love it. Benji smirks at me, like he knows what I'm thinking.

Jordie comes around, passing sparklers to all of us. Andi lets go of me and eagerly grabs one. Benji pulls out a lighter, gesturing to my sparkler. "Want a light?"

I nod, removing my mittens, and watch as the sparkler lights up. Around us, bright, colored sparks slowly fill the rooftop as everyone else does the same, becoming little constellations that hiss and crackle. Some of the guys immediately begin using their sticks as lightsabers, adding their own sound effects.

I meet Andi's gaze and we both roll our eyes. "Men," she mouths, but we're both smiling.

"Are we sure this is safe?" I ask Benji as he lights his own.

He shrugs. "As safe as can be. Just wait until they bring the bottle rockets out." My mouth falls open, and he laughs. "I'm kidding, L. Those aren't legal in the city. We'll let the professionals handle the big boy fireworks this time."

I relax, and he tips his sparkler to me. We toast, and I watch intently as our sticks collide, the sparks combining into one large fountain of light. I smile, watching the sparks pour down to the ground, disappearing before they hit.

When I lift my eyes to look at Benji, I find him already watching me. "How are you?" he asks quietly.

My throat instantly burns with emotion as I consider his question.

To be perfectly honest, I'm doing better than I thought I would be. Austin is going to be dealing with legal troubles for a good long while – not only for what he did to me, but for the breaking and entering, and the scuffle that followed with Jordie and Grant after I left the gym. Paul's video footage from the gym will answer any questions about who started what, and Benji's family lawyer from the case with his brother has already agreed to help.

In a strange way, knowing that the worst has already happened and that I was able to fight my way through it has helped. I fought, and I *survived*.

I expected to have nightmares the night it happened, or not be able to sleep at all. But once the panic subsided, I was able to drift off in Benji's arms, and I slept for almost twelve hours. It was like my body did a hard reset.

Since then, Benji and Andi have been by my side constantly. I'm suspicious that they have a group chat going on, because the second Benji leaves for hockey, Andi is texting me, asking to hang out. And as soon as Benji is back from hockey, Andi slips away, leaving the two of us. They're definitely taking shifts to make sure I'm not alone, but I can't say that I mind.

Most surprising is a conversation Grant showed me on his Instagram last night. Of all the names I would have suspected to show up, I didn't expect Patty's.

Pattycake1450: *Hey. I don't expect you to check your random DMs, but just in case...*

Pattycake1450: *I heard what happened with Austin and Lyssa in Minnesota. When I looked it up, I saw your name tied to some of the charges. I haven't found any contact info for Lyssa, so I'm taking a chance that you know her and hoping you can pass a message along.*

Pattycake1450: *Please tell her I hope she's doing okay, and that I'm glad she took the chance and got out when she could. Tell her Ethan is okay, and neither of us have been in contact with Austin since that night. We both know we should have done more when we suspected what Austin was doing in the beginning. I was scared that if I pushed too hard, I would lose Lyssa for good...and I wanted to stay close enough to be there if she needed help. But it turned out all I could do was tell her to run.*

Pattycake1450: *Anyways. I'm assuming she got a new number to escape that bastard. And though I wouldn't blame her if she never wants to hear from me again...please just let her know I'm still here for her, I love her, and my number hasn't changed if she ever wants to talk.*

"This is your only chance. *Get out.*"

For months now, I thought Patty meant something completely different with her words. What I'd interpreted as a shattered friendship was really her plea to me, telling me that she knew what I'd been dealing with, and that I needed to save myself.

I'm glad she took the chance and got out when she could.

I've reread the messages half a dozen times now. I already know I want to respond, but I need a little bit of time before I do. I have to process how I let my mind run straight to the worst interpretation of my best friend's words, expecting her to blame me instead of Austin. My trust in our friendship was just another thing I let him take from me without even knowing.

"L?"

I blink, bringing myself back to the moment. Benji's face is etched with concern, and I realize I haven't answered his question.

"I'm...really good." His expression is doubtful, and it makes me laugh. "No, I'm serious. I know it sounds strange, but I really am." I pause. "But I'm very ready for a new year."

A slow, somewhat sad smile spreads across his face. "So am I, little fighter."

I nod in understanding. We both have so much from this year that we'd like to leave behind. A fresh start might be cliché, but I think it's something we both desperately need.

"What do you hope the new year brings?" he asks, and my gaze goes back to the fiery light, now almost at the end of the stick, as I consider.

We haven't discussed the fallout from our fight a few days back. The words he said, and the ones I answered with. I'm not entirely sure we need to, because our actions the last two days since have said it all. He came for me when he knew I needed him, and I ran right into his arms. We've been inseparable since.

Even though we haven't kissed, he's come over at night, a silent question that I answer by letting him in and curling up with him in bed, our bodies a tangle of arms and legs.

What do I hope the new year brings?

The revelation crashes like a tidal wave. I know him. I know he isn't Austin. And I'm more terrified of losing him than any fear I had before of being with him.

This has been his request since day one, hasn't it? He asked me to choose him. So that's all there's left for me to do.

"You."

His gaze is fiery with the last lights of the sparkler and the heat of emotion. I swallow and continue. "I want a new year filled with you. I don't want to leave here. I have a home here now. I have Paul, and Bella, and Andi, and...you. If you'll still have me."

I add the last part quietly, and my heart stutters as I wait for his answer. I've taken the leap, and now all there is left to do is freefall, until he decides if he'll catch me.

"All right, let the countdown begin!" Grant bellows, and a chorus of hoots and hollers go up alongside his words. They begin the chant.

Ten! Nine!

"You've always had me, little fighter. I was just waiting for you to decide if you feel the same."

Eight! Seven!

"I do." My heart beats painfully in my chest, and I decide, fuck it. All in.

I discard my drink and the remnants of my sparkler and twist my hands together nervously. Finally, I voice what's been bubbling under the surface for weeks, desperately trying to break free from the layers of ice I've kept it under. "I love you, Benji."

Six! Five!

Benji gazes at me, and I know the pure, raw emotion on his face is surely reflected on my own. It solidifies everything I just chose. I feel safe here, and it feels like home. I'm growing stronger every day, physically and mentally. I'm surrounded by people who have taught me not only to love them, but to love myself, too. I can't imagine being anywhere but here, in this moment, with them. Especially Benji.

Four! Three!

He steps forward and reaches for me, pulling me to him. "I love you too," he rasps out, his hand reaching up to cup my cheek. "So much."

Two! One!

Cheers explode around us, but they're a hazy backdrop as Benji dips his face toward mine, and I take the briefest second to absorb the beauty of him. His dark brown eyes light up with the brilliant light of the sparklers around us, and the fireworks leaping into the sky at a distance. As our mouths collide, I melt into him.

He's everything I never thought I would have. I was too busy running away to realize I ran right into the true love of my life.

Even after we break our kiss, our hands can't seem to leave each other. He wraps one arm around my shoulders, intertwining his free hand with one of mine. I fold my other hand over the top of his and lean into him, enjoying the warmth that fills me inside and out.

Andi beckons us over, a new sparkler in hand. She draws a heart in the air with it as we approach, sparks flying as she whips it around. "Happy new year, you two lovebirds!"

"Happy new year, Andi." Benji says, then turns to look down at me. "And happy new year, little fighter."

I grin up at him, my heart so full, it's near bursting. "Happy new year."

And I know it will be.

ACKNOWLEDGEMENTS

This book is a long time in the making...like, several years long. This began the first time I ever saw a hockey romance book in the wild, and thought to myself "Huh...so that thing I love, I can write about it?". So I wrote, even as everyday life did its best to get in the way and slow things down. By the time I got around to querying Iced Out, the market was well and truly 'oversaturated'. If you made it this far, the most I can say is **thank you**, dear reader, for not being over the hockey romance hype and giving Iced Out a shot!

Though I did my best to bring the levity that's inherent to most groups of hockey players into this, obviously, there are some very hard topics that I tried my best to handle with grace. I want to thank Jess for the thorough sensitivity read-through, and Di, Kayla, and Mara for beta reading, providing sounding boards for my general fears, and overall being the best hype people around as this grew its baby wings.

To Lindsay, for the beautiful cover art and the business advice: Thank you for being the type of friend I go to when I need an adultier adult. Everyone needs someone like you in their life.

To Beca and Charlie, thank you for never letting me second-guess my foray into contemporary romance. I don't know what I'd do without you two.

To my hockey teammates, who may or may not ever read these books (you honestly probably shouldn't, so if you got this far, let's never speak of this) – thanks for providing some A+ content. Yes, I took some notes. And yes, I saved some for the next book.

MORE FROM JAYME HUNT

The Marked Trilogy

Marked by Fate

Marked by Gods

Marked by the Crown

The Lakewood Leopards Series

Iced Out

Book 2 – coming soon!

ABOUT THE AUTHOR

Jayme Hunt studied marketing and data analytics in college, and continues working a full-time job in the marketing field. In early 2022, she rediscovered her love of reading and writing, and has rarely put down a book since. *Marked by Fate* is her debut novel, followed by *Marked by Gods* and the epic conclusion, *Marked by the Crown*. She is also an avid hockey player, the finer details of which can be found in her debut sports romance, *Iced Out*. She resides in Colorado with her husband and two dogs, who often make cameos in her social media posts.

@authorjaymehunt
www.authorjaymehunt.com